Abou

James Warden was a teacher for forty years and retired in 2006. During those years, he wrote about twenty play scripts for children; these included the one that formed the basis for his children's story *The Great Gobbler and his Home-baking Factory at the North Pole,* which he wrote in 1982.

He now enjoys his retirement, as much as he enjoyed his time in the education service, and is catching up on those things which he left undone and ought to have done – in particular, his writing. He writes every morning between nine o'clock and noon, for thirty-six weeks of the year.

He is married – for the second time – and lives in Norfolk. He and his wife travel as much as possible; they have visited Italy (where they were married seven years ago) several times, Canada, Bermuda, Egypt and India. They have also taken several holidays in various Mediterranean resorts – the basis for his first published novel *Three Women of a Certain Age.*

He is lucky enough to be able to act in several Norwich theatres – the Maddermarket, the Sewell Barn and, with the Great Hall Players, at the Assembly House – and this experience informs his writing. He is not trained for the stage, but has learned much from those actors and directors who have been; over the past two years alone, he has appeared in eleven plays, and had his stage adaptation of Laurie Lee's *As I Walked Out One Midsummer Morning* performed at the Sewell Barn Theatre in November 2009.

He has three sons by his first marriage and they inspired two of his novels – *The Vampire's Homecoming* and *The One-eyed Dwarf.* With them and his first wife, he also travelled to the southern states of North America, France, Germany (West and East), Estonia and what was Czechoslovakia.

Three Women
of a Certain Age

by

James Warden

Grosvenor House
Publishing Limited

This book is published by
Grosvenor House Publishing Ltd
28 – 30 High Street, Guildford, Surrey, GU1 3HY.
www.grosvenorhousepublishing.co.uk

A CIP record for this book
is available from the British Library

ISBN 978-1-907652-52-3

To my wife, Lindy,
whom I did not meet on holiday,
but with whom I have had many hours of conversation,
and who gives me the space to think
and the time to write.

Acknowledgements

Many articles read over the past decade or so have contributed to this novel. Some of these have been in newspapers but, more usually, in women's magazines.

One letter in particular – from a lady who had formed a sexual relationship with a local man while on holiday, knowing it to be transitory and feeling bad about the casual nature of it, yet knowing it had been a good experience for her – was the mainspring of the idea. She re-called how her lover, a hotel worker, had always placed a rose on the pillow when he left, without waking her, in the morning, and this gesture stayed with her forever.

I cannot acknowledge these articles and letters because, once read, the magazine was placed back on the table and passed on.

I cannot, also, acknowledge the half-heard but long-remembered conversations to which I have been privy over many years: it is not so much what people say, but what they leave unsaid, between the lines so to speak, that remains in the memory long after the talk.

Two books I can and should acknowledge, however: Kate Fox's *Watching the English* and Patrick Blackden's *Holidaymakers from Hell*. Kate Fox's very readable book is packed with witty insights into the English character, and some of these must have found their way into the minds of my characters. Patrick Blackden's book is a collection of stories and incidents from those aged 18-30 and these accounts, some fictionalised in the novel, form a background to – and a comment on – the story of the main characters who are up to thirty years older: Three Ladies of a Certain Age.

I should also like to thank Michael Stanislaw for his permission to use the photograph he took of me as Laurie Lee in *Cider with Rosie*, and which appears on my website (www.jameswarden.co.uk); likewise, my thanks goes to Andrew Evans for his permission to use the photograph he took of me as Speed in *The Odd Couple*, and which appears on the back cover of this book, as well as on my website.

Lastly, thanks to Sandra Dean for her painting, which I have used for the cover picture.

Watching the English by Kate Fox: published by Hodder and Stoughton in 2004
Holidaymakers from Hell by Patrick Blackden: published by Virgin Books in 2004.

Chapters

Day 1: Arrivals

Frank:

It was four thirty in the afternoon when I stepped on to the tarmac at Craphos. The air closed in on me like glue. You know how it is when you come out of an air conditioned plane? Suddenly, everyone is having a hot flush. Sweat poured from every orifice in my body and stuck like wax. I'm not greatly enamoured of hot places. Give me the temperate climate of England any day – a little bit of sunshine and a little bit of rain. Undiluted heat just gives you a prickly rash. But then, that's what we go abroad for, isn't it – chalky white from an English winter to return as the proverbial lobster?

I hadn't actually arranged this holiday, of course. My ex-wife had done that in a last ditch attempt to forestall what I saw, once I'd made my mind up, as the inevitable. Once the decree nisi was in her hand, however, she withdrew, so I came on my own. I was looking forward to it, although I wasn't sure – as I walked towards passport control – exactly why. It wasn't the obvious – so don't go jumping to obvious conclusions.

I'd read about the Brits abroad, of course. In fact, it was one of our long conversations around a newspaper article that had made my ex-wife suggest the idea of a resort-based holiday. She thought a couple of weeks of sand, sea and sun might liven up our sex life, but as far as I was concerned, that wasn't the problem. Apart from that, I was a trifle apprehensive about the fourth "s"– cystitis – with which, according to the article, many of us are now returning home. Evidently, promiscuity abroad is now rife among those of "a certain age" (shall we say?) and – with an estimated three or four partners each in a couple of weeks – the sensation of having a screw of tin foil unfurled as it is whipped out of your essential tubing is becoming a more and more common holiday present. So no, it wasn't the lure of the delectable that attracted me.

I think more than anything, it was the thought of being totally irresponsible. Don't get me wrong, I am a most moral man, but the thought of being amoral for just fourteen days in my life was fascinating. I've been a father for thirty years with all that entails in terms of time, energy, resources and ingratitude. I've held down a demanding and responsible job for a little longer than that. And you get tired of it: there are times when you just want – as the Americans say – "out".

As I showed my passport, I had only ten essentials to worry about – visiting an open air theatre, finding a quiet beach, having a drink in a village café, joining a plate-breaking session, getting invited to a wedding, going water-skiing, having an alfresco meal off the tourist track, driving to a cliff-top for a view of the sunset, joining in a local dance and walking a forest trail. And they didn't seem too taxing at all. What's more, on my own I stood some chance of achieving them. Don't get me wrong, I'm not saying that my ex-wife – had she been with me – would actually have tried to stop me, but you know how it is with women. You spend hours poring over the books and planning the best holiday ingenuity can buy – and then, on the word of a perfect stranger who has been there before, they change their minds.

The flight had been pleasantly uneventful – free from those little catastrophes without which women seem unhappy. A delayed take-off, of course, but did I fret? Not at all: it gave me a chance to read the paper. We were served an uneatable meal of what appeared to be soggy cardboard that was intended as lasagne; but, then again, there were no needless and endless conversations along the lines of "was I going to complain when I got home?" I simply sent it back, quietly. I don't like the idea of these foreigners laughing at Brits because "they'll eat anything". I simply said to the air-hostess – "Would you serve that to your family?" She smiled and dropped it in the gash can; there was no fuss and no tensions. I've always felt sorry for air-hostesses. After all, most of the time they're little more than glorified waitresses, aren't they? As a doctor friend of mine once put it, "trolley dollies".

And now all I had to do was follow a lovely backside in a pair of blue floral trousers to the baggage collection point, and look forward to my fellow travellers opening up as the sea, sand, sun and alcohol got to them over the course of the evening. I'm a great believer in the liberating influence of alcohol. It brings out the best – or is it the beast? – in all of us.

The lovely backside belonged to a woman in her late forties – and aren't women lovely at that age? Don't misunderstand: I wasn't imagining what she would look like without the blue floral trousers. It was just pleasant to follow her hips across the tarmac, as they swayed gently from side to side. She was quite stylishly dressed too. The trousers were a snug fit and calf length, but they weren't the usual ubiquitous jeans, and she had a loose, flowing top with little straps on the shoulders. She was a real contrast to most of the women on the flight. This was the summer of the Britney Spears look – you know, hipster jeans and tight tops that exposed the midriff, which is OK if you have a midriff like Britney Spears. What we had been subjected to, of course, since April was fat bellies hanging over studded belts and fleshy hips oozing out of tight trouser tops. Why don't women ever realise that they are better off being stylish than fashionable?

The chap at passport control looked me over several times, and I couldn't make up my mind whether he was being officious or whether it was because the photograph made me look like a convict. I'm not particularly good looking and the passport photograph did give me a menacing appearance. I thought he might have suspected me of being one of the many British gangsters, or even civil servants, seeking refuge abroad. However, through I passed, and arrived, unhurried, at baggage collection. This was the first holiday I'd had without my wife for thirty years and, believe me, I was already feeling more relaxed than ever. With a wife, you always feel impelled to rush to get the suitcases. Why? They're not going to come any quicker because you're working up a sweat, are they?

You can't really blame English women for going weak-kneed over foreigners, can you? I mean, it's simply the lure of the unknown and a curiosity as to how it might be different. Looking at all the local talent as we passed out of the airport, I could well understand how they felt. The black hair, dark skin, large eyes and finely chiselled noses certainly had me wondering how different it might be. I've always loved hair and the thought of running your fingers through a dark mane of it down to slender shoulders and beyond certainly turns your heart over. Is it an illusion or are all foreign women slim?

We loaded our cases onto the tour operator's coach and began the long round of hotels. Our holiday rep, Vera, was as English as steak and kidney pie and just about as stoutly built. I found out from her, later, that she had retired early to Cystos and dropped immediately into this "nice little earner". British tour operators liked to employ home grown talent where they could; they found that they had less complaints that way. It isn't easy for foreign reps to enter into the psyche of the English loose abroad, and dangers were more readily averted and problems solved when the likes of Vera were around to sort things out the morning after. She gave us the usual warnings about avoiding the drinking water, watching the exchange rates and keeping out of the sun.

"Adapt to Mediterranean time, go out late, eat late, don't rush, and take everything as it comes," she said. "When you visit churches and mosques, leave your shorts in your bags and no bare shoulders. Take an afternoon siesta or spin out a relaxed lunch. Browse the bazaars for unrivalled value and local colour. Buses and taxis are a cheap alternative to rented cars. Don't get drunk in public – the locals don't, and they'll be offended if you do."

I appreciated the advice, of course, but it didn't sound terribly convincing. Did we build an empire by staying in bed and eating late? I don't think so. Even on holiday, the Brits like to be on the go. Had she taken her own advice,

Vera would now be relaxing in the shade of a convenient tree, sipping the local wine. And who were you to take the siesta with on a hot summer's afternoon?

Already, those I had glimpsed on the flight were splitting off to their own hotels. The blue floral trousers had disembarked at the Aphrodite, together with her husband and three teenage children. It was now six in the evening and old love's dream was fading fast. I felt I might end up buying the local handmade lace for my mother and hiring a pedalo. Why is it that your own hotel always seems to be last "en route"? The coach was now twisting and turning through endless side streets and passing half finished hotels. The flashing signs of burger joints, Chinese, Indian and English restaurants, Irish bars and Scottish pubs made me feel mildly depressed as I looked desperately for just a touch of local colour. And then we arrived at the Poseidon and were met by Stavros and his wife, whose name I heard, perhaps not correctly, as Skeggy.

Stavros was everything a Cystonian should be – he had thick, curly hair and dark, brooding eyes. He was tall and well muscled, with a deep baritone voice. He welcomed us while his wife offered a smile that took in the entire reception foyer. Although she had two children, she still looked like the women at the airport so, while the female tourists watched him, the men watched her, and we learned about safety deposit boxes, air-conditioning and where to put your toilet paper. I later learned that they both worked at least a twelve-hour day and usually a fifteen-hour one and that their restaurant, the best in town, was due to open for business in about an hour.

A dark young man took my suitcase, led me up two short flights of stairs, unlocked the apartment door, showed me the room with a flourish of his hand and smiled.

"You're not from around here?"

"No, I come from Bangladesh."

"Working here for the summer?"

"Yes."

"From Bangladesh?"

"I am studying at the university."

"At Craphos"

"At Abydos – the capital of Cystos."

"What are you studying?"

"Tourism and Systems Management."

"Ah."

I handed him a small gratuity. Always keep on the right side of those who look after you. A few cents now could mean a great deal of comfort later: evening meals on time: a lounger by the pool. A little bit of thought goes a long way. I was in Africa once at one of the crappiest hotels you could imagine. A few words with the pool attendant and we changed not only our hotel but our holiday experience – excursions out, the best food in, meetings with the most influential locals, personal guides to the bazaars – you name it and it was ours!

The room was all I could really have expected – a kitchen combined with a small lounge area leading onto a balcony, a bathroom and a double bedroom with air conditioning. Oh yes, I'd paid for that as soon as Stavros opened his mouth. With daytime temperatures at 35 and the nights only a little cooler, air conditioning wasn't optional. How many nights in the past had lovemaking turned into two waxen bodies congealed together? Running your mouth over the cool of a woman's skin loses its attraction if you're lapping up grit and sweat as you do it. Not that I had any plans for that this holiday, of course. No involvement – no pain.

I unpacked my case, hung my clothes and ran a cooling bath. I was tired after the flight and wanted to wash away the grotty feeling left by nearly half a day's travel. I'd arrived at the airport for eight o'clock that morning and it was now after seven in the evening, local time. I wanted a cool bath, a catnap and then to slip into my holiday slacks and a white silk shirt. I look OK for a man ten years younger than myself. I've taken care of myself and I exercise regularly. Besides, I dislike sunbathing and had taken a short course at the local tanning centre before coming. I was lightly tanned all over – nothing obvious, but that awful English whiteness had gone before I arrived. No creams, no burns.

I must have dozed in the bath, because when I became aware, it was nearly nine o'clock. "Adapt to Mediterranean time, go out late, eat late, don't rush, and take everything as it comes." Well, it looked as if I now had little choice.

The main street of the resort was alive with holidaymakers and locals enjoying themselves. Mingling with the crowds, giving myself over to the flow of the night, I felt worlds away from my daily life. Summer after summer we're drawn away from home and, floating with the crowds in Craphos on that first night, I knew why. It isn't that you can behave abominably; after all, you've got to wake up with yourself the next morning. It isn't that you can do those things you always imagined you wanted to do; at my age I had no illusions about what constituted happiness. It is, quite simply, that none of us realise ourselves; we're all hemmed in by other people's expectations, and the constraints of who we are, within our own communities and families. None of that existed here. Had I come to live in this place, instead of simply holidaying here, I would have had to find a personality for myself – something that was, in part, me but also something that was acceptable to the people I had come to live amongst. I could experiment with those aspects of me that had lain dormant for years.

I stopped at the first restaurant I came to; the patron accosted me and led me to a table. Why resist? These tourist restaurants all serve up much the same kind of food at much the same kind of prices – unless you're lucky and find one used by the locals along a side street and, at something after nine o'clock on my first night, I was too hungry to be troubled. The usual range of international cuisine presented itself on the menu: Italian, Chinese, Indian, English – and then I saw Local Specialities and chose moussaka. Yes, OK, but I happen to both cook and like moussaka; getting those aubergine slices the right thickness and grilling them in olive oil so that they are neither sloppy nor dry is an art form. I was not disappointed. The moussaka was superb: not your usual tourist moussaka, each one cooked in its own little dish and then microwaved to perfection. No this was a slice of real slow-cooked-in-the-oven moussaka. I washed it down with a half-jug of the local red wine. My eating and drinking habits are European (much as I love my own country) and I thought half a jug was enough with the meal. I didn't want to spend the remainder of this lovely evening dozy with alcohol. Have you noticed, for example, how the Italians never appear to get drunk? Your average Brit is reeling around, everyone's mate and ready to right wrongs, after a few lagers, but the Italians can drink all night and walk home in a straight line. Why? Because they pace themselves, combining food and drink in one mellifluous evening; it's an art we Brits have yet to learn.

"Enjoy your meal?"

The question came, not from the patron, but from a glorious redhead at the next table. I had noticed her and her two friends when I arrived, but only casually. It's overly easy to become quickly involved with other holidaymakers and, as I said earlier, when I arrived at the taverna, I was too hungry to be troubled by anything except the need to eat.

"It was great. I can thoroughly recommend it."

"We played safe and had scampi and chips."

"Never do that."

"What – have scampi and chips?

"No – play safe."

I don't know why I said that; I hadn't really meant to but, of course, it was met with triple gales of laughter. It's easy to flatter a man with laughter, isn't it – for a moment, there, I felt like Jim Davidson. As I spoke, I'd given the redhead a good look over. Well, you do, don't you? She reminded me of one of those models used by Rabelais or Monet – not by any means fat, but big; there was plenty of her, but it was firm, and she exuded joie de vivre. I could picture her in one of Monet's boating pictures, leaning over the side rails, a table full of food behind her, laughing into the face of whichever man happened to be talking to her. As far as it is true of anybody, she was wonderfully unselfconscious.

"Have you been here long?" she asked.

"First night."

"Ooh – nice tan."

"Gardening, mainly."

Well, what man of my generation can admit that he's been to a tanning parlour? It opens up too many other questions. And, anyway, I do garden regularly – it's one of my creative outlets.

"A touch of the Alan Titchmarsh, eh?"

"Ooh, he's sexy, isn't he?"

Until now the conversation had been with the redhead, but this last comment came from the second of the trio. She was black-haired, with the kind of skin that carried a natural tan all year. Someone who knew their craft had cut her hair into a cropped style. She was beautiful in a hard kind of way – a bit like a dark-haired version of Sharon Stone. Her eyes, too, were on the flinty side, but dark – the kind of looks which young men think of as those of a "man-eater".

"Why?" I said.

"Why what?"

"Why is Alan Titchmarsh sexy?"

"He just is."

Asking her why had been a mistake, of course – the kind of mistake I often made in conversation; for a moment it had made her think, instead of simply tripping out the latest patter from the newspapers. And after all, we were on holiday, weren't we – who needs to think on holiday?

"Well, it's nice to have a role model," I said.

She laughed. The moment had passed. Quick as a flash, the redhead said,

"Perhaps we'd better introduce ourselves. I'm Lorraine. The lady who fancies Alan Titchmarsh is Caran – C, A, R, A, N – and this is Joyce."

Joyce smiled and said hello. There was sadness in her eyes just waiting to well out. If anyone could be said to have come on holiday reluctantly, it was Joyce.

"Frank."

Lorraine and Caran both laughed.

"Is that so funny?"

"I'm sorry," said Lorraine, "it's just a funny name, isn't it?"

"Like Brian?"

They both laughed again.

"Yes, like Brian."

"Why are some names like that?" said Caran.

"I don't know," I replied, "It must be the picture they conjure in your mind. Could you ever feel threatened by someone called Frank? What image do you see when you hear it?"

"Someone doing the washing up or in the garden," began Lorraine.

"Like Alan Titchmarsh?" I asked.

"Touché," said Caran.

"Sorry, Frank. We didn't mean to take the Mickey out of you."

"It's all right, Lorraine. No offence taken. You get used to your own name."

The laughter and my self-deprecation had eased us into a pleasant conversational mode. I could see that both Caran and Lorraine were relaxed; even Joyce betrayed a faint smile. Lorraine said, quietly,

"You're not here on your own, are you, Frank?"

"Yes I am, actually."

"Oh."

I forget who said it, but that didn't matter – all three looked it. The next question, of course, they couldn't ask, but Lorraine did:

"Are you divorced?"

"What makes you think I'm not a bachelor boy?"

Lorraine's laughter was reassuring. Joyce said:

"You're not a widower?"

The other two looked at her, surprised either by her question or the fact that she had joined the conversation.

"No, I am divorced."

"Well, I wouldn't have thought that," said Joyce.

"Joyce?" said Lorraine.

"I'm sorry. You just don't look divorced."

"I try to."

I couldn't resist the take on the Humphrey Bogart line and they all laughed, which let Joyce off the hook and eased the conversation once again. You have to admire women, don't you? They had, in the space of perhaps fifteen minutes, established that I was newly arrived, had a garden presumably attached to a home, and was divorced; more than that, they knew I had a sense of humour and could laugh at myself. They had also established several conversation points, inroads into my psyche, for later use.

"What are your plans for the rest of the evening?"

"I haven't got a clue. I fell asleep in the bath when I got here, so I'm not tired. I suppose I'll take a stroll."

"They say the place doesn't come alive until the early hours."

Caran's comment bore the gentlest suggestion that this was a good thing. Lorraine said:

"We're thinking of taking in a night club."

"Are we?" responded Joyce.

"Come on, Joyce. It's our holiday," said Caran.

"We've also been travelling all day."

"It'll do us good," laughed Lorraine, "You'll enjoy it when you get there. Would you like to come, Frank?"

My God, I bet she could turn a car on a sixpence! A reluctant friend and a stranger drawn into her plan for the evening without either of them wanting it or fully realising, at the time, what was happening.

"Where is it?" I asked.

"According to our rep, it's in the main street, just off The Square. She says, it gets really wild from about one in the morning. But this place is all right for starters, Joyce – cocktails, a great mix of house and trance, definitely worth a visit."

Lorraine laughed from the bottom of her lungs, and said, "It's called 'Gasoline'. Nice name?"

I found myself walking along the main street of Craphos with my three new acquaintances; it seemed I had known them all my life. How trite can you feel? Lorraine was the lynchpin, and the conversation was easy between strangers brought together simply by being in the same place, surrounded by the unknown. That night, the town was fairly quiet; there was nothing here that would have made the British Sunday papers. Families drifted alongside couples and groups of young people, and the locals watched and mingled. Occasionally a group of local youths would close in on a few young women, obviously newly arrived and at a loss as to where to go; but then, the holiday brochure had said the local people were very helpful. Café touts – pulling trade for such establishments as Tap Donahue's, Gary's Bar, Keystone Korner, Los Banditos, Pagoda, Downtown Taste, Belly Full and Il Cavaliere – called out incessantly, but politely, as we passed and, in the end, you patted your stomach, smiled and moved on. The shops were similar to any you would find in a British seaside town – full of junk and local souvenirs made in Taiwan or China. The harbour walls – for this had once been a quiet fishing village – were lined with people enjoying the night air. Along the centre of the promenade, buskers sang and played and African traders offered temporary tattoos or hair braiding at "knock down prices". Lorraine and Caran walked slightly ahead, keeping their eyes open and looking for Gasoline, leaving Joyce and I together. She seemed relieved at what she later called the "normality" of it; she had been expecting gangs of young men and women baring their chests, breasts and bums. What struck me was how alike we all appeared – most of the women dressed as Britney Spears look-a-likes: most of the men in calf length trousers and T-shirts advertising somebody else's place of education or hobby. Apart from the lack of fighting, vomiting, singing, chanting and sex, the promenade at Craphos was like any reasonably sized British town on a Bank Holiday. Across the harbour, a boat sporting bright lights headed out to sea carrying tourists on a night excursion.

Faintly, across the water, we could hear the sound of laughter and music: Western pop music and western prices – just what the discerning tourist travelled thousands of miles to find. Lorraine turned down a side street, passed a sea sponge stall, and we found ourselves suddenly cut off from the bustle and walking along a dark alley towards the bright lights of The Square. It's funny, isn't it, how women always tighten their grip on you when they find themselves in a dark alley. Joyce had been a foot or so away from me and suddenly she was on my arm as though I might save her from any assailant who lurked in the doorways. Some chance – I'm not built for the mean streets.

The Square was what – in Italy – would have been a beautiful piazza but the British tourists and local entrepreneurs had put paid to that: the central fountain was completely surrounded by bars, all pumping out dance music. It was just getting busy at eleven o'clock. Holidaymakers were appearing from the alleys that led on to it, lingering for a moment and then being enticed into the clubs. Local youths spun round the fountain on scooters, cutting out and homing in on the groups of teenage girl tourists. We passed The British Pub, situated opposite what once had been a monastery (perhaps it still was?) where the waiters, all young men in tight black trousers and red vests, were serving pina coladas and "special cocktails". Here, they told us, we'd find "a great party atmosphere" and "live music with a difference". The resident singer –Vassilis – would entertain us with classics from the Chili Peppers to the Beatles.

"Come in, pussycats."

They giggled but neither Caran nor Lorraine was enticed by the compliment. Gasoline beckoned. Gasoline was definitely worth a visit: the rep had said so. And then we found it – along another alleyway aptly named Nightlife Street. A sign outside promised us not "special", but "lethal", cocktails. I wasn't quite sure whether that meant we would end up dead or just with our brains smashed. One thing I did know, however, was that we'd be ripped off. It was a young woman who beckoned us in and she was gorgeous – well she would be, wouldn't she? No vest here to hide those romping breasts, but a nicely low-cut dress that showed all to perfection. We climbed a few stairs but it was worth it to escape the heat of The Square and find the air conditioning. Before the young woman's smile had faded, we were sitting at a tubular steel table with drinks menus in our hands. The relief of the air conditioning soon gave way to the horror of the music – a hard relentless, battering ram of sound that crashed into your eardrums and fragmented your conversation.

It's hard to recall the next two hours or so as the resident DJ played his great mix of "House and Trance" and the cocktails poured down our throats. My early protests faded into a cacophony of sound and alcohol.

"Like nothing else matters."

"You're in good company."

"We don't do whisky."

"What do you mean – you don't do whisky? You serve Blood and Sand, don't you?"

"Yes, sir."

"Manhattan?"

"Yes, sir."

"Rusty Nail?"

"Yes, sir."

"Shamrock?"

"Yes, sir."

"So what's the problem with serving me a whisky? Skip the crap and just pour me a whisky into a glass. No ice – unless you're using Jack Daniels."

"Ah – you want a Jack Daniels?"

At that point I gave in, and along came the Jack Daniels, together with an Adonis (Lorraine), Cosmopolitan (Caran), Mimosa (Joyce) and then the inevitable string of tourist bar rubbish – Sex on the Beach, Sex Behind the Bar (was there any difference?), Orgasm,

Between the Sheets, Va-Va-Vroom, Crazy Jack, Bliss, Shaguluf, Viagra for Two (which had a nice sense of sharing), Craphos Sunset, Long Screw Against the Wall and an endless stream of unremitting alcoholic concoctions designed for laughs rather than drinking.

We did make the dance floor. I was glad of that because I actually like dancing. Any pretence at real conversation had long since been suspended. We blended with the crowd on the dance floor. Sweat, gyrating bodies, shoulder and bum banging all added to the fun. On that tight, heaving floor, I tried to dance properly – well, why not? If you can actually do something no one around has a blind idea how to do, strut your stuff. Touch at the hips and lean slightly back. I'd taken Caran to the dance floor first – or had she taken me? I had her wrapped tightly in my arms at the edge of the floor, spinning and dipping, hip to hip, gazing deeply into each other's eyes. Dancing is so natural: the rhythm takes you over and soon we had commandeered the floor while the youngsters stood around whistling and clapping. They aren't used to that kind of dancing nowadays. Once rock 'n roll gave way to the Twist and those silly dances from the Seventies onwards there was no more touching. Limbs thrashed around all over the place, or twitched and jerked close to the chest, but you never touched the girl: which is strange considering how much closer, sooner, sex has got. Maybe that's it – dancing was foreplay to music: now that it's shag time on the second date, foreplay is hardly necessary.

I danced with Joyce and then with Lorraine and neither Caran nor Lorraine was ever off the floor for long. Joyce turned down several offers, but not the other two. Sitting there with three women, I was like the stud of the street, king of the sidewalk, the cat who got the cream. And so the night wound on. "If you don't dance you're crazy – wow! – and you're totally crazy if you do. It's a real chill out, groove with the chicks, chat with the lads. Who's got more energy than anyone else? The lights get lower and the music gets louder. You'll feel like nothing else matters and you're in good company. Love the show and the DJ is something else! Check out the bar for the coolest drinks in town".

Joyce:

"Frank, will you walk me back to the hotel?" said Joyce.

Day 2: Welcome to Craphos

It sounded forward, asking Frank to walk me back like that, but I couldn't bear that disco any longer. I cleared it with Caran and Lorraine, and then just asked him. He seemed a decent sort of man and I didn't think he would misinterpret my intentions: at least I hoped not. I just had to get out of the noise and the heat and that incessant movement of bodies. I don't necessarily dislike discos – although I can't honestly say they are one of my favourite pastimes – but it had been a long day and I'd had enough by the early hours.

It was wonderful in the square. These clubs seem to go on all night and hadn't yet emptied on to the pavements. The only sign of life was some splashing in the fountain. A youth, somewhat the worse for drink, seemed to be propping himself against the sides, while another stood facing him with his back to the fountain itself, the water pouring all over him. I couldn't quite make out what was happening but a young woman seemed to be bending over, stretched between them, with her bottom towards one and her face toward the over. Frank frowned as he saw them, then smiled and steered us away along the sides of the square. He looked at me and said:

"Three coins in the fountain?"

"Which one will the fountain bless?"

"I suppose it depends on your point of view."

"What are they doing, Frank?"

"Ever seen those Greek mosaics – *Nightlife in Athens* and the like?"

"Eh, no."

"Good – your education has obviously been a cultural one."

We walked out, along Nightlife Street, on to the promenade. It was quiet now: the crowds had gone. Frank and I seemed to be the only people in the world. The night was still warm and we could hear the water lapping gently against the hulls of the ships. It was the kind of night on which you had dreams and aspirations, when you were young and in love for the first time: when you would have died for the touch of a boy's lips or hand. Now – older but no wiser and certainly less sure of myself than I had ever been – I felt like laying bare my feelings, as I had done all those years ago, when Robert and I had fallen in love and walked together. When you love someone like that, you can talk, can't you? That's part of being in love – sharing your soul.

I wasn't in love with Frank, of course, but as we walked together on the promenade at Craphos I was aware of a quietness about him that encouraged me to want to say something. But where could I begin? I was vulnerable, now, to rejection as I had never been with Robert. Do you say, to a perfect stranger, that you are divorced and desolated? Do you talk endlessly about your ex-husband on the first night of your holiday? Frank looked at me across the silence of my doubts.

"I'm sorry. I'm not very good company, am I?" I said.

"What's good company? Is walking quietly with you any less good than pounding the dance floor back at Gasoline?"

"Is it?"

"No. At our age, we're interested in each other whereas when I was young I was far more interested in myself. All those youngsters back there are concerned about is what they are going to get out of the night. To me, it doesn't matter. There'll be other nights."

"Why are you divorced, Frank?"

"Why shouldn't I be?"

"I'm sorry. I shouldn't have asked."

"I don't mind, but if I tried to tell you, I wouldn't know where to begin and, if I started, I wouldn't know where to stop."

"Do you want to be?"

"I suppose I must do, since I did the divorcing, but it's hard to say."

It would have been the moment, then, to tell him that I was divorced, too, but I couldn't. Suddenly, I didn't want to. He was right. It was somewhere between two and three in the morning, we hardly knew each other and he had been kind enough to walk me back to me hotel. Cans of worms could wait.

We walked into the foyer of the Captain Karas Holiday Apartments. The night porter looked up and I knew I was blushing to the roots of my hair but he merely smiled and went back to whatever book he was reading beneath the counter.

"Where's your room?"

"I can make my own way from here."

"No you can't. If I walk a lady back to her place, I walk her all the way back. What if something should happen to you on the stairs?"

"I don't think it will."

"Nor do I, but I'm not taking the risk. How would it look, later on this morning, if you didn't arrive back safely?"

"It really is all right, Frank."

"I know, but English women tourists have the reputation of being "easy" and I'm responsible. Don't worry, Joyce, I shall stop at the door."

I laughed and so did he and, somehow, I knew that he would. When he wished me good night and turned away, I felt so silly. I watched his back, with its slight stoop, move off towards the lift and then I shut my door. I was very tired and glad that I had returned to my room. I was glad, too, that I had asked Frank to walk me there. I needed someone to talk to and Frank was that someone.

Caran:

Lorraine, who had been laughing like a drain all the way home, eventually collapsed with all the cocktails she'd had, so when I saw Frank leaving the Karas, my relief was palpable. I had struggled with my drunken red-headed friend long enough, needed some help and didn't fancy asking the concierge when I got to the hotel. Frank turned as I called and sauntered towards us along the road. A motor scooter zoomed by; we'd been harassed by those all the way from Gasoline – young men eager to help themselves to a couple of English women. If there were to be 'helping yourself', I'd be the one to do it! Island studs!? Who the hell did they think they were? Who the hell did they think we were?

"You OK, Caran?" asked Frank.

"Do I look OK?" I responded.

"Only asked."

Lorraine started to sing as Frank arrived. I wasn't sure whether or not it was because she recognised him or whether she would have sung for any man at that point in the evening.

"Little Lorry Tucker sang for her supper".

"What shall we give her …?"

"Knock it off, Frank. She's drunk enough."

"Forget the bread and butter, and run the …"

"OK, Lorraine, let's get you to bed."

"Oh, Frank, did you think our first date would be as romantic as this?"

"No, Lorraine. Nothing could have prepared me for this."

"Sugar tongue."

Having had her say, she slumped into unconsciousness, leaving us to sort her out. Frank didn't seem too bothered. He crouched close to her, pulled her left arm across his shoulders and stood up, nodding to me to support her right arm. He then slipped his right arm around her waist and we walked steadily through the hotel foyer, Frank smiling at the concierge.

He was very good when it came to putting Lorraine to bed. He lifted her on to the bed and, before I really knew it and with little help from me, removed her dress (which was a little strappy number from Next) and pulled the duvet up and over her; he then reached underneath, removed her bra, tights and knickers and handed them to me.

"Doesn't pay to sleep constricted when you're drunk – I'll leave these to you. Good night."

"Don't go."

"Pardon?"

"Don't go. You aren't supposed to leave the hotel grounds after dark."

"We have just arrived back from outside the hotel grounds."

"But that's not the same as leaving them. There are muggers about."

"Really? I didn't see any."

"I wouldn't feel happy, you going back to your hotel alone."

Frank looked at me as I stood there, Lorraine's underwear in my hands, and I could see that he was puzzled. Mind you, so was I. I hadn't expected to say what I did, and didn't know why I had.

"You've helped us out tonight, Frank, and we hardly know you. How about a late night drink?"

"A late night drink?"

"Well, you know, we are on holiday."

"Yes."

I don't suppose he had slept since the early hours of the previous day, any more than we had, but you lose all sense of time on holiday, don't you, and this was so unusual I wanted to hold on to it. Don't ask me why. I wasn't attracted to Frank. I didn't want him to take me to bed. I think I had half an idea that Lorraine might walk through with the duvet around her and we would sit talking until morning. I wasn't use to this. When you have a husband and two boring little shits of teenage daughters, you don't get moments like this. Your life is centred round their needs. "Shall we do this? Drive me there!" Frank wasn't going to ask anything of me – I knew that. He would sit and listen all night. I can't tell you how much I had enjoyed tonight. I think it was the first time I had felt free since my college days.

"We bought some duty-free gin on the flight here."

I knew that the last thing Frank wanted at that moment was a drink of any kind – duty-free or not – but I also knew that he wouldn't refuse me, and I wanted to sit on the balcony listening to the sounds coming up from the late night bars, watching the drunks staggering home. He opened the door and arranged the chairs while I got the gin and tonic from the fridge.

"Do you have teenage daughters, Frank?"

"I did do. Helen must be thirty-something now."

"Do they get any better?"

"She's always seemed a nice enough girl. She and her mother had their scraps at the time, as I remember."

"I feel drained by mine. They're like vampires, sucking away my energy and my looks."

"You look fine to me, Caran. In fact, you're something of a stunner. You've obviously taken care of yourself. You don't have a body like yours at fifty unless you've taken the trouble to look after it."

He said this in a matter-of-fact, conversational tone, without taking his eyes from the sea and with no apparent attempt at making a compliment. Englishmen of my acquaintance making such remarks either do so with lashings of irony or a "nudge-nudge, wink-wink" leer.

"Do you have any lemons?"

"Lemons?"

"To go with the G-and-T."

"No. Eh, no, I don't think so."

"Never mind."

There was the briefest of pauses and then he said:

"Your daughters get on your nerves, do they?"

"They're so rude and ungrateful. They don't seem to think anyone has a life but them. They were lovely little girls and then – overnight, it seemed – became teenagers. I don't think a day goes past without one or the other being rude. They treat my husband and I like servants. "Are you going to take me, then, or have I got to catch the boring old bus?" With a grunted "please" to make it sound all right, but which clearly almost chokes them. And then, having kept you waiting in the car until the last minute, they complain that you're not going to get them where they're going on time."

"They're just children in adult bodies. Would you let a child speak to you like that?"

"They didn't when they were children."

"Exactly. Then, if they behave like children, treat them like children."

"Did you?"

"I found the more I intervened in support of my wife, the more we quarrelled about it. She would ask for my help and then, when I sorted Helen out and laid down the law, she'd tell me I was being hard on the girl."

Just like my husband, in fact. Frank didn't understand women, any more than Simon does. Perhaps we do need our bread buttered on both sides.

"So I opted out, like most men, and left it to my wife. I couldn't see the point in us falling out over something we agreed about."

"No."

I laughed; I couldn't help it. I wanted to ask him about his divorce at that moment because I couldn't quite see why any woman would let him go, but it didn't seem appropriate. And then the gin kicked in.

I'd taken some trouble getting ready to go out that evening and suddenly it felt quite sexy sitting with Frank on the balcony, watching the harbour lights and listening to the night life returning to their hotel rooms. He was right. I was an attractive woman, not just the mother of two selfish teenage daughters, who gave a thought for nobody but themselves, and a husband caught up with his work and ducking his domestic responsibilities. I was fifty; how much longer was I going to look as I did tonight? And I did take trouble with myself, as Frank had said in that offbeat way of his. I'd let Lorraine have her bath first because I wanted the luxury of lying in mine until the last possible moment – or, at least, the last moment before your skin starts to wrinkle. I'd relaxed, watching the bubbles float between my thighs, every now and then opening and closing my legs so that the warm water washed against them. I'd pictured the black dress I had laid out on the bed with the black silk panties and black bra. I know, black is a fashion cliché! Yet it always looked good against my naturally tanned skin and dark hair. I'd chosen those clothes – all from Hobbs – for a laugh really, to get Lorraine and Joyce going; but I did want to look sexy on our first night and I knew that men's eyes would follow me around any bar in town. And wouldn't I look stunning against those teenage girls with their cheap Topshop outfits! Standing by the side of the bed, I actually wondered whether or not to wear the bra; when I looked in the mirror, lifted my arms and saw my nipples rise, I decided – no bra.

Joyce was going to pass out and I could hear Lorraine's laugh; now and then you have to feel good about yourself. Looking at myself in the mirror, naked except for the panties and with the dim light of the hotel bedroom accentuating the darkness of my skin, I saw a tart – in the nicest possible way, of course – looking back at me. I'd played the tart for Simon in the early days of our marriage – and enjoyed it. I twisted and turned, admiring myself, pushing my hair up and away and tossing my head about. I used a little eyeliner, just to make my eyes larger and darker, and a slash of red lipstick.No more make-up: my skin was already glistening with its summer tan. I swept the brush through my hair until my scalp tingled, shook it out and let it fall. Lauren had cut it well. "At fifty-something you need a good cutter". I think Joan Collins said that. Perfume (if your feeling classic, why settle for less than Chanel No 5?) at the neck, wrists and just a touch (for vulgarity's sake!) in the valley between my breasts. The dress had slipped on, casually caressing the flow of my body; there was no fat on me, but neither could you see any bones. At my age you have to exercise sensibly and diet on the best food money can buy – otherwise you grow pot-bellied or have wrinkles of flesh hanging on your ribs. When I moved, my muscles moved with me!

I stood and looked at Frank, the noise of the harbour bars now only a murmur in the distance. He had that rather bemused look on his face but his eyes followed every curve of my body, until they rested on the valley of my breasts and then my mouth, which opened for him – just enough. He seemed to hesitate, so I reached out for his hands and drew him to me, placing one hand on each hip and arching slightly towards him. He ran his hands along the curve of my back and cupped my shoulder blades in them and then bent his mouth gently to mine. I returned his kiss, pressing my body against him; my breasts stroked softly across his shirt and I reached for his crotch. I knew I had aroused him, knew that his penis was straining for release against the thin cloth of his slacks. I was reminded of the first time I had unfastened a man's belt, unzipped him, taken out his penis and held it in my hands. Why don't we make time for that in marriage? Frank stepped back and ran his fingers along the underside of my breasts and then slid the straps of my little black dress down my arms; he bent and took first one nipple and then the other into his mouth, flicking them gently with his tongue until my breasts ached, wonderfully.

It was an exquisite moment for me in the bedroom when I heard the slide of the zip; my dress slithered to the floor and Frank took down my panties and tossed them aside. I hadn't been naked in front of any man but Simon since we married a quarter of a century before. It seemed so easy, so natural – and then Frank took my hands and led them to his belt. As I pulled his pants and trousers to the ground I noticed, with a shiver, that his socks and shoes were already kicked across the floor. It was my only moment of apprehension. I'd wanted to unfasten the belt, let his trousers down, touch his penis and run my hands over his buttocks. I wanted him to satisfy that enormous aching in my breasts.

He seemed to know where I wanted him to kiss me next, placing his mouth on my throat, chest and belly as he made his way around my body. At times, he drew back and impelled me to kiss him, and I covered him with light, feathery kisses until he could bear it no longer and he opened his mouth and drew mine to him in a long kiss that held and stirred me until I felt my juices run. Frank suited me: I'd always enjoyed long sessions of love-making – before the children came – and he seemed in no hurry. His lips returned again and again to the small hollows of my body. He placed his lips gently into the small cavity above my collarbones and breathed kisses, brushing his nose along the side of my neck until he reached my mouth where he paused and then retreated along the sensitive underside of my arms to the perfumed wrists.

Have you ever had your fingers kissed one by one, the man's mouth returning again and again to the hollow of your elbow, knowing that he would then move across your breasts, pausing to taste your nipples as he passed, to the other arm? I hadn't, not for a long, long time. It felt good. It felt exquisite. He nuzzled my navel a score of times – breath, mouth, nose – stroking and rousing and passing on. I remember, at one point, he turned me over and found the hollow at the base of my spine. He took my buttocks in his hands and gently parted them – nosing, kissing and tonguing persistently until I opened to him. I wished, at that moment, that I'd dabbed a little Chanel there, but he enjoyed me nonetheless. I thought he would enter me, taking me from the rear, but he didn't. I could smell the sweat on my body by then and the juices ran freely down my inner thighs and, although he opened my legs and ran his fingers from my tuft to the inside of my knee, he moved on to the hollow behind the knee and I felt his breath and kisses once again.

His kissing never ceased throughout that night, even as his caresses took over and became more and more urgent. He caressed me with every part of his body, stretching across me, rubbing his chest over my breasts, his penis along the length of my thighs and all the while his touches were silky and light. It was me who became violent – if I can call it that – falling on him hungrily, using my teeth wherever I could reach, nipping him and reaching for his mouth time and again. I mirrored his every movement: lying, kneeling and sitting on the bed we touched and tasted every part of each other.

You cannot pull back from love-making. Finally, I took him to me, raising my legs across his back and over his shoulders, stretching muscles unused for years. I wanted him to take me furiously and he knew it, but he made me wait, bending over me, watching the tangle of our legs. I felt him come into me again and again, each time with slightly more penetration and each time I would experience that aching for him to be deep inside me. I didn't want to be left unsatisfied. I felt myself widen and close, widen and close until I went into spasm and then he came – hot and quivering, he exploded and the tension went from me and I was relaxed and easy in his arms.

I don't know how long we were together that night but it could not have been less than three hours. I lay in his arms when we had finished and watched the corner of his chin and that smile across the wrinkles of his face. Occasionally, he turned his head and kissed me and one of his hands cupped and fondled my breasts. I recall crossing a leg over his stomach and down between his thighs and his hand leaving my breast for a moment and stroking my hip, wandering carelessly down along the line of muscle to my pubic hairs where it tickled and played. I didn't want him to speak. I didn't want words – not at that moment – and he seemed to understand, crooning gently, saying nothing until I fell into a deep sleep.

Frank:

It was after six o'clock in the morning when I left Caran asleep and made my way quietly from the hotel apartment she seemed to be sharing with Lorraine. I couldn't believe I'd been on Cystos only fourteen hours. No sleep and a "welcome meeting" to face at ten thirty. I gave the concierge a nod and he gave me a long look and then a fixed grin. 'The English', he was thinking, 'what pigs they are. If any race deserves to be wiped out by AIDS, it's the English abroad'. I couldn't bother to think up a counter-argument: I was too confused. How had it happened? Why had it happened? Did it matter that it had happened? What did I know about Caran other than that she had two, difficult, teenage daughters? And a husband – yes! And the daughters treated them both like servants – I remember her saying that.

"Frank?"

I looked up. Joyce was leaning over her balcony.

"What are you doing?"

"I've been taking a kip on Lorraine and Caran's settee ...."

"I can't hear you. Come on up. I couldn't sleep. It's so muggy."

I didn't want to go up; at the same time, I didn't want to continue a review of the last few hours of my private life outside a Craphos hotel at six-thirty in the morning. I was shattered and I just wanted to sleep – for a long, long time. Ten minutes? You can't be rude, can you?

Why not – why can't you be rude? Joyce was nothing to me; I'd met her less than ten hours ago.

"They said you might be mugged?"

"Yes. Hadn't the hotel warned you about going out alone after dark?"

"Hmm. How was Lorraine?"

"Zonked out. We got her to bed and then had a quiet gin-and-tonic."

"And a cat nap on the settee?"

"Something like that."

"You've had less sleep than me, then?"

"I suppose so. Time to crash out. We've got the welcome meeting at ten-thirty."

"Well, at least have a coffee before you go. I've given up trying to sleep in this heat."

"Thanks."

I hope my voice carried more appreciation than I felt. I wasn't so much tired as desirous of sleep. You know how it is after you've made love? You just want to turn over, cuddle down and sleep.

"Would you like a poached egg to go with it?"

"You've got eggs?"

"We went shopping soon after we got here – for the essentials. You know – bread, milk, eggs, butter, tea, coffee – that sort of thing."

"And a poacher?"

"No, I brought my poacher with me. I couldn't go without a poached egg for two weeks."

"You brought a poacher with you?"

"Yes – and marmalade. I don't like foreign marmalade. It doesn't taste the same as what you buy at home."

"No. And they never provide a poacher in hotel apartments, do they?"

"Isn't it annoying?"

I didn't answer. My comment was meant to have a touch of irony (is it irony or sarcasm?) about it.

We ended up eating a three-course English breakfast – Joyce had also bought a grapefruit – and washing it down with coffee. Joyce looked really at home in the apartment kitchen, preparing breakfast; I could see that she was enjoying herself.

"Thank you, Frank."

"For what? I should be thanking you."

"For sharing breakfast with me. It's a long time since I cooked breakfast for anyone."

"A breakfast shared is a pleasure doubled?"

"Yes."

She laughed; it was a heartwarming sound.

"You miss your husband very much."

It was neither a statement nor a question. It sat somewhere, comfortably, between the two but, as I spoke, I realised I might have opened up a long conversation. When Joyce turned to look at me I realised that I had: her face was quietly convulsed.

"How did you know?"

"I believe Lorraine mentioned it during the evening."

"Yes. People don't understand. All this talk about "today being the first day of the rest of your life"! How shallow are people who really believe that? Did all those other days mean nothing to them? Is everything so meaningless that they carry nothing forward?"

She paused, clearing the table slowly.

"And if you carry forward joy, then mustn't you – by necessity – carry forward grief?"

"You've been alone for some while?"

"Yes. I've tried, but it's no good."

"Tried what?"

"Those things that people advise you to try."

"Like?"

"Singles holidays. That kind of thing."

"Not for you, Joyce?"

"No."

There was another long, long pause. This was a woman who had, for how many years I couldn't guess, been used to sharing her thoughts with one man – easily, knowing that he would listen and sort out her problems. Now she was talking to a complete stranger, wanting to do the same thing but unsure whether it was right and how I might respond.

"How long were you married?"

"Twenty-nine years. Robert was the only man I ever knew or wanted to be with. He was a very untidy man. When he left, he left his tie thrown over the arm of the settee. I picked it up to put it away but realised, if I did, that I would never ever have the chance to tidy up behind him again. So I left it. It's still there. I keep kidding myself that he dropped it there yesterday evening when he came in from work. Can you believe that?"

I could believe it – my wife and I had been that close. It wasn't the closeness that had got me down; it was those other times – the monthly strings of verbal abuse that became a habit that Stella couldn't break. I, perhaps, had more sympathy for Joyce that she might realise. I was tired; I didn't want to listen anymore, so why did I feel obliged to ask, to move the conversation on?

"You've never met anybody else?"

"I don't want to."

"And yet you can't, or won't, come to terms with your loss."

"Yes – put like that, I suppose so."

We weren't getting very far. There was another long pause and then Joyce said:

"I'm sorry, Frank. I don't mean to …."

"Joyce, stop saying that you're sorry. You need to talk. I'm happy to listen. Really – quite happy."

"Really?"

"Yes – really."

She suddenly laughed. From the little I knew of her, I felt the laugh to be uncharacteristic. It became almost a giggle and, for a moment, there was this little girl, full of fun, her amusement ringing out from her balcony. A woman, on her way to work no doubt, looked up from the street. 'The English enjoying themselves,' said the expression on her face.

"What are you laughing at?"

"It's our conversation. 'Really – quite happy.' 'Really.' 'Yes – really.' It sounds like that funny playwright."

"Harold Pinter?"

"I don't know his name."

"Yes, it's Pinter. He's noted for his 'realistic' dialogue."

"You're well read, Frank."

"Not really – there we go again! In my line of work, you tend to keep your eyes and ears open, that's all."

"What do you do?"

"I'll tell you in a fortnight's time. It may put you off."

I laughed, then, and said, knowing somehow that it would cause no offence, since we had "opened up our channels of communication":

"Look, Joyce. We'll talk later. OK? When we're both less tired?"

"Yes. Thanks, Frank."

"And thank you for the breakfast. It's a long time since I had somebody cook me breakfast. It was very nice."

"Enjoy your 'Welcome Meeting'."

Down in the street once again, I hurried back to my hotel. Which one was it? The Karas Apartments? No, no – that was where I had spent the night. Mine was the Poseidon with Stavros and Skeggy. I must have been over an hour with Joyce; it was now getting on for seven-thirty. Young men whizzed past on scooters, not a care in the world, hurrying towards the hotel kitchens where they would soon be cooking breakfasts for the tourists. Women in their twenties walked more slowly towards the hotels where they worked, carrying with them the worries of their homes. Such was life.

"Frank?"

It was Lorraine's voice. She was walking towards me along the street, a newspaper in her hand. I suppose the expression on my face said it all; my utter surprise at seeing her actually on her feet. She laughed the laugh that must have turned so many men's knees to jelly.

"I've got the constitution of an ox. Don't take me on in a drinking contest. It's Caran who's out cold. Anyway, what are you doing here? I thought your hotel was further on."

"I spent the night in your apartment. Caran said that you had been advised not to go out after dark because of muggers. When I left this morning, Joyce was on her balcony and invited me up for breakfast."

As I spoke, I realised that what I was saying might seem implausible, and the expression on Lorraine's face was one of utter disbelief; although, looking back on it later (when I knew more about Joyce in particular), I don't see why.

"Well, Frank – take me under that beach table and you'll have shafted the three of us in one evening. Not bad. What's the record on Cystos for the number of lays on the first night?"

I don't think any woman had actually spoken to me like that before – at least not under normal circumstances. I wasn't quite sure how to respond; I didn't want to get involved in what might, later, make me look a liar and yet I couldn't let her think that Joyce and I had slept together. Lorraine saw my bewilderment.

"It's alright, Frank. It's what we girls are here for – a good holiday shafting. Only I think we all thought it might be from Tom Conti or someone like that. Come to think of it, there is a resemblance. You're better looking in daylight, Frank. It enhances your tan."

"Lorraine, we need to get a couple of things straight."

"I should guess you've done that already, Frank."

She laughed again.

"Come on, buy me a coffee first."

I bought her coffee and croissant and sat with her while she read through the morning papers from home. The article that particularly took her fancy was one on celebrity men who are "bad boys". Lorraine found it quite amusing that her own sex was inordinately attracted to men who were "shits".

"It's evidently the charm that gets us, Frank. They can be alkies, druggies or love-rats. As long as they've got charm, it appears that we go back for more. What makes them charming is their vulnerability. Security is boring. What we girls desire more than anything is a "walk on the wild side". What we don't want is a loyal bloke who works hard, helps out with the kids, listens to us, gives a hand with the housework and keeps the garden looking nice. That is definitely "boring". Give us a sensitive, warm druggie any day because he'll open up our soul to endless possibilities. Ooh, yes, and if he sees us chucking up after a binge night out, he'll understand and show us he loves us by ignoring it. I wonder if his understanding would stretch to clearing up the sick afterwards."

It turned out that Lorraine was an avid reader of the papers and we must have sat for an hour while she ate and talked her way from the front page headlines to back page sport. My head was nodding forward when she put the paper down. She looked at me with that laugh in her eyes and said:

"OK, Frank. Let's find that quiet spot on the beach now – or would you rather go home to bed?"

I went "home", although not to bed. It was after nine when I arrived at the Poseidon Apartments. Skeggy was at the reception desk looking wonderful at this hour – the black hair, dark skin, large eyes and finely chiselled nose I'd noticed on the local talent at the airport all on display. She smiled and handed me my room keys.

"You must have had a good night?"

I was too bewildered to answer. In my room, I wondered what she and her husband really thought of British tourists abroad. The religion here was termed 'orthodox'. Did that mean they took it seriously or was it rather like the 'Church of England' at home? Did it form the moral basis for the way the islanders lived their lives; were its teachings on sex the same as ours? Most religions were pretty clear on this sort of thing but, of course, we accommodate their teachings to our own particular needs at the time – don't we?

Such were my thoughts as I undressed and fell into the shower. I just wanted to sleep. As Shakespeare has it 'Sleep that knits up the ravelled sleeve of care', or something like that; but I had the Welcome Meeting in just over an hour, so there was no point in going to bed. At the same time, I had been up and active for twelve hours, ever since I had strolled along the seafront for a quiet meal last night and bumped into the three weird sisters. Half consciously, I showered, shaved, did what I needed to revive myself for the meeting and then put on some fresh clothes. I know – why didn't I jump into a pair of shorts and slob down to the pool-side as I was? Because I can't, OK? I was brought up to go out clean, not covered in yesterday's sweat. I'm around sixty and can't shake off the teachings of my childhood.

The Welcome Meeting was all I had expected it to be; I was glad I hadn't missed it. There was a glass of red or white wine for everybody and orange juice for the children, the initial milling around and then Vera covered the usual topics with slickness and brevity – where not to change your money, time, customs on the way home (yes and no), tourist offices are best avoided, don't worry about opening hours because everything is open all the time, use public transport because the taxi drivers will fleece you, you can't rent a car if you are under 25, expect to be stopped at random by the police, get a crime number for insurance purposes if you have anything stolen which is unlikely, tips are expected everywhere except in toilets or at the cinema ("give about ten percent unless it's a hairdresser, tour guide or porter, when fifty pence will do"), few concessions are made for elderly visitors, and so on. Finally, she came to what these meetings are really about – booking your excursions through the rep.

"Don't trust regular tour operators. We do it cheaper and we have insurance." Her sales build-up was a joy.

"It's always hot here in August. You've come for the sun, so enjoy it. There are plenty of places to go and we can take the hassle out of organising it by doing all the tedious stuff for you. So, what's on? Well, it's a democratic country, so you can choose anything you want. Versatility is our speciality! If you want nightlife, we can whirl you away to Karavi Limani – the place for clubbing: in fact, once known as the 'Club Capital of Europe'. Or there's the whole day, two-centre visit to the dream-like beaches of Trootaras in the morning and inland to the mountains of Graphos in the afternoon, where you'll find the coolest shower on the island – the waterfall at Koodos. It's an absolute must for fun-lovers and nature-lovers alike.

Or .... you might prefer the sophistication of Abydos. That'll be a whole day trip, where you can visit the markets, stack up on those souvenirs for the family back home – and take in a nightclub to round off the day! And if that sounds too quiet for you, you adrenalin freaks, we can also offer day and half-day excursions to go bungee jumping (yes, and do a reverse bungee), skydiving, gliding, para-jetting, helicopter rides, off-road motor bike safaris, go-karting, horse riding, water parks, kite surfing, scuba diving, water ski-ing, jeep safaris, windsurfing, jet ski-ing and some wild night rides with a barbecue thrown in! And that's just for those of you who want to party!"

At this point, Vera wiggled her hips and moved her forearms backwards and forwards – rather like a child imitating the movement of a train, but actually intended to give the impression that she was a party person and "couldn't wait to boogie". Realising, too, that she had probably exhausted at least some of her clients, she took a deep breath, paused quite dramatically, and then carried on.

"Are you getting the drift? There's something for everybody. And ...for those looking for more relaxed leisure, we have the two-centre visit to the Graphos Bird Park and the archaeological remains at Napa, ten-pin bowling at Porfos (that's an evening trip), the beauty lounge at Xylotnos where you can spend a day being pampered *and* have a 'Hot Stone Massage' – how about that ladies? Or ...why not try a trip on a pirate ship; fun for the kids and adults alike. This is a crazy island – so get ready to slap on the Factor 20, get ready to chill out to the max, get ready to put on a few pounds, get ready to pump some adrenalin, get ready to drop all those inhibitions, get ready toooo parrrrrrrty!"

At this point, she waved her hand broadly over a range of brochures and sat down to collect our money. As we surged forward to pick up leaflets, it occurred to me that this £450 a head all-in holiday might just prove to be a little more expensive than my ex-wife and I had originally anticipated.

A few leaflets in hand, I sauntered to my room. It was midday; I hadn't stopped for fifteen hours and had only been on the island for about twenty. I was, in Princess Anne's words, "absolutely knackered". "Adapt to Mediterranean time, go out late, eat late, don't rush, and take everything as it comes," Vera had said as we arrived. I didn't feel like lunch. It didn't feel like lunchtime. I went to my room, drew the blinds across to keep out the sun, turned the air-conditioning off (have you ever tried to sleep with it on?), stripped off, folded my clothes onto their hangers and crawled in between the sheets (yes, sheets: cool, cotton sheets!) and slept. 'Sleep; the balm of each day's life' – or something like that.

It was past seven o'clock in the evening when I woke and my first thought was that I must, if I wanted to enjoy this holiday, avoid the three weird sisters. I crawled from my bed, turned the air-conditioning back on – so that when I got out of the shower I didn't have to get back in again immediately – and made for the bathroom. By nine o'clock I was dressed in a fresh silk shirt and slacks, enjoying a quiet drink in the Poseidon bar and wondering once again about a late evening meal. It turned out that Stavros was opening an extension to his hotel on the following Sunday and that we, as his guests, were invited. This was to be a big occasion; at some point in the proceedings, the archbishop was coming to bless what would essentially be a bar-cum-restaurant and children's play area. Stavros had spent many months travelling between Cystos and England looking for what he wanted to achieve and ordering the right equipment; Skeggy had stayed on in Craphos, with their three children, managing the hotel.

"We are a good team," he had said, as he served me my vodka and lime.

As we spoke, I noticed the children running about the hotel and popping back into the kitchen occasionally for a snack. He saw me looking at them, and said:

"We have a flat here in the hotel. When they are tired, they go to bed. Then we take them home when we have finished. When they are school age, we shall see."

It turned out that he and Skeggy had a large house with a swimming pool somewhere up in the Craphos hills.

"It is cool there."

He laughed, showing a full set of natural, white teeth.

"You are wanting a meal?"

"I certainly am. Thanks."

He disappeared into the kitchen and a moment later, a young man was rearranging some tables, whipping out a fresh tablecloth, setting cutlery and leading me to a seat.

It was a really good meal cooked by Stavros himself – did all the evening meals in his restaurant. It consisted of a tuna fillet weighing about half a pound which had been marinated in olive oil, garlic, red onion, jalapeno and lime, with a dash of cumin and minced cilantro; it was barbecued for a few minutes on each side and then served with a salsa of papaya, mango, pineapple, red pepper and red onion with a good handful of chilli flakes and Italian seasoning.

"The secret is in the freshness of the fish," said Stavros. "You can buy them from the harbour, but make sure the fish has bright eyes, bright red gills, a shiny skin, and that it smells of the sea!"

He breathed in lustily:

"My restaurant is the best in town."

"It was excellent."

"Of course ... You now need to 'walk it off', eh? The English always need to 'walk it off'. Try Coral Beach, Frank. Have a nice evening."

He laughed again as he spoke. I looked at my watch; it was close to midnight.

Day 3: Coral Beach

Out in the street I turned right – away from the main centre where I had met the threesome on my first evening – and made for Coral Beach. I felt like a vampire; having slept most of the day, here I was, out at night, seeking my prey. I began to question why I was here, what I was hoping to do. Was it the thought of being totally irresponsible after thirty years of fatherhood? How long had I been here? We arrived on Saturday afternoon, and it was now (what?) the early hours of Monday morning: sort of a day and a half, then. I hadn't visited an open air theatre, found a quiet beach, had a drink in a village café, joined a plate breaking session, got invited to a wedding, had an alfresco meal off the tourist track, driven to a cliff top for a view of the sunset, joined in a local dance or walked a forest trail.

So what had I done? Had two local meals, gone dancing at a tourist nightclub, attended a 'welcome meeting', had sex with one woman, breakfast with another and coffee with a third. It was the sex which worried me. I'm not a promiscuous man and I knew nothing of Caran, other than that she had clearly wanted to do what we did – or had she: was it simply the gin? Should I have left the room, gently? My ex-wife had said that I was a drifter, and went along with things to "keep the peace". "What did I really think; what did I really want to do?" My work had always demanded my thinking and planning so, in my private life, did I just let things 'take a natural course'. Did I accept no moral responsibility for what happened? Was I feckless, amoral, thoughtless or weak? Did I owe Caran at least the chance to talk – or was she just as responsible as me for what had happened? Why didn't I feel the need to give Lorraine and Joyce another chance to talk; is sex more important than breakfast or a cup of decent coffee?

With these thoughts running through my mind, I arrived at Coral Beach. I knew from the brochures that this was considered a local beauty spot. How shall I begin to describe it? If you can imagine a junk yard of the old-fashioned kind (nowhere near as well designed as our current 'household refuse sites') which has been subjected to a violent sand storm and then sprayed with dried effluent to give everything a dull, grey appearance then you can picture Coral Beach. This wasn't just a trick of the moonlight, as I discovered on a subsequent visit; it looked exactly the same under the sun. I stumbled down a rough track from the car park; to my right stretched a line of cafés and bars, which had been built into the cliff face, their terraces jutting out over the beach and supported on stilts.

Litter (the usual detritus of the tourist spot) was everywhere: coke cans, crisp packets, ice-cream cartons, take-away boxes from the kebab house, wrappings that had once held chips, drinking straws, newspapers, magazines, posters, tourist information pamphlets, plastic water bottles, beer bottles, wine bottles, olive oil bottles, olive oil cans, empty gas cylinders, plastic cutlery, balloons, broken plastic spades and buckets, wasted food (soon to be picked out by those scavengers of the night – rats), lost baseball hats, bits of swimming costume, hair bands, sun tan lotion bottles and scraps of make-up tube; but this was only the surface mess of what made this beauty spot more unkempt than a shanty town.

I decided to take a look at the café and bar area first. The steps leading from the rough track were worn and the banisters broken. Everything had been nailed together (there wasn't a screw in sight) and was now beginning to twist apart: the steps were askew and wobbled as you placed your weight on them, and the banisters had begun to rot. The once-white paint was now flaking away. When I reached the wooden walkways, I felt the grey sand crunch under my feet. There was no pride here; none of the bar owners cared enough to keep their patch clean. The first bar, the Athene (did they know she was the goddess of wisdom?) was described in the brochure as "a classic venue where you can enjoy your post-dinner tipple on a stool on the terrace, overlooking the sea; hey, at this rate you'll never get out of here!" It actually sported an unsightly assortment of peeling and rusting tables covered with half-empty drink cans and bottles, and featured ashtrays half-full of dirty butts. It was also half-full of happy Brits in various stages of drunkenness eating chips with gravy, chips with curry and chips with squid; by each table stood a bucket in case anybody wanted to be sick – with booze being so cheap, this was an essential requisite in such bars.

I passed through the Arithea and found myself, having avoided the public toilets that stood between the restaurants, in the Crazy Moon Disco bar. This hosted a screen which must have measured about three metres by two and was showing a "live" football match; again, it was half-full of happy Brits eating and drinking much the same as I had seen in the previous bar. Notices around the bar advertised Newcastle Brown, Stella Artois, Carling, Guinness, Caffreys and Hoegaarden. I asked for a pint of the latter and was handed it by a young Cystonian girl full of smiles and covered with sweat; I felt glad I hadn't come for a meal and decided to try to get to the beach.

This was easy provided you descended the rickety stairway, which led down from the terrace, carefully and I found myself quickly on the grey sands. In front of me, stretching towards the sea and spread casually around, were more peeling tables; this time they were topped with umbrellas that were tattered and torn beyond caring, all lounging at disturbing angles from their hole in the centre of the table, some actually lying flat on the sands. I felt the gritty sand beneath my feet again and sipped my beer; it was ice cold and, after a couple of deep pulls on the glass, I began to feel better, more at home with my surroundings.

Stavros told me later that each year, the beach was re-created by bringing sand from Africa and dumping it in the bay. One year the sand had come by boat from the Sahara and turned out to be full of black scorpions; for a while this had deterred tourists from coming to the beach but the local entrepreneurs immediately had the sand removed, dropped out at sea and replaced. You cannot help admiring such enterprise, but why did such energetic people not re-paint their premises each season? Was it simply that the punters would notice a lack of sand and the scurry of scorpions, but remain oblivious to their tatty surroundings? It didn't seem much of a deal for the scorpions either.

As I stood downing my Hoegaarden, a couple of young women, half-cut and half-dressed, came lurching up to me. One was a natural blonde (I could tell that even in the moonlight) and the other was what used to be called auburn. Both had huge manes of hair tumbling across their shoulders and halfway down their backs. They both sported the bare midriff look but could afford to do so. There wasn't an ounce of fat on either of them; long, lean legs that used to be described as "going right up to their necks" stretched down from denim skirts frayed just below crotch level. There was some conflab and then the blonde, an absolutely stunning looking girl with a beautifully even tan, fell towards me and said:

"Twenty-two?"

"Sorry?"

"Twenty-two?"

I looked at her friend, who was leaning on the table and put what I hoped was a quizzical expression on my face.

"Twenty-two?"

"She wants to know if you'll be twenty two."

"It would be nearer sixty two"

"Oooh – how long you been here then?"

"A couple of days."

A look of utter admiration crossed the girls face.

"You pulled sixty-two birds in two days?"

I had been somewhat surprised to have "pulled" one, but thought I might lead them on for a while.

"Men of my age are in great demand. We make excellent and caring lovers. A little slow in coming, perhaps, but worth the wait. Any man in his fifties, fancy-free and owning his own house can reckon to pull a bird every night of the week. A girl-friend told me that."

It was a lie, of course (I'd read it somewhere – probably in *Grumpy Old Women*) but it had the desired effect. Adolescents can't really bear to think that people of my age might actually indulge in sex and might even be quite good at it; after all, what they are discovering is unique, they are the first people ever to have been young.

"You fancy yourself, don't you, you dirty old man."

"It was you who approached me – number twenty-two wasn't it?"

It had only dawned on me as I started my "men of my age" speech what the blonde girl had meant by "twenty-two" and, of course, the "slow in coming" reference would have had the desired effect; mention of anything specific always got a "Daaaaad" from my daughter when she was in her adolescence.

"Well – twenty-two?"

"I don't think so. Thanks all the same."

"Are you turning me down?"

"Yes – it certainly sounds like it."

"You speak posh, don't yer – for a dirty old man."

"Well, I don't know where you've been. Who was twenty-one?"

"You old git."

At that moment, a group of three young men, who had been swilling 'San Miguel' (the kind of drink which you and I let out the other end when we've had a real beer) and listening to our conversation, lolled over, bent on being chivalrous.

"Trouble, girls?"

"Yeah – this old git made an improper suggestion to Sharon."

"Is that right, mate?"

"What's it to you? An improper suggestion is one thing – and no, I didn't – what you have on your mind is an improper act."

There were several conflicting concepts contained within this sentence as the frown on the youth's face showed; he hadn't expected me to stand up to him – this surprised me, as well. I had apparently defended improper suggestions while deploring improper acts and I had read his mind – all part of the training!

"Whaaa?"

I saw no need to respond; they were on the run. They had come here to shag openly on the beach, drink themselves sodden, show off their love bites and do all those things they were unable to do at home. Being abroad brings out the beast in the Brits and places like this had been set up for them – any vomit, blood or semen would be washed away in the morning tide.

"How about you, then – twenty-two?"

"Yeah – all right. I'll see to you later, mate."

He and the blonde girl put their arms round each other and staggered off to "make out under the pier", so to speak. Her auburn friend looked at one of the other young men.

"Well?"

"Yeah – OK"

"Your turn next?" I said to the third man.

"Don't know if I fancy it."

"Take my advice, son. You don't know where they've been – steer clear. How drunk are you?"

"We've been here since about nine o'clock. I reckon we've shifted a few."

"Let's hope your friends are up to it. They may have got Brewer's Droop."

"Those girls will get somefink out of 'em. We've heard about them. They're determined. They've got a points system for getting off with blokes – twenty for getting laid, ten for a blow job and just five for a really good snog. They're making their way round the island."

"Enterprising young women! What you might call the 'entrepreneurial spirit'. You're a mine of information son. Fancy another drink?"

"Whaaa ? You're not queer are yer?"

"What? No – Christ, no. I'm just interested in what you've got to say."

We walked back towards the steps that led up to the bars, missed the Crazy Moon and found ourselves in Miklos' Black Velvet Pub – "free jukebox and over 5000 songs. Wow!"

Sitting over a pint of Guinness (me) and a pint of Stella – what else? – (Glynn), I said, once more:

"You're a mine of information. You and your friends have done your research?"

"Yeah – well you hear a lot just sitting in the bars and that."

I waited: patience always pays off. Years of experience have taught me that people want to talk. Eventually, Glynn – who was from Cardiff – said:

"It's what it's all about really, coming here. Anyone can pull here. The first night we were here, we met these girls at a club and they were pretty fit so we played 'scissors, paper, rock' to see who got who. I got the younger one – the riper one – and we got out on the dance floor. I could tell she was into me and soon we were having a snog and I could feel myself, like, coming, so I pulled her off the dance floor and we went to look for a bit of privacy. Eventually we made our way upstairs to a bar that was 'off-limits' and we did it there behind the bar. You can always get a fuck when you're on holiday."

"Did you see the girl again?"

"Oh no – you never see them again. You move on."

"And the girls are happy with this?"

"Eh – course they are. They reckon to have sex with at least ten blokes in the two weeks they're here."

I had read somewhere that the average time between arrival at the resort and the first "lay" was just under four hours; I assumed at the time that this didn't include honeymoon couples who were, hopefully, a little quicker off the mark – or perhaps they're not these days. At that moment, Glynn's two mates appeared at the top of the beach steps.

"The blonde one is a bit of all right. She's looking for you. She wants to make it twenty-five tonight."

I thought it sounded like time to go, so I wished Glynn the best of luck and made my way back to the Poseidon. He seemed a nice lad and I was puzzled although I don't know why I should have been. The Sunday papers, over the summer months, are full of stories of the Brits having a good time abroad – the combination of cheap booze and holiday-makers wanting to indulge in one-night stands. One paper reckoned that there wasn't a single square inch of – well never mind, let's say one of the Mediterranean islands – that hadn't been used for sex at some time or other: the beach (of course), the top of a speaker in the night club, a rubbish bin at the end of the street and a bar stool in a pub called Tramps.

As I went through the Arithea, a 'Eurovision Thong Contest' was in full swing; a girl, wearing two stickers over her nipples and a sequinned thong, was gyrating around one of the umbrella poles which she was using as a phallus. The crowd were yelling, "get 'em off, get 'em off, get 'em off". As I passed through the door she removed the stickers, danced for another ten seconds and then collapsed. I wondered whether she would remember anything about it in the morning.

Caran:

Lorraine, Joyce and I had beaten the Germans and secured prime places at the poolside: it felt good. Lorraine had actually been leaning over the balcony and seen one of them come down, as the pool attendant put out the loungers early on, and place towels for about ten of them; so, when we arrived, she slung four of the towels on to the fence and we spread ourselves. Joyce was embarrassed, of course, and started with "What if …?" but Lorraine brushed it aside, saying "Leave it to me."

"Why four?"

"Why not? They pinched ten. I need one for my sun tan creams. We can always give it up to a nice family later."

It had been just over twenty-four hours since I arrived back at the hotel with Lorraine and asked Frank for help – the early hours of Sunday morning and it was now Monday afternoon – but it seemed much longer. When she returned with her Sunday paper, Lorraine had made a remark and passed me a look but that was all, and

Joyce had said that she gave Frank some breakfast when he left – in that innocent way of hers. To be honest I didn't know whether to say anything or not. I wondered whether it would be more cool to make an announcement or more sensible to keep quiet. A huge percentage of women, according to a *Women's Hour* programme I had heard, thought that one night stands left them feeling bad about themselves. On the other hand, one of the women who they interviewed called herself "a rapscallion in my love life" and it didn't seem to have done her any harm. After all, why had we come here if not to find our Tom Conti? Not that Frank was exactly my idea of Tom Conti and, but for the gin, I wouldn't have done it. So yes, I did feel bad but not that bad. Simon hasn't been very keen for a long time. I used to need him to get me going, but not now – it must be the menopause. It's a shame the way it works out, isn't it? When they're all keen you're too tired – having been with the children all day – and when they go off it, you get the hots. I find myself looking at other couples at parties, wondering when they last did it.

And my daughters don't help. I can't tidy their rooms without finding a condom case – used, of course – somewhere or a magazine telling them how to do a blow job. To be fair on Simon, he wasn't into all that; he reckoned that they did more for the man than the woman. When he was younger, he did give good value. I got married knowing nothing about sex. It seemed to take months from having a crush on someone to building up to the first kiss, but you did get to know each other that way. The slow build-up was beautiful in its own way; I can remember lying beside Simon, when we were first getting to know each other, aching for him. There was always that anticipation, but a shag on the second date seems standard, now.

"Penny for them, Caran", said Lorraine.

I looked at Joyce; if I shared my thoughts, could she take it?

"I was thinking about sex and how different it is for my daughters these days."

"The world is obsessed with it," said Joyce. "You can't turn the television on without seeing some couple in bed. And the way they kiss these days. Actors used to close their mouths; these days you can actually see them stick their tongues in each others."

"And not just in their mouths," Lorraine laughed.

"Not just in their mouths? I don't understand."

"Never mind, Joyce – the odd bit of late-night viewing on the satellite channel has depraved me."

"It can't be very pleasant for the actors, can it? I mean, would you want a perfect stranger sticking his tongue in your mouth?"

"Not while a group of techies filmed it."

"Have you ever wondered what it would be like to have an affair?" I asked Lorraine – or rather, I threw generally into the conversation.

"I wouldn't know where to begin," said Joyce.

"It isn't the beginning that is difficult, Joyce: it's coping with the end," said Lorraine.

"It's not me. It's not my world. I found that singles holiday they persuaded me to go on awful. Men groping you."

Lorraine and I exchanged glances. I must admit, I quite fancied the idea of being groped – by the right man, of course: nothing vulgar. I'd had a dress made once. It cost the earth but was unique, and the fashion designer who measured me for it was really macho – not one of those nancy boys you usually get in the fashion world. I'd enjoyed that, and he fed my fantasies for a long time. I'd developed quite a crush on him. He was dark and hairy and foreign – a Spaniard or an Italian: something like that. I said, mostly to Lorraine:

"Do you think foreign men are sexier?"

"I think they're more attentive. I went out with an Italian once and he never took his eyes off me the whole evening, whereas if Barry and I are chatting in a restaurant or anywhere, his eyes are all over the place."

"On other women?"

"No – just generally."

"An evening isn't a lifetime, though, is it?" said Joyce. "Any man can be attentive for an evening. How long does charm last?"

"Stavros is an attractive man, isn't he?" I said.

"Sshh, keep your voice down."

"Oh, Joyce, no one can hear us. He is, isn't he?"

"Yes – I could quite fancy him. Lucky Skeggy," said Lorraine.

At that moment, a young man walked past wearing a T-shirt to protect him from the sun; he couldn't have been more than seventeen or eighteen at the most. On the T-shirt was the slogan 'Fancy a Blow Job?'

"It's disgusting," said Joyce.

"Ssshhh, Joyce. His parents might hear."

Lorraine laughed out loud and said:

"Do you really think he's with his parents?"

"Is he old enough to be on holiday on his own?"

"Joyce, my daughter took her first holiday 'on her own' when she was seventeen. I don't like to think what they got up to," said Lorraine.

"They?"

"She went with her current boyfriend."

"And you let them?"

"What can you do? Teenage girls want their own way, and if they don't get it, the atmosphere in the home is awful. Didn't you find that with yours?"

"No, not really. My son was fine. Our daughter was more difficult, but then girls are. It didn't occur to us that she would be going on holiday – alone - with her boyfriend and she didn't. She just wouldn't have asked. Anyway, it's no preparation for life, is it, to get your own way all the time? And this 'sex before marriage' thing is highly overrated. Look at the divorce rate."

Lorraine and I exchanged another glance. My two had both been bonking whenever they could from about the age of sixteen or seventeen. I had been worried at first, but then I read somewhere that 86% of unmarried girls in Britain were sexually active by the age of nineteen and decided to try and ignore it. Simon hadn't been remotely interested: "Not in the house" was all he'd said, hoping, I suppose, that that might cut down the opportunity somewhat. By the time they got round to marriage, which seems to be later and later these days, they would both have had more men than I ever dreamed off.

I'd always thought that when they grew up they would be fun to talk to – like having another woman around all the time – but it wasn't like that. If I asked anything, my two sort of grunted, pulled a face and made me feel as though I had intruded on their privacy. There's nothing like a teenage daughter to make you feel you're past it.

And yet they keep coming to you for things ("Where's this?" "Where's that?") because they're quite incapable of looking after themselves. It never seemed to be like that for us. I can't ever recall lolling about like my two – aimless and gormless – and then expecting the whole house to jump to attention when they received a text message to join their friends "in the ci'y". They don't seem to have any life outside the current boyfriend; if he isn't around, they're "boooored" and expect you to jump in and fill the gap – take them shopping and spend a fortune on those silly clothes. You know, the 'here's my belly button, here're my boobs' look or, worst still, those over-long jeans which soak up everything from the "ci'y" streets. And why can't they say "city"? Is it so difficult to sound a "t"? After all, they 'tut' enough! It's not as though you can sit them down anymore, and offer some sound advice, either – like my mother did. You get the faces and the eye-rolling and the puffing and the 'err-ing'. They always used to hate Harry Enfield's 'Kevin the Teenager'. I can see why – it was so true to life.

"I thought you'd come on holiday to get away from them, Caran?"

"You can't, can you, Lorraine? Wherever you go, they're with you."

"Are they worrying about you at this moment? Were they worrying about you when they were with their boyfriends in Ibiza? Relax! Enjoy yourself! You only come this way once – teach them a lesson; show them you have some life left in you!"

"We've got the excursions to look forward to," said Joyce.

"Ye-es, they should be fun, but we need to get out and about anyway. We're not going to find what we're looking for lying around here everyday."

"I'm particularly looking forward to the Evening Boat Trip and the Ethnic Night Out."

"Not so keen on the Pirate Ship, then, Joyce – or the Jeep Safari?"

"You wait!" I said, and Lorraine and I laughed out loud.

At that moment, one of the waiters passed by, gave us a smile and asked if we wanted anything to eat or drink.

"Have you got anything we might fancy?" said Lorraine.

For a moment he froze, having – no doubt – heard this line in jest many, many times before, and then he said:

"It depends on what madam has in mind."

"Well how about something to round off our lunch – something cool and crunchy?"

"We have an ice-cream sundae … "

"With a dark chocolate sauce?"

"If that is what madam wants."

"My name is Lorraine – and you?"

"I am Dakos."

"Married?"

"No … Lorraine. May I get you that sundae?"

There was some discussion, but Joyce's expression was such a picture that Lorraine and I could hardly keep a straight face, then Lorraine said:

"You can do better than that – how about a date when you finish work tonight?"

There was another frozen moment; his face was now a picture, and he faltered.

"I do not finish here until – oh, maybe ten o'clock …."

"Ten o'clock suits me fine. I'll save myself, and you can take me somewhere special for a really nice meal. You know, somewhere in town where the local people go."

"It will be my pleasure … Lorraine … Do you still want your sundaes, ladies?"

"Yes, please."

As Dakos left to get our order, we all followed him with our eyes. It was hard to place his age – it could have been late thirties or early forties: maybe older. He was tall and dusky; he moved between the loungers, tables and poolside with the easy glide of the experienced waiter.

"I can't believe what you've just done," said Joyce, her eyes popping from her face.

"Why are we here, Joyce?"

"For a holiday!"

"No. We are here – especially you – to get a man."

"Really!"

"Yes – really! I must say, I don't feel particularly desperate about it myself but you, Joyce, are on the look-out. You want a husband, someone to look after and nag at a little when you've had a bad day. You're not going to find one sitting at the poolside eating sundaes and going out for a quiet meal with Caran and me in the evenings. You've got to work at it. It isn't going to just happen. I must say, I thought you'd latched nicely on to Frank that first evening when you asked him to walk you back to the hotel."

"Frank is different. We sort of know him."

"We met him one evening, late, after we'd all just arrived."

"Well …."

"You didn't like that singles holiday, did you? You're not going to join a dating service, are you? How are you going to meet anyone, Joyce – by accident?"

"We are going off the point a bit, Lorraine. I was thinking about you."

"Don't worry about me. I have made a few enquiries about Dakos. He is one of those experienced waiters employed by these hoteliers to keep the cheap labour in line – a kind of maitre d'. The lads who work here are mostly from places like Bangladesh – they study at the university in Abydos and work in the hotels, bars and restaurants during the season. The owners need people like Dakos to see that things run smoothly. And he isn't married."

"But you've got Barry at home."

"Joyce, I'm in my fifties and Barry and I have been together – not married because we didn't want it that way in the feminist seventies – for thirty years. I've probably got another forty years ahead of me. Barry and I are fine but things have, shall we say, gone slightly off the boil ...."

At this moment, Dakos arrived with the sundaes, arranged them neatly in front of each of us, smiled at Lorraine and glided away. Lorraine continued:

"I don't mean, by the way, just sexually, although it is a fact that we no longer chat while we're having sex. I used to rather like that – a lot."

Joyce blushed to the roots of her hair, but Lorraine ploughed on.

"I've never actually been unfaithful to Barry – or he to me, as far as I know – but people can drive each other mad, after thirty years of exclusivity, which we had never intended. That's one of the reasons we never married.

But am I never to make a friend of another man – ever? We are all living longer – there is life after the children have left home: a lot of it."

She laughed, suddenly, in that infectious way of hers, as though she'd had a dirty thought and then said:

"You've heard of Club 18-30? Who hasn't? Well, our generation of women are Club 48 – 60. Fifty isn't what it was in my mother's day. Sixty is the new forty! What moron said that? But there is some truth in it. Don't look so worried, Joyce. I'm just going out for a Mediterranean dinner with an attractive man – a man who has led such a different life to me, probably. It will be interesting. We're not just sexual fodder. We have brains and minds and feelings and concerns. We are fascinating people, the liberated women of the seventies. Men have to learn that they must be interested in us, not just our bodies."

"You are a one, Lorraine. I must say that. Excuse me, I won't be a moment."

Joyce made her way from us, up to our rooms. I said to Lorraine:

"Do you think you've upset her?"

"I hope not. I didn't intend to but she does need to be a little more – what's that horrible word they use? – proactive."

"I think she was a bit taken aback – you asking him for a date."

"The devil was in me. I hadn't planned it. Still, perhaps it'll show Joyce the way."

"Have you really checked up on this Dakos?"

"I asked a few questions. He'll be all right. You can always tell with men. We'll have a nice midnight dinner and see a bit of the town by moonlight. Live like the locals – adapt to Mediterranean time, go out late, eat late, don't rush, and take everything as it comes."

"I must say I admire your nerve."

"It's funny, Caran, that Joyce of all people sees what I have done in sexual terms. I'm not planning to sleep with this man. I mean, can't a girl have a night out without it having to end in bed?"

"But does he see it like that?"

"It's all the same if he doesn't. I assume he's taking me out because he's interested in me – not my fifty-something body."

Joyce:

I'd felt a little uncomfortable listening to Lorraine, so I went for a walk. I knew she meant well and I could see that no knight in shining armour was going to gallop by on his white horse and whisk me away but, at the same time, I couldn't see myself joining a dating agency or anything like that, and I certainly couldn't ask a man out as Lorraine had done. I really had to "just bump into somebody": that's how Robert and I had met – at a dance, but I was nineteen then, not fifty-nine.

I had tried: I had been to dances and sat there like a wallflower while everybody else danced. I went with a friend of mine – a widow – and she was all right, but I only danced three times in the whole evening. Nobody wants to dance with a divorced woman when there are attractive women about. Divorce does make you less attractive; I feel less attractive now. They call it "losing your self-esteem" these days, but it's simpler than that: you're nearly sixty: there are younger more vivacious women about, so why should anyone want you?

I've never been like Lorraine: I couldn't do what she did. Fancy asking out a man you had never met before! I hope she'll be all right. But she is attractive, of course: that mane of red-blonde hair – natural or not – and those firm breasts of hers, no need for any uplift there! And she is an attractive person – always laughing and seeing the funny side of things. People are drawn to her.

I just can't get away from my thoughts these days. Ever since Robert divorced me, I've been thinking about it. When Lorraine and Caran persuaded me to come on this holiday, I didn't really come to find a man. I came to get away from my thoughts: just to find something to "take my mind off things". I walked a little faster.

The seafront was busy despite the afternoon heat. Families were coming and going to and from the beach; none of them took any notice of the many warnings about "staying out of the sun between twelve and three", but then the advice is so contradictory. One moment they're saying to use a sunscreen lotion of at least Factor 30 and the next that you should be in the sun to make sure you get enough vitamin D! I certainly felt better in the fresh air; there was a slight, warm breeze from the sea and it lifted my spirits a bit to feel it on my skin.

The bars and restaurants were busy, of course; they're never empty, are they? I think that some of these people spend all day and night in one – and usually the same one. Robert always said he couldn't see the point of coming on holiday and sitting in a bar all day, that you might as well stay at home in your local pub.

The shopkeepers gave me a smile as I passed. I was reminded of Blackpool or Great Yarmouth. Apart from the sun, it wasn't much different – the same fast food stalls, the same beach equipment for sale, racks of dirty postcards, cheap souvenir shops – but I began to feel better as I walked. They say that walking is good for your health. I read in one of my women's magazines that some university (Essex, I think it was) had done research to show that people who exercise outdoors reported increased levels of self-esteem, that exposure to nature had "positive mental effects and that physical activity is good for us".

Their 'research officer' called it "green exercise". She advocated an hour's gardening instead of an hour's housework, and said that a real bike ride was better than half-an-hour on an exercise bike. I suppose she was a young piece who left the housework to her mother; the picture that went with the article showed this young woman, who didn't look as though she knew what a Hoover was, cycling through a park. She had a beaming smile on her face, but I couldn't see her tidying the children's bedrooms or getting home in time to get the family's evening meal on the table. I expect they'll be setting up 'Green Gyms' next and have us all meeting up in the local park – "everyone welcome from seventeen to seventy". I know who'd attract the looks!

I reached the end of the row of bars and shops but decided to walk on a little further; the road led towards Coral Beach which we had heard so much about. I eventually found a car park and the rough track that led down from it; to my right stretched a line of dirty cafés and bars with crowds of young people sweating over the tables. The beach was littered with tatty umbrellas and loungers. It was awful. I had turned to go when I heard my name called.

"Joyce?"

At that moment, I knew why I had come. I'd not just wanted to get away from Lorraine and Caran for a while – I'd wanted to "bump into" Frank. It was his voice. He was coming up from the beach.

"Frank?"

"Hello, didn't expect to see you here. What do you think of the local beauty spot?"

"It's awful."

"You should see it at night! I came down after I'd eaten last night and couldn't believe it so I thought I'd wander back this afternoon."

There was a pause and I didn't know what to say. Frank seemed at a loss for words, too. He smiled and then said:

"I've been catching up on my sleep. I think I've recovered from that first day now. Do you fancy a drink?"

"Here?"

"Why not? This is "the mythological playground of the Mediterranean". I think it was on this beach that Aphrodite first appeared in her shell. We'll find somewhere with clean glasses."

I must say I didn't really fancy eating or drinking here, but I didn't want to seem standoffish so I said yes, and Frank led me down the steps and across the beach.

"How do they make this sand grey, Frank?"

"I don't know. Perhaps it's 'the curse of the black scorpions'."

As we sat at the bar, he explained what he meant.

"You're very well informed, Frank."

"Men are expected to know these things, aren't they? Didn't you always ask your husband questions he couldn't possibly know the answer to?"

"I haven't thought about it."

"One of my wife's favourites was "Frank, what's round the next corner?" We were once in Germany – on a Rhine cruise – and we had stepped off to explore the Lorelei Rock. We had never been in Germany before, you understand? Halfway to the top, she says, "Frank, what's round the next corner?""

I couldn't help laughing.

"What is the Lorelei Rock?"

"Hmm? Oh a maiden – not many of those about these days are there? – is said to have thrown herself off the rock in despair over a faithless lover. She became a Siren whose voice lured sailors to their doom."

"How long have you been divorced, Frank?"

"About six weeks. I started proceedings in March and the divorce came through in June."

"You mean your decree nisi did?"

"That's right."

"So you're not properly divorced yet?"

"Hmmm?"

"You haven't had your absolute?"

"Joyce, you do not sue for divorce in jest. As far as I'm concerned, the nisi is absolute. I'm not going through that again."

Here I was, within minutes of meeting someone, talking about divorce again; I decided to change the subject – rapidly.

"We've booked some excursions, Frank. Have you?"

"Oh yes – 'Historic Cystos', a trip on a pirate ship, an evening cruise and an 'Eco Day Out' which should "flow with local wines". I'm looking forward to them."

"What days are you going?"

"To be honest, I have no idea, Joyce."

"We're going on our Pirate Ship on Thursday – this week, our Jeep Safari on Monday, our Evening Boat Trip next Tuesday and our Eco Day Out next Wednesday. A bit close, I know, but it's the only way we could fit them all in."

"Right – you've got that well sorted, then!"

He laughed at me, but I didn't mind too much. It was so nice to be talking to someone – to a man, to be honest. With Robert, our whole social life had revolved around me organising everything, but now that he'd gone I had no social life at all. There was a lesson there, somewhere.

"What did you do last night – more clubbing?"

"Oh, Lorraine and Caran won't hear of it otherwise. I would have preferred an early night in, but we went back to the square in Craphos."

"Not to Gasoline?"

"No, this was worse. It was called Seventh Heaven Rock Garden. The young man on the street said we'd be crazy if we didn't go and crazy if we did, so Lorraine and Caran couldn't wait. After dark, the music – if that's what you can call it – became unbearable. There was a 'Tattoo Competition'. They were all going up on the stage showing off what they'd got. You can't imagine what some of them had had done to themselves. There was one man who'd had what looked like a snake inserted under his skin and it wound its way down from his elbow to his wrist. One girl showed her bottom and ...I can't tell you what she had written on each cheek."

"An invitation to dance, perhaps?"

"An invitation to something – but it wasn't dancing! There was a restaurant attached to the club and it was called Love Bites."

"A neat play on words, Joyce. It's where you would take your girl for a romantic evening."

"But there was no romance, Frank. When they kissed, they seemed to be gnawing at each other."

There was a moment's pause. Frank seemed to be weighing something up in his mind, and then he said:

"Joyce – did you just happen to bump into me here? ... If you don't mind my asking. It just occurred to me that it was quite a coincidence, considering the number of people here."

"I wanted to get away from Lorraine and Caran's interminable sex talk ... I knew your hotel was this way and ...yes, I did hope to bump into you but it was only on the off-chance, of course."

"Of course ... well since we have, why don't we have dinner together this evening – purely as a couple who like to share a little chat? You might be able to get your early night in, that way."

"Oh, I don't know. Um, it's not as simple as that."

"Why not – are you girls always intending to eat together?"

"No – it's just that Lorraine has a date and I don't like to leave Caran on her own. It's one of the waiters. She just chatted him up."

"Good for Lorraine. That's why you girls came here – to go places and meet people?"

I felt odd: I'd come here hoping to "stumble across" Frank, I had stumbled across him, and yet I was refusing to have dinner with him. I suppose Lorraine would have said that I had "pulled". Perhaps that's why I felt odd.

"I didn't mean to be rude, Frank. I was just thinking of Caran ...I know – why don't we have dinner at the Captain Karas? Then Caran can eat with us."

Frank seemed to hesitate for a moment but only for a moment; I thought perhaps that he didn't like Caran for some reason, and then he said, crisply – as though he'd made a decision:

"Why not? What time shall I get there?"

"Oh, about eight, I suppose. Nobody seems to eat any earlier than that."

Frank:

Lorraine sat with us while we ate, just drinking, and the occasion was pleasant enough. Caran gave me a 'look' when I arrived, but there was no 'atmosphere' which was what I had been afraid of; Joyce chatted about our afternoon at Coral Beach and then all three launched into a detailed description of their night at the Seventh Heaven Rock Garden. When Dakos arrived, I could see that he was a "man's man": one of those guys who would treat a woman with respect. Too many of these foreigners – especially in tourist spots – have the idea that English women are "an easy lay" and I had wondered what the evening might hold for Lorraine when Joyce had described Dakos to me. He shook my hand, helped her from her chair and then they were off and away.

We continued to chat for a while after they had gone, Caran and Joyce both looking forward to the excursions they had booked, and then Joyce said, suddenly:

"I hope you don't mind, but I'm going to get an early night. I think a third night up after midnight will do me in."

I was taken aback, but managed to mumble:

"Thanks for the dinner. You must eat at the Poseidon with me, sometime."

With a wave and a smile, she was off, leaving Caran and I at the table.

"What's the arrangement, Frank? Are you supposed to get rid of me before midnight and then follow her up?"

"I don't think so, Caran. I think Joyce just sees this as a chance for 'an early night' without being rude to her friends. She's enjoyed her dinner, she's had her digestif and now it's bed-time."

"Have you always been such a gentleman, Frank?"

"Probably."

"Aren't you going to offer to take me for an after-dinner walk, then?"

"If that's what you would like. Where do you fancy – a quiet stroll along the prom-prom-prom?"

"How about showing me Coral Beach? Joyce seems to have enjoyed it."

Day 4: Early Night

I had no intention of taking Caran to Coral Beach; Stavros had laughed, when I arrived back, and said "It used to be a beauty spot. Tourism has spoilt it. We prefer a little beach just to the north of the harbour". The following morning I had found it and so I said to Caran, as we set out along the seafront:

"Are you dead set on Coral Beach? It is ghastly by moonlight and just a little worse by day."

"OK. A walk and a drink anywhere would be nice."

We passed The Hippopotamus; loud, beery voices belted out "Do you want to be my girl?" This song, together with "Sex on the Beach", was the adopted anthem of the Brits abroad. I never managed to hear any of the other lyrics, but these two phrases reverberated through my head on every evening stroll I took. As we passed the bar, a row of red faces leaned over the rail of the terrace and leered, giving us the main phrase full volume, off-key and scented with Stella. The singers were irrepressibly cheerful, quite sure that everyone else shared their view of the night and, indeed, probably the world.

Caran and I walked on; as we passed the Sienna which, according to the billboard, offered an "extensive a la carte menu, blending culture and cuisine" a young couple, sitting at a roadside table, were clearly upset with the waiter. The young man, wearing a T-shirt announcing "fcuk mon amour", was waving his arms and pointing at his dish.

"This is fucking rigatoni init? I ordered penne din I?"

The waiter was also young and clearly less than fluent in English; his lack of understanding seemed to enrage the customer even further.

"Let's go, Frank," said Caran.

"It'll be all right. This might be fun."

"It's the wrong fucking shape, init?"

"Does it matter, Aron?" said his girl who, according to her T-shirt, also appreciated the pleasures of "fcuking".

"Course it matters. We're paying for this. They're quick enough to take your money. They ought to fucking get it right."

"Can I help?" I said.

Aron looked at me in utter bewilderment.

"Wha ....?"

"The waiter doesn't understand you. Can I help?"

"Fuck off!"

"Aron!"

"What's it fucking got to do with you?"

"The man was only trying to help."

"I don't need his fucking help."

At that point I beckoned the waiter over and had a quiet word in his ear.

"Efcharisto", he replied.

"What's he say?" asked Aron.

"Thank you. It's a word you might learn, sonny – oh, and 'parakalo' can get you a long way, as well. It means 'please'. They're quite ordinary words. You haven't got to choke on them. You'll get your pasta now. No need to shout. Enjoy your meal."

We walked on as a string of abuse poured after us down the street.

"Do you set out to make friends and influence people, Frank? Does it come naturally to you or do you have to work at it?"

"Part of the job. I have a very calming influence on people."

She laughed, and it was a nice sound. I hadn't quite made Caran out, but I had gathered that she seemed to appreciate a little social conflict.

"You enjoyed embarrassing that young man didn't you – in front of his girlfriend."

"People like him annoy me. He probably wears Union Jack underpants."

"So?"

"So every time he farts, he farts into the flag!"

"Frank!"

"I don't approve of that kind of thing. Anyway, when we're abroad we represent our country. He wasn't doing that very well – yelling at a waiter who spoke English, however poorly, better than 'fcuk môn amour' speaks the local lingo."

"How come you speak it?"

"I don't. I just took the trouble to look through a phrase book before I came. You can get a long way on 'please', 'thank you', 'hello', 'goodbye' and the numbers one to ten."

By now, we had arrived at the far end of the row of bars and – in true Brit Abroad style – would have crossed the street and walked back down the other side. Caran laughed at the idea, and didn't feel like another drink quite yet, so I suggested a stroll down to the beach. She gave me a brief, questioning look but the natural innocence of my expression took the day. So we made our way along what, in England, would have been a lane, but over here was simply a sandy track at the end of which the beach opened out before us. The sea was out and the sand shone silver in the moonlight.

Stavros had been right about the beauty of the place: it was only a short stroll from the main street and yet secluded by the idleness of most holiday-makers and the lack of commercial interest. Thickets of thorn and mimosa bordered the track from the road, and the little cove swept round to the east, where the beach met the foothills of Craphos, and to the west where the pebbly shoreline separated it from the harbour. The bay was truly Mediterranean, with large tracts of impenetrable maquis giving way to the long stretch of the beach and interspersed by pine trees. Here, too, were cyclamen and juniper bushes. The sea, which by day would have been a clear turquoise, now broke gently on to the sand in bands of black and grey. The lure of water on this balmy night tugged at me.

"Do you fancy a midnight swim, Caran?"

"I think they call it "skinny dipping", these days, Frank – and no, I don't."

"Do you mind if I do?"

"What if someone comes?"

"They won't. The holidaymakers hardly use this beach and the locals have never understood our passion for the sea. They use the beach but even during the day consider the water far too cold for swimming. We could stay here all night and no one would disturb us.

The most we're likely to see is the odd fishing boat way out there – and, perhaps, a turtle coming ashore."

"Did you bring me here deliberately?"

"Yes – I thought it would make a nice stroll – and no – I didn't have any ulterior motive."

"All right – if you're sure."

I kicked off my sandals and stripped quickly – dropping my trousers, shirt and pants on to the dry sand. What a contrast to this time last night on Coral Beach when I had been accosted by a dirty, foul-mouthed teenage slag. Here I was with a beautiful woman – fifty-something and looking every inch as though she had cared for herself – anticipating my first midnight swim in over thirty years. I glanced down at my body – I'm no less vain than most men – and felt OK: I was, at least, firm across the chest and free of any beer gut, and subdued lighting is always good for the wrinkles. I reached out for Caran's hand and looked at her; the moonlight made her naturally tanned skin look almost black, and picked out the small hollows and dimples of her body as little patches of silver. I felt myself rising and said:

"Let's go."

We raced across the beach towards the night-lined sea, leaving two tracks of footprints behind us in the sand.

What I had said about the locals was true: more than that, they felt that the Brits were virtually shameless – people who could barely wait for the first opportunity to get their kit off and lie nearly naked on the first available beach. Midnight swimming was seen as almost pagan, connected with some long-forgotten fertility rite, an opportunity for uninhibited sex and viewed with real disapproval – but as we raced for the sea, I had nothing in mind more than a bit of fun.

We hit the water at full tilt. I just had time to glance across at Caran, as I let go of her hand, and saw the laughter on her face, saw her left arm swing out from under her breasts, saw the long stretch of her abdominal muscles, saw the shadows of the moon lapping the curves of her muscles, and then the waves were at our feet and lapping around us and the water closed, warm and soft, over and across our shoulders. I love swimming in the sea – pools you can keep for the kiddies – and I threw my arms forward and then pulled back twice in a long, slow breast-stroke. I felt the water rush past, curling around my body, caressing each part of me, and then I tucked my legs under, twisted, turned and shot to the surface. Caran was about three or four metres away, treading water, and I reached her in seconds.

"All right?"

"It's lovely. I'd no idea it would be so warm."

I kissed her then, just once, but supporting her head gently with one hand so that her lips remained on mine, soft and open. Our bodies drifted together; I felt her breasts float against my chest and my penis rise to her tuft and then we pulled back from each other and gave ourselves up to the sea which was calm and dimpled with moonlight. She was a good swimmer, using long easy strokes; her body looked so beautiful, elongated and silvered by the water. I dived down; the bottom was visible and I swam along, scooping up handfuls of sand and letting them drop back gently to the seabed. I pulled myself along on the odd rock, sea plants brushing casually against me. I turned and swam towards Caran. Her threshing legs were blurred and I wished I had brought a mask but I swam under her, gave her legs a tug as I passed, and then came up behind her, sliding my hands around the hip bones so that she turned to face me. We kissed again, briefly; we laughed, dived, came up for air, pulled away from each other, swam alone for a while, but always returned. I was unaware of this at first – this returning to one another – but it gradually took on a pattern, almost as though the sea was guiding us. The shore became a distant black and silver bar.

As we moved further and further from the beach I lay back against the swell of the sea and she came to me, drifting up through my legs and on to my chest; she lay there for a long time as we rose and fell together on the pulse of the sea. I held her gently, moving my legs breast-stroke fashion, listening to the water lapping against our outstretched bodies, making the same slap-slap sound as it would have done on the side of a boat. It was so effort-less, this floating, and so relaxing was the warmth of the water that we began to drift away and then towards each other, away and then together again; the touching of our bodies was like the stroking of a new silk shirt as you slide into it. I embraced Caran, holding her shoulder blades firmly, and we rolled in the water, first her head under and then mine, and each time I heard her quick intake of breath just before the water closed over her and then the laugh as she bobbed to the surface.

They say that you cannot make love in the water because there is nothing to push against, but that is not true. Caran drifted down on to me and the tip of my pe-nis touched her again and again in time to the rhythm of the sea until she opened and slid on to me. I held her there then, by cupping her buttocks in my hands, and the muscles of her vagina tightened, and I felt her tuft brushing gently against my stomach as the sea plants had brushed against me earlier.

How long we floated like that I do not know, but it was one of those glorious moments that I shall take with me to the grave – whatever the rights and wrongs, it was something I could never regret.

We came apart eventually and I felt myself leave her, still erect and eager, but in a quiet, contented kind of way, and with a sense of gratitude. We swam back to the shore together, not touching now, but occasionally diving so that our bodies curled around each other, with only the swirl of the sea between us. Her breasts swung in the water and, as she dived and turned on her back to face the surface, I would swim over her and then up between her legs as they kicked outwards. Once again, this coming together and drifting apart – this time, without touching – took on its rhythmic pattern, a teasing arousal of our desire.

When we reached shallow water, our feet gripped the sucking sand and we stood together, the sea running from us. We held each other then, loosely, and kissed, my left arm draped across the top of her right hip, my fingers resting on the swell of her buttock. Caran's lips held mine, but otherwise we hardly touched; there was only the delicate prod of her right nipple against my ribs, the touch of my penis as it rose and swept across her belly, the fingertips of her right hand caressing my shoulder and our other hands in a loose hold.

We sat together, resting against a little mound of sand; she was close to me now and we had our arms around each other, sharing the warmth of our bodies. Caran's skin felt soft and I could smell her hair drying in the warm night air. She hadn't spoken since we left the water – neither of us seemed eager to break the silence of the occasion. I felt the ache in my testicles, distended now with semen, as a distant thing, almost as though they were not part of this moment. We watched the sea, as the tide gradually brought the shore-lapping waves closer, and were part of its beauty. Small really, aren't we, adrift in the eternity of life? It was good to feel like that, at sixty-something – and I was nearly sixty-something – you are very aware of your own mortality. How many years had I left to know such a moment; would there ever be another time like this?

"Thanks."

Caran did not answer, but her quiet was enough, her quiet and the slight movement as she settled more firmly against me. The moon had dipped by now, closer to the horizon, and the bars of Craphos were a far distant sound that seemed to blend in with the night. The moonlight and the sounds – of the sea and the bars – conspired to encircle the cove, cutting it off from the world and the reality of our daily lives.

Caran:

I didn't want to think about what had happened – not at that moment. It was too nice just lying there with Frank. For that brief time, nothing existed but him and me and the sand and the sea and the sounds of it lap-lap-lapping on the shore. Neither of us were drunk – we had both shared only one bottle of wine with Joyce at dinner – so I had no excuse, but neither did I want any regrets. I didn't want to let my mind wander back into my childhood, where I had learned that you had sex *after* you'd fallen in love and, probably, *after* you were married – although the edges were already beginning to blur, even then. I didn't want to think about any of that, because I had this fear that a moment like this would never come again so I turned to him after a while; he was lying naked on the midnight sands, and I knelt between his spread-eagled legs and roused him again by running my lips along either side of his penis. It didn't take long; his balls were like rocks and he groaned when I gripped them with my fingers. I straddled him when we were ready and let myself slide down on to him, and it was glorious, feeling him come into me and holding him there. I leaned forward to give myself more leverage, so that my breasts almost touched his chest, and began a slow rocking movement, letting him slip almost from me, tightening on his glans for a second or so and sliding back down again. I had control; I was giving him pleasure and was mistress of my own coming. When I felt my juices flow, I fell on to his chest, increased the speed of my movement and brought him off.

"Come, Frank. When you're ready. Don't hold back."

He came, flooding into me – hot and soothing. He held me, then, and we must have fallen asleep, because when I woke he had covered me with his shirt. I was curled into him, my head was on his chest, and he was watching me.

"What time is it?"

"My watch is in my trouser pocket and I can't reach it, but I would guess that it's three or four in the morning."

"What!"

"'Adapt to Mediterranean time – go out late – and take everything as it comes'."

"Take me back, Frank."

"You don't fancy another swim?"

"Yes, but not now."

When we arrived back at the Captain Karas Apartments, I was wide awake and wanted to talk, but Frank hovered in the doorway.

"Are you coming in?"

"Do you want me to?"

"For God's sake, Frank! Stop being so considerate. Do you want to come in?"

"It would be very nice."

He undressed me as he had on that first night, slowly and gently, and I said:

"Frank, I don't want to make love anymore – not tonight."

"OK."

"For God's sake, Frank. Aren't you going to ask me why?"

"You'll tell me when you're ready. Anyway, I'm not sure I could."

"What?"

"Men of my age don't recover as quickly as a younger man."

He laughed and I wasn't sure whether he was just teasing me, so I said:

"Did you really not plan to have that midnight swim, this evening?"

"Certainly not. I'm of the Michael Caine School of Chivalry."

"Michael Caine?"

"He once said, on a chat show, something to the effect that you don't take a woman out for what you might get at the end of the evening. You take her out for the pleasure of her company. The rest – if there is any rest and that's up to her – is just a bonus. I've never forgotten that, and I subscribe to it. Think about it. It takes any tension out of the date – you're there to be with each other, not for what you might get out of it."

"That's lovely, but it's not very modern, Frank."

"People always say that as though there is some virtue in being 'modern'. Is 'modern' necessarily 'good'? Do you have to be 'modern' to be happy, contented .... whatever?"

"I don't think my daughters get much beyond the second date before they're buying the condoms."

"Then they're fools. Shagging every boy you happen to go out with is no way to find happiness."

"And what about us?"

"Well, that first night was a mistake, wasn't it? You were drunk and I shouldn't have let it happen. Tonight – it was a special occasion. You could feel it in the air, in the water, all around us. I have no regrets about tonight."

"And tomorrow?"

"Tomorrow, as they say, is another day."

There was a pause while he waited for me to speak. I had my daughters on my mind, as well as myself. You don't like to think that your daughters are .... well, shagging around, but everything, today, primes them for that. I found magazines in their bedrooms when I tidied up – 'Seriously Sexy! Turn-on tips for a HOT summer'.

"I was reading a magazine recently. It talked about turning your partner on. Men like a woman to groan and gasp in bed, it said. It makes them feel like great lovers."

"You mean faking an orgasm? No man's taken in by that – a boy might be, but not a man. Some men might pretend they are – or simply aren't bothered, as long as they get their end off. Personally, I'd be offended. I don't expect you to make it every time, but when you do, it's worth it! You can't fake a real orgasm and why the hell should you try?"

"It also talked about ... oral sex. It said no man ever forgets oral sex, 'so you might as well get on with it'."

"Really? You mean do something you don't really want to do because the man wants you to do it? I don't think so. If you're happy with it – fine. If you're not – forget it. We're not into 'sex by numbers', are we, Caran?"

"These girls are, Frank. They take these magazines seriously and they're all full of this kind of thing – virtually every week. It builds up an expectation about what love is about."

"Not love, Caran – sex, mechanical sex. For heaven's sake, you're a woman – you know more about the difference than I do! "

"Do you want a drink, Frank?"

"What? God, I do find it disconcerting the way you women suddenly change the topic of conversation."

"I'm wide awake now."

"And you can switch on and off, can't you? I'm still on the beach!"

"You enjoyed tonight?"

"I shall never forget it."

"Oh yes?"

"Caran – it was lovely. I didn't come on this holiday hoping to make out, and if you wave me goodbye tomorrow morning ...."

"This morning!"

"This morning … I'll not be resentful, but nothing will take from me the memory of our swim tonight and all that went with it. I don't take the moment for granted. Someone, in one of Tolstoy's novels, once said that happiness is about living each moment for itself. There's a lot in that."

"You're well read, Frank."

"I didn't read it – it was in a film. I have a memory for the things people say, that's all."

"Well, that puts you in a different class to most men."

"So they tell me."

"Do you still want that drink?"

"That'd be nice."

"I'll get it."

"Thanks."

Frank:

Watching Caran slip out of the bed and walk towards the bedroom door was another of those wonderful moments a man never forgets: this one was purely visual. I can remember being haunted for years by a picture of a nude I once saw as a boy. There was nothing intentionally erotic about the picture; it was just a photograph of a woman's beauty, and the photographer had managed to capture the natural lines of her body as she moved across the room. The way in which her waist flowed naturally into the swell of her hips had stayed with me forever. Caran was slim and her waist and hips were clearly delineated in the early morning light that filtered through the curtains, but it was the ease, the naturalness, with which she moved that held my attention. She reached for her bathrobe and I said:

"Don't do that. Don't cover yourself. You're lovely."
She smiled and returned naked with the drinks, lifting the glasses higher than she needed to elongate the lines of the stomach muscles.

"How often do you go to the gym?"

"Twice a week at least. Does it show?"

"Oh yes, it's well worth the effort."

"Frank! I didn't think old men could make it twice in one night!"

I had risen again, much – I might say – to my surprise, and I slipped across the bed and sat on the edge so that when she arrived I could take the drinks from her and Caran could sit on my lap, her legs either side of mine. She wriggled on to me and I slid into her once more. I didn't "come", as they say, that time but the feel of her, of being inside her, was honey-sweet and – when we sat with the drinks – I said so.

"I didn't need stockings and suspenders, then? That's another of the recommendations from the glossy girly mags."

"No – you just needed to walk across the room as you are."

"And take a bit of trouble to keep in shape!"

"All woman – no fat."

"Frank – that's not exactly PC!"

"You make an effort to keep yourself looking wonderful, Caran! Take some credit for it. You've got a better figure than fifty percent of the country's teenagers."

Caran:

Was it really the afternoon of our fourth day? I lay on the beach thinking about what Frank had said. There were the three of us – Lorraine with her sun-tan lotion, Joyce with her book and me with my thoughts.

"What day is it, Joyce?"

"Tuesday. It's our fourth day."

Lorraine looked up from her sun-bed and caught my eye.

"The day after tomorrow is our first excursion – the pirate ship."

She returned to her sunbathing; there was nothing either of us could talk about in front of Joyce, somehow. I returned to my thoughts. What was I doing? Did I come on holiday to have sex with a man in his late fifties – or was Frank over sixty? Mind you, what was I expecting – George Clooney? Where was I going? Where was all this leading to? Apart from the boy at nursing college who took my virginity, I had never been with anybody else, except Simon.

We talk about all these things, don't we – women that is, when we are together – but it is all talk. None of us actually expects it to happen. When Lorraine suggested we all come away for a "girlie break", I was all for it and, to be honest, I did rather hope something might happen, but I didn't plan for what might be the consequences if it did. It's all very well in the films; they can roll up the credits before anyone has to face the music. What do you do with your newfound freedom when you've got it? Am I going to have an affair with Frank? Do I want an affair with Frank?

So what are all those journeys to the gym about? Why do I want this beautiful body? Why am I working so hard to fight off the years? I don't think Simon actually notices; he doesn't look at me like that anymore. When we do it, it's usually after a party or something and he simply rolls across to me in bed. I wonder if Frank was like that with his wife, or did he look at her as he looked at me last night? It is nice being looked at like that: it gives you a lift to be desired. And I stopped thinking about it when I was with Frank: stopped thinking about all that stuff you read, that is – "Top 10 turn-ons every woman should know". Why? "Get creative, get a sex book and find a new position to try out." Why? Simon would think I had flipped. And yet I enjoyed doing what I did with Frank; it seemed so ... natural. What is all that advice about? Is it just something to fill the column inches? "Gaze at him adoringly" What? Simon would say – "Are you feeling all right?" He is attentive like that: it's being a nurse, I suppose. I wanted to marry a doctor – there was that gorgeous Irish intern – but I ended up with Simon. "Tie him up and pleasure him in unimaginable ways." What does that mean? "Take the lead, lust after him once in a while." I can remember lying beside him when we first got together; I used to think about it all day on the ward. Isn't that funny? I don't really think about Frank at all until I am with him, and yet when Simon and I first started, I thought about him all the time. So what is it I want? Do I want to get away from Simon, and all that goes with it: home, friends, family, social life?

Maybe it was better in our parents' day – when you just drifted into retirement, when there wasn't all this advice about what you should be doing. But it isn't like that anymore, is it? At fifty-something, you now have thirty or forty years of life left – I could be only just over halfway through! It's a long time to be stuck with just one person, from twenty-something to ninety-something.

And I know what Simon will do with his retirement: he'll take up golf again, and I shall never see him. He gave it up when we had the children but I know what's in his mind. "What are you going to do when you retire?" "Well, I don't know about you, but I shall be playing golf." So what am I going to do – keep house, look after the grandchildren, have affairs?

"It's your life, Caran," Lorraine said later, "You have thirty or forty years ahead of you. What are *you* going to do with it? Nobody else can decide for you."

"Simon and I have attended all those 'life-building' courses. You know – aromatherapy massage, working out together, learning a foreign language together…."

"There's a very interesting watercolour weekend coming up, how about going to this theatre skills course, … yes, I know what you mean."

"And it doesn't make any difference, does it? We started going to a wine-tasting club, but it just became a booze-up. I still can't tell a Gamay from a Chardonnay."

"And did you spend nights massaging each other after the aromatherapy weekend?"

"No! It just didn't happen. Can you imagine the girls coming in and finding us like that? They'd wonder what the hell was going on."

"Tell them. Your father and I are having an erotic evening together. Bog off."

"Would you do that?"

"Barry and I have. We made Mummy and Daddy's private moments a priority from the very beginning. And to be fair, Steph has always respected that – irritating though she is in other ways."

I must have paused in thought then for a significant period of time, because Lorraine looked at me and said:

"We have always been open about things like that. Barry and I have what used to be called 'an open marriage'. Yes – we've both been free to have other partners."

I must have paused again because she laughed and went on:

"No – funnily enough, we have been remarkably faithful, although both of us have had weekends away."

I frowned, and Lorraine went on:

"If someone I met, man or woman, was interested in going on a – say a dance weekend – I wouldn't hesitate and Barry wouldn't expect me to. And he's the same."

"So you'll tell him about Dakos?"

It was her turn to pause.

"I might. All that's happened with Dakos so far is that he has taken me for a meal."

"Where did you go?"

"To the Ariadakos. It was a lovely restaurant with walled and paved gardens. You know, those little courtyards they create with all those lush plants growing up the walls. They seemed to know him there, because every now and then he disappeared into the kitchen and came back with a tidbit for me to try."

"He was very attentive, then," I said, picking up our conversation from – when was it, yesterday afternoon?

"Yes, he was."

"What did you find out about him?"

"It was true that he isn't married, but he is divorced and lives in a little flat in Craphos with his son. In the evenings – when he works – he puts the little boy to bed and then leaves him in the care of a neighbour."

"What about his wife?"

"I didn't ask. After we had eaten, he took me for a walk along the harbour. He said his family had all been fishermen when Craphos was a fishing village and that his father still had a boat and went out each day. The fish in the restaurant was caught by him, fresh. And then he walked me back to the hotel."

"Are you going to see him again?"

"Yes – he's offered to show me the island tomorrow. You don't mind if I go?"

"No, of course not."

"You'll be OK with Joyce?"

"Yes – we might go into town or something."

Lorraine looked at me long and hard:

"Caran – it's your life. You can't go on holding other people responsible for what you do. You can't go on using your teenage daughters as a spur for your actions, or an excuse for not acting. They are all intensely self-centred – enough said. What you've got to ask yourself is – what do I want to do for the next thirty or forty years? Take charge. You don't come this way twice."

"Sometimes I think that if I had my time over again I wouldn't have children. There are other things to do with your life these days, aren't there?"

"There always have been. Children don't ask to be born. We make that choice for them. Steph wasn't planned. She happened after a Christmas party at the arts centre and we've brought her up with as much love and care as we can. I don't expect her to be grateful – except in the sense that everyone should appreciate what others do for them, otherwise they simply grow into intensely selfish human beings. At the same time, I don't expect to be at her beck and call – if she loses a skirt because she's an untidy slut, then she can find it. She's nineteen now – at university – and I want to get on with my life. There is so much out there, Caran. Your children come to a point where they are – or should be – independent. They can't have it both ways. "Treat me like an adult." "Mummy, take me into town." Sorry – you're grown up. Get yourself into town. I've got a life to lead."

"Who are you trying to convince?"

"Oh, I mean it. You're not just a mother, Caran: not just a wife. You are an independent, unique person with the right to lead a full life – not a dogsbody for your lazy daughters. What are you going to do with all those years ahead now that you are free?"

"I don't know. I've never thought about it quite so ...."

"Specifically?"

"Yes."

"Decide, or drift hopelessly into old age – and get like those bitter old women who blame their children and their husbands for what they haven't done with their lives. It's up to you."

"You are a comfort, Lorraine!"

"Sorry," she laughed, and then said "No I'm not. Someone needs to point you in the right direction. You're a beautiful woman, Caran. There's a lot you can do with your life. It doesn't have to involve a man."

"How do you see this Dakos?"

"Stop finding your salvation in others! Dakos is a friend. He might become a holiday romance. I don't know. I'm not looking to him for my future. Treat Frank the same. See him if you want to. I imagine he's quite nice, isn't he?"

"Yes."

"Then enjoy yourself. Don't take it too seriously. And take some time – while you're away from the demands of your teenage daughters – to think about yourself and what you want to do."

"Where are we going tonight?"

"Let's get Joyce to a night club. She's the one who should be "on the pull"."

"She won't want to go."

"We'll tell her that it's only for a little while – that we'll be back by midnight. We'll make it an early night!"

Joyce:

I didn't really want to go with Lorraine and Caran but I didn't want to be a killjoy, either. I'd hated that first night. Only Frank made it bearable, and I was glad to get away with him at midnight. Anyway, they'd looked up some nice places and there was one called Pebbles – not a very original name for a seaside resort bar, really. It was described as "sophisticated ... By day, a stylish, cosmopolitan café ... But at night it has a comfy, loungey, candlelit ambience with cool Mediterranean breezes and smooth chill-out sounds", which we were "never gonna forget". I wonder why they always use those Americanisms: they could simply have said "which you'll never forget". I suppose it's to give the impression that they're "with it". So we were going to be able to sit down and enjoy a meal. We wouldn't be stuck on a bar stool waiting for someone to ask us to dance.

We decided to go for a *meze*, but I didn't quite realise what this was when we ordered. Evidently it's a large meal that you can take all night to eat and, as the waiter put it, "dance it off as you go along". He was dressed like they all are – tight trousers showing his crotch and a brightly coloured shirt open nearly to the waist. I can't think why they assume that a sweaty chest is attractive. I could imagine beads of it dripping onto the food as he served us. He seemed clean enough, otherwise: his nails were nicely cut.

We started with salads that were fresh, and lots of little bowls of dips that you were supposed to eat with slices of that bread that's soft in the centre but has a very hard crust, so that it is difficult to chew. These were followed by plates of a local cheese that almost took my breath away. The waiter explained that this was haloumi. He said "Aaah" and kissed his coiled fingers into the air, but I thought it too strong to be pleasant. The haloumi had been cut into thick slices and sprinkled with basil, garlic, lime juice, sun-dried tomatoes and olive oil. Not exactly what they recommend at Slimming Worl', and the usual olives were sprinkled all over the plate. I must say that, whatever they look like, these waiters do take their job seriously. I don't go a bundle on foreigners per se – as Robert used to put it – but they certainly know how to serve at table. At home, waiters seem to almost resent serving you at all.

Lorraine certainly tucked in. She really enjoys her food. Mind you, she isn't exactly small, although men find her very attractive. We had hardly finished the salad course before one of the locals, who was lounging at the bar, asked her for a dance. He was very polite:

"Excuse me. My name is Antonis. May I ask you for a dance?"

Of course, she was up like a shot, her breasts all over the place. I think it's that red-blonde hair of hers that attracts them. She has so much, it's almost too good to be true. She hadn't done too badly since we arrived had she? Morning coffee with Frank, a night out with that Dakos and (as I understood) a day out tomorrow, and obviously this Antonis quite fancied her! He sat down at the table with us when they came off the dance floor – something an Englishman would never have done, but these locals get pushy once they have their foot in the door.

"Aaahh, you are having a *meze*. You like this?"

We all said that we did, and suddenly he had an aunt who could make us a "traditional" one and asked would we like to go one night. When the meat arrived, he gave us a guided tour around the plates.

"Most Cystonian kitchens will hold a few surprises. Are you ladies the "try anything once" kind of people?"

Caran's left eyebrow shot up; her face took on that "come and try me" expression, and so he continued:

"You have here the pork sprinkled with the herbs and slowly spit-roasted and dotted with cheese. This is a great favourite. And the lamb with the red berry glaze. And the salsa beef. And the chicken – this has the honey coating. And this is heart – pickled, and this – the liver. Aahh yes – the rabbit with the sultanas."

The dishes continued to come. I could see that Caran was wilting at the sight.

"I really think I need to let this go down," she said.

"Then, please, we will dance," said Antonis.

Lorraine's appetite only seemed to be whetted by each dish as it arrived and she and Caran never seemed to stop dancing; by the time we had reached the final meat course, several of his friends had joined Antonis around our table.

I do think English women have to be careful abroad. I remembered that black dress that Caran had worn on our first night had drawn a lot of attention. She'd had no bra on: you could see her nipples under the cloth. Tonight she was wearing red: somewhat risky for women of our age I always feel, and this dress plunged to her waist at the back. I could see when she was dancing that the men all tried to slip their hands in there. It was obvious she had no bra on – we had those nipples on display again – and I began to wonder if she was wearing any pants, either. I don't imagine she got much change out of two hundred pounds for the dress – perhaps she couldn't afford the pants to go with it.

Lorraine was as bad, but then she always shows off her breasts: winter or summer, work or play, Lorraine always wears low-cut dresses. She must wear a bra with breasts that size otherwise they'd never stay in place, but the neckline of her tops always seems to hide the straps. I must confess she really has lovely skin and her face is always so fresh and healthy looking – apart from that bright red lipstick she splashes across her mouth. Her dress tonight was floral and it floated in layers around her – the floral patterns, which were abstract rather than real flowers, tossed and floated on the white background. She somehow managed to dance with two or three of them at once. Not that she could really dance – not what I would call dancing, no recognisable steps: but then that's hardly the point, is it?

I was quite relieved when the band stopped playing and they both sat down. I noticed Caran didn't eat much when they returned to the table, but Lorraine continued to tuck in; by now they had served chips – as though we needed chips with all that food! Antonis and his friends didn't leave when the band stopped. I had thought they might do, but no – they obviously thought the evening might hold something else for them, no doubt, although I could have told them they were on to a loser with Lorraine and Caran. Lorraine had a day out planned with that Dakos and – although Caran was all "come hither" with the eyes – I didn't fancy they'd get very far with her.

Some more dips followed the meats and with these came sweet biscuits and cakes of some kind. At least having the men around the table helped to clear it – otherwise I don't think I could have borne the waste; but then, we waste more as a nation than any other on earth – except the Americans, of course.

It was as we sat eating these, with me looking at my watch, that the disturbance occurred. The band had stopped for a drink and left their instruments on the stage. Two young men – part of a group that had been drinking heavily in the corner (I'd watched them pouring away pint after pint of what they called Kronenbourg) – went on to the stage and began to play around with the instruments. To be fair, I think they could play and – at first – the band didn't seem to mind, but when it came to the time for the band to start again the young men refused to move from the stage. In fact, one of them began to cry. I couldn't see any reason for this, but he got down on his knees and began to plead with one of the musicians:

"You know man, you're lucky," he said, "You have music in your blood. Me – I have nothing."

And he began to cry, saying over and over again:

"You're killing my mother and father."

When the musician tried to move him, the young man grabbed at his throat, although only in a half-hearted way, with the tears running down his face. The young man's friends came over, but instead of removing him they began to argue with the band.

"Can't you hear what he's saying mate? You're killing his mother and father."

The bar staff then closed round the group of youths and a scuffle broke out, but only for a moment. The youths were frogmarched back to the corner and sat firmly in their chairs and the bar staff brought them more drinks. The young men then began to sing:

"They'll always be an England,
And England shall be free,
If England means as much to you
As England means to me.
Red, white and blue
What does it mean to you ....?"

When they reached "blue" their voices faltered and faded into a squeak on "you". Antonis looked across the table and said:

"The English."

"What do you mean – 'the English'?" asked Lorraine.

"They always hide behind their flag ... I do not mean you, sweet lady! These young men cannot hold their drink ...."

He never got any further; Lorraine stood and poured her drink over his head, tossed some money on the table and gave us a nod.

"What did you do that for?" said Caran, as we walked back along the street.

"Can't have them insulting the English, can we Caran?"

"But those young men were drunk."

"Antonis and his friends would have had their hands inside your knickers as quick as a flash – if you'd let them. What these people have got to learn is that if they dance with us, they respect us."

I didn't understand why, but I found myself agreeing with her; I just wasn't sure if Caran had any knickers on. Still, it was only just midnight and we could look forward to what, in Cystos, was going to be an early night.

Day 5: Day Out

Lorraine:

My night out with Dakos had been as I described it to Caran: nothing, of the kind that female Brits of a certain age are supposed to dream about, happened. The Ariadakos had been a lovely restaurant with little walled courtyards and they did seem to know him there: in fact it was almost as though he owned the place. He was very attentive and astutely avoided any little queries I slid into the conversation about his ex-wife. I rather got the impression that she was still involved in some way with the restaurant – which, I suppose, would have made sense. He had spoken lovingly about the flat and his little boy, and talked proudly about his father as we walked along the harbour. Dakos was also proud of Craphos and its traditions as a fishing village; he had taken me on to the beach and run his fingers along his father's boat and, in his mind's eye, could see the old man catching fresh fish for the restaurant.

I was looking forward to my day out. It was the first time I had been abroad since Steph and I took a holiday on the Spanish coast when she was sixteen: that had been a laugh. I've never been fazed by teenage girls and their horrendous PC attitude to life – what they can and cannot do, what their parents can and cannot do would fill a book; their "rebelliousness" is within such closely contrived limits – unlike ours in the late sixties, when we really did break away from the conventions of our parents. I knew she found me a pain in the neck and I rather enjoyed it. She hadn't wanted to come on the holiday, but Barry was deeply involved in one of his projects and I could see that it was going to be 'one of those summers' unless I got her out of his hair for a while. She'd been a goth or something at the time; her hair had been died an awful black so that she looked like one of those old women who can't afford to fork out two hundred quid on some pretentious hairdresser, and have to resort to dyeing it themselves over the sink. Her skin had been so pale that I had wondered whether the sun might shrivel it – like a vampire's.

Anyway, we went and Steph quickly got 'pally' with some other youngsters which left me rather freer than I'd expected. Teenage girls are quite selfish aren't they? It never occurred to her that she'd actually left me alone. Not that I minded that, particularly: it was quite a relief to have her happy, instead of sulking and snapping at me about everything from my bikini to the shape of the suntan lotion bottle. I wandered down to the row of the usual tourist shops on my own – you know, over-priced gift shops full of crap from China, and those restaurants serving the same tired-looking pseudo-British food. I had it half in mind to get myself tattooed, or to buy one of those 'Barbie Doll' T-shirts – I knew Steph would love me like that! While I was there I bumped into Malcolm who we'd seen on the plane. He was obviously on the make, but I've always been able to handle men so that didn't bother me; when he invited me to join him at "a beach barbie" that night, I accepted.

Steph, of course, went (what's the word they use when you tell them off in the mildest terms?) "ballistic" and when I had eased myself into a pair of white jeans – ensuring that my top did my breasts full and firm justice – I saw her give me the dark look they are so famous for: it's more than they dare acknowledge, isn't it, that "Mum" might be attractive to men? She never got round to mentioning Barry: it was purely the embarrassment factor for herself that concerned Steph.

She'd refused to come so I told her not to leave the hotel grounds and to lock herself in when she went to bed. I knew she'd be OK – the girls she'd been with all day would spend the night in the pool, and I had a quiet word with their parents.

He did try it on: we'd gone skinny-dipping and Malcolm's approach – like most British men – had been awkward and, later, after a few drinks, boorish. British men just do not seem comfortable, do they, with putting their cards on the table? He had started with the "nudge-nudge, wink-wink" approach, trying to imply that we both knew what this was all about and that there was no point in wasting time, we might as well get on with it, and then – after the Stellas had taken hold – he had tried the direct grope. His tone had changed to what you might describe as "soppy", not to say maudlin, but only because we were "on holiday" and far from home; he was off the leash and could let the beast come to the surface.

We'd gone off to one of those holiday discos after we left the beach and Malcolm had jerked around a bit – all elbows and hip thrusts, like a poor man's John Travolta – and then returned to the hotel at about two in the morning. The evening had finished on a truculent note – rather surly, really – with him muttering something about me "not being his type", and then we'd both gone our separate ways to bed.

Steph, of course, was immensely relieved the next morning, even though she still couldn't believe I had actually gone skinny dipping with a man.

So yes – I was curious about Dakos – although I felt certain that his offer to "show me the island" meant exactly that, not what an Englishmen would have intended to imply by such a statement. I was expecting Dakos to be attentive and free with his compliments: I'm more Kate Winslet than Kate Moss so I supposed that the 'Earth Mother' one might come my way.

Dakos had asked me to meet him on the beach near the Queen Vic Pub which promised me "Karaoke with Keef" if I liked to turn up on a Monday night. I wasn't quite sure why he asked this, but I guessed it had to do with fraternising with the guests – so I made my way towards some palm trees next to the bar where someone with 'Big H' on his T-shirt was emptying the trash. It was Dakos who had asked me out this time and he was a little apologetic about not picking me up at the hotel. I've always liked good manners in men – Barry is very partic-ular about that kind of thing himself. I waited under the trees and wondered what the day would hold. I will admit I was excited. A friend of mine once told me that, following her divorce, she had joined a dating agency and couldn't wait to get home at night to see what had come in the post. It was a bit like that waiting for Dakos. The beach was already crowded and I could sense the afternoon heat building; I rather hoped he would take me inland, perhaps into the hills.

When he arrived, it was in an open-top car and Dakos immediately leapt out and held the door for me; Barry still does that but, even among decent Englishmen, it's a dying tradition.

"Is there anywhere in particular you wish to go, Lorren?"

Isn't it funny how the mispronunciation of your name by a foreigner always sounds exciting?

"Oh, anywhere. Surprise me. I shall enjoy anywhere."

"You have brought something to cover those wonderful shoulders?"

"Yes," I laughed.

"Then I would first like you to see the monastery at Nykos. It is very cool there and there is a nice restaurant where we can have lunch – al fresco, as you say. My brother, Mikolos, is one of the monks. The monastery is one of the ten top sites on the island. During our struggle for independence it was used to store guns and supplies for the freedom fighters."

We drove up into the hills north of Craphos. Grapes grew on the slopes and we passed through vineyard after vineyard that stretched along the southern terraces until we reached the pine-clad slopes of the higher ground. There was spiky scrub relieved occasionally by dry, bright flowers. Dakos stopped the car whenever I asked and by the time we reached the monastery, I had an armful of splendid blossoms.

"The monastery was built, nearly a thousand years ago, for the icon. It is said that St Luke painted it, and it was given to a Cystonian monk by the Emperor Commenos for curing his daughter's sciatica. It is encased in silver. Do not look directly on it, or you will suffer a horrible punishment."

His face as he spoke was deadly serious, but I didn't like to ask him if he was religious. When he pulled his car over to stop by the dusty roadside, he said:

"You must cover your shoulders now."

A monk stood near the door and smiled as we approached. Dakos spoke to him.

"This is my friend, Lorren. She is from England and staying at the Captain Karas Apartments."

The young monk inclined his head slightly but did not take my hand.

"Είναι ο αδελφός μου περίπου;"

"Είναι στο φυτικό κήπο."

Dakos turned to me and explained that he had asked about his brother who was in the vegetable garden. I was suddenly in another world. I was out with an attractive man: a man who was leading such a different life from mine. It was interesting – and exciting.

The icon was beautiful – a Madonna in deep blue against a background of gold mosaic. She sat on what looked like a stone bench – it had a cushion for her – and the Christ child was in red and gold. Dakos explained that the painting, though depicting Jesus and his mother, was in memory of the emperor's daughter who had been cured of her sciatica.

"What was her name?"

"Who?"

"The emperor's daughter."

"Elousa."

"Have we looked long enough?" I asked, intending a joke. His reply was deadly serious.

"I think so."

We wandered into a little museum and then out into the cloisters, and they were so cool, it was wonderful. Dakos said that many tourists did not come here because the roads were rough, and without safety barriers, as they climbed the steep hillside. We found his brother, after a while, with a hoe weeding the vegetables. Everything was so still and peaceful – we seemed to be a million miles away from Craphos. Mikolos took us to what I can best describe as a bower – a small seated area raised on stone slabs and roofed to keep it cool at all times. These monks certainly knew how to look after themselves (it was almost palatial!) and yet they lived frugally, eating only small meals: there was no fat here, no obsession with diets. He admired my armful of flowers and named each one as though he knew them all personally, and we talked for a while in a strange mixture of Greek and English. I learned that Mikolos was a novice monk and that Dakos was concerned for his happiness and peace of mind.

"I come out often – at least once a week."

"So your father is a fisherman, your brother is a monk and you look after the tourists ...."

"And my mother makes lace – the famous Kleftara lace your guide books tell you about. We are a very talented family," he laughed.

"And your brother is happy?"

"It would appear so. His faith is alive and well."

Outside, we walked down a little track into a wooded valley towards the restaurant and Dakos pointed out a cave in the hillside.

"During the struggle for independence, the guerrilla leader Syprianous was betrayed by a local shepherd and he took refuge in that cave. The soldiers surrounded it and he chose to fight. He fought for eight hours before he was killed. That was in nineteen fifty six."

I had been just six years old, learning to read in primary school.

The restaurant was a roadside coffee shop and a group of local men looked up as we approached. Among them were two priests with white beards and those tall hats with the flat tops.

"A male preserve," whispered Dakos, "but, slowly, things are changing."

Well, needless to say, Dakos knew the owner (this time, one of his cousins) and we were shown to a little wooden table under an awning at the rear of the bar, away from any possible traffic. A linen cloth was laid, drinks appeared without our asking and a menu was placed before us: all delivered with a huge smile and a bristling moustache.

"It is a simple life we have here on Cystos, but a good one. Always there is plenty of fresh food and we take a pride in what we serve. May I recommend?"

"Ye – es ..... uhm, I've never heard of this one before .... soov – la?"

"Souvla – kebab. It can be any meat – chicken, pig, sheep or goat - and the chunks can sometimes be a little fatty for the English taste. May I suggest the afelia – pork and potatoes casseroled in coriander and white wine, wonderful with a salad – or, perhaps, the kleftiko, which is my favourite? Here it will be lamb, not goat, and will have been cooked for at least five hours on a bed of cinders in a sealed clay oven. The cooking allows the meat to steam in its own juices – it will simply fall off the bone."

I didn't like to say that kleftiko is served in every Greek restaurant in Britain (still this wasn't Greece, was it?) so I thought I'd have a go and said yes, then changed my mind and went for the afelia. I didn't want to feel bloated. Dakos laughed.

"Women – you always change your minds. Why?"

"There's always the feeling you might have made a better choice."

He gave me a quizzical look, so I said quickly:

"The wine is nice."

"It is made ...."

".... by your brother, in the monastery?"

"Yes – how did you guess?"

We both laughed. I was feeling more and more bemused: ever since that moment when he had spoken to the monk at the monastery door in Greek, I had experienced the sensation of being out-of-body. Have you ever felt like that – when you are watching yourself, as though looking at another person, doing things, being somewhere? I know we all have this sense of un-reality on holiday but this was more than that – I was being drawn into another world and, for the moment anyway, I didn't mind.

The meal arrived and the afternoon drifted further from the world; the afelia came with not one, but several salads, including a delicious cacik – cucumber in yogurt. We also had little dishes of olives and that wonderful bread with the hard crust and large holes like those you find in Emmenthal cheese. The wine also flowed and Dakos kept up with me, drinking steadily. When I wondered out loud whether he would be able to drive us back, he said, simply:

"Oh yes, the roads are quite safe."

"It wasn't so much the road ...."

I never finished the sentence: just then the cheese arrived, although I couldn't remember either of us ordering it.

"This is one way we take our siesta – relaxing in the shade over a long lunch. It is too hot to drive. If you wish to take a sleep after the meal, then my cousin will find you a room."

Yes – anywhere else, from anyone else, it would have been a try-on but there was nothing in his manner that suggested this: Dakos seemed concerned solely with my comfort and he later said that he had noticed my head nodding forward.

"You are a dancer, Lorren?"

"I was. I don't do so much now. I'm a little ...."

I was going to say "on the heavy side" but didn't want to so added, quickly:

".... out of practice."

"You never lose the skill. I saw it in you the first time you walked across the foyer. There is a grace in every move you make. It is lovely to behold and, tonight, I have a surprise for you."

"A surprise?"

"A surprise."

He winked, smiled and waved his hand over a plate of biscuits which were placed before us:

"Baklava – they may be a little sweet for your taste, but try one. They are a speciality of the island. And the wine – Commandaria – for the dessert. Sweet, yes, but exquisite. It is said to have been created for the goddess Aphrodite herself ...."

"But not by your brother – or cousin?"

"Aahh, the English sense of humour. No, not by my brother but, perhaps, by one of my ancestors. Hmmm? It was drunk on the festive day of the goddess. A little, to try?"

What can you say?

After the meal I wanted to lie down, to be undressed and lie in that room with its yellow-white walls, the afternoon sun peering in through the window, the iron bedstead and the crisp, cool sheets on my body but I didn't like to ask: I thought it might be misinterpreted. Instead, we sat in the shade of the awning and were joined by Dakos' cousin and his wife – a big, Cystonian woman whose skin glistened with olive oil. I had the impression that the balance of relationships was different here, that men were men and did manly things, that women were women and did feminine things. I know! It's an attitude I've fought against since the 70s but doesn't it make life easier: aren't there less arguments about who does what, and aren't we all struggling less to do everything? From the way that he looked at his wife, it was clear that Dakos' cousin simply revered her; he had cooked and served our meal because that was the way of things – his work – but I knew, without asking, that it would be she who cooked for the family. Her name was Ayia which seemed tall and slim to me – and, somehow, I knew that was how she thought of herself.

While Dakos and his cousin, Karystos, talked business she took me round their little home. In England we would immediately have wondered about how we could improve, extend or enhance it – "make-it-over" – but Ayia saw only its joys: here her daughter had learned to sew, here her son had learned to read, in this oven the

113

family meals were cooked. The wooden table in the kitchen was scrubbed clean, the broken stones of the floor swept free of the ever-intrusive dust; their little sitting room – with rugs over the stones - was furnished only with a few cupboards and soft chairs, but she showed them with pride.

"This is Kleftara and that is my mother's shop."

Dakos had drawn his car up alongside a house of glistening stone walls and was holding open the door for me to get out. I was awake now. We had said our goodbyes – "Perhaps not goodbye, perhaps another time?" Karystos had said as we drove away, with his wife and himself waving furiously.

His mother sat by the doorway in a rocking chair; behind her stood a younger woman whom Dakos introduced as his sister. Around them hung their work – lace dresses, tablecloths, doilies, waistcoats, curtains, pictures: I say 'work' because they made it to sell, but perhaps 'art' would be a better word. Before they even spoke there was pride in the eyes and in their smiles. The introductions were formal and attentive; why can't the English introduce each other like that? Here was a man who loved his mother and his sister because they were his mother and his sister, and there was love in the introduction. At home, introductions are always so awkward, clumsy and inelegant: even among people we know well, we never seem sure about what to do with our hands – except teenagers, of course, who rather over-do it by pointing at each other in the street and screaming. In complete contrast, Dakos led me across to his mother and, still holding my elbow, brought his arm around her, kissed her forehead and drew her eyes to mine in one smooth, continuous movement.

"Η μαμά, αυτό είναι Lorren. Είναι στις διακοπές στον καπετάνιο Karas. Της παρουσιάζω το νησί. Lorren, you will be pleased to meet my mother."

"Hello, I am very pleased to meet you."

I didn't quite know what to say; I suddenly realised I didn't even know the Cystonian word for "Hello", so I smiled and shook her hand. Dakos then passed a few words with her, presumably about her health, and then drew his sister into the circle by simply stepping back on one foot and introducing her; her name was Mara – I think that was what he said – and soon she was showing me their workroom.

"It was Leonardo da Vinci who first ordered our lace for the cathedral in Milan. Now we sell to visitors. Dakos had this little window built to display our work and Mama sits outside to attract the visitors. In Cystos, every new bride has to have 100 sheets and pillowcases in her dowry – but you can start with one beautiful piece."

I couldn't make out why they were both dressed in black and didn't like to ask. Mara showed me around the house, which was very small – the living-room doubling as a workroom, while Dakos spoke with his mother. Mara spoke English easily and I said so.

"Dakos says the future is in the tourist – especially the English – so we learn the international (is that what you say?) language."

"I don't think many of us would say that. We're just grateful that everyone else is learning English, but it makes us rather lazy."

She laughed:

"We like the English. Not down in the towns, but those who come here are always polite. They are rather frightened of Mama when she waves our lace in their faces."

"No, we wouldn't like that very much. We are rather reserved."

I thought of Caran: was she reserved? Yes – very, despite appearances and the way things had gone with Frank. I felt overwhelmed for the third time that day as we sat down to coffee and more baklava. I wasn't just on holiday: I was being drawn into another world.

"Lorren is a dancer and tonight we go to Napagia. Napagia, μαμά, για το χορό."

The old lady chuckled and her eyes wrinkled in a knowing look:

"Napagia - για το χορό."

It was a very pleasant end to the afternoon. Dakos stayed speaking with his mother and Mara took me for a walk around the village. Mara explained that the village was in two halves and that the lower part was neglected but worth a visit because the streets were narrow and so there would be no traffic. We visited the church of St Paul, who had brought Christianity to the island, and looked at the icons: from the church we looked out over the valley.

"You are content to live here?" I asked.

"I have always lived here," replied Mara.

The houses here were rundown and some were unin-habited; steps were broken, windows missing and the stone walls were their natural sandy colour only bleached to a yellowy-white by the sun. As we made our way back towards the upper part of Kleftara, I noticed that the villagers had painted their homes a distinctive white and blue. Mara steered me away from the main street, a bustle of tourist shops, through narrow alleys where it was cool and peaceful to wander; here we visited a small museum dedicated to the history of lace making.

"You see the Venetian ladies followed Leonardo and they could not buy enough of our lace."

She laughed and the phrase "vagaries of fashion" came into my mind but they had given this village a livelihood over five hundred years ago: Kleftaritika, the lace of Kleftara.

"Now some of the shops on the main street are selling lace from China. We do not like this – beware."

As we walked slowly up the steep alleyways my feet began to tell me I was tired, and I realised that Dakos had picked me up at coffee time; it was now late afternoon and it seemed as though some dancing was planned. I had been on the go for about seven hours – even if "on the go" had included a long lunch! How was I going to dance the night away without a rest? This little problem he seemed to have anticipated, however, and, when we returned to the shop, Mara led me to a bedroom – hers, I learned later – where I was told I could lie down.

"Please – 'make yourself at home'. You will need to rest."

So I undressed and lay in that room with its yellow-white walls and iron bedstead, the late afternoon sun peering in through the window, the crisp sheets (bordered with Kleftaritika) cool against my skin. Did I expect Dakos to appear, stripped naked, through the doorway and make love on the cool, crisp sheets? No – not in his mother's house; as a Cystonian he would have considered that the height of vulgarity. O Lord, where have we gone wrong at home? How can we so easily confuse simple lust with love? Why is it now a public event rather than a private act? So I slept, and when I woke the sun had gone down, the evening was cool and Mara stood at the foot of the bed holding a dress – yes, of kleftaritika – that you would have died to dance in.

Dakos, too, had changed and, as we drove further into the hills, he said:

"I keep some clothes at my mother's house for special occasions."

"Where are we going?"

"To Napagia for the dancing – real, Cystonian dancing. When you come to the island, what are the ten things the reps tell you that you must do?"

"Oh, visit a famous site, find a quiet beach, have a drink in a village café, join a plate breaking session, get invited to a wedding .... oh, I don't know ..... "Buy some hand-made lace, have an alfresco meal off the tourist track, drive to a cliff-top for a view of the sunset, join in a local dance and walk a forest trail. Yes?"

"Something like that."

"And today?"

"We have visited a monastery ....."

"*The* monastery of Nykos ...."

"Had an alfresco meal with your cousin and his wife, visited your mother and her sister in their lace-making shop ....."

"Bought a dress of hand-made lace ....."

"Bought?"

"Of course – a gift to the lovely lady."

"Dakos, I thought it was on loan. I couldn't possibly accept."

"Not to do so would cause offence beyond reparation."

He knew more English than I did!

"And now we are off to 'join a local dance'. You have enjoyed your day so far?"

"It's been lovely."

Was I being worked on, "set up" as they say, or was this simply Cystonian hospitality? After all, we take holiday visitors on days out in England, don't we? But this wasn't quite like a visit to the local wildlife park, was it? I still felt in control of the situation despite the fact that he was doing everything. He was guiding the day through visits to his friends and family, and was selecting where we went and how long we stayed; but then I couldn't expect to have discussed it, could I (as I would have done with Barry) since this was his treat for me? Not that Barry and I would have actually discussed it, of course; he would have decided where, I would have disagreed and we'd have ended up going to a compromise place – somewhere neither of us actually wanted to be. Yes, all right, so it was easier having the man making the decisions (even if you couldn't disagree) and I was enjoying the day and Dakos had made no demands upon me.

The dance was local and it was in a *taverna* – and there were no tourists or, at least, only a few who happened to be in the know. The taverna was like a barn and so naturally rustic it made your heart squirm at the pseudo "make-overs" we see at home: you know, the kind of thing they are doing to our country pubs – ripping out the old woodwork and padded settle seats to replace them with artificial beams, hard chairs and high tables.

"You like it?"

"Oh, Dakos. It has been like this for a hundred years?"

"Ever since we first built farms on the island."

The taverna was wonderfully untidy – but naturally so: jugs and bottles had been pushed to the side on shelves and into niches in the walls, old wagon wheels were propped against the side or used as candelabra, herbs dried in bunches. At one end a stove burned, giving the room a smoky smell which suggested food. Shadows flickered across the walls and up into the rafters; a pile of dry logs was stacked against the end wall, next to the range. The windows were high up and only shafts of light shone through them. There was the smell of olives and baking; a woman stood near the range tossing something like pancakes. Flames leapt, pans hissed as the oil touched the hot metal. Tables were pushed to one end of this huge room and a few people sat around these in family groups, but mainly they were filling up with food; the rest of the floor was clear for dancing – wood scrubbed white – except at the other end of the barn where a local band was setting up. I saw a violin, two guitars, an accordion and a mandolin.

"This is Resistance Day," said Dakos, "when we celebrate the beginning of the fight against our oppressors, when the freedom fighters first rose against them."

A procession of young children from the village marched into the barn, flowers in their hair, flowers in their hands, led by a young woman of, perhaps, seventeen who was obviously some kind of May Queen; a brief crowning ceremony took place, and the band struck up. I couldn't help but be taken by the young woman – there was something so innocent about her: you rarely see that look in any teenager at home these days. She took a natu-ral, not hysterical, joy in being the centre of attention; a young man took her hand and they led the dancing. There was respect in his face, and instinct told me that they weren't going to be off behind the taverna for a quick shag when the night came to an end.

If you've seen Zorba's dance then these dances would seem familiar, but they are indulged in by both men and women. The dancers moved in pairs but as part of a whole sequence so, although you never changed part-ners, you did change position within the dance. There was lots of hugging and arms across shoulders, lots of knee bending, dips and rises, and you had to keep a straight back, which automatically thrust your breasts forward; the women were dressed for that and were enjoying the fact. Blouses were low and off the shoulder – or on the shoulder but designed to fall off as the danc-ing progressed. I've always felt rather sorry for men in these circumstances: everything was being done to push up their testosterone levels but, at the end of the evening, was there going to be any fulfilment? The lace dress I was wearing was similarly cut and, fortunately, brought in under my breasts; it was well cut and hung beautifully from the hips down so that every swirl lifted it high to reveal my legs. Although I'm a bit big in the boob area my legs are shapely, so I was really enjoying myself – and so was Dakos; he took many an eyeful as we made our way from set to set, and was very aware that the other men in the room were casting admiring glances at his English lady. I didn't mind being on display: in fact, it was very nice.

We stopped occasionally for a drink of the local wine – poured from stoneware jugs, cool as a mountain stream on our lips and throats – but only for a moment; it was an evening of non-stop dancing – the food and the drink was just to keep us on our feet. Despite the stove and the heat of the summer evening it was cool in the barn because of its size and the thickness of the walls; so we built up, only gradually, a healthy glow rather than a sticky sweat, and isn't it wonderful when your skin begins to glisten? The dancing cleared my head; the concentration needed pumped up my adrenalin; I felt more alive than I had done for so long. The rut of working, rushing home, getting the meal on and collapsing in front of the box seemed (and was) a million miles away.

Suddenly the floor cleared and Dakos and I were the only dancers. He smiled and said:

"They have admired you. Most tourists are cack-handed and make a great palaver of learning our dances but you – you dance them as though you have danced them forever."

I had no time to wonder where he had learned phrases like 'cack-handed' and 'great palaver': the crowded barn was clapping an insistent rhythm and we had no choice but to dance. Since I had no one to follow, I decided to improvise a few steps and sequences of my own.

Dancing is flirting and only a few steps away from the act of sex itself: at times, it is even more intimate. Like lovemaking, it can't be faked successfully – not with a sensitive partner. Watch those couples on television and notice their eyes – however well they place their bodies, the dance never reaches their eyes unless the dance creates more between them than a series of planned moves. A really sexy man, as distinct from one who is pretending, will flirt with his eyes and the dance gives him the chance to do just this; call it "courtesy flirting", a compliment paid with the body, rather than the mouth. Some men can make you go weak at the knees when they bring you a drink; dancing is just like that and I wanted to show off to Dakos' friends. We're talking here, as I say, about social flirting – the kind of thing that goes on in every workplace – a bit of fun, with no promises made.

Dakos was not a trained dancer, but he had led me well through the steps he knew, and I had the feeling that he would follow any changes I made to the sequence; in some cultures, the man supports the woman, in others, he leads – we were about to combine the two approaches in such a way that Dakos lost none of his machismo. Between the sways and the dips, I introduced a few fancy steps in the fashion of the flamenco, so that our heels drummed on the floor; then, as we moved forward, I eased into Dakos' arm, curling my far shoulder against it and turning my head the other way to face him. This brought my near shoulder away from his chin and my body turned naturally from him; he had no choice but to follow so that we began to move backwards in the style of the Gay Gordons. Dakos got the idea and soon he was leading. The other dancers loved this little variation to their traditional dance, and the floor began to fill up again to the drumming of heels, the curling of shoulders and the backward sway of bodies.

At the end of the set, they all stood around us and applauded: it was wonderful. Dakos smiled and I knew he was more than pleased; he had entertained me with great gallantry all day and this had been my way of saying thanks. Foreigners take such pleasure in others admiring "their woman" and for that moment, I was his woman.

We only come this way once (what a cliché!) but you may as well enjoy it while you're here and while you can.

At eleven o'clock, almost to the minute, the evening ended as joyously as it had begun with the young people of the village processing out of the taverna led by the "Queen" and her escort. Dakos must have noticed a certain look on my face because he smiled and said:

"These people are at work early tomorrow – cleaning the hotels, gathering the harvest, and there are young children."

"Yes. We may be on holiday but you are not?"

"Sometimes – it is different in the resorts."

The band closed around us, laughing and clapping.

"Thank you, thank you. The English lady is a fine dancer."

My evening was made!

As we drove back into Craphos, the warm night winds blew up from the bay, blowing my hair, and I felt glorious. Watching Dakos at the wheel I realised that, despite a day in his company, I actually knew little about him; I felt serious despite the fact that I was on holiday and wondered how the day – which had been fun – had managed to do that to me. I didn't like to ask too much and had ended up asking nothing.

"A penny for them, Lorren."

"For my thoughts? I was thinking that I know very little about you."

"And what do you want to know?"

He was attentive – he couldn't have been more concerned that I enjoyed the day, astute – although I wasn't quite sure why I thought that, loving – as far as his family was concerned, admired – by his friends and family, proud – of his father and his town, courteous – he had opened the car door for me, intelligent – he could see the importance of tourism to the island, knowledgeable – about his home, complimentary – he had taken the trouble to say things that made me feel good about myself, a hard worker – he seemed to have his finger in many pies, generous – he would have paid his mother for the dress I was wearing, modest – he had danced for me and not himself, sexy – oh yes, and kind, humorous ... So what the hell did I want to know? Lots!

"Who is looking after your little boy?"

"Aah! You need not be concerned about Michael. He sleeps in our little apartment and my neighbour sees that he all right. You understand I do not normally leave him all day and all the evening. Today was special and he understood. He played with my neighbour's children and eats with them and now he sleeps safely. You will see."

I wanted to ask, of course, why a neighbour? Why wasn't Michael with his mother? Did Dakos still see his ex-wife? What was his relationship with "his neighbour"? Was he always as smooth as he seemed? Had he a hidden agenda in showing me around? I'd found out more about Frank in fifteen minutes on that first evening than I had about Dakos all day, but I'd joked with Frank, drawn his conversation along through humour. Its funny how we rely on humour isn't it? It's a constant factor with us English. There is always an undercurrent of humour in our conversations and social interactions and we dip into it. It is like breathing and without it – without the surety of knowing how Dakos would react if I probed a little – I felt apprehensive that I might cause him offence.

So it was a quiet drive back, and I reflected pleasantly on the day. I felt relaxed, perhaps a bit vulnerable, and listened to his soft voice talking about nothing much at all until the car pulled up in front of an apartment block and he opened the door for me and led me up a narrow flight of concrete steps. This wasn't romantic Cystos: this was modern. This was where Dakos lived with his son: the place from which – every day – he went to work. He tapped on a door as we made our way up, passed a few words with his neighbour, opened his front door and gestured me in.

The flat was small (no larger than our holiday apartment) with a bathroom, two bedrooms and what we would call a lounge-dining room which opened off the kitchen. He immediately placed his finger on his lips and beckoned me towards his son's bedroom door. The little boy – he must have been about ten – was sleeping peacefully and as deeply as only children can sleep; Dakos made his way around the room, tidying the books and toys, straightening the duvet cover – generally making the room nice for the boy to wake up to in the morning – and all the while looking at his son, the expression on his face being one of unremitting love.

He closed the bedroom door quietly, took my arm and led me gently into the lounge:

"You would like a drink – a ....?"

"Nightcap? Thank you."

"We have ...."

"Whatever ... It has been a lovely day, Dakos. I have learned so much about your island and met your family. Thank you."

"Thank you, Lorren. It has been my pleasure."

I decided it was now or never. Well, curiosity doesn't always kill the cat.

"You look after your son all the time?"

"Ah – you are wondering about my wife? Yes. I was not having all this chopping and changing – here one minute, gone the next. That is no good for children. They need a place to be, a place to call their own. And he was a boy and a boy needs his father. Had it been a girl, then my wife would have taken her."

"But your son sees his mother?"

"Oh yes, whenever she wishes. She calls and he is here. This is his home."

"And how do you manage your work?"

"Around him."

"With the help of your neighbour?"

"Stephy and her husband are good friends, but I manage my work around Michael. I am here most of the time in the day for the school holidays. I work at night. At other times I am working while he is at school."

"Always in the restaurants?"

"Yes – Ariadakos is mine. My family's restaurant. We all "do our bit". Yes?"

He laughed. As he spoke, Dakos moved around the apartment, drawing the curtains almost to close, putting on lights, and then sat beside me on the couch. Finally, he placed the drinks on the little table, took my hands and lifted me to my feet. Those Cystonian eyes of his were so dark and they glistened in the swarthy face. I knew he'd be hairy; I've always liked dark, hairy men. He lifted his hand and brushed my hair aside.

"Your hair is so lovely."

"All over the place?"

"That is part of its loveliness."

He ran his forearms along mine and then stroked my upper arms with his fingers, sliding them gently under the short sleeves of my kleftaritika dress. His movements were firm and positive but – I gathered – exploratory. When I offered no resistance, his right hand fingers moved carefully across my breasts, along the top edge of the low bodice and then into the valley between them. Oh dear, those breasts caused me no end of trouble when I was a student; it took me a long time to understand men's fascination with them – indeed, I'm not sure that I really do to this day. I'd always wanted a pair like my friend Alison who was small and petite but mine 'stood up for themselves' and so I made a feature of them.

"Your skin is so soft and smooth. It is like that of a young girl."

His left hand had not moved from under my sleeve, and he continued that slow stroking movement with his fingers while his right hand came to my neck and lifted my chin. I turned my head for him (well, why not – we were both adults and it was the end of a lovely day) and he kissed my lips with a tenderness so exquisite, it really did quite take my breath away – you can be surprised, even at my age. I've often thought that kissing was, in many ways, more intimate than lovemaking itself. There's something about a man's lips on yours that invites you on; it isn't simply a question of what a good kiss is doing to the rest of you – it's the act of kissing itself which is so delightful. A couple experienced at kissing can – well, shall we say, 'infiltrate' each other so deeply.

He didn't attempt anything that might have been thought vulgar – I didn't have a foreign tongue halfway down my throat within seconds. Dakos just held the kiss, gently but decidedly, so that his breath brushed my face on alternate sides of my nose as the kiss moved across my lips. He eased back but never lost touch and drew my own lips towards him. I've heard it said that the mouth is the signpost to sex; a full mouth, generous in its kisses, promises a good time when you actually get between the sheets, and Dakos' mouth certainly tantalized me – the way it parted for the kiss, the insistence of its caressing touch.

I felt my breasts resting lightly on his chest, my neck stretched to reach for his mouth and then he dropped his hands so that they were holding mine, our fingers just touching, our lips still pressed gently together. When he stood back I looked into his eyes – you know the kind of thing you get in women's magazines – they were "a deep rich brown, the colour of dark chocolate and whipped cream".

Well, perhaps they were, but it was the expression in them that disturbed me. I'd expected his hands to begin exploring, of course, but they didn't; instead, he led me to the little balcony that led off the lounge. He had opened the windows and a light breeze blew the lace curtains against us. The soft light of the night was seductive as the breeze drifted from the harbour; it enhanced the mood his kisses had begun and then he talked about his family, his friends and his town, his vision for the island, his home and his son. All the time, we looked at each other; not for a moment did he take his eyes from me, as though he was trying to divine my thoughts before I could speak them. I felt unnerved, I admit: if he had simply suggested that we went to bed, then I could have said yes or no – and feeling as I did at that moment, would probably have ended up under the duvet. I would have had control because this was not a man who was going to force the issue or dash off in a sulk

My mind was still full of the day. I was taken back to that moment when Dakos had spoken to the monk in Greek, and then turned to me and explained that he had asked about his brother who was in the vegetable garden. I was taken back to the sensation I had then of being in another world, to the excitement in being out with an attractive man who was leading such a different life from mine. I was taken back to that moment after the meal when I wanted to lie down, to be undressed and lie in that room with its yellow-white walls, the afternoon sun peering in through the window with the iron bedstead and the crisp, cool sheets on my body, and my realisation that things were different here. I remembered, too, his mother's chuckle and her eyes wrinkling in a knowing look as she said *"Napagia – for the dancing"* and, at the end of the dancing, when they all stood around us and applauded, Dakos' smile and pleasure in the others admiring me.

All this passed through my head so I reached for his shirt, undid the buttons and ran my fingers across his chest. I had to do something as a distraction – for him and for me. It was nicely hairy and, like a gentleman, he folded his arms around me, drew me close and this time kissed me deeply. I felt his tongue flicker across my lips and into my mouth and then that unbearable tenderness again as his lips almost withdrew and began caressing mine, but he would not be distracted. Once again, he eased us apart and looked into my eyes:

"You have enjoyed today?"

"You know I have."

"Some of the ten essential things every visitor to Cystos must do."

"Visit a famous site, enjoy an alfresco meal, buy – or in my case have as a gift of – handmade Kleftara lace and join in a Cystonian dance."

"Or, in your case, make variations to a Cystonian dance."

We both laughed; isn't it wonderful, enjoying a laugh together?

"There is one more of the ten essentials I would wish to do," he said.

"Today?"

"It may start today ….would it be nice to get invited to a Cystonian wedding – our wedding?"

Somewhere across the town a church bell struck midnight.

Day 6: Pirate Ship

Caran:

Lorraine was up, out, and back with her paper before either Joyce or I were properly awake; she and I had really been looking forward to this excursion, so I wasn't surprised. She looked up at me over her coffee, as I came out of my bedroom, and smiled. She'd obviously had a good day with Dakos. I'd heard her come in not very long after midnight as I remember: rather early, I thought – and that did surprise me a bit.

"Have a good day?"

"Yes, thanks."

I waited, but she carried on reading the paper; she obviously wasn't in talking mood, so I stood waiting by the bedroom door and Lorraine looked up.

"I'll tell you later. I need to think about it – get it straight in my head."

"That serious!"

"It was a lovely day ...."

She proceeded to tell me all about it – at least where they had been and so on – but actually, I knew, was telling me nothing, so I scrambled a couple of eggs and listened, wondering. She didn't seem upset, just surprised.

"Was he nice?"

"Very nice. He's a lovely man."

"And he treated you with respect?"

"And he treated me with respect."

"That's a shame," I laughed.

"No, it wasn't actually, Caran. That was part of the niceness. How did you and Joyce get on?"

"Went out, had a meal and a drink. It was all right. Came back here early and chatted with the staff and other guests. There're several going on this trip today."

"Let's get ready."

We arrived at the harbour dressed like French matelots – all stripes and clean lines. I'd bought my little number from Kookai – the navy and white suited me well, and was by far and away the most expensive outfit in sight; I noticed several of the "pirates" giving me the eye as we arrived. Lorraine, as usual, had her boobs on glorious display, but had been sensible enough to wear a loose top that hid her tummy; that strawberry and cream complexion of hers was tanning beautifully and the sun was bleaching her hair to suit; any man looking for a buxom blonde need look no further! Joyce – well she was dressed nicely but with a straw hat that really took the sharpness off her appearance; she reminded me of one of those *memsahibs* you see in television series like *Jewel in the Crown*. But, as a threesome, we were presentable, which is more than can be said for nearly everybody else. God – no French or Italian woman would have been seen dead in some of the outfits that the others, mostly Brits, had arrived in. There were the usual bikini tops worn with old shorts which looked as though they'd been dragged out of the bottom of a suitcase; how can people live like that – does it take so much effort to fold your clothes nicely or hang them up? It was the summer of the

Britney Spears look, of course, so they were all wearing three-quarter length trousers with short tops whether their bellies hung over the trousers or not: great rolls of dead flesh, tanned or not, are so unattractive aren't they? It would have been bad enough if this had just been the teenagers, but older women, too, had those tight, clinging tops pinching into their fat.

As we made our way up the gangplank, with the crew lending many an unnecessary helping hand, one woman in a white top and black shorts (there are times when even black isn't slimming, aren't there?) asked:

"Does the island have water all the way around?"

The crewman looked at her for a moment – I suppose he wondered if this was some special form of British humour – and then said:

"Yes, Ma'am, all the way around – and there are fish in the sea."

"Really – how exciting! How many?"

"How many ....?"

"How many fish in the sea?"

He caught my eye and I gave him a sympathetic smile – it was so embarrassing, I just had to let him know that we weren't all stupid.

On deck, there was a scramble to make sure you got a place for your towel and then we wandered around to take a look at the ship. The crew, I must say, were well dressed in dark blue T-shirts and knee-length denim shorts; they put most of the tourists to shame. There were two, naked to the waist – one with black trousers and a red cummerbund and the other with red trousers and a white cummerbund, but they were the clowns. They were extremely 'muscley' in a wiry way, which

I don't find particularly attractive in a man; but they were fit – they clambered up the masts and rigging like monkeys at a zoo.

The bar was already in use; I overheard one lout saying to his friend:

"No shortage of totty walking around, is there, Kev? Glad we got tanked up before we came. I'm ready for action, man."

"Yeah, right."

I suppose somebody might be attracted to that kind of person (some of these teenage girls have no taste at all), but you just hope that it isn't your own daughters. The first one carried on:

"We'll make our way up on deck in a minute, see if we can find a couple of likely shags and get them pissed up, ready for lunch."

"Yeah, they'll be starting them games once we're underway. See who we can touch up as we go."

"Right on. Another Stella just to get us in the mood?"

"Don't mind if I do, Neville."

Lorraine was in stitches as we passed out through the bar. Joyce said, in that voice of hers:

"I don't see what's so funny, Lorraine. They're disgusting."

"That's about all they are, Joyce. Can you imagine either of them being in a fit state to do anything within half an hour?"

"We'll see."

The ship had already left harbour by the time we reached our towels and the crew were roaming round looking for the giggly girls to get the party started. It was going to be one of those games where you stood in lines and passed things through your legs. I remembered going on a similar trip with Simon and the girls in the Canary Islands when they were young teenagers. It was one of those holidays nobody wants to go on – you know, Simon and I would have preferred a gourmet wine trail in France; they wanted to dress up like tarts with their friends, pick up pimply boys and have a snigger. Anyway, our compromise – since they weren't going on holiday alone at fourteen and fifteen – was a fortnight in the Canaries, where we lay awake half the night wondering what they were doing in the pool bar and waiting for them to come in at the agreed time.

On the pirate ship from Los Cristianos, we had played a game which involved having a doubloon placed between your cheeks; you then had to grip it there, turn without losing it and drop it in a tin can. I was quite pleased, actually; I'd just started Pilates, my pelvic floor was in good condition, and I managed it time after time – much to the delight of the crew and Simon's annoyance. My daughters, of course, were speechless with shame and would have gone to hide in the bar if the crew hadn't stopped them and made them clap Mummy; but, I must admit, it was a vulgar game – even with my Noa bikini bottom intact – and I could see that we were in for more of the same today.

Sure enough, lines of tourists were organised and a small rubber squid attached to a long piece of string was passed back from one to the other; needless to say, the lines were arranged with men and women alternately placed. The idea was to pass the squid down the front of the person behind you, pull it out through the legs of their shorts or swim gear and on to the next person. The winning team – the one that got the squid to the last in their line first – all got a free drink from the long-spouted flagon carried by one of the crew; in addition, of course, they stood the chance of having a good grope around the private parts of the person behind them. I don't mind this sort of thing (I'm no prude), but I noticed that the teenage girls who had been co-erced into line by the crew certainly appeared to. It's funny isn't it – they're all 'knickers down' as soon as they get the 'boy-friend' these days, and yet squeal and shriek at a little bit of innocent fun!

Of course, it does depend who you get in front of you; I wouldn't have been so happy had I ended up with Kev or Nev – but then they wouldn't have got their dirty little paws anywhere near me. As it was, I found myself behind one of those men who is always the life and soul of any party. He was tall and, as a younger man, would have been considered handsome; he wasn't too bad now at fifty-something, but had allowed his paunch to sag. He introduced himself as Noel when he slid the squid between my breasts with his left hand and whipped his right hand up under my matelot top to pull it down; his smile suggested that he would be quite happy to pass it through my bikini bottom, too, but I declined and did that myself. The man behind me was young – nineteen or twenty – and quite good looking in a rough kind of way, so I insisted, much to his embarrassment, in not only sliding the squid across his chest but also dropping it into the top of his swimming shorts and reaching for it as he hurriedly tried to work it out. I saw him harden and blush furiously; I couldn't resist saying:

"Girls, can we interest you in a package holiday?"

He flared up until his face was a beetroot red. The 'package holiday' slogan had been one of those used by

Club 18-30 some years ago. It had appeared on some holiday advertising alongside a photograph of a man's enlarged crotch in boxer shorts, and caused quite a furore. It had been banned, but still appeared in those magazines young people like to think of as "sophisticated"; it's funny isn't it – they can snigger along with it until someone brings it out into the open? Anyway, it was nice to know I could pull them young: just a pity the girls hadn't been here to see me!

"Where are you from?"

As soon as the game was over and we'd had the wine poured down our throats, Noel introduced himself.

"Stafford," I said.

I gave him a good look over. He reminded me a bit of that French actor – Gerard Depardieu or something like that, the one who was with what's-her-name in *Green*-something. He had the same kind of bulbous nose – not unattractive in a French kind of way – and his eyes twinkled all the time; you could imagine him enjoying sex and knowing a thing or two about it.

"I'm Noel, as I said briefly in the line-up – from Matlock. It's in Derbyshire."

He was certainly quick on the uptake: the fact that I had no idea where Matlock was must have been apparent from my expression and he noticed it at once.

"I'm Caran. I'm here with my friends Lorraine and Joyce."

"Let's get acquainted. I'll introduce you to Tony."

"Tony?"

"We're here together. It's OK – we're not limp in the left wrist."

Again that sharpness: his eyes hadn't left my face and, within minutes, you felt you had known him all your life. The five of us stood looking each other over with drinks in our hands and smiles all over our faces.

Noel:

I was glad to have met Caran; she and her friends looked as though they might be up for a good time. She was a bit of all right herself and her friend Lorraine was something else – I've always liked a firm bird. I didn't quite take to the dowdy one, Joyce, but I thought she might turn out to be Tony's cup of tea – he needed a shoulder to cry on and she looked the type. We'd come away together because I thought he needed cheering up; we go to the same pub and play in the pool team. He'd lost his wife about a year before and had been as miserable as sin ever since; we kept telling him to look on it as a fresh start – after a respectful interval, of course – but he couldn't get over the loss. I suppose marriage takes some men like that: I was glad to be out of it myself. Maureen and I have been divorced for years but we're still on hatchet terms, so to speak: she still phones me up when she wants something. I was in the middle of a sales conference one evening – I sell sports equipment, not that I'm a very good advert for it – and she wanted to know how to mix a Manhattan. Anyway, here we were in Cystos, and things were looking up.

We'd booked this trip at our 'Welcome Meeting' in the heat of the moment, persuaded by the ersatz charms of two of the ladies at our hotel. They were in the room above us and, on that first morning, we had made their acquaintance when – after an early dip in the pool – they had hung their towels over the balcony so that they dripped on to our breakfast table. I didn't mind myself (live and let live) but Tony gets a little tight-arsed over that kind of thing, and he'd gone to have a word with them, so we ended up at the meeting together, full of apologies, the best of friends. I later learned from one of the waiters that the two ladies had come to the hotel every year for the last three or four years; they were called 'Siesta' and 'Fiesta' because one enjoyed sex and the other enjoyed eating. Tony hadn't liked that (he didn't think it "nice") but as I said at the time – "What's the point of taking a lady to a restaurant if she doesn't enjoy eating, or to bed, if she doesn't enjoy sex?" I became a little worried about both of them after a prolonged conversation which boiled down to the fact that it had been hotter last year when they had booked through Thomson!

Things were beginning to hot up now that the first game was over and the drink had been pouring liberally down our throats. Caran pointed out two lads called Kev and Nev who were leaning over the side vomiting, and we all had a good laugh when a girl passed and accused one of them of pinching her backside:

"Don't pinch my arse!"

Kev's hands went up to heaven, as though beseeching the Lord to proclaim his innocence but the girl continued to scream, laughing with her mates as she did so:

"Don't touch what you can't have."

"Stupid slut."

At this point one of the crew intervened, leaning his arms on the girl's shoulders and steering her towards the next game. This was played in couples with the men standing in a circle over one of the hatchways while their partner tried to pour wine down their throats from the long-spouted flagon; the crewman partnered the girl, much to her friends delight. Caran dragged me into it and we did pretty well; I'm a seasoned drinker and she had a steady hand. I have to say I much enjoyed the cuddles afterwards; she had a nice pair of Bristols on her for a woman of fifty. I guessed she was fit.

"It's not lunchtime yet and half these young people are drunk already," said the dowdy one – Joyce.

"They're only enjoying themselves, Joyce," said Lorraine.

"They should be ashamed – and besides, how are they going to swim safely?"

"The crew seem to know what they're doing," said Tony.

"They're used to the English. Binge drinking is a national pastime. We even send our policemen abroad to advise the locals on how to deal with it," I said.

"It's frightening. I'm sure the locals don't like it."

"Joyce, stop worrying, we're on holiday."

"I agree with Joyce," Tony cut in, "They'll begin undressing in a moment and we'll have them running around the deck naked."

"Ooooh, we should be so lucky."

Caran said that, and we laughed; well – she, Lorraine and I laughed and I said:

"Don't you ever go into the town centre at home on a Thursday, Friday or Saturday night, Joyce?"

"I certainly do not."

"The locals think it's obscene," said Tony.

"But they encourage it and take our money. They can't have it both ways."

"It's a British phenomenon, Noel. You don't get it anywhere else in Europe."

"So we like to get drunk! Who's for a swim?"

At that moment a cry went up from the starboard side of the ship and we all lurched across, rubbing bare arms and shoulders quite nicely together as we leaned over the side. A cliff face towered before us and the crew were in earnest negotiations with some of the young bloods aboard; it turned out that the ship was about to navigate a headland of which this cliff was part. Traditionally, those who wanted to were put ashore here; they then climbed the cliff, passed through the caves in it and joined us for lunch in the bay on the other side. It seemed simple and a bit James Bond-ish: something to impress the women. At the same time, I was a little troubled; you don't reach fifty-something without gaining a bit of caution – where was the catch?

"Do you fancy having a go, Noel?"

"What's in it if I do, Lorraine?"

"One of us gets to take you out for dinner – right Lorraine?" said Caran.

I saw Lorraine pause and caught the glance which passed between her and Caran: perhaps I wasn't Lorraine's cup of tea – or was there something, or someone, else?

"OK – I'll take you out," said Caran.

"Well toss for it," said Lorraine.

This was Dreamland – two beautiful women vying for the honour of taking me to dinner! I dropped my trousers, hauled on my shorts and joined the young men in the water. It was only cold for a moment and then we splashed our way to the shore.

Joyce:

"I don't understand Noel," said Tony, "You can't get him out of the chair at home – unless it's to play pool at the pub."

"You don't fancy having a go then, Tony?" I asked.

"I most certainly do not, Joyce"

Tony seemed quite sensible; I'd preferred him from the start. Noel's type has never appealed to me – "Hail fellow, well met" as my father used to say: all right on the day but nowhere to be seen when you need them most.

At that moment, two women – very common – came rushing up to us, screeching:

"Was that Noel? Was that Noel in the water, Tony?"

"Noel, Noel, come back, come back!!"

They really caused a scene; everybody on the deck was staring at us. Noel heard them, turned and waved.

"He doesn't know what he's doing."

"Call him back. Noel, Noel!"

"What's wrong, ladies, what's wrong?"

It was Tony who spoke; he appeared to know them.

"It's the other side ….,

".... the other side. It's a hundred foot drop.

"Noel, poor Noel."

"What are they talking about, Tony?" said Lorraine.

"I don't know. Dot, Lorna – what is it?"

"It's the drop."

"When he comes out on the other side of the cliff?"

At this point one of the crew came over and spoke; he was very calm.

"Ladies – what is the problem?"

"It's Noel."

"It's a hundred foot drop."

"Ah – the dive! It is nothing. The Cystonian children do it all the time."

"What exactly is going to happen?" asked Tony.

"When your friend comes out on the other side of the headland – through the caves – it will be high up on the cliff face. He will dive into the sea and we shall take him aboard."

"How high?" said Tony.

"You see the cliff? The caves come out near the top on the other side."

"Oh dear, what have we done?" said Caran.

"What did you do?" screeched one of the women; I couldn't make out whether it was Dot or Lorna.

Caran looked at both of them as though wondering whether or not to answer. I could see what was going through her mind – they both wore baggy T-shirts, for a start. She'd been holding forth about those the other night – "a complete beach disaster because all they really do is make you look completely shapeless. It's far better to wear a simple loose-fitting top that stops at your hips for that refreshing 'I've-been- to-Marrakesh'-look; and don't go for cap sleeves unless your upper arms are perfect." Neither of them were exactly 'beach babes' and the cutaway bikini bottoms did nothing for them, it is true, but they did seem genuinely concerned about Noel. Then Caran said, in that cutting way of hers:

"Who exactly are we talking to?"

"Oh, I'm sorry, I should have introduced you," said Tony, "This is Dot and this lady here is Lorna. They are staying at the same hotel as Noel and I."

"Oh."

Isn't it funny how one word can say so much? I saw both of them give Caran 'the look' and then Dot, who had what men call "bedroom eyes", said:

"We came together, didn't we Tony?"

"We booked the trip at our Welcome Meeting".

"Oh, I see. Well we rather dared Noel to have a go," said Caran in her silkiest voice, "If he did it, then one of us – Lorraine or I – would give him a night out to remember ...."

"Only we didn't realise that it might be as dangerous as it seems," said Lorraine, trying to soothe things a little.

"It is not dangerous," cut in the crewman, "We always do this."

"Well, you'll be sorry if he's hurt," said Lorna.

"Yes, we should be. Let's hope for the best," said Caran.

Caran:

What a couple of baggages! It was embarrassing to be standing with them; I could only hope that neither Noel nor Tony, who seemed quite nice men, saw anything in them. Apart from the baggy T-shirts, they had cutaway bikini bottoms in pink! There was little they could have done, I suppose, to enhance the shape of their bottoms – but they could have tried; perhaps a shorts-style bikini to hold them in?

Fortunately, it wasn't long before we rounded the headland, but long enough for another group of roughs to make an exhibition of themselves: they'd got some sparklers from somewhere and had begun dancing round with them. That wasn't so bad and the crew joined in, laughing with the rest of us – but of course, they couldn't stop there could they? One of them stuck three or four in his mouth to have his picture taken, so the rest of them plonked him on that rail that goes round the ship and dumped a load of lager bottles in his lap.

While they lined up the picture, with all of them piling in and making those stupid faces you see on the Clubber's Page in the local paper, one of his mates lit the sparklers. I mean, can you credit the intelligence of people like that? The sparks were flying everywhere, the pirate crew were clearly getting anxious and the lout himself was having his eyebrows singed, so he decided to spit out the sparklers, one of which got hooked in his wristwatch. He leapt into the air screaming as the sparkler burnt into his arm, showering lager bottles all over the deck. Broken glass and beer bounced and splashed around, all of us yelling as we tried to get out of the way. The girls who had been egging him on now began that cats' chorus of screams (largely designed to draw attention to themselves) pushing and shoving each other, in that way they do, until several of them were literally dancing on the broken glass. "The English – they are mad," one of the crew muttered to himself as he ran around with a mop and a bucket trying to clear the debris; by now, there was blood amongst the beer and the yelling and screaming had reached a fever pitch. You have to admire these foreigners: they closed in on the roughs, sorted those who needed first aid from those who were just making a lot of noise, washed the broken bottles over-board and had us all dancing to 'Sex on the Beach' before Dot – the slag-eyed one – was shouting:

"Noel, look Noel. It's Noel on the cliff!"

You'd think he was her personal property: I just hoped he wasn't.

"Dot, are you sure?"

"Yes, of course she's sure," I said, "We can all see that it's Noel up there."

"I only asked," replied the slightly fatter of the two. What was here name – Lorna?

There was no doubt about it. Noel and some of the others who had swum ashore on the other side of the headland had now come out, through the caves, on the far side. We all gathered on the starboard rail and, of course, there was the usual chorus of raucous laughter – the kind of thing you get in evening classes with everyone trying to out-laugh each other to prove how matey they are; only now, with teenagers, it was accompanied by an increasing number of belches as we neared the cliff face. The girls, increasingly cranking up their hysteria, were almost beside themselves, like toddlers at a party. Occasionally they stopped roaring to have the obligatory snog, or rather slobber, with their boy-friend – or any boy really; as long as they could wobble their breasts against a chest and ram their tongue halfway down another throat it didn't seem to matter much.

"Noel isn't going to jump, is he?" said Joyce – real concern in her voice.

"I don't think he has any choice," said Tony, "He can't climb the cliff either up or down. His best chance is to jump clear of it into the water."

"But it's three times as high as the ship!"

"There is no worry," said the crewman with the red trousers and the white cummerbund, who was now perching on the ship's rail grinning like a monkey.

"If you say that again, I'm going to thump you," said Tony, quite quietly but with meaning.

The crewman laughed, more like a pirate than ever. Then one of the teenagers piped up – he must have over-heard Tony's comment to the pirate:

"Here, we've got a fight coming up here."

"You mind your own business," said Tony, "I wasn't talking to you."

"You what?"

"You heard."

All the time he was speaking, either to the pirate or the youth, Tony never took his eyes off the cliff face. He seemed such a quiet man, but the youth, now mouthing and belching more furiously than ever, didn't seem to bother him at all.

"Here – I'm talking to you, mate!"

"Yeah – we're talking to you," chorused a group of his mates – their girls on their arms – as they gathered round us.

"Go and play with the fish."

"What?"

"You heard, son," said Tony, "I'm worried about my friend. Now go and play with the fish – or yourself, if that's easier."

I don't think I've ever heard anyone be so rude to a group of drunken louts in all my life. Lorraine was killing herself with laughter, Joyce was clutching herself as though she was about to have hysterics and the two baggages just looked at him open-mouthed, in the way those fans look at spotty boy bands, but he was so calm – he never so much as looked at them or took his eyes off Noel on the cliff face. Then one of them lunged at him, grabbing his shoulder. Tony turned – he had no choice, the youth pulled him round – but before anything could happen, six pirates had intervened among us, separating our group from the teenagers and easing them away.

"Shan't forget this, mate. We'll sort you – you see. We'll fuck you up."

When Tony didn't answer, it seemed to infuriate the youth even more; still ringed by pirates he yelled:

"You got a problem, mate, or do you want one?"

"Why? Are you going to "make my day", sonny?"

At this, the youth went ballistic, kicking and struggling to get at Tony.

"Fuck you!"

"Take it easy, sir. Take it easy! You're winding him up."

"Really? If he can't handle his beer, he shouldn't be aboard. Chuck him over the side to cool him off."

"I'll chuck your dick over the side, mate. Let me fucking get him."

"Yeah – get him, Neil."

"Sort him out."

"Give him a good hiding."

The girlfriends now chipped in, waving their cans of lager threateningly.

"The next generation of motherhood, Caran. What price the children?" said Lorraine, but not loud enough to be heard.

"He's jumped. Fuck me, Ian's jumped."

We all turned and, for a moment, the impending fracas cooled. The first youth had jumped. There seemed so little distance between him and the ship but in seconds he'd dropped past the mast and into the water. He surfaced, spluttering and yelling but triumphant: I must say it was impressive. The girls cheered, thrust their breasts over the side and wobbled their bottoms; several of them scrambled over the side and jumped in the water. Soon he was surrounded by admirers, each trying to get into the photographs that were being taken from on deck.

Tony:

It was so high, the drop from the cliff top, that I was angry with the crew for not warning Noel of what he was letting himself in for; now the girls were in the water, there seemed even less room for Noel and the others to jump. To be honest, I wouldn't have dared, but then another of the young men leapt clear and splashed to safety. The chorus on deck was getting more vocal – making chicken sounds, bending their arms at the elbows and flapping imaginary wings.

"Cluck! Cluck-cluck-cluck-cluck-cluck-cluck!"

There must have been about a dozen men up in the mouth of the cave; as one found the courage to jump, another stepped or was pushed into his place. A small group, including Noel, stood to one side: they were all ages, all shapes and sizes.

"Does he have a head for heights, Tony?" asked Dot (the one Noel calls Siesta). Before I could reply, Caran cut in:

"He doesn't have much choice, does he?"

She's a hard case: she and Dot were daggers drawn from the moment they met and I don't know why – they're as different as chalk and cheese, and neither is really Noel's cup of tea. Dot's just a good-time girl but a bit given to the drink and Noel is fussy about drunken women; he always has a lot to say and likes them to listen. The other one – Caran – well, you might get more than you bargained for with her; she looks a bit, shall we say, 'experimental'. I could see him going for Lorraine; big but firm, what he would call Rabelaisian – whatever that might mean – and straightforward.

The whole ship was now alight with anticipation: everyone waving and cheering, making chicken noises or holding their breath as the men in their lives faced that awful leap.

"I just hope he has the sense to keep his legs closed," said Lorraine.

"Hmmm?" said Lorna – the tubby one Noel calls Fiesta.

"If he hits the water from that height with his legs open, he'll split himself in two," said Lorraine.

"Noel, Noel – keep your legs together," Dot and Lorna called at the top of their voices.

"There's no point in shouting, he can't hear you," said Caran.

"You think he might damage his equipment, darling?" called one of the youths, "That's all you old girls ever think about, innit – sex? Heh?"

Gales of laughter rippled along the deck rail, followed by more belching; the mood had switched from anger to good humour.

"Ignore him. They're only looking for trouble," said Caran.

Those in the cave mouth were all jumping now; one after the other, they hit the sea, sank and then kicked their way to the surface. The water was awash with bodies: finding a clear spot seemed to be the main problem. As each jumped, a roar of encouragement went up from the ship's side; as the next one hesitated, the chicken sound swelled from the deck. The crew had opened up the side and run a plank over the edge so that, as their boyfriend hit the water, the girls were made to walk the plank at cutlass point.

The ship was already in the bay and at anchor. During the mayhem, the crew had furled the sails and dropped rope ladders over the side. We were in reach of the beach and several groups were already ashore. The crew ran around dishing out life-jackets in quite a haphazard fashion. There was no way that any of this met any kind of 'Health and Safety' standards – if Cystos joined the European Community, then all of this would have to stop.

"He's jumping!"

All five women spoke at once but their voices together sounded little more than a whisper. I saw Noel drop, feet together and – as he flashed past the ship – I saw that his eyes were closed. I could never have done it – they would have had to call out the fire brigade to lift me clear to the cliff top. He is a big man and hit the water with an almighty splash.

"Who's his woman?" called one of the pirates, with a cutlass.

Caran and Dot looked at each other.

"I don't swim," said Dot.

It must have taken an effort for her to say that: the alternative, I suppose, was to risk drowning.

"So who gets to give him a night to remember – Lorraine?"

"I think you'll look better on the plank, darling."

"If no one objects, I'll join our hero in the water."

She did look stunning. There aren't many women of her age who can wear a bikini and actually look better than an attractive younger woman: they either look scrawny or pinched – but not Caran. The week's sun had done her no harm – a tan always covers the blemishes – and she had chosen plain colours, navy blue shorts across the stomach and a white top; the bra looked as though it had been made to measure. She had short dark hair that curved into her neck. Isn't it funny how some women never seem to have a hair out of place? It was like that with her now: the sea breeze just ruffled it slightly. The pirates wrestled each other aside to help her; she stepped on to the plank, walked to the end and turned with a face that said, "Eat your hearts out, girls. Will you look like this at fifty-something?" A big cheer went up from the men, and a chorus of wolf-whistles that received some elbowing from their girl friends, and then Caran turned, waved to Noel – the cutlass just nudging the small of her back – and dived: yes – dived! Not for her the usual jump and splash; she cut the water pretty neatly and surfaced next to him. Their arms went out; they kissed and swam together towards the ship.

"Bitch."

I heard Dot say it quietly, but quite distinctly, to Lorna.

The return of the heroes was quite something and their women lapped up every moment of their glory. I admired them – as I said, I could not have jumped from that cliff to save my life.

"You were like the man from the Black Magic ad, Noel," said Lorna.

"Do you fancy a bit of black magic, Lorna?"

"I wouldn't mind a box of chocolates."

"Umm! Give me the man any day," said Dot.

We were all sitting on the beach – Noel and I, Dot and Lorna and the three new ladies; the crew had run us ashore after the barbecue and I could see that we were here 'for the duration' – as my parents used to say. The barbecue had been all right – basic, of course and cooked on the back of the pirate ship: none of your lamb kebabs with mint, oriental spare ribs or pork chops Provencal or even Greek souvlaki. Simply, chicken, chips and salad'; I avoided the salad. The only time I have ever been tempted to eat salad abroad was in Kathmandu and I ended up with "Delhi-belly" for a fortnight.

Noel was in his element, surrounded by a harem of five women, and had already told the story of his jump half a dozen times. I could hear him now sounding off in the pub when we got home; by then the "jump" would have become a "dive", no doubt, and, eventually, a dive with a cutlass between his teeth. I like Noel – you can't help it – and I suppose I envy his easy way with women. They don't seem to bother him at all; he's had several "partners" since he and his wife split up and, according to him, they've all left him – not the other way around. "Don't you care? Doesn't it upset you?" I'd asked. He shrugged and replied "Why should it?" "You don't feel a failure?" He'd simply looked puzzled and given me that quizzical grin, and then said "You're too open to life, Tony." He was right, of course. I'd worshipped Bev until the day she died; I always put a little poem in with every card I sent her – Valentines, Easter, anniversary, Christmas. It took me hours to write them sometimes – I'd sit in the car on the way home from work, otherwise Bev would have asked me what I was doing. We didn't have any secrets from each other. We lived in each others laps rather too much, I suppose, but I don't regret that at all.

"Penny for them, Tony?" said Joyce.

"I wouldn't know where to start. I don't want to put a damper on things."

I whispered this, but Noel looked up; he's quite solicitous in that way.

"It's time for the banana boat!"

The boat was moored alongside the ship and already full of youngsters; we were going to be here all afternoon.

"We'd better get back to the ship."

"They'll pick us up from the beach. Give them a wave, Caran," said Noel.

"Why me?"

"You're more likely to attract their attention than I am. You can repeat your performance on the gangplank. Give them a flash of your bikini bottom."

She did and, sure enough, two of the pirates waved back immediately. This attracted the attention of a group of youths further along the beach who had also been waving at the ship from the top of a rock; they, of course, had actually taken their swimming shorts off to use, and were presumably naked under the long baggy T-shirts they wore. Certainly, judging from the girls with them, who were on their backs looking up from the base of the rock, this was the case. They'd been drinking heavily all morning and how they managed to stay on the rock, I don't know. Anyway, they seemed annoyed at Caran's success and, as the pirate dinghy made for the shore, the youths and their girls made for us.

"Here mate, what's up with you? Are you some sort of wanker?"

"What does he mean?" asked Joyce.

"He doesn't mean anything, Joyce. He just likes the sound of his voice using the word," Noel replied.

"I said, 'Are you a wanker?' mate."

"Our friends are unsure what you mean by the word," replied Noel, "Perhaps you could explain exactly what a "wanker" is?"

"What?"

"Wanker – could you define the term?"

"You being fucking funny?"

"Well since you ask, I have fucked for fun and I have been funny, on odd occasions, when I've fucked."

"He's trying to be fucking funny, Keith," said one of the girls – her size 14 squeezed into a size 10 bikini.

"But to return to the term "wanker" – could you elucidate for us?"

"Careful, Noel. They look nasty," I said.

"They could certainly have dressed more tastefully," said Caran.

Noel and Lorraine laughed; Joyce, Dot and Lorna just looked stunned.

"What she say?" yelled one of the girls.

"Her concerns were largely sartorial," said Noel, "Can we return to your "wankers"?"

"What?"

"Perhaps we could have the declension of the verb 'to wank'? 'I wank, you wank, they wank?"'

During this exchange, the group had been tottering slowly towards us across the beach – eight or nine of them in all, youths and girls – and I began to wonder whether Noel had gone too far. The girls, in particular, looked hostile and one of them (Tracy, I think her friends called her) said:

"They're old, Keith, old wrinklies. You can smell 'em from here. Ignore 'em."

"Old we may be, sweetie, but your young men fancy us more than they fancy you," said Caran.

"Wha?" said Tracy.

"Isn't that right, boys? You'd give a lot to get your hands on us, wouldn't you?"

"Don't flatter yerself."

"Men are roused by what they see. You need to learn that, little girl. What they see in us are clean, smartly-dressed women glowing with our summer tans. What they see in you is a fat old laundry bag stuffed with dirty clothes."

The girl's face was a picture; I don't think she'd ever been the recipient of such direct rudeness before. Caran went on:

"We washed this morning which is more than can be said for you, I imagine. I expect you just rolled out of bed, sweaty from the night, and covered yourself with perfume, didn't you? I should think you're as grubby as your clothes."

"What's wrong with my clothes, you fucking snob?"

"You and the way you wear them – oh, and the fact that you could lose a stone or so. Don't think that "young" means "attractive" because it doesn't. And here comes our boat."

One of the pirates leapt into the water and steadied the boat while two more jumped over the side of the dinghy and made towards us; they were all smiles.

"Are you ready, lovely ladies?"

The remark was directed at Caran who promptly dropped her odds and ends into a bag and walked over to him.

"Could you give me a hand to get in the boat?"

"Here, just a minute, mate. We were waving first," yelled one of Keith's mates.

"It was the lady we noticed."

"What about us?"

"We can return for you – or, you can swim out to the ship as you swam ashore."

"And while you wait," said Noel, his eyes twinkling, "perhaps you could discuss the meaning of the word 'wank' and its relevance to this situation. Have you been wanked? Does that make you a wanker?"

This was too much for Keith who ran at Noel and lunged out with his fist. Noel stepped aside and Keith was so drunk that the strength of his lunge swung him round and over on to the sand. His mates moved forward, fists clenched, and the situation would have become very nasty, indeed, if the pirates hadn't intervened; the two in the water – eager to help the ladies into the boat – stepped between the youths and us, raised their hands in a gesture both of supplication and warning and then said to Noel:

"You shouldn't wind them up, sir. It isn't worth it."

"Right! You heard that, mate. You wind us up, you're for it."

"My concern is primarily for the sanctity of the language ...."

"OK, sir, shall we get in the boat now?"

In minutes, they had lifted all five ladies into the dinghy (including Lorraine whose face bore an expression of bewilderment and joy) and were rowing us to the ship and the banana boat which was completing another circuit of the bay.

"You're best to ignore them, sir. They can get quite nasty. We had a group in town the other night calling out insults across the market square. They were in one of the bars and began insulting the king ...."

"King?"

"For some reason they think we have a king on Cystos. Don't ask me why! They were calling out insults. The police arrived and they abused them, told them to ...you know. So they waited – the police that is – while the insults became a chant, and one of the youths knelt down asking the police to shoot him."

"Really?" said Joyce.

"Yes, madam, really. It quietened down after a while and the youths wandered off and the police followed them – with a few of the bouncers from the bars, you understand, armed with canes. When they were out of sight, they caught up with them and gave them a beating."

"The police beat them?"

"The bouncers beat them. Just enough to let them know that certain behaviour is not tolerated. One or two ended up in hospital – a few cracked ribs, cuts, bruises – nothing serious. All quietly done – away from your people who are here to enjoy themselves."

"Right," was all Noel felt able to say.

Caran:

I don't know why I said it and I don't care; it was something I had been meaning to say to my two daughters for a long time, so I suppose Keith's girlfriend got the sharp edge of my tongue, but I enjoyed it. What I do know is that I would not have said it a week ago – not with that amount of confidence. It was true, of course – she did look like an old bag stuffed with dirty clothes and it did her no harm to know that; these young girls assume that youth is everything – the fact that fifty percent of them are fatter and less attractive than their mothers doesn't actually occur to them.

The rest of the day went wonderfully – or shall I say, swimmingly. We were next on the banana boat, slotted together like After Eights in a box – but unwrapped and with every reason to hold on to the shoulders of the man in front of you, and I made sure I was between two of the younger ones. High speed is always sexy; I remember reading one of those Harold Robbins novels years ago when one of his heroines has an orgasm in a racing car. It was rather like that as we whizzed around the bay.

The pirates had helped us down, holding us close against their hairy chests while they waited to lower us on to the banana boat; there's something about being lifted into place by a man, isn't there? Then we were off, bouncing up and down over the waves; it was a bit like sex when you're young, first married and trying out the new bed in your own house. The noise was part of the thrill and we yelled every time the banana hit a wave and threw us upwards. All you could do was to grip tight with your thighs and go with it: quite different from the gentle sex I'd had with Frank (what, two days ago?) but exciting. There were two banana boats by now – every one was at it – and Lorraine had got herself a place on the other one, so we waved and laughed at each other as we whizzed past. Noel was behind her, obviously enjoying himself, and Dot (the one he called Siesta) was behind him. I think the others stayed aboard the ship. I "came", as they say, several times during the trip and slid gratefully into the sea when it was over; Lorraine swam over to me.

"God, Lorraine, this is the life, isn't it?"

"We came here to enjoy ourselves. Let's not forget it."

"It's the first time I've ever holidayed away from the family."

"Glad you came, then?"

"Need you ask? And you?"

"Oh yes."

"Are you seeing Dakos again?"

"I told you, I'll tell you about him later."

Lorraine:

Caran and I were too excited to stay in that night as Joyce wanted, so we forced her out to a nightclub. We'd made a casual arrangement to meet up with Noel and Tony sometime and exchanged hotel names (they were staying at the Aeneas Hotel), but we didn't meet up that night and simply danced with whoever invited us, returning to the Captain Karas alone – and sober-ish. I had Dakos on my mind, of course: I just didn't know what to do about him. "Would it be nice to be invited to a Cystonian wedding – our wedding?" I'd never been married: we didn't think it "cool" in the seventies – not those of us who were liberated.

Day 7: Poolside

I was ready to talk the next morning – not to Joyce, only to Caran – because, in a way, I'd already made up my mind and wanted to test it out on somebody. I needed somebody to argue with, but somebody who might agree with me – or was it that I needed somebody who might persuade me? So we sat over breakfast a long time – pretending, later, to Joyce that we had overslept; she was nice enough to believe us. I didn't have to introduce the subject: Caran was agog.

"Well?"

I laughed; I couldn't help it. It was a bit like Les Dawson and his friend over the garden fence.

"He proposed to me."

"He did what?"

"He proposed to me."

"What did you say?"

"Caran – we're not going to get very far if you keep interrupting me with questions. You'll have to let me ..."

"OK – I'm mum."

"As I said yesterday, we spent the day visiting his relatives. First of all, his brother in the monastery, then we had lunch with a cousin and his wife and in the afternoon, I met his mother and sister. In the evening we met his friends at a dance. All day it had seemed to me to be more than just a trip round the island doing the things tourists are supposed to do. He was showing me his way of life – the things that are important to him. And then, late in the evening I saw his son ... "

"Saw? Sorry."

"He took me back to his apartment and showed me his son, Michael, who was asleep in bed. We had a drink. We touched and kissed. The only decision I was going to have to make – or so I thought – was going to be whether I would say 'yes'. And it would have been my decision. I knew that. I wasn't worried by him. That was part of the attraction, really ... "

"So you didn't actually? Sorry."

"No, we didn't. Dakos began by talking about the 'ten essentials'. You know the things tourists are supposed to do on holiday – one of which is to get invited to a Cystonian wedding. And then he said – "our wedding?" I remember that somewhere across the town a church bell struck midnight. I couldn't speak. I was gobsmacked. I just stood gawping at him and gulping down lungfuls of air. And then he said "You are offended, Lorren?" That's the way he pronounced my name. I'm sure it wasn't intentional but it had sounded so sexy all day. I said "No, no – just surprised." And he said "Why should you be surprised. You are a beautiful and lovely woman." I said "Thank you but I am fifty-something. I didn't expect ... " and he said "I am in my forties. It is not such a gap. We are both mature people." I asked him for another drink and sat down on his settee while he got it. He came and sat beside me. He said that it was not so difficult to know whether you were in love or not. It was that special feeling you had about someone, and he had that feeling about me. And that if we liked each other – and he thought we did – then what was there to stop us? He knew it would be a change of life for me and that was why he had shown me some of the island and some of his family. He realised I might need time to think about it and when I had – if I accepted him – he would introduce me to his father and propose properly."

"Bloody hell, Lorraine."

"Is that all you can say?"

"Well, it is a bit unexpected, to say the least. What did you say?"

"I asked if he would bring me home – which he did – and said I must think about it. Yes – I was honoured he had asked, but I must have time to think. I couldn't get out of his apartment quick enough."

"And he didn't try to …"

"I've said – no!"

"Why?"

"Why what?"

"Why didn't he try it on?"

"I don't know. I haven't thought about it."

"He must fancy you."

"Well, I would hope so."

"So why didn't he ...."

"Caran – you're obsessed with sex! Aren't you interested in how I feel?"

"Of course I am … I just wondered …Where do you go from here?"

"Exactly. What would you do?"

"Do?"

"Would you accept?"

"I'm married. There's Simon and the girls."

"But I'm not."

"You have a partner – Barry – and a daughter, Steph."

"Steph's nineteen and at university. She's a grown woman ..."

"Or thinks she is."

"We won't argue about that. She's old enough to look after herself."

"Are you actually thinking of accepting his proposal? You can't. There's Barry."

"Barry and I never married. We wanted to leave each other free. But we have been together for nearly thirty years, yes."

"Do you fancy this Dakos?"

"It's more than that. People make too much fuss about sex. We'd be OK. We'd settle down quickly enough to a pattern. What he's offering is more than that: it's another way of life – his life. I was quite flattered – I was very flattered that he "didn't try it on" as you put it. He took that for granted."

"That you'd be OK?"

"That we'd hit it off sexually, yes. He was more concerned about my understanding what his way of life was about."

"He's not just after a mother for his little boy?"

"If it was that, there must be any number of young women on the island who would fit the bill. No, no. It's me he wants."

"But what about Barry?"

"Yes – what about Barry? I'm fifty-four, Caran. I've probably got another forty years ahead of me – longer than Barry and I have been together. Nearly half my whole lifetime. Do I just stay around and "see it out" with Barry? When we got together, it was an attraction of like minds. He was an artist. I was a dancer. I was a feminist – still am. He was Renaissance man – oh, yes. Barry was doing all the things these "modern" men are doing – and more – thirty years ago, in 1974. We saw marriage as an "institution" – society's way of tying people down into a contract to keep the social order intact. We looked at our own parents' marriages and asked – "Were they happy?" My own parents have been married nearly sixty years, now. How many of those years have been happy? I'm not saying that the pursuit of happiness should be an end in itself. I'm not a hedonist – they're essentially selfish people. What I am saying is that Barry and I foresaw all this – that a couple may not want to be tied together for seventy or eighty years – that they may want to take another direction at some time in their lives, and should be free to do so – that staying together out of a sense of duty or "for the children" – once the children were grown up, that is – was not a viable or sensible attitude to take. We haven't actually ever been desperately unfaithful to each other sexually, you understand; I'm talking about a greater freedom than the freedom to hump whoever takes your fancy on the odd occasion."

"Thanks, Lorraine."

"You and Frank are a holiday affair – accept it for what it is, take it as it comes. He will. You're not what the papers love to call a 'serial adulteress'. In a weeks time you'll go back home to Simon and the girls – if that's what you want. It'll be a fond memory, not a life-changing experience – unless you want it to be. As I said the other day (God you lose track of time on holiday don't you?) it's your life. We can't go on holding other people responsible for what we do. What we've got to ask ourselves is – "What do I want to do for the next thirty or forty years?" And then take charge. We don't come this way twice."

"So you've said. Where does that leave you and Dakos?"

"I don't know. As you said – "What about Barry?" "

"Do you love him still?"

"Oh yes – I can always go to Barry, talk to him, have him put his arms round me ...Oh yes, Barry's special to me."

"Then why think about leaving him?"

"Because ... because I am asking myself that question ..."

"Where do I go from here?"

"Exactly! I don't want to end up as one of those bitter women 'who could have done better'. You see them around town all the time, looking as miserable as sin, picking on their husbands who seem perfectly decent men, blaming the world for what they haven't done for themselves, wondering 'where it all went wrong' and why their husbands spend half the year away on golfing holidays .... you've seen them around."

"I can't say I'd actually noticed them until now, Lorraine."

We both laughed then. I got the impression that Caran and her husband don't do a lot of talking whereas Barry and I never stop – well we do, sometimes! We don't talk much during lovemaking, anymore, but we do talk about the people we see and wonder what they're thinking and feeling.

"Why should you end up 'bitter'?"

"Because I haven't achieved what I wanted in life. As I said, when Barry and I started out it was a coming together of like minds. We were both artists in our own way, we supported each other's aspirations but neither of us has got anywhere – if we're honest about it. He couldn't earn a living through his painting and I never became a professional dancer. We both ended up teaching – not that there's anything wrong with that, but it isn't what we wanted for ourselves. So what do we do? Carry on together attending the theatre and art exhibitions – an ageing couple looking at the achievements of others – or do we strike out in other directions? I liked what I saw of Dakos' life, here. I liked the sense of community, family – the whole holistic thing. He seems to have completeness about him. We haven't got that. None of his people seem to measure themselves by a single standard; they don't seem to have a sense of failure, they seem happy in what they do."

"And you want a share of that?"

"I want to be part of it."

"And Barry?"

"You keep saying that, Caran! Barry loves me. He will give me his blessing and settle back into doing his 'projects' – odd thematic weekends and holidays when he paints the odd thematic painting!"

"So you're going to say "yes"?"

"Yes – I think so. I think this a chance I can't miss. It's like waiting to be called for a part and then – when the call comes – being too nervous to take it on. I don't want to miss my chance."

"God – I do admire you, Lorraine. You certainly know what you want out of life."

We did eventually get down to the pool and join Joyce who had commandeered three loungers – definitely a move forward for her!

"I wish Robert could have seen me," she said, "He was always saying I wasn't assertive enough."

Somehow, after we'd settled down, I couldn't pretend any longer and told Joyce about Dakos; talking to Caran had settled my mind, I suppose, and I felt I could face Joyce now. She didn't say a word – just stared open-mouthed, like the proverbial fish. When I'd finished, her mouth tightened and she said:

"You must be mad. You don't know when you're well off."

"It's up to Lorraine, Joyce. It's her life," said Caran.

"You don't know what you're doing, coming to a strange country to live with a strange man. Why can't people settle for what they've got?"

"I didn't mean to upset you, Joyce. I just thought you ought to know."

"Thank you."

There was a long pause, then; long enough for Caran to call a waiter – one of the young men from the university in Abydos who worked here during the summer – and set us up with drinks. I could see that Joyce's mind was running over her own situation, and finally she said:

"You could end up with nothing."

"I could cope with that, Joyce, but I don't think it will happen."

"You could end up looking for a husband – dating!"

"That wouldn't be so bad, would it?" laughed Caran.

"It would be awful. You've never had to do it – not since you first got married. You've no idea what dating at our age can be like."

"Are you thinking of your 'singles' holiday?"

"Partly – but after Robert left me, well-intentioned friends tried to get me together with different unattached men. Can you imagine what it's like being set up for a date?"

Her tone and demeanour were such that even Caran, perhaps one of life's shallow people, didn't make the obvious joke.

"They even persuaded me to join one of those dating agencies. Oh, I didn't have to go along and meet anyone and tell them what kind of man I was looking for. It's all done 'online' these days but it's just as horrible. You go into what they call a "chat room" – no one can see you – and then you put in details about yourself. Well – where do you start? How would you describe me, Caran?"

"Well ..."

"Exactly! Short, grey-haired and frumpy."

"I wouldn't say that, Joyce," I said, trying to be reassuring.

"I know you're not like me, Lorraine: you are lovely. But what I am trying to say is that starting out again at our age isn't all dreams. If things don't work out for you with this man, you could find yourself worse off than you are now."

"How did you describe yourself, Joyce?" said Caran.

I couldn't believe she had asked the question; Caran was either being remarkably insensitive or astute enough to be turning the conversation onto more fruitful lines, and I didn't have her marked down as 'astute'. Joyce looked at her for a moment and then laughed. Don't people always surprise you?

"Petite!"

"What about the grey hair?"

"Ash blonde!"

"And the frumpy?"

"My daughter took me to Debenhams and made me buy a new outfit from Coast."

"So you did get a date?"

"It was awful. I arranged to meet this man in the local shopping mall. I was told it was safer to meet any stranger in the open where there are plenty of people about. Well, we have this Italian-style café with seats outside and it seemed as good as anywhere. He was supposed to be short and dark – dark-haired, I mean – and a bit like Robert De Niro."

"Really?" said Caran.

"Of course it was a foolish place to meet, wasn't it? It was 'open' all right – too open: the place was packed. When I got to Le Fonticine, as it was so pretentiously called, I could barely find a place to sit. Even if there were no people at a table, it was full of rubbish – cups, spoons, half-eaten food, dirty plates. Not exactly a romantic setting. Mind you, I wasn't really looking for romance. I didn't really know why I was there. I eventually found a table and sat down, trying to avoid all the mess on it. I didn't want it to spill over my new suit. It was quite a nice suit in a speckled material – light purple on white. My daughter said it suited me and it did look summery.

I tried to find room on the table for my bag which matched the outfit and then, when I couldn't, tried to catch the eye of one of the waiters. They were all too busy, of course, dashing about, looking important while the tables they were supposed to keep clear piled up with rubbish. Eventually I caught a girl's eye and she came over with a shrug as though she was doing me a favour. Then there was an almighty huff when I asked her to clear the table before I ordered – she said it wasn't her job, another girl did that …"

"Did he turn up, Joyce?"

"Hmm?"

"Robert De Niro – did he turn up?"

"He was nothing like Robert De Niro. Well, he was thickset with a heavy face, and walked with a stoop. I suppose he looked moody like Robert De Niro, but that's all."

"What was he like to speak to?"

"I don't know. I didn't wait. We'd arranged to be carrying a magazine – I was to have *Woman* and he would come with *What Camera?* He thought it would give whoever arrived first something to read while we waited. Anyway, when I saw him coming along the mall I put the magazine down on the table and left – quickly."

"Why?"

"I couldn't face it – all the 'getting to know you' chat. I was used to Robert. I knew what he was going to say."

Tony:

I should never have come on the holiday with Noel – I know that; I allowed myself to be persuaded against my better judgement. It had been arranged that he and Caran – the dark, tarty one – were to meet at the Il Cavaliere at nine o'clock. Noel had picked the restaurant himself from the brochure. "Listen to this," he'd said, *"..... the finest Italian restaurant this side of Italy. Frederico the owner, has been in the business for years and it doesn't go unnoticed. Everything is finely tuned, from the staff to the bottle holders for the wine. With an expert chef cooking a variety of pasta, meat and fish dishes, the menu here has something for everyone .... It's so good because it's made by Frederico. We think he should be in the kitchen all night but the atmosphere in the restaurant wouldn't be the same without him!* Hey – are we going to have a night." He'd got out of bed early (unusual for Noel; he was usually sleeping off the night before) and had been dancing around the apartment singing 'Tonight'. *"Tonight, tonight, won't be just any night. Tonight there will be no morning star ...."* I couldn't share his enthusiasm so I'd said:

"What am I going to do?"

"Do? Take out the other two."

"On my own?"

"These girls have come here for a good time. Give it to them."

"I don't know."

He began to iron his shirt for the evening, but he hadn't got a clue: you always start with the collar, move on to the saddle, do the front, then the back, and finish with the arms, but Noel was all over the place.

"Give it to me."

"What?"

"The shirt, give it to me. Don't you know how to iron a shirt?"

"I don't normally bother, but this Caran looks a bit particular – somewhat classier than the kind of woman I normally ask out. I don't think she'll be turned on by a creased shirt."

"How long do you think you'll be?"

"How long?"

"With Caran?"

"Hopefully all night."

"You don't mean ..."

I couldn't finish the sentence.

"Tony, we're on holiday, they're on holiday. We're all here to enjoy ourselves, to rub against a little female flesh, to feel a soft arm around us. You're making a good job of that shirt."

"I always did the ironing at home. My wife got irritated, so it was easier for me to do it."

"It's a good thing she didn't get irritated with the cooking and the cleaning as well – eh?"

"She did."

"You mean you did the ironing *and* the cooking and the cleaning."

"It kept the peace. It was easier that way."

"And what did your wife do – the gardening, the decorating? Did she clean the car, drive the kids around?"

"No, I did that too – or most of it."

"Tony, you are a gem. You could take your pick. How did your wife fill her time?"

"She worked."

"And you didn't?"

"Oh yes, I worked, too, but I found it easier to combine the two. I work in local government – my hours are more flexible. Bev was a hairdresser. She had to be at the salon by a certain time, but I could drop the kids off on the way to work and leave early enough to collect them and get the tea on ...."

"You collected the kids *and* got the tea on?"

"I liked to have them settled and the meal on the go before Bev got home."

"Right!"

"She loved to smell the meal cooking as she came through the door."

"She certainly had things well organised."

"We always got the children to bed by seven when they were younger, so we had the evening to ourselves.

Bev liked to get her feet up. She'd been on them all day. I'd tidy round, clear away the dishes, get the children's clothes ready for the next day and then we'd sit and talk or watch telly unless I'd had to bring some work home, but even if I did, I got that finished by nine. Bev didn't like me working after nine. She said we needed some time to ourselves."

"Sounds the ideal set-up."

"I liked it. I like order. There's no fun watching telly on your own, though. It's not the same. Neither are the weekends. After you've cleaned through, dusted, Hoovered, polished, changed the bed and got the laundry out of the way where do you go on your own?"

"Where, indeed?"

"I don't have your lightness of touch, Noel."

"Tony, you're a unique person – advertise yourself in the marketplace. You could go to the highest bidder. In fact, you could take your pick!"

"The joy seems to have gone out of my life with Bev's death."

"What did you and she do for fun?"

"We went out with friends, went round to theirs. When the children were younger, we took them out. Pictures, barbecues – you know the usual things. But it's no fun on your own, Noel. It's a couples' world."

"Then couple up! There are women out there with their tongues hanging out for a man like you. If you don't fancy the market place, open your own website – 'At home with Tone'."

"It wouldn't seem right. I'd feel that I was being unfaithful to Bev."

"You think Bev would mind?"

"We were very close."

Noel:

I suppose you've got to admire a man like Tony. His wife had been dead over a year and he was talking about being unfaithful to her – but you could see his loneliness going on for ever and, let's face it, he had a lot to offer! I didn't like to say too much in case he thought I was being critical of his wife but she seemed to have it made. What was it she actually did – apart from a job, like most of us, and putting her feet up? My wife, on the other hand, played merry hell because I didn't do anything around the house, or the garden, or anywhere else! Watching him iron that shirt I could see that he needed someone to look after and when he went on to press the creases out of my white linen suit I was sure of it.

I'd begun to take him for granted, I suppose. Every morning it was Tony who served us breakfast on the balcony. His tidying round the lounge got on my nerves a bit, but you can't have everything. He'd become a creature of habit brought on by his wife's hysteria when she had to get anything done. I just needed to loosen him up a little, to go forth and dally! I've never found that women have much respect for a man who does too much – especially too much around the house: the more you do, the more you can is my experience. Not that I'm speaking personally – I'm a bit of a slob myself; a beer can on the mantelpiece for the twelve days of Christmas doesn't give me too many sleepless nights! But it did give me a divorce: even an empty beer can has its uses. A friend of mine was like Tony; an idealist from the sixties who believed a man should do his share – change nappies, cook meals, clean houses – and he did, only he never quite did it properly. You know what I mean? He'd spend all

Saturday afternoon – he'd been in the garden in the morning or doing the week's shopping – cleaning the lounge and when his wife arrived home from her shopping trip she'd complain that he'd forgotten the light shades!

Don't get me wrong, I like women; it's just that you've got to see them for what they are, and not take them too seriously. When I said that to Tony, his response was predictable:

"You didn't take your wife seriously?"

"You especially don't take your wife seriously."

"That sounds neglectful to me, Noel. I listened to everything Bev had to say."

"How did you stay sane? How can any man who takes his wife seriously stay sane? Did she take you seriously or pooh-pooh what you had to say?"

"Bev and I always talked a lot."

"But did she listen? Have you noticed how women never listen to what you have to say?"

"That's what she used to say about me."

"They all do. Women have a collective intelligence; they all know what each other are thinking. They all treat men in the same way and – more to the point – they treat all men in the same way. It doesn't matter what you do, you're treated the same as if you hadn't done it."

"I don't quite follow, Noel."

"Tony – be yourself! You are not placed upon this earth to please your woman. She'll love you or loathe you anyway – for what you are, not for what you do! Loosen up, take life easy. You and Bev had a way of going about things and you're caught up in it, but you can't want to spend the rest of your life playing 'house-husband'. Ignore their nagging side, clue in on their assets."

I was as near now to insulting his wife – his deceased wife – as I dare go.

"Their assets?"

"The things that make them different from us: they're women! They have hair that smells of the night, they have perfumed shoulders, they have arms that hold you softly, they have breasts you can nuzzle up against, they look wonderful in a low cut dress, they spend inordinate amounts of money on clothes and never have anything to wear: they're from Mars – hence the collective intelligence."

"Do you want anything else ironed?"

I gave up then and said:

"Do you think it would impress her if I took the creases out of my underpants?"

"I always iron mine."

"You iron your underpants?"

"I like the feel of ironed clothes against me – underpants, vests, but shirts in particular, of course."

"You're a nice man, Tony. If you don't mind – and thank you for the shirt and suit – would you iron me a T-shirt?"

"T-shirt? You're not going out with Caran in a T-shirt?"

"No, no but I might wear it under the shirt – so that is just shows under the open collar. The Italian look."

"Which one?"

"Does it matter?"

"It will need to tone in with your trousers."

"Why?"

"It gives a complete top-to-bottom look that way."

"OK, thanks. Then make it the white one."

"Wouldn't the stone-coloured one look better? The suit isn't white and I always think that a white T-shirt under a shirt colour gives an unwashed look."

"OK – the stone one it is."

Was it me going nuts? I hadn't had a conversation like this since Maureen and I were mercifully divorced; maybe I was hoping for too much for Tony, maybe he was too stuck in his ways.

Anyway, I was looking forward to *Tonight*. I would have preferred the blonde with the magnificent breasts but I wasn't going to turn my nose up at Caran – she looked as though she might go a mile or two. I wasn't quite sure how I'd ended up with her, though; I'd put my money on the blonde. It was the thought of a bit of rumpy-pumpy with her that kept me from screaming on the cliff face. Ian Fleming used to put his hero through the mangle, but he did come out with the bird in the end: I deserved tonight.

I'd joined a dancing class once. It had been Maureen's idea (those sorts of things usually were) and the teacher had insisted that no one danced with their own husband or wife. She said that it led to too many arguments and left people who had come on their own out of things, so I ended up with this gorgeous blonde who turned out to be a near neighbour we'd only met in passing. I'd seen her husband a few times down at the boozer and in his garden, but never really got to know the lady. He was a right prat – one of those smug bastards who always knows how to replace leaky washers and cuts his grass every Sunday morning throughout the interminable grass-cutting season. He was into DIY – always building something or extending something so that the rest of us, who were happy just to *sit* in the garden, felt inept. His name was Clive (it would be, wouldn't it?) and his wife's name was Sharon. She and I got on like a house on fire – much to Maureen's annoyance; she was having difficulty actually getting her new "partner" to put his feet in the right place. Anyway, Sharon was rather like Lorraine – nice knockers, a mane of blonde hair that flopped everywhere and a pair of shoulders to die for; there was more sensuality in the hollows around her collarbones than in a year's supply of page three girls tit-to-tit. You can't actually dance with a woman, can you, without getting horny (unless it's your wife of course) and this Sharon had everything going for her. She must have noticed me looking at those hollows – let's face it I was losing myself in them – because when I looked up, she was watching me, and not just watching – know what I mean?

Well that was the start of it – Sharon, sweet Sharon! I could feel the heat coming off her. If any lady was looking for a chance to let off steam it was Sharon, and I wanted to be there when she blew! I got my chance one weekend when the lawnmower decided to pack in and we had friends coming round for a barbecue. I was content to leave the grass as it was (after all, we were only going to sit around on the patio, drinking – we weren't planning a croquet tournament), but no, the grass had to be cut. Perhaps I could borrow Clive's lawnmower now that we had got to know them? Well, I didn't exactly fancy going round to ask that little shit for his lawnmower but I was – shall we say, persuaded? It turned out that he wasn't in – off somewhere to negotiate the price of upgrading his fencing – but Sharon was, and we started to samba around the kitchen. Then we tango-ed into the lounge and before I really knew what was happening Sharon was giving me the rumba on the sofa. It just about blew my head off that first time with her, although it couldn't have lasted more than minutes; she was the first and, in some senses, still is the only woman I have known who had a real taste for sex – she actually, physically, enjoyed it! It was the beginning of a fond relationship. Sharon and I got together whenever we could for ten years or more. It bothered no one, took the pressure off at home, and gave us both something nice to look forward to every now and then – you couldn't really ask more of a woman, could you? Of course, my break-up with Maureen put paid to the relationship because I had to move away – not that Sharon had anything to do with that; Maureen divorced me because I was a slob. But Sharon did give me a taste for buxom blondes, and that was why I had been hoping for Lorraine tonight, but faint heart never won fair lady, and I had won Caran and was going to make the best of it.

Caran:

I wasn't looking forward to an evening with Noel – not looking forward to it ecstatically, that is. When you talk about these things with your girlfriends, it's always George Clooney or (if you think you might like a bit of rough) Sean Bean who is going to ask you out. On the other hand, as Lorraine said, it might be fun; Noel sounded like good company.

When I arrived at Il Cavaliere, he was waiting – big smile lighting up his big nose. He really did remind me of that French actor whose name I can never pronounce – the one who was in (what was it called?) where he played the man who also had a big nose. He bent and kissed me on the cheek, but I noticed his arms went round me in that actorly way and he had a good press with his chest.

The meal went well; he'd soon prised out of me that I was a nurse – well, that's always good for a bit of 'nudge-nudge-wink-wink' isn't it? 'Bath-time should be fun', 'let's share a shower' – that sort of thing; all the time with a twinkle in his eye. His ex-wife provided a good deal of amusement; she, evidently, had been a real hygiene "nut" but not, as Noel put it, actually hygienic – "If only I'd caught her occasionally with a sponge and Mr Muscle in her hand I wouldn't have minded but all she did was talk about it".

I've never been able to resist not looking at what is going on around me and our waiter kept catching my attention so that I had to remind myself of one of the big 'Dating Don'ts' – don't fall in love with the waiter! Noel was so busy talking he didn't seem to notice, but this particular waiter was the kind who hovers around you and is very attentive. Noel made great fun of the menu names; you know the kind of thing – *Risotto con pancetta, mozzarella e cavolo* ('Risotto with cheese and cabbage') or *Spezzatino di pollo con torta al testo* ('Chicken stew with bread'). It was nice being dated and feted, however. Simon always orders a steak with chips and trimmings, without looking; but Noel took his time, 'taking the mick' out of the menu, and was enjoying making me laugh.

He admired my body and kept saying so, in not so many words. Although he didn't put it as bluntly as that, he was clearly fascinated by how I kept so "trim and lovely". "I tried jogging to work once but all I did was damage my knee, sweat all morning and sit around all day in crumpled clothes – but you don't, do you? You're fresh and neat and smell like heaven." He wondered if I had a personal trainer and how often I went to the gym and, of course, we had a laugh over Jim Fixx.

He got me talking, too – I think he realised that I could be quite a bitch and that "other women" might well be a favourite subject of mine. I've always been annoyed, for example, by what used to be called 'horizontal promotions' and they do happen, even in the National Health Service: women who get promoted faster because they're prepared to drop their knickers for their manager. The coming of feminism only seemed to make that sort of woman more ruthless – they'll do anything to get their careers on the move. Their attitude seems to be that they can shag their way to the top and when they arrive they still have their self-respect intact! And, of course, while you're struggling to get the kids to school, they're driving around in the latest Mini Cooper with a soft top! And with their hair always in place – and in the latest fashions!! He got me going and I loved it! And then he capped it and made me feel rather good with a story about meerkats: you know – the ones who hopped around for David Attenborough. Evidently each group has a dominant female, so dominant that she reduces the testosterone levels of all the others in the group, both male and female. "So that kind of woman ends up getting nowhere: she simply crunches the balls off everyone around her. You chose the right path, Caran – stay soft, stay warm, stay feminine."

He spoke like that all evening – in the grand manner. He was a very interesting man in that he was both a slob and a gentleman; by the time we got to the *Biscotti a forna di cuore* ('Heart-shaped Biscuits') I was ready for the night club.

Lorraine:

An evening with Joyce and Tony was a bit hearts and flowers; his main topic of conversation was how much he missed his wife, and hers was how much she missed her husband. I think I'm a sympathetic person – Barry has always said so, anyway – but I was finding it a bit tedious, I must admit.

We'd chosen The Meze House because it was quite close to Il Cavaliere and Caran hadn't wanted to be "too out on a limb, just in case" as she put it. The Meze House was run by Paul and June who had *'years of experience providing local cuisine in perfect and peaceful surroundings. Using a blend of local and regional produce and exciting spices'*, they were going to provide *'a unique and delicious menu'* – and they did! We couldn't have asked for more, but Joyce didn't like the waiters hovering, "listening to your conversation". "We're not ready to eat, we're not ready to order, we just want to enjoy a quiet drink and look at the menu in our own time". When we did order, of course, it came too quickly – "was it microwaved?" No, I didn't think so. "Still," she said, realising she was casting a shadow over the evening, "I do like small gatherings, I'm not a party goer, I'd much rather read a book". Tony agreed.

It seemed, listening between the lines, that she and her husband – the adored Robert – had never quite seen eye to eye over parties. He relished them; they were an opportunity to get together with your mates and their wives. The women would sit at one table talking about Young Wives or the WI and the men would gather round the bar drinking and discussing that afternoon's football results. There would be plenty of drink – usually cans of Boddingtons or Carlsberg – and the food would have been bought quickly and without fuss that afternoon at Sainsbury's. Later on, when everyone was drunk enough, there might be a bit of dancing to Status Quo or, on the other hand, you might fall asleep until it was time to go home around 1 o'clock in the morning.

I'd never met Robert, but I thought I might rather have liked him. Joyce presented all of this as a virtue, showing us what good company he had been, but trying to make the point that she tended to prefer quieter evenings like the one we were having. Tony agreed, saying that the parties he really liked were when everyone had taken the trouble to dress properly. He couldn't see the point of going out for the evening in T-shirts and trainers – after all you weren't cutting the grass. He just liked a few friends whom you could chat to over a few glasses of wine and who weren't going to wake up your neighbours when they left.

I commented on how much they must both miss their partners (it seemed the only way into the conversation!) and said how nice it was that they only had good memories of them: strange, I know, in Joyce's case but she does only ever speak well of Robert, despite the fact that he divorced her and they seemed so unsuited.

This launched Tony into how much he loved coming home to his house at night: how he would always, in the winter, close the curtains and turn on the wall lights before settling the children down and starting to cook the dinner: how he loved the fact that the house always smelt of flowers – his wife always had big bunches in every room – that, however hard he tried, his house now lacked "a woman's hand". I think our home has always been comfortable but not, somehow, quite up to Tony's mark.

And there was Joyce – dying to create a home around someone.

Dot:

Lorna and I were a bit pissed off that the stuck-up one should have got a night out with Noel, but we decided to make the best of it. We tarted ourselves up and toddled down to the Belly Full to have a blow-out. As I said to Lorna we could end up lucky, with a blow-out and a blow-job – who knows? Not that Lorna found that very funny – she's more interested in food than men, but she's a good mate and would go along with it for my sake. We've been here together a few times now and you never fail to pull; it's always so much easier on holiday. Well, no one knows you, do they? You haven't got to explain anything the next morning. Of course, a lot of them are a bit on the rough side but you do have some nice experiences.

A few years ago, I fell in with one of the local men almost as soon as I got here. He was a cleaner at the hotel, so he worked mornings, which was handy, because he had most of the afternoons and evenings and – more to the point – all night free. He was a lovely man – gentle, considerate, kind. He treated me as though I was the Queen – no disrespect, you know what I mean. I used to love the way he would take all his clothes off and stand there, absolutely starkers. He didn't seem embarrassed at all, but then he hadn't got anything to be embarrassed about – not with a six pack and a dong like his; and when he undressed me, he looked me all over and always folded my clothes and laid them carefully over the back of the chair. He was never in a hurry and it wasn't just sex. He took me all over Craphos – to the market where he made the stall-holders charge me right: to the local cafes where everyone seemed to know him. We'd go dancing and then make love all night and when I woke up there was a rose on the pillow beside me, every morning. I knew it had to end of course, that it was only for the holiday, but it was lovely at the time.

And the thing is I'm no sight for sore eyes – any more than Lorna. I know what they call us at the hotel – Siesta and Fiesta – but we don't give a toss. I'd live here if I could afford it. I was hoping to get off with that Noel until the tart turned up. Mind you, there's still time. I dress young even if it does hang out a bit – you know, skinny tops, hipster pants and I'm not afraid to wear leather and leopardskin. Lorna's a bit more conservative but she keeps the boobs on display. It's what attracts the men, isn't it? There's no good being modest if you're on the pull. These young girls get a bit pissy when the lads grope them, but what can they expect, walking around with everything hanging out – after all, who have they got it hanging out for? They should think themselves lucky. When you're fifty-something, you have to work at it. I've got a dressing table full of creams and stuff and I have my hair done every week – after the weekly swim, which can be a good place to meet blokes except they're all just that bit too old. And I always book in at the tanning parlour before the summer starts so that I look good even in the garden.

Lorna tried dating – properly, I mean, through an agency, but that's no bloody good. You've got to get out there and hustle if you want to pull it in. She reckoned she felt like a cow at a cattle market when she went to the pub and the blokes were looking them over. But if you want to score, there's no good being too picky. If a bloke looks interested, get in there is what I say! Mind you the pub can be a funny place – especially if you get pissed too early. We were out in Craphos one night – it was the Queen Vic, I think – and they were doing a two-for-one offer on Miller Lights or one of them drinks – it might have been Guinness. We'd been there quite a while when this group of blokes turned up – there must have been about twenty of them; they were like a bleeding rugby team – filthy songs and hairy arses all over the place. I said to Lorna – if we don't pull here we don't deserve to pull anywhere, might as well order your coffin. Anyway, one thing led to another. There was dancing and a lot of singing with all of us getting drunker and drunker, and the last thing I remember was sitting on the floor looking up at this circle of blokes. I think I must have passed out then because the next morning I found myself in this bedroom – alone. I got dressed and went to leave and when I picked my handbag up there was a wad of cash in the top of it. Talk about creating the wrong impression! Still whoever he was he was a gentleman, I suppose. At least he paid – even if he didn't have to.

Still - you only come this way once. I mean, sex is what makes the world go round isn't it?

Lorraine:

I thought I might just leave Tony and Joyce to finish off the evening in their own way when Caran's "diabolic duo" arrived at our table. They had come from Belly Full down the road, spotted us, wondered how Caran and

Noel were getting on and whether they "could join the party". I didn't want to appear rude, but I really didn't have the heart to stay; what was there to do but drink more? I had Dakos on my mind, of course – I was going to have to see him tomorrow and wanted a clear head; but I sensed that I couldn't leave Tony and Joyce alone with Dot and Lorna, so the conversation turned once again to 'parties'. I somehow got the impression that the word meant something very different to each of us.

I shared Robert's view: they were a chance to get together with your friends, to relax and enjoy each others company but not, unlike him, a chance for the men and women to sit at different tables. Barry and I never took much trouble with preparation. We just got some drinks and food in and sat around eating, drinking and talking. The only thing I didn't like was tomorrow's hangover.

Tony clearly enjoyed a more formal and organised occasion – little groups of people standing around with glasses of wine and everyone circulating politely until, by the end of the evening, you knew everything about everybody but actually couldn't have cared less. He liked people to be "polite".

Joyce didn't like parties at all – she had made that quite clear. The preparation, which had to be painstaking, was too much trouble and so was clearing up the mess afterwards – or, probably, during the party. The only party she really enjoyed was "a dinner party where you can organise what is going on and where you can get people to go home when it's finished".

Lorna saw them as a chance to get stuck in to some real eating; she didn't mind what as long as there was plenty of it. She could sit as happily over a traditional

English barbecue – the inevitable parade of chicken, burger and sausage – as she could over vol-au-vents, cream cheese whirls and flaky pastry parcels. She also liked to sit down and couldn't see the point of "standing around all evening balancing a few bits and pieces on the edge of your plate".

Dot saw them as a great get-together and a chance for some dancing but preferred "*big* dos" where you stood a chance of pulling someone; she wasn't particularly taken with back-garden parties just with your friends and their husbands. Mind you, she had to admit that "these days I need less and less drink to get fucking legless". She liked them "wild" and the more you upset the neighbours when you left the better.

We were swapping party stories, when who should turn up but Noel and Caran. I looked at her, she looked at me and raised that eyebrow, Joyce looked relieved and Dot looked delighted. Lorna did look up from the table but not for long.

"Hi – we've just been thrown out of Gasoline," said Noel.

"Noel insisted on showing off his Latin American dance techniques."

"They threw you out because you were dancing?" asked Tony

"Out-dancing the clientele. Some of the girls were fascinated by our tropical rhythms and their studs didn't like it."

"You and Tony do seem to have the knack of putting these kid's backs up."

"They should learn to dance," said Noel, "'if you don't dance, you're crazy and you're totally crazy if you do. It's a real chill out, groove with the chicks, chat with the lads.' That's what the DJ said."

"And then the bouncers asked us to leave before there was trouble."

"Come and have a drink with us then, sweetheart," said Dot.

They might have done if Dot hadn't said that; later, I felt sure that Caran had intended to end the evening there, at our table, at The Meze House. It would have been enough for her, but she sensed a certain gloating in Dot's tone, was aware of an 'I told you so' note in her voice. She said:

"We're not ready for a cup of Ovaltine yet! The night is still young. Let's make it one to remember, Noel."

"Lead on, sweet lady. I am yours to command."

Day 8: Tomorrow is the first day of the rest of your life

Do we live by clichés? Are they the forces that drive us? Is it easier to go along with the accepted wisdom than to think things out for ourselves?

Caran was not in her bed when I got up the next morning, but as I came back with my daily paper, she was getting out of a taxi. She didn't speak until I put a cup of coffee in front of her on our little balcony table.

"Not a good night?" I asked.

"An awful night," she answered. "What's it all about, Lorraine?"

"How many women have asked themselves that the morning after the night before?"

"I feel grubby."

I sat down beside her and buttered my toast. For a long time, she didn't speak, but simply sat staring out across the bay; when she did, eventually, say something, Caran continued to look straight ahead.

"I don't think it would have happened if Siesta hadn't been sitting up waiting for him. Oh, yes! I thought we'd left her at the Meze House, but there she was when we got to Noel's hotel, by the pool, chatting up those young lads who look after the bar, and pouring rum and Cokes down her throat. And I just knew that she would be on his arm – or, more exactly, leading him by the dick – to his room. I couldn't face that, somehow, and so I went up with him. He was nice. I can't blame him. I could have left at any time, but I couldn't bear the thought of walking out of the hotel past her. We'd trumped her cards on the pirate ship, but she still had that look on her face. It was different to what happened with Frank. I was drunk the first time – no excuse, I know, but I was – and then, when we went skinny-dipping, it was somehow romantic out there on the beach. But this was, well, more cold-blooded, if you like ..... an obligatory shag!"

She sipped her coffee absent-mindedly, and then went on:

"We can't just blame our hormones, can we? I know, some days when you think (when I think!) Simon should have shown a bit more interest the night before, I wake up a "quivering mass of hormones" – as they say in the women's magazine stories. You – I – still feel young and neglected and wonder where the romance has all gone. Do you still get crushes, Lorraine."

It wasn't a question, so I didn't answer.

"I fancied the instructor down at the gym. He was the one who gave me my 'induction'. God – how can a word like that sound sexy? But it does. He must have been in his thirties, so it was ridiculous, wasn't it?"

This time it was a question so I said:

"You're an attractive woman, Caran. Your age wouldn't be a barrier."

"Thanks, Lorraine. Anyway, nothing happened, of course. I just burned with lust for about six weeks. I couldn't organise an affair if I tried. Where would you do it? Obviously not at home, and I can't really imagine doing it in the back of a car and the idea of actually booking a hotel room! Do you remember Dustin Hoffman in *The Graduate*? That Anne Bancroft got it together quickly, didn't she? How many years ago is that? It was a sixties film, wasn't it? How far have we travelled since? I wasn't born until '54. Fifty years later, I can't do what she was doing then!"

Another long pause, so I went and made some more coffee and Caran smiled as I poured it for her.

"I've only ever really been with Simon. We met when I was training as a nurse in '72. The halls of residence had just about gone co-ed when we started, but all that swinging sixties stuff you hear about didn't really swing into the seventies. OK – some girls did, but there are always those who will drop their knickers at the drop of a hat. Most of us were still worried about getting pregnant and what our parents would say if we did.

I met Simon at a dance – a place called Trentham Gardens. They used to organise coaches to get us there. Lads would be bussed in from the surrounding colleges, too. There were quite a few lusty ones from the local agricultural college, but the coaches went back at midnight and that was that, really – a long snog in the gardens, but nothing else. I can remember getting really excited about a snog. We used to talk about how good you were at snogging! It was quite something, the snog. It was almost an art form – first the feeling of his breath, the lips brushing softly and then with more pressure, the tip of the tongue moving gently over your lips, opening your mouth to him – gradually... it was poetry in motion, wasn't it? It didn't always happen first time around, either. There was a slow build-up and actual petting came much later. Only a real slut would let a boy touch her breasts before she really got to know him! I remember lying awake at night and aching for Simon. It was all anticipation, wasn't it? Not that I liked him at first. We'd meet at dances, but we never went out together. He was a bit on the short side and I thought the other girls would laugh at me.

Anyway, I fancied this doctor. I could see myself married to him. I didn't want to waste myself on a male nurse when Dr Kildare was just round the corner. The one I fancied was an Irishman. God, he had a lovely voice! I could really imagine being married to him – looking at him over the breakfast table, sharing his bed, talking and laughing together, a touch here, a hug there. I could feel my juices flowing just thinking about it. I used to go on diets. We would spend weeks eating nothing but Pontefract cakes – do you remember them? I fancied being married to a doctor, of course – giving dinner parties to the consultants and their wives. I can cook, Lorraine, really cook and I would have been a "wow" rubbing shoulders with the county set – the councillors and the merchant bankers these people attract. But it wasn't to be and I ended up with Simon."

"You did love him?" I had to ask.

"Oh yes. It was just that he was short. As I said, I used to lie awake at night aching for him. We were well matched in many ways – still are. He's got a sharp sense of humour and we enjoy laughing about our friends after a party. He's a bit short-tempered but only with the situation – not me as such – and you know when not to rile him, although I always do. I can always choose the right moment to flare him up. Usually when he's doing something and I think it'll be a good idea to mention that something else needs doing."

She laughed (what Barry calls the "heartless laughter of women"), and I could imagine her stoking Simon's fires at, deliberately, the wrong moment.

"Did I ever tell you about the barbecue? He was in the middle of cooking the meat and the guests were arriving, so I said, "Aren't you going to get our guests a drink, Simon?" I suppose I did choose my words carefully. And he said "Right. OK. I'll do the drinks. Perhaps you'd like to keep an eye on the chicken pieces, Caran?" He stormed off to get the drinks and the whole bloody barbecue went up in flames. It was funny really; but – of course – he was responsible for cooking the meat, wasn't he, so Simon wasn't amused."

"You love him still, then?"

We both laughed at the collective animosity only understood by women and which perplexes men so much.

"Yes – I suppose so."

We laughed again.

"But I know what he'll do in a few years time when he retires – he'll be off playing golf and he won't have any thought for me. He'll just remember the barbecue and suggest I invite some of my girlfriends round for one – when he's away! And he's passionless, Lorraine. Oh, he'll do it. He's very efficient. He has a saying which he always quotes at weddings, much to everyone's embarrassment – "Long and thin slips right in, short and thick does the trick". He's short and thick and if I'm in the mood he'll do the job – rash, nipples, juices, widening, spasm – but no foreplay, unless you count turning over; and when we've finished he's likely to put on the light and carry on reading his book – he enjoys Wilbur Smith. He's got it down to a fine art, so I can climax within no more than five minutes."

"Some women would be grateful for that."

"I know – ungrateful bitch – but there is more, isn't there?"

I didn't answer; I didn't really want to be drawn into Caran's longings. Barry and I had never had any real problems. Maybe it was because I didn't read the magazines. We made love anywhere – as long as Steph wasn't around, of course; but even then we'd always made it clear that "Mummy and Daddy need their time together". Barry always put off any lights; he hated making love in artificial light and would draw back the curtains – if we were upstairs or even downstairs at night; feeling and touching, looking and seeing were all part of it; he'd always undress me and me him – body confidence had never been an issue and he always took his time.

"Frank was very good – in a casual, almost off-hand sort of way. I felt real excitement with him, and when I came it was different. He took pleasure in it. It was more than just a job well done."

"It was illicit."

"You think that was what made it exciting?"

"Partly. I'm sure what they call affairs are exciting – all that chasing round with just one thing in mind."

"I watch the girls sometimes with their boyfriends – not just them, all these teenagers. How can they be so sure of themselves? And they treat the boys like personal servants, rolling over on the sun-bed with a "Do my back." No please or thank you. No negotiation. And the boys just do it – and not out of courtesy; it's more of a faithful dog syndrome. They'll sit for hours talking about nothing or making wishes together, chatting, giggling until the early hours, losing track of time, carefree. No thought of the chores that lay ahead. They're scatter-brained, of course, and everyone scurries round looking for the things they've lost. They'll decide to cook a meal when they get in at night, and in the morning – yes, all the mess is there for you to clear up, everything they've used to prepare a meal for "the boyfriend". And the tone is, "Well, you don't really expect us to clear it up, do you?" And you can't say anything, can you? You have to go along with it for fear of losing them. Simon just says that it's part of growing up, but doesn't offer to clean up after them; there's no good talking to him about it.

I spend quite a lot of time on my own now. I'll go for short walks along the beach – on the surface to take the dog for a walk but actually to be alone with my thoughts. But thinking gets me nowhere: my walks are mindless. They simply take me away from the house. I listen to the seagulls and watch the young families walking, but it's no good, my mind always comes back to them – the girls. My mind goes back to their child-hood – the little girls they once were and the dreams we had for them – and I find myself talking to strangers, especially men, and trying to share these thoughts with them. Young men are useless, of course – they stare at you as though you're nuts – and older men are either dismissive, or so solicitous that you want to cry.

We have a little café near the beach and I often drop in there for a cup of tea – on my off-duty afternoons when I'm walking the dog. The owner doesn't mind dogs as long as you keep them under the table. It's a lovely little place, so cared for. They have gingham tablecloths and napkins – yes, napkins. The owner folds them himself for each place setting. And on the table, real flowers ...We just talk about anything and he always listens so thoughtfully and is so attentive. He knows how I like my tea and teases me about having a cake – which I always do – and he gives the dog a piece of cheese scone! Time stands still in that café and the outside world is closed off, but the moment I leave it surrounds me again and in rush the jobs, the children, the church flower rota, the family planner!

We have a clock in the hallway – a grandmother clock. You know how they tick. But it isn't a relaxing tick like in the films; it's ticking away time. When I hear it I'll rush around doing unnecessary washing up, straightening pictures, even writing abusive letters to the electricity people about last week's power cut. Then I realise that there are real things to be done and I rush to get the dinner on. The girls like it as soon as they get in because – yes, they're going out with the boyfriend aren't they? And they aren't really interested in the kind of day I might have had – whether at work or at home. They've got their own lives to lead, as Simon says, and soon they'll be gone to university. And nowadays they won't even write that weekly letter when they get there, will they? It'll just be a text message – curt, unintelligible and dashed off in the odd spare moment, while for me tomorrow is another day … the first day of the rest of your life, as they say."

"And you think another man is the way out of all this, the way forward?"

"I don't know."

I sensed, somehow, that Caran had spent much of her life "not knowing", feeling that there was something out there, not knowing quite what but that – if she weren't quick – it would pass her by; I knew from things she'd said previously that she and Simon had moved house at least six times in their married life. I felt that said some-thing. Deep down, however, she must have realised that finding another man wasn't the answer and that all that work on her body wasn't going to take her to where she thought she might want to go. I said, by way of being complicit with her:

"I know that instinctively, I'll know when it's right – that fate will bring it together. I don't mind being a bit reckless. The time will come when I no longer can. I told you, didn't I, that we've joined …?"

"… life-building courses? Yes, we talked about that – aromatherapy massage, working out together, learn-ing a foreign language, watercolour weekends, a the-atre skills course to improve your communication tech-niques and build your self-esteem …the list goes on?" Caran queried, but not with any real interest.

"A friend of mine decided to have an affair once," I said, "She was like you – younger, because this was some years ago but, like you, attractive and passionate. Also, like you she had the feeling that somehow she was "missing out". The man she fell for was charming and intelligent, one of those artistic types who act a bit at the local theatre or paint. You know. Oh – and he could write. Could he write! Poems about her poured from his soul – soon they had a book of them and he'd begun work on a novel based on their affair. This was all quite genuine – I'm not skitting the relationship. It was intense, lustful, all-consuming: it went on for two years and then her husband found out. He wanted to know everything about it and the more she told him the more it destroyed him. Nevertheless, he asked her to give the marriage another chance and because she felt guilty and wanted her family back – there were three children involved – she agreed.

They tried marriage guidance, they moved away – but it was no good. There had been too much destruction. For two years they struggled on and then she moved out. Whatever love there had been between her and her husband, she reckoned she had killed. To this day, she has never come to terms with the fact that she betrayed her husband who was not only a good man but her closest friend – before the affair they could talk about anything. At the end of the day the thrill wasn't worth the emotional fall-out – the hurt it caused her family and friends. She lost her husband, her children for a while and their whole social circle which had come together over twenty years. She said that, if she could have turned back the clock she would have valued her husband more and made more of an effort to keep their passion alive, and that if there was still that vital spark missing she would have walked out of the marriage. That way, at least, she would still have had her husband's friendship."

"Did she ...?"

"No – the artist type wasn't the "love of her life". Oh Caran, the point I'm making is that you need to be very sure about what you want and what you're doing. A holiday fling is one thing. You can forget that when we arrive home in a week's time – bury it if you need to or talk about it ..."

"To Simon?"

"That's between you and him. All I am saying is, be sure about what you want to do. Ninety-nine percent of "affairs" end – there's no mileage in them – and ninety percent of women say they feel "used" after they've been involved in one. I can't think why – presumably no one forced them into it …You just need to know what you want and what you're doing."

Joyce:

I'd felt depressed after yesterday; the whole holiday had suddenly turned dirty. There was Caran off with Noel. He'd have been better to have spent his time with that Dot: more his type – common. And there was Lorraine talking about leaving Barry. I mean I don't approve of couples "living in sin", as they used to say (to me it doesn't show the right commitment) but they had been together for thirty years. I can't imagine what she could see in that Dakos – a foreigner in a strange country.

Anyway, they hadn't given me the usual ring – I imagined Caran would have a lot to talk about over breakfast – so I left a note with reception and went for a walk. It was nice along the front; the resort is so different in the morning, when the drunks and louts are out of the way – they start drinking early enough as it is. The shopkeepers are always friendly although I don't trust their prices. I think they would twist you without thinking twice about it, but they are pleasant. One man gave me an orange as I passed. I bought a newspaper and made my way towards a quiet little café that we had found. It didn't attract the rougher element so it was pleasant to sit there. The owner recognised me. You could tell it was the owner by the way he cared for the place; that's what sets foreign cafes above those awful places on the high street at home – Starbucks and places like that. In those places, a few loud girls, who are more interested in chatting about what they've done the night before than in serving you, just clutter the place up. They don't take a pride in serving you. But here, along came the coffee on a coaster on a saucer, with the milk – hot – in a separate jug; and it was placed in front of me with a smile. I didn't have to queue for a paper bucket of the stuff and pay some girl who was looking at her friend while she took my money: no, the owner was attentive.

It's one of the awful things about being divorced, not having anyone to chat to; but the owner paused and passed the time of day and suggested I should sit outside in the sun. He adjusted the umbrella so that I didn't burn; he was very attentive. Robert used to fuss round me. He'd always make me a cup of tea or coffee when I arrived home and he saw to it that the house was tidy. That's why I never understood why he divorced me; we were so happy and comfortable.

I always blamed her – the other woman; she latched on to him when he was vulnerable. We were going through a bad patch – all couples do; the dog had just died and Robert was very attached to her. Our eldest, Mark, was away at university and Mark and he were as close as brothers. Jessica was just about to take her 'A' levels and at that awkward stage. I think Robert got caught between us. Trying to defend both sides was just like him. And she was waiting there, wasn't she – a sympathetic ear? Although I don't think Robert would have actually discussed his problems with anyone. He was very close and didn't always talk to me until he'd sorted things out in his head. It was just someone sympathetic to be with, I suppose. All I know is – we would have got through it if she hadn't been there!

Mark suggested that Robert may have wanted something else out of life; he said his dad was a bit "wild" at parties when he drank. He said Robert never discussed personal things with anybody. I didn't understand, so he went on to say that his dad was one of those people who "bottled things up" and the cork had blown! We weren't, he said, one of those families who discussed intimate things. I didn't really understand him. Robert and I talked about everything. "Maybe, there were things he couldn't broach with you, Mum. Maybe there were things he couldn't talk about that he should have." "But why?" "Perhaps he thought you'd hit the roof. I'm not saying he was right – just that he may have seen it that way."

I could be a bit hysterical, I know – if I thought that our happiness was threatened. I used to shout, then, if Robert brought up awkward things. And he could go a bit over the top. I remember once we were at this get-together with some friends of ours – we'd known them for years. *Lady Chatterley* had been on TV – the one with Sean Bean and one of the Richardson girls – and we were talking about it – the women, that is. The men were over by the food and drink. Anyway, the talk drifted from that to the church flower rota and Robert must have overheard us because he suddenly cut in with a crack about draping forget-me-nots around a "penis". He actually used the word! I was so embarrassed and we had a row about it when we got home. I told him that our friends didn't expect that kind of language and that they were disgusted with him and did he think we'd get invited out again to any "dos". He couldn't see what the fuss was about: would I have preferred him to use a euphemism like rod, dong, member, organ ...? He rolled off a whole list! Oh it was awful … but most of the time we were happy.

We had a lovely home – not materialistic but homely. We'd fallen in love with it from the start. We'd seen it on Sunday walks and couldn't ever imagine living in it and then one day it came up for sale. The vicar told me, and Robert went down and made an offer – in fact he simply offered the asking price. The children were brought up there; it's the only home they remember. We took such care with it, choosing everything together – curtains, furniture, carpets. Everything toned in, nothing jarred – it was a lovely, quiet, peaceful home and I know Robert loved it. Some of the times we loved best were when company had gone and we were alone; we'd flop into a chair and just be with each other.

All this was going through my head, when I looked up and saw a man watching me; he was on the other side of the street and had just come out of a grocery store. Well, they sold everything from pears to pornographic magazines; it wasn't a shop I liked. I waved; he hesitated and then waved back. It was Tony.

"Hello," he said. "All alone?"

"I'm waiting for Caran and Lorraine. I'm an early riser. I had breakfast at half-past six."

"You always have breakfast that early?"

"I'm a creature of habit. My husband and I were always up by then. 'Best part of the day' he used to say."

"I couldn't get my wife up. It took at least three cups of tea before she would stir."

Robert had never brought me tea in bed. Well, he did at first, and then it stopped – suddenly. I forget when and never liked to ask why, but it had been in the first few years of our marriage. I knew Tony was a widower, but wasn't sure if he knew my situation, so I thought the safest thing was to talk about his, and said:

"You miss your wife very much?"

"It's been over a year now, but I can't get used to it. I don't want to get used to it. We were so close – Bev and me. I see other couples sitting in cafes enjoying a drink together and it all comes back. I don't want to be a widower. I loved my wife."

"Have you tried bereavement counselling? People say these things help."

"I've been bombarded with help. Pamphlets and free advice are everywhere. Everyone has been very kind – my relatives, the doctor, the vicar, the bereavement coun-selling nurse. I have advice coming out of my ears – 'Throw yourself into something else', 'Others have been this way before you' – but, at the end of the day, there's no one to go anywhere with, no one to be with."

"No."

It was a simple enough word, and I would have been hard pushed to find a shorter one, but it made him look up. I suppose it was the tone of my voice.

"Oh, I'm sorry, talking about myself. You're alone, too, aren't you?"

"Yes."

There was no good beating about the bush, so I said:

"I'm divorced."

"I'm sorry to hear that, Joyce. You seem a very nice lady. These things never work out fairly, do they?"

"I didn't feel I deserved it – no."

The bitterness came out in that (didn't it?) but it was how I felt. I had worked hard. I had been a good wife and mother. I didn't think I deserved to be on my own at this stage in my life. It wasn't just the financial situation. It was the loneliness and the humiliation.

Tony looked at me quietly for a moment as the owner came up and – after a little hesitation – he ordered a coffee. "Noel can get his own breakfast this morning", he said and then turned back to what we had been discussing:

"Have you ever tried a 'singles holiday'? People do say …"

"Don't talk to me about 'singles holidays'."

"You have tried one, then?"

"It was awful – the most humiliating experience of my life."

"Really?"

"You've not been on one I take it?"

"No."

"Then don't. My family suggested I should. I think they were tired with my complaining and felt that doing anything was better than doing nothing."

"It was a really bad experience?"

"On the first night, they sorted out the divorced and the widowed and – believe me, Tony – the divorced are the pits. At least the widowed had some dignity but there was none for the divorced."

"I'm really sorry to hear that, Joyce. No one deserves to be humiliated."

"There were just certain assumptions made about you if you were divorced."

I didn't want to say what, and Tony seemed too well mannered to ask so we sat quietly as his coffee and croissant arrived.

"Do you mind if I dunk the croissant?"

I laughed; I couldn't help it. He seemed so concerned about not upsetting a stranger and I said so.

"Bev said I used to worry too much, but these things are important. I think I irritated her a bit"

"I'm sure you didn't," I said, softly.

"I'm sure I did."

He smiled – a long-lost, lonely smile – and then said:

"But we were happy. We suited each other. My being a little obsessive may have irritated her at times but it suited her, too."

"You find your house unbearable without her?"

"You understand – that's nice. I love my home. It's like a person to me. All my memories are there – all those meals together, birthdays ..."

"Christmases?"

"Don't mention that. I went away this year – on my own. The children invited me round, of course, but I said no. I knew I'd spoil it for them. I told them I wanted to be alone. I just hired a cottage in the Peak District to get away from everything. I took a few things that reminded me of Bev – a picture, some anniversary cards, a cushion she'd made – that kind of thing. Then I stoked up the fire, closed the curtains and shut out the world."

"What did you have for Christmas dinner?"

"Pork tenderloin baked in pastry. It's something I used to cook for us when the family was together. It's a poor man's version of Beef Wellington, but it was different from the traditional Christmas dinner. It's a wonderful meal – stylish, great for weddings and special occasions. You wrap the pork in slices of Parma ham before draping it with the pastry."

"What vegetables did you serve with it?"

"Seasonal – whatever I could get at the local store in Castleton."

"You shut yourself away with your memories?"

"Yes."

"Mine aren't that kind of memory."

"You must have good memories of your family life together."

"Oh yes, but the divorce pushes them out. It spoils everything."

"Especially at Christmas?"

I nodded.

"Christmas Day was awful this year. I argued with Mark, fell out with his partner. I apologised, of course, but in a way the harm's done. You say things you wish you hadn't. He sided with her, of course. But she's so untidy; I just had to clean up."

"You are house-proud, Joyce?"

"I suppose I am ... I just want to get back to normal, to have the family together again."

He sat quietly dunking his croissant as though we both had all the time in the world, which, at that moment, I suppose we had; I knew he was thinking about what to say next. Tony was a considerate man; he chose his words with care. When he spoke, he changed the subject completely, and said:

"Some friends of mine sent me 'speed dating'."

"Speed dating?"

"You have to book in advance and they did it for a birthday treat. I found myself in this room with a lot of people around my age. It was very civilised. There was a glass of Champagne and nibbles. A lady presented me with a card on which I had some questions to use as conversation starters, and there was a list of names of people – women – who I was to talk to. If I got on well with any of them I had to mark the card and the dating agency would arrange a meeting – if the lady liked me."

"It sounds like a cattle market."

"It wasn't for me, but I could see it might suit some people. Bev had not been gone long. Friends are so keen to push you into things, aren't they?"

"I couldn't bear it. It makes my flesh crawl. If I am going to meet anybody else, it will have to be ... naturally. The singles holiday I told you about was a disaster. I couldn't wait to get home. I did meet one nice man but all he wanted was his wife back. The others were just ...well ...."

"Out for what they could get?"

"Yes."

I was rather keen to get away from talking about my singles holiday; being pawed by strange men isn't my idea of fun. One or two of them had almost felt obliged to "touch you up" – I think that's the expression. I'd never liked that, anyway. One of our friends – Ken – had been a bit "handy". He used to grope the women in the group and I hadn't wanted to make a fuss. I remember asking Robert what I should do and he said, "Just go with it. He means no harm". But I never liked it. My sister's husband, on the other hand, actually had a word with Ken when he tried it on her. He'd grabbed her from behind and had been "hard", as she put it, but her husband put a stop to that and no mistake.

"My friends actually gave me a 'dating card' with a list of 'dating don'ts' on," said Tony, laughing.

"Dating don'ts?"

"Don't be late, don't forget your wallet, don't talk about religion ...that sort of thing. Oh yes, one of them was 'Don't talk on your mobile'."

"That's so rude, isn't it? How often do you sit with a friend chatting over a cup of coffee and they answer their mobile part-way through the conversation. Such bad manners! Is the conversation they're having on the phone more important than the one they're having with you?"

"The etiquette of the mobile phone is in its infancy. I have lots of meetings in my job, and people just can't handle the mobile phone with good manners. They either rush out of the room to answer it, apologising as they go, or they take it out of their briefcase and make a big show of switching it off – as though to say, 'Look, you're more important than whoever is ringing me up'. I have seen people actually take calls during a meeting – supposedly to show the rest of us how indispensable they are!"

I laughed; for a moment I could hear Robert talking.

"Women carry them because it makes us feel safer. If there's a problem, you can always ring someone ...."

I paused, not wanting to add "... or I could when Robert was there." Tony sensed it anyway, and smiled.

"They make you feel just a little less vulnerable – and alone?"

"Yes."

My "yes" was as simple as my "no" had been, and produced the same look of empathy on Tony's face. He smiled, that shy, tight-lipped smile.

"People don't understand do they, Joyce – all this 'Tomorrow is the first day of the rest of my life' nonsense? You can't just start over again like that. Like you, I don't want anybody else. My friends say, 'Life goes on'. Does it? It isn't as easy as that, is it? Not when you've lived all those years with someone."

"I know. I'd give anything just to see him walk up the path again."

Lorraine:

Talking to Caran, I had more or less made up my mind about Dakos. I was going to accept his offer and start a new life. I wasn't unhappy with Barry; it was just that we had another lifetime ahead of us and I could see nowhere to go – nowhere that we hadn't been, that is – and, as I had said to her, there was no way that I was going to end up as one of those bitter women whom "life has passed by". Barry wouldn't have wanted that any more than I did.

"How about a date when you finish work tonight?" I laughed to myself, recalling my cheek; it had been a purely chance remark, and now look where I was. I had quite fancied him out on that first evening and es-pecially after our day together but, thinking back to his proposal, I was still breathless.

I've always enjoyed the physical side of love-making: some women don't, do they? But I always have: the sun beating down on my belly and legs after that time on the beach with Barry always came back to me in moments of pleasure. We'd been out for the day – just the two of us; it had been one of those gloriously hot days of an English summer. We don't get them often, but when we do, they beat foreign sun anywhere in the world. The sun was warming my breasts through that thin cotton blouse; there was nobody about and so I took it off and walked in my bra. Barry had said "You be careful of the sun" and I had replied, "Sod the sun". Barry was good-look-ing in a Roman Polanski kind of way; he had a quirki-ness about him which had immediately attracted me and all he was wearing that day was a pair of swim shorts. The sun was burning down through that mane of tangled brown hair and it really turned me on – as they say today.

"Don't argue, let's find some shade," he said and picked me up (I was lighter then and dancing regularly) and walked off with me towards a steep dune surrounded by marram grass.

He lowered me gently against a north-facing slope and sat beside me. "I shan't get a tan here." "You'll get tanned enough. You don't want to end up looking like an English lobster". My skirt had dropped when he lifted me and I had felt the warmth of his forearm against my under-thigh and the pressure of his chest against my tummy. Barry had one of those direct stares that women can misinterpret: in his case it was "simply an appreciation of beauty", he'd said. "To me you're a vista of tone, shade and colour." He was painting madly at the time, mainly landscapes (he had this tremendous sense of the "spirit of the place") but he had painted several nudes of me. He looked at me now, his eyes roving from my ankles to my "wonderful, wonderful mop of red-blonde hair".

"My word, you're lovely, Lorraine. Have we got a drink?" I smiled and pulled a flask out of the bag. "Here." "You first?" he said. "No, go on." Barry drank, knelt facing me, placed his hand on my thigh and then our lips brushed. I've always loved that word – "brushed": it has a gentleness and anticipation about it. I could taste the water from the flask on his breath. I ran my hands over his chest and then my bra was off into the grass. I'd reached for the tie of his shorts as he wriggled me out of my skirt and then we were together on the sand. Barry's arms cushioned me and he held me there, hard within me and in no hurry; all the time we made love, the sun – shielded by the slope of the dune – shone down at us through the rough, spiky grass. We climaxed together, which is always nice, and then lay there, the sun warming our bellies and legs. "I'm going to paint this when we get home." "What?" "You, just you, lying here. I can't tell you the tenderness I feel for you, Lorraine."

Thinking about this, I slipped into my blue dress and went to meet Dakos; he had asked, quite apologetically, that we meet again by the Queen Vic Pub. It was another world here, of course, and I was soon immersed in it. Dakos arrived in his open-top car, tall and dusky with that hairy chest and chocolate-brown eyes. He was smiling broadly as he spoke:

"Where would you like to go, Lorren?"

"Somewhere quiet to start with – just off the beaten track."

"The beaten track?"

"The main road."

"We shall have to learn each other's language properly."

As we drove out to a little restaurant on the edge of Craphos ("The Andria," Dakos told me, "and no I don't own it, part-share it or work there!") my thoughts turned back to my day and evening with him. I remembered the warm night winds blowing up from the bay, watching Dakos at the wheel, his attentiveness, his astuteness, the love he bore his family, the admiration in which he was held by his friends, his pride in his town, his courteousy, his intelligence, the compliments he took the trouble to pay me, the fact that he was a hard worker, sexy, humorous and his love for his child. I recalled that moment when he had spoken to the monk in Greek and turned to me and explained about his brother who was in the vegetable garden, the sensation I had then of being in another world, of the excitement in being out with an attractive man who was leading such a different life to mine, that moment after the meal when I wanted to lie down in the room with its yellow-white walls, his mother's chuckle and her eyes wrinkling in a knowing look as she said *"Napagia – for the dancing"* and Dakos' pleasure in the others admiring me after the dance.

We arrived and ate, but I could not tell you what it was although Dakos explained each dish as it came. The Andria had a little terrace that overlooked the beach and we walked here after the meal, taking off our shoes so that we could stroll at the edge of the sea. Dakos made no attempt to kiss me although he might have thought that the romance of the occasion would clinch it for him. It was almost as though he stood at a distance watching me, waiting for an answer that would change not only my life, but his, beyond measure. The evening was soft – the warm breeze from the sea, the light from the restaurant, the touch of the water on our feet, the sand between our toes.

"Dakos ... I am honoured by your proposal, I am flattered. I loved your family, your way of life, your mother, your son. I am overwhelmed by what you offer me. I think you are an exceptional man – sexy, humorous, kind, intelligent, astute ... I would love to be here and share all this with you. I think I could make you happy, give you what you want ...."

He was smiling as I spoke. An Englishman – with that oblique approach of ours – would have caught my drift after the fourth word, but not Dakos; he was a foreigner and took my compliments at face value, accepted my outpouring of emotion as straightforward and genuine, direct and unequivocal. He smiled and the more I said, the wider his smile became; I almost gave up, and then thought of Barry and thirty years and Steph and unravelling everything and the whole rotten unfairness of it all.

"I'm sorry, Dakos. I would love to, but I can't."

His face fell like that of a little child who has had a simple gift rejected by an uncomprehending grown-up.

"I do not understand. You have such wonderful things to say and yet you will not consent to be my wife. I love you, Lorren. Love is not difficult to understand. I have this feeling that you are special to me, that I want to protect you, to love you, to share my life with you ...."

"I know. I came here to say 'yes' but I can't."

"But you are not married. You wear no ring."

"I am not married but I have had a partner for thirty years and we have a child. She is a woman now but ...."

"I do not understand. You approached me. You asked me for ... for ..."

"A date – yes."

"But why – when you already have a man at home?"

"I thought it might be fun. I fancied you."

He strode off along the beach, into the shadows, away from the light cast by the restaurant. There was anger in him, the anger of a man humiliated, but the expression on his face showed more bewilderment than anything when he turned to face me.

"Let me understand. You wanted me to take you out for a meal – that is all?"

Looking back, later, I realised that I should simply have said "yes" to that question. He would have understood that, apologised for his mistake and we might have parted friends: but I didn't say "yes". It wasn't simply that I realised how silly he would feel, having driven me round the island to meet his family and friends; it wasn't even desperation to be totally honest with him; it was a desire to reach some kind of understanding. Facing him on the beach, I was suddenly aware of the huge cultural gap between us. In a way, I think, I wanted to justify what I had done.

"No – I did fancy you. You are a very attractive man. I thought it would be nice to spend a day together, and you offered to show me the island."

"And if I had suggested that we spend that night together, what would you have said?"

Nothing like putting you on the spot, is there? I had to be honest – I would have agreed. I remembered how I had felt that night in his flat.

"I might have said yes."

"You might have said yes, and yet you have a man at home?"

"Yes."

It was rather a bald statement, but I wasn't going to be browbeaten; somewhere at the centre of this was my relationship with Barry, my whole view of life over thirty years. He turned and walked away again, his hands over his mouth, and then he spun round.

"So – you reject my proposal of marriage, but you would have spent the night with me?"

"Marriage is a bigger step than one night, Dakos."

"So – shall we go back to my flat and make love? You would be happy with that?"

"Not now – things have changed, but it would have been nice."

"Would have been nice! And how would your man feel? Would you have told him?"

"That's between me and him, Dakos."

"And if we had married – if you had said yes, would you betray me, too?"

"Barry and I have been together a long time. He wouldn't see it as a betrayal."

"Then he is spineless."

"No! Actually, he is far from spineless. Barry is a generous man. He has intelligence and understanding. He and I have an open relationship. We've had that relationship for thirty years."

I struggled for the words then, the words I had used with Caran – "We saw marriage as an "institution", society's way of tying people down into a contract to keep the social order intact. We looked at our own parents' marriages and asked, "Were they happy?" My own parents have been married nearly sixty years, now. How many of those years have been happy?" I realised that none of this would have any meaning for Dakos. His whole view of marriage and the family was so different from ours; the word "duty" reared its head.

"If he is an honourable man, then you dishonour him."

"Now just a moment! We have different ways of looking at things, that's all."

"Tell me, how are we on Cystos to treat you English women with respect?"

"I would assume that you would respect all women."

"And you wonder why you have such a reputation on the islands?"

"We have a different view of sexual freedom."

"The English – they are easy; they will sleep with anyone and you don't even have to pay."

"Would it make it better if you did?"

"The women of the streets have more dignity."

"So you have nothing but contempt for a woman who chooses to sleep with a man – freely and without obligation to anyone but herself."

"You have no right ...."

"Oh, I do – that's exactly what I have. Barry and I are not married. It would be different if we were."

"But you have a child – you are a family."

"I have enormous respect for your view of the family, Dakos, but it was not our view and are you telling me that single women on Cystos do not sleep with single men?"

"We do not sleep around. A fiancé would be different, nowadays."

"I have decisions to make about my future. When I was attracted to you and especially after that lovely day out I wanted to make a new start here with you, but I have known Barry a long time. It's a bit like a marriage."

"Marriage is forever."

"Yes – and it would be for me, too."

"But already you are unfaithful to your man. Why has he allowed you to come here?"

"Allowed? Barry wouldn't have tried to stop me. That is part of our relationship."

"It is wrong that you even think about sleeping with me."

"Your island will change, Dakos. Your women will want more say."

"There will always be respect for the family on Cystos. None of our women will ever offer themselves to men as you do. When I took you to see my family, I thought you would consider marriage to me. I treated

you honourably. There was no ring on your finger.
I thought you were a free woman."

"It is true I am not free. I thought I was, but Barry has
claims on me – the ties of affection. I see that now."

"It is not good that you wanted to marry me despite
your man."

I had come here so convinced that a new start was
possible: talking to Caran it had seemed the way
forward. I had even rehearsed what I was going to say to
Barry and Steph. I had seen his face, but I knew what his
reaction would be. I was tired. I had really messed this
up, and come out of it feeling worse than a whore.
I wondered what he would think of Steph, what he
would think of the eighty-six percent of modern English
womanhood who lost their virginity before they were
eighteen. Would he put them "on the streets" as being
not worthy of marriage? That was clearly how he saw
me. I wanted to go and think, find a drink and think, and
I wanted to go alone.

"I want to go now. Which way is it to Craphos?"

"I will drive you back."

"No, I want to be alone."

"Please ...."

"It isn't far along the beach, and I want to walk. I am
sorry about the anger, Dakos. I do respect your ways"

"You need to respect yourself."

"Oh I do. You have no idea how much," I said, with
far more certainty than I felt, "but your ways are not
mine. Maybe they could have been."

Day 9: Theme Park

I insisted, against all his protests, that I wanted to walk back alone and, within half an hour, was in the main street of Craphos where the nightlife was still sprawling along the harbour wall. As I watched it, I couldn't but have some sympathy for his point of view. What have we come to? How do others see us? And yet, as I'd said to Dakos (or was it Joyce, so many days ago when I'd poured that drink over the head of that Cystonian jerk in the bar?) this may be their country but they had moulded it around an image of us. That surely is their responsibility isn't it – not ours? I passed a bus stop; on the side was a McDonald's ad that said 'Your world changes. Big Mac doesn't. It's just that good.' I hadn't put that ad there – Dakos and his countrymen had; this was the world they were welcoming us to – the world of 'Big Mac', which is so good that it has no need to change. It was tawdry, vulgar, shoddy, a cultural obscenity ...but it was part of the island the Cystonians had created for themselves – just as were the pole dancers, the free pub crawls offered to tourists who will take off their clothes, and so on.

When Steph and I had arrived in that Spanish resort three years ago it had been the same. We'd arrived on a cheap flight and were greeted in the most offhand manner by the airport staff; the arrivals lounge, which smelt vaguely of urine, looked as though it had been furnished with the leftovers from a shut-down garden centre, and cats and dogs wandered in looking for scraps. We'd been kept waiting while some pompous little men made a great show of examining our documents, as though they expected to apprehend an international villain; we sat around patiently, as only the Brits can show patience – tired, cold and hungry, on cold marble floors. Then the music had started and the alcohol appeared from nowhere (you couldn't get a cup of water!) and the youngsters began to party.

Officials shouted in protest and security arrived, but the alcohol kept flowing, and in no time we had to contend with the usual teenage drunks. The looks we received became more and more hostile, but the Brits were having a good time – after all we were on holiday! Of course, the loud music and the alcohol didn't help a group of people already queasy from the flight and soon we had people vomiting in waste bins – the toilets being either full or so nauseous that it only made you feel worse to go there. Then police turned up, lightly armed with pump-action shotguns and an assault rifle. Someone dropped their flight bag and the duty-free gin they had bought shattered, making all of us feel worse. "This is not a nightclub", one of policemen had said, "You cannot drink and dance here." Steph had gone ballistic (yes, that word again!) when I had replied, on behalf of the youth they were harassing, "If you turned off the music, hadn't sold them the alcohol on the way over and moved your butts so that we could get to our hotels, it wouldn't be a nightclub and they wouldn't be drinking!" The copper had looked at me – not, I imagine, ever having been spoken to like that before, especially by a woman – and was speechless. Looking round, I could see that we weren't great ambassadors for our country but, at the same time, our hosts had to take some responsibility for that.

I made my way to a bar, guessing someone might try to pick me up, but not caring. I wanted a drink, and a chance to sit quietly and think before going back to the hotel and facing Caran. I had to tell her, after all, that I had completely changed my mind between talking to her and reaching Dakos. Why?

The bar was like all the others – 'playing 70s-90s' music and all the latest tunes'. What happened to the '60's? 'Tri Nations Rugby and Grand Prix AND Olympics LIVE on SKY AND the new Premiership Season Football LIVE. 3 HUGE screens AND 6 TV's with full ENGLISH commentary.' Tonight, however, I was spared the sport and could simply enjoy 'A real Aussie pub with a true Aussie Atmosphere' although, if I came next Saturday, I could 'meet the KING'. Not their King – the Cystonians hadn't got one. This was Elvis – the old rocker who had dropped dead, drunk and drugged, while on the toilet seat; but he was now alive again, and did I know he was Australian? The waiter who sold me the drink certainly wasn't, but thought he looked as though he was – all checkshirt, jeans and crotch. Do these young men wear jock straps permanently to keep themselves prominent? I remember one of the stars of *Neighbours* being asked why he thought English women found Australians so sexy. He responded with the comment "Perhaps it's the way we stand." Watching the waiter, I could see what he meant.

I hadn't been seated more than five minutes when one of the loungers from the bar wandered over to try his luck.

"Hi, my name is Stan. Remember that, 'cause you'll want to scream it at the top of your voice later."

I looked at him (I hope disdainfully) for a while (I find that always disconcerts men – if you meet their eyes, that is), and then said:

"Not with you, numb nuts. Now bugger off!"

I'd heard that – or something like it – in a Clint Eastwood movie. I forget which one – it was something Steph and one of her boyfriends had been watching on the telly – but it worked. He looked at me as though I'd shot him straight between the eyes, opened his mouth, closed it and then buggered off; it would give me the peace and quiet I wanted. None of the others would bother me now. What is it about Englishmen? He could have asked me if I'd like a drink with him, or a chat. But no, it had to be a shag, didn't it? As though a shag is some-how less personal than drinking or talking: less personal and therefore less embarrassing when approaching a complete stranger.

While my thoughts came and went, I looked along the street. From where I sat, on the terrace of the bar, I had a good view of the early hours in Craphos. Some youths were walking along the middle of the street – deliberately or not it was hard to tell. One of them was naked from the waist down, but strolling quite calmly with no apparent desire to impress. He had his shorts in his hand, and his mates in fits of laughter. Further along, some more were busy pushing one of their mates into a large plastic wheelie bin, which they then whirled along the road. I could hear rugby songs coming from the bar next door and an occasional bottle hitting the floor. Across the street was a stripper bar where a bouncer, looking incredibly self-righteous, was refusing entry to another group of drunks. Eventually, money passed hands and he let them in, but they didn't stay long. About fifteen minutes later, one of them flew out on to the street, stripped down to his boxer shorts and followed by his clothes. His mates came after him and a chorus of "Happy Birthday" faded into silence down the street. I wanted someone to talk to – not Caran and certainly not Joyce – but here I was in a foreign country, for the moment friendless. I always find it easier to think when I am talking to someone, rather than when I am simply sitting with my thoughts.

"Lorraine?"

I looked up; like manna in the desert, there stood Frank! We hadn't seen him for days, not since before the pirate ship, and all that followed for Caran.

"What are you doing here?"

"I might ask you ..."

"... the same question – yes – but what are you doing here?" I insisted.

"I'm on holiday and I've been in a bar down the road beating the locals – and some of the lads – at pool. And you?"

"Thinking."

"Alone?"

"Well it would be easier if I had someone to talk to."

"Can I get you another drink?"

"Let me get you one, Frank. It will upset the boys at the bar."

I signalled to the waiter, who brought his crotch over in a hurry; soon Frank and I were looking at each other over, in my case, a glass of tequila and, in his, a double whisky and Canada Dry. He'd been spared his usual bit of banter with the waiter – running through the series of whisky-based cocktails he'd listed on that first night – because this was just a bar and they did actually just sell whisky, even if it was spelled 'whiskey'. We now sat smiling at each other while the noise of the bars seemed to fade into the background. He didn't speak, just smiled and waited; he knew I had something to talk about, something important to me, and he wasn't going to distract me by filling the first few minutes with small talk.

There was something disconcerting about Frank's silence; it seemed to insist that I should talk. I didn't discover what it was until later in the week. Then, that night, I just began to talk and poured out to him all that had passed between Dakos and me. He listened without speaking. No one in all of my life had ever listened to me like that except, perhaps, Barry who – after thirty years – knew me so well that he had developed the irritating habit of anticipating everything I was going to say. When I had finished, Frank reached across the table, took both my hands, squeezed them and said:

"I'm sorry. It really is one hell of a predicament you're in, isn't it?"

"Well, was in. I've burned my boats, as far as Dakos is concerned."

"I wouldn't say that. There might be a bit of negotiating to do, but 'burned your boats'? No."

"What makes you think that I would want to "negotiate" with Dakos?"

"Male logic? If it was over and done with why are you sitting here thinking about it? Not simply because you want to get it square in your mind before facing Caran.

You'd just say to her that you had changed your mind and given him his marching orders."

I laughed.

"We are complicated, aren't we, Frank?"

"Yes. I don't pretend to understand women, Lorraine, but I was married so long that I have arrived at an intuitive acceptance of it all. It just keeps me sane and saves me losing my temper."

I laughed again and said:

"But you didn't enjoy being married?"

"Yes, I did."

"But you did divorce your wife?"

"Yes."

"So ....?"

"I thought we were here to talk about you? What are you going to do – a life with Dakos, or a life with Barry? You have the world at your feet, Lorraine. You have but to 'screw your courage to the sticking place' – or something like that."

I nearly said, then, "What would you do?" and realised how silly that would sound. It really annoyed Barry when I had a decision to make – whether it was going for another qualification, or simply deciding whether or not to have a drink – when I asked him that question, so I asked Frank.

"What would you do?"

He laughed; years of marriage had prepared him for the question and the impossibility of his giving a sensible answer.

"How about another drink?"

"Love one."

Frank looked up and the crotch came over again, bringing a smile and Frank's whisky and Canada Dry with it: me, he was less sure of because he smiled and asked what I wanted. There was that same manner about him as about all bar staff in Craphos; they seemed to have the impression that a crotch and a hairy chest were all they needed – perhaps it was, if you were after a teenage girl.

"Keep the tequilas coming, my friend – steadily, but in no hurry," said Frank.

"You're not trying to get me drunk, Frank?"

"No – you can be sure of that. To answer your question – "What would you do?" – in a sense, I have already done it. Divorce."

"And do you regret it?"

"That's not an easy question to answer, Lorraine. No – I'm not being evasive, just trying to focus on you and Dakos. Cheers."

"Cheers. And Barry?"

"Haven't you already made up your mind about Barry and your life back home in England? You're not unhappy but you cannot see it going on for another thirty years? Maybe Barry feels the same?"

I hadn't thought of that; I knew Barry would support me – he always had – but it hadn't actually occurred to me that he might be feeling as I did and for similar reasons.

"Oh, God, Frank, you're making me think."

"You think all the while. You're an intellectual, Lorraine – an intelligent woman who wants to give her life some purpose. This isn't going to go away. You've faced the question. Back away now and it will still be there next year and the year after. And when you're seventy …."

"All right – you've made your point! Let's just leave it for a moment ...there is this other thing, isn't there – the way Dakos and the islanders see Western women? It's all part of my dilemma. Have we ourselves to blame?"

"I tend to agree with what you said to Dakos – and history is on our side. This has always been 'party island'. Dakos should read his own tourist propaganda. The guide books tell us that, as far back as the Romans, conquering armies had a tradition of rewarding their returning soldiers by sending them to Cystos for a fortnight with a ship full of women and wine. It didn't say whether all the women agreed to come! Cystos has emerged as – and I quote, roughly – "one of the hippest destinations on earth. Mix a cocktail of clubbers, holiday makers, stars, celebrities and models – and what do you get? One of the summer party places of the world!" And with clubs open until four in the morning and with names like 'Shagwells', who can doubt what the Cystonians have to offer?"

"Is that true?"

"What – Shagwells? Oh, yes. Care for a "hip" night in Karavi Limani? You can't blame the locals entirely, of course. We are responsible for our own behaviour. I've never gone along with the 'making bullets for the others to fire' brigade, and we are disgusting at times. There was that outcry last year about 'Shameless Britons'. Remember? One of the Mediterranean countries wanted us tried for indecency. The article went something like – 'It is four o'clock in the morning. Loud, thumping music accompanies swarms of sweaty, red-faced young Brits as they make their way along the seafront downing pints of cheap lager. A pretty, semi-naked blonde writhes around on the counter of Nobby's Bar. Further along the street we have the neon-lit bars, clubs and strip joints. An amorous young couple sporting wet T-shirts are having sex leaning against the wall in an alleyway. At the Baywatch Bar an all-night sex party is in progress with tourists enjoying themselves naked in foam pools while, around the pool side, men are licking cream off the breasts of naked women. Two club reps are showing the way by having oral sex shielded only slightly by a table umbrella cocked at a rakish angle. In Tramps a young couple have decided that it isn't necessary to leave the bar to have sex because she is wearing a skirt – with no underwear, of course – and all she has to do is unbutton her beau's trousers ...and so on."

I couldn't help laughing – the picture he painted was so ludicrous.

"Ludicrous maybe, but I'm not making it up. Read your Sunday papers when you get back home. But, of course, as one of the locals pointed out – "anyone with an ounce of decorum and self-respect gives those bars a miss." The local businessmen – not unlike your Dakos – took a rather ambiguous stance I thought. It went something like 'Business is business. I have seen bar owners pay young, provocatively dressed girls to dance on the bar and entice more customers to come in' followed by 'I don't tend to go out in those areas.' Yeah – right."

"And what did the young Brits have to say for themselves? As you say, we are responsible for our own behaviour."

"Well, Cheryl – or was it Sharon or Tracy? Anyway, the journalist got a quote from one of them, when he'd prised her off her beau at the bar, no doubt. It went something like 'It's just a good night out. You get more trouble back home. Here it's just about going out, having a drink and a good laugh'."

"So Dakos has a point about Western women?"

"And you did offer yourself to him, but declined marriage."

"Thanks Frank!"

Frank:

I'd enjoyed meeting Lorraine by chance. She was a woman you could talk to without going through the usual pretensions of being sexually interested in her; this always seems par for the course when you first meet a female stranger on holiday or, indeed, at home. On that first night, when the three of them chatted me up, she'd reminded me of Monet's models – not fat but big, plenty of her but firm. She exuded joie de vivre. I'd pictured her in one of Monet's boating pictures, leaning over the side rails, a table full of food behind her, laughing into the face of whichever man she happened to be talking to; I remember thinking how wonderfully unselfconscious she was. I had fancied her, and still did, but I wasn't trying to get her drunk to take advantage of her – anyway, who'd actually want to make love to a drunken woman? She was a nice lady and I would have been happy to listen to her all night. It's quite pleasant, isn't it, just to chat to a woman without having to go through the rigmarole of flirting – pretending you're after something you're not; at least – not at that moment?

The other thought I had in my head as we sat there – with no disrespect to Lorraine who, as I said, I liked – was how ruthless women can be. Here she was, considering leaving a man she'd been more or less married to for thirty years and she wasn't really questioning the rights and wrongs of it or – at least, on the surface – showing any great concern for her Barry. When I'd gone through my divorce, although it had been me who instigated it, I was wracked with guilt and uncertainty.

"So you think I will be seeing Dakos again?"

"Don't you?"

"Do you always answer every question with another, Frank?"

"It's you we're talking about tonight, Lorraine. When you wake up in the morning, you want this 'sorted' – as they say on *Eastenders* – don't you?"

"I'd like my mind clear about what I am going to do – yes."

"And your approach will be a direct one? This is too important for the preliminaries to get in the way?"

"The 'preliminaries', as you put it Frank, wouldn't be very appropriate in the circumstances, would they?"

"No – Dakos might get the wrong idea."

Lorraine:

He laughed; I laughed. The English turn everything to do with sex into a joke, don't they? Frank and I could see the humour of the situation, but would Dakos? With Frank, as with Barry, I shared a cultural heritage; we saw sex – at least the social aspects of sex – from the same perspective; we had the same expectations of each other's behaviour.

"It is another world, isn't it, Frank? I was watching one of those women's programmes some time ago – those American-influenced ones where they talk about their personal lives in public? I don't mean *Trisha* and that kind of rubbish where they set people up to humiliate them; this was a group of relatively intelligent women talking about themselves in front of an audience. Anyway, one of the women was saying that she wished she'd kept a particular relationship as simply an 'affair' but, knowing how the bloke had felt about her, she'd said the dreaded words 'I love you', knowing she didn't. She talked openly about a relationship with a man she didn't love and had no intention of marrying – the relationship was, presumably, largely sexual and a matter of social convenience. How would Dakos have seen that – would he have said 'The women of the streets have more dignity'?

"The view they have of sexual relationships out here is still one based on a moral perception of behaviour, Lorraine – so, yes, I expect he would. I suppose she would be considered a 'woman of loose morals' – not worth marrying."

"So that is how he sees me because I have lived with Barry for thirty years – a woman of loose morals?"

"I don't know. There are always gradations of behaviour, of what is and is not right within any moral code – at least for worldly people, and this Dakos is worldly, I take it – at least within his own view of things?"

We sat quietly for a long time, looking out along the street, sipping our drinks; Frank seemed in no hurry and the conversation was making me more confused than ever. I thought of Dakos as being "out of touch", but with what? He was well in touch with his own world. It's always the English who are seen as sexually inhibited isn't it – but are we? On even the simplest level of sexual contact – flirting – we are at it all the time. It's almost obligatory and women are as up-front as men. Where I work, it oils the wheels of the day. It goes on between people who are married to someone else and who have no sexual interest in each other at all; but that's it, isn't it? We make teasing comments, we banter, but it's all safe. It's sometimes a way of sussing out another person's feelings, but there's always a line you never cross and – when you do – sex rears its head and you're into another ball game. I just can't imagine any of the women out here behaving like that: flirting with a man they had no sexual interest in. I think, in the first place, that it would be the man who made the approach, and after that, the woman might show her feelings by flirting sexually but – by then – the intentions of both would be clear. Frank said, suddenly, as though continuing our previous line of conversation:

"I was reading an article in one of my daughter's magazines – oh, way back. It was an interview with one of these teenage celebrity types – some girl who'd sung a song or appeared in a film. You know the kind of thing – she's appeared in one film and is now 'one of the brightest actresses of her generation'? She talks about the all-night parties and the string of boyfriends, but has now become 'a respected actress'?

"Get to the point, Frank!"

"This is the point – it's all part of the casual way we treat sex. There'll be loads of pictures of this girl; she'll be at least half-naked in most of them, in one she is almost certain to be on a bed, and in another they will be some stud with a swollen crotch. The look in her eyes in all of them will say – "Well come on buddy, if you fancy your chances."

I laughed. We don't take this seriously (do we?) but in Dakos' culture we would. So why hasn't television and the glossy mag market brought the world closer together? Frank continued:

"She has a string of 'conquests' – as though sleeping with a man implies you have conquered him – and they're all Hollywood big names. That says a lot about them as men, if they've slept with a young woman barely out of her teens, doesn't it?"

"You don't approve, do you Frank?"

"Anyway, in this particular case, the girl concerned had a reputation for 'liking men, partying and getting lots of attention'. Natural enough in a young woman, of course; but she does have this reputation for 'dating several men at the same time' so the interviewer asks her about this and she says 'I'm not dating just one person. I don't want to put myself in a position where I'm in a monogamous relationship right now.' Fine! The interviewer goes on 'How many times do you sleep with someone before you're officially dating them?' You get that, Lorraine – 'sleeping with' comes before 'dating'? Now that's casual sex."

"But we don't take it seriously."

"Don't we? Oh, I think we do. It becomes part of what is "normal" in our way of looking at things and it is so different from Dakos' world. It's a long bridge you have to cross, Lorraine, to get back to that other world. The girl went on to talk about having the right to 'give her body' to someone she fancied, but she'd rather they weren't sleeping with someone else at the same time. She talked about how 'her Mom would kill her for talking about sleeping with people' but, in the next breath, she's saying she likes a variety of partners and finds married men to be 'more alluring than single guys' because 'you always want what you can't have'.

"But I repeat – we don't take this kind of thing seriously."

"And I repeat: I think we do. This young woman went on to say that 'Sex in the city' ..."

"'Sex *and* the City', Frank – it's a TV series!"

"OK – 'Sex *and* the City' – this series had "changed everything for me because those girls would sleep with just anyone'. The whole article was a mish-mash of what her rights were, what her Mom would say, what she did and why she did it. None of it had any coherence, especially no moral coherence. It was simply about what she wanted to do, and it was laced through with a tone of moral self-righteousness. Now a moral society has a relationship with a code of behaviour. Does ours? This girl and her 'string of conquests' is part of the amoral climate you now inhabit in Dakos's eyes. You're part of the morally sloppy West."

He was right, of course. Whatever the rights and wrongs, I was part of that world. How would Dakos see the way we had brought Steph up? This had been pretty freely and, by his standards, perhaps almost licentious. Had I come a bridge too far? Did I want to retrace my steps back into that other world we had all inhabited as children? Was that part of Dakos's attraction for me?

"Have I upset you?"

"No, Frank. You're just making me think through things I have taken for granted for years. I just don't seem any nearer to approaching Dakos again – in fact, I seem further from him than ever."

"Well, even if things had gone well with him tonight, it strikes me that you would have had to face this sooner or later. You couldn't have hidden Barry and your daughter away. Better that you and Dakos talk these things through now – before you bring Barry and Steph into a situation that is going to cause them pain, however you handle it."

"Have we become morally sloppy, Frank – pushed on by this self-ordained right to do what we want without reference to anyone or anybody other than ourselves?"

"That was a nice mouthful, Lorraine – straight out of the *Moral Maze*."

"Don't joke, Frank. We dodge out of thinking by making a joke of everything."

"Yes – well maybe we do. Very good, Lorraine – I knew talking to you would be fun. The answer is, I don't know. If we have, then I'm floating along on the sea of slop just like everyone else. Some would say that we are on the point of an ethical breakthrough, others that we're sliding back into the Dark Ages of the Soul. I don't know, and it's three o'clock in the morning."

"Don't back away from me, Frank. Keep me thinking."

"It's three o'clock in the morning."

"We're on holiday."

"That was my point."

Frank had got me going: I was beginning to fancy him. It was a long time since I'd had a discussion about morals with anyone of my own age – only the intelligent young seem to talk about these things. The art students and those I taught at the drama centre were all afire with moral debate – not that it necessarily seemed to impinge on the how they lived their lives, in any obvious way, but perhaps I wasn't the best judge. The young actress in Frank's article was hardly responsible for what was written about her either, was she? I suppose she could have repudiated the title –'one of the brightest actresses of her generation' – but then humility isn't an attribute of the young in any age is it? As far as her 'morals' were concerned, she was as much adrift on Frank's 'sea of slop' as anyone.

I noticed that Frank's comments held no tone of moral censure; he seemed to place himself firmly on the sea along with the rest of us; but in society there is a 'moral backlash', as they say. Some years ago – following the upsurge of pseudo-American management styles forced upon us in the eighties and nineties – there was an attempt by 'top firms' to stop even flirting in the workplace. I suppose feminism must take some responsibility for that, because it was seen as chauvinistic, but the move was actually made by management in line with their view of political correctness. It didn't work, of course – you simply cannot stop something that is so deeply ingrained in the human psyche – but the disturbing thing is that the attempt was made by quite reputable firms. In the States, I understand, it actually worked – led on by puritanical forces.

"Where were you educated, Frank?"

"I left school at sixteen. Never went to university. I picked up an education as I went along. Thank God for BBC2 and Radio 4. I take it you did get a degree, Lorraine?"

"Oh, yes. They were the best years of my life in many ways. I've never had that amount of freedom since. It's where I met Barry. It's where I thought through my view of the world. It's where my creativity found an outlet for a while."

I paused; I'd found this evening that you could always pause in a conversation with Frank – he didn't find it necessary to fill the space with a quip or an inanity.

People like Frank – free from a formal education – often have a fresh way of looking at things and I wanted that now so, eventually, I said:

"What would you do, Frank?"

"You've asked me that once – several hours ago."

"No, seriously. I can't tackle the moral decline of the West with Dakos. It's simply too big an issue for me to handle alone."

"I don't think he'd be interested anyway, Lorraine," he replied with a grin, "If he loves you, he'll want to find a way forward for you and him – nothing else."

"There is a concern though, isn't there Frank, about the moral turpitude of the West? People like Dakos don't want his children growing up into the moral quagmire that our children find themselves in."

"He will expect you to adopt his way of life. It's as simple as that – church, family, society. Is that what you want?"

Frank:

I'd enjoyed my "night out" with Lorraine – unintentional though it was and certainly lacking that sense of joie de vivre one associates with a holiday. Still, holidays are about doing something different and discussing "putting the world to rights" was certainly a change for me. I normally had conversations like that with Michael Buerk and his guests but, of course, they never took much notice.

I could see what Lorraine meant about the "moral turpitude of the West" – not that "turpitude" was anything but a new word in my dictionary. In fact, I didn't ever recall hearing it before – not even on Michael Buerk's programme – but I got the general drift.

I suppose women do worry about these things more than men. They have such an eye for the detail of things, don't they? And, of course, they worry in a way that we don't. I remember my wife never really stopped worrying; Michael Buerk (again!) in his 999 series had her on the edge of her seat. After that episode with the car in the river she had me driving along the Haddiscoe Straight at twenty miles per hour with the car in the middle of the road.

Being a bloke, I tend to take the long view and, generally speaking, I think things are better than they have ever been as far as moral turpitude goes. We're a kindlier people than we were: more concerned about the world, eager that children should get a better deal from schools; we respond generously to emergencies, are pro-active (what a word!) in acknowledging our responsibilities, more accountable for what we do – although that can go too far – and are far less tight-arsed than our parents' generation. The other side of the coin, however, is the relaxed view we take of other people's behaviour. We don't dish out the moral guidelines we received from our teachers and parents, and so our children are left to find their own way through the 'moral maze' – like the confused young woman in the magazine – and they are a prey to crappy drama series that also take the line "anything goes". The only way to go, though, is forward from where we are; only the most crass of politicians really believes in "back to basics". Dakos' people will find this, too, as they move into the twenty first century. They have yet to approach the battlefield on which we are already fighting. That's rather good that – I'll have to send it in to Michael Buerk.

The mayor of one of these Mediterranean islands once said that the reason the Brits are so loutish is that they are not used to the permissive atmosphere they find abroad. "Life in England is more restrictive," he said, "the rules of behaviour abroad are so relaxed that the Brits cannot cope with them". He wasn't, of course, referring to the behaviour of his own young men towards their women – the rules for which are anything but relaxed – he was referring to the licentious climate of holiday resorts which he and his kind have helped to create for commercial reasons. His particular island attracted over half a million Brits a year, offering package deals at £200 a time; he wasn't exactly aiming for the elite market, was he? He, also, obviously hadn't wandered round the centre of a typical large British town on a Thursday, Friday or Saturday night, although I blame the holiday resorts for that – we have simply imported the uncivilised behaviour we find abroad.

But, to be honest, I didn't think any of this would really affect Dakos' attitude to Lorraine, if she cared to get in touch with him again. People tend to live their own lives without constant reference to the wider picture; he was simply put out because he supposed she was unmarried and – to be fair on the guy – his comments were largely about the Brits he'd seen, not the world picture.

We walked back towards our hotels together arm in arm like old friends. Her mind was clearing and I was glad of that. Friendship is a lovely thing and, although we would almost certainly never meet again once the holiday was over, we had been friends tonight. I was a stranger to her but Lorraine knew I was concerned for her happiness.

Walking at four or five o'clock in the morning is always a pleasure, at home or abroad. At home you have the quietness of the nation asleep with the early risers just beginning to stir – even the market vendors and delivery vans are silent at that time. Abroad on holiday the clubs are just turning out the detritus of the night. I had come to know Craphos quite well during the past eight or nine days and decided to take the back streets home, not because it was nearer – after all it's not every day you have a glorious redhead on your arm at that hour of the morning – but because it would be different to the walk along the harbour.

We passed the fort built by the Lusignans with its battlements and dungeons, which I had visited alone earlier in the week, and crossed by the mosaic pavement, screened off to preserve it from tourists. The road was now tarmac and began to slope slightly downhill; here we passed the Odeion, a restored Roman theatre, dating from the second century, which I intended to visit before my final week was out. A young man ran by us, naked from the waist down and sporting an elephant mask on his penis; his penis formed the actual trunk, while the large ears – I took it to have been inspired by an African elephant – shielded us from the sight of his pubic hairs. He smiled, somewhat sheepishly, I thought for such a brazen exhibitionist. I smiled back as Lorraine whistled; she was enjoying herself and more like the Lorraine I remembered from that first night. We had both drunk too much but were not actually inebriated, which was nice because we could enjoy each other's company and the night.

I kept the lighthouse top in view and steered her gently away to the right of it towards another tourist attraction: Gregory's Pillar, the site where an early Christian martyr had been flogged by the Romans. For such a civilized people they were a tad on the rough side, weren't they? However, undeterred, Gregory pressed on and eventually converted the governor and – subsequently or consequently – the rest of the island to his point of view. They bred them tough and purposeful in those days. A group of youths lurched from a side street carrying a goldfish bowl as though they had just left a funfair. I'd come across these earlier in the week. Local bars, in order to ensure that the young Brits got well and truly pissed and carried on spending, provided these on the tables; they were a concoction of white spirits – locally produced rum and vodka – mixed with orange juice. The challenge was, of course, to empty the bowl in one swallow. Later in the evening, they were useful for the youngsters to vomit in; on the side of this bowl was the inscription 'HMS Victory' – the locals encouraged us to take pride in our heritage. I'm sure that Nelson would have approved. They ignored us more or less completely and staggered away together towards the harbour.

It was at that moment, when the street was suddenly quiet again and we had just turned into an alleyway that I noticed two youths lurking in the doorway of a house. It was too late to turn back: as soon as Lorraine and I were off the main back street, they were on us. One – the taller of the two – pushed what appeared to be a gun at my head and the other shoved Lorraine back against the wall. They were sweating: I could read anxiety in every twitch of the tall one's eyes.

"Quick."

"Quick what?"

"Your money – quick!"

"Why?

"What?"

"Why?"

"This is a gun, mate."

"Really? And you're going to shoot me if I don't hand over my money?

"Right."

"Wrong."

"What?"

"I said, 'wrong'. You would need to be really stupid to kill me and face endless years in prison for what I have in my wallet, wouldn't you? Besides, my father, and doubtless your grandfather, fought a war so that you and I could walk down any street in Europe as free men – free from having some Fascist stick a gun in our faces and threaten to shoot us. Right?"

"I'm not a Fascist."

"You're behaving like one."

As we had talked, I kept my eye on Lorraine, hoping she wouldn't panic or react violently; her assailant had a stick to her face but was watching his tall companion and me. If she would just keep calm we might actually get away with this, I thought. The tall youth looked at me and something in his eyes told me he wasn't going to shoot. At that moment there was the noise of laughter from the main street. He stepped back, kicked me in the chest and ran; his mate followed. Lorraine looked at me, speechless with anger, and I couldn't help laughing: it was partly nerves, partly the release of tension, partly the look of total incomprehension in her eyes.

"What the hell were you doing, Frank?"

"I just couldn't bear the thought of handing my money over to a punk with a gun. What is the world coming to?"

"He could have killed us! They always tell you to hand over your money, offer no resistance ..."

"I know, I know – but you should always try talking to people. He didn't like to think his granddad would be ashamed of him. These Cystonians are very family orientated."

"How did you know he was a local youth?"

"He didn't use the 'f' word."

Lorraine laughed, then, that hearty, sexy laugh of hers.

"You mad bugger. They could have killed us."

"Are you all right? Apart from the shock, I mean?"

"No thanks to you."

"At least you've got your purse intact."

When we reached her hotel, the shock had set in and she asked me up to her room. Caran's door was closed. Lorraine and I sat on the balcony where, on that first night, I had sat with Caran. Lorraine talked the tension out of her over the next hour or so while we drank a few gins, held each other close once in a while and convinced each other that we were safe. Eventually, we agreed to report the matter to the police in the morning. Lorraine kissed me good night like an old friend and I made my way down to reception. The concierge gave me a wink.

As I left, a scrawny youth was having an argument with a taxi driver. They stood on the pavement yelling at each other. The youth was out of breath as if he had just run a half-marathon and the taxi driver was raging with anger. It transpired that the youth had hailed him for a lift home and then thrown up in the taxi; not only was the youth refusing to pay his fare, he was also refusing to pay the penalty for vomiting in the cab. I thought it was as well neither of them had a gun. The concierge followed me through the doors to intervene, as I walked off down the street, half-expecting Joyce to call me up to her balcony for breakfast. I could have polished off a Full English at that moment.

Stavros was really pleased to see us at the official opening of his theme park. His face beamed as we arrived. I had persuaded Lorraine to bring Caran and Joyce because I got the impression that Stavros saw virtue in numbers. The extension to his hotel with its bar-cum-restaurant and children's play area was a big occasion in the town. Stavros' trips to England over many months had now borne fruit and Skeggy, who had stayed on in Craphos with their three children managing the hotel, was basking in the glory. I had noticed that the "good team" rarely exchanged a smile; about both of them there was intensity of mutual purpose, and yet a distance between them as though their marriage was a formal matter. I hadn't seen them at their large house with the swimming pool somewhere up in the Craphos hills, of course, but they never seemed to rest anyway: fifteen-hour days were the rule and with the Brits demanding tourism all year round they were looking at more or less a forty week working year – if that is what they wanted, of course.

The children ran past, dodging in and out of the gathering crowd. Stavros flashed us a smile with his full set of natural, white teeth. Skeggy passed, looking wonderful – the black hair, dark skin, large eyes and finely chiselled nose – and I found myself wondering again how different it might be, how it would feel running my fingers through a dark mane of hair down to slender shoulders and whether, indeed, all foreign women were slim. There were so many of them here – a huge crowd spilled from the hotel across the road and into the theme park and they all looked so cool. Holidays are OK but I've never enjoyed living out of a suitcase and I felt scruffy next to them. At home I had a smart summer suit but it was doing nothing for me tonight.

Without exception the Cystonians here tonight were smart, dressed for the occasion. I suppose Stavros was the town's Richard Branson – a "hands-on" entrepreneur. I couldn't imagine a whole island of people turning out at home for the opening of a theme park of this size – or an archbishop turning up to bless it. The 'theme park' was, as I said, essentially an additional bar and restaurant with a children's playground attached and yet he had pulled them in, and it wasn't just the lure of free food and drink. This was a special occasion for the island, almost a religious event – not even to be compared with one of our celebrities opening the village fete or cutting the ribbon at the latest supermarket. Yet it was so informal – everyone was dressed by Versacci but seemed unaware of their glamorous appearance. The islanders wore their designer clothes as casually as you and I might slip into a T-shirt and jeans to mow the lawn. This was not lost on Caran who, having given me a strange smile, had cast her withering eye over the crowd.

"There must be money in tourism, Frank!"

"But do you fancy a fifteen-hour day, forty weeks of the year?"

"These people aren't all hotel owners."

"True – perhaps they're in what the Yanks call "real estate"? Can I sell you a holiday home? We're building them down on the beach and they're packed together like rabbit hutches in a pet shop."

She laughed that cruel laugh of hers so I went on:

"Or perhaps a 'time-share' apartment? We'll seduce you into thinking you can't resist the idea by having a piece of twenty-something crumpet in reception at the poolside. We'll keep you hanging around for two or three hours while we pretend to explain everything, and then make you feel cheap when you refuse to pay us an extortionate amount for the privilege of using a fart-arsing apartment one week a year."

"You've been collared?"

"I'll tell you about it tomorrow – or when we meet up again."

"It won't be tomorrow. We're on the 'Jeep Safari"'

"Oh yes – booked at your welcome meeting'. Enjoy yourselves!"

The crowd swirled across the road towards the theme park, making their way through the debris of the builder's rubble, which littered the site. This was something else I couldn't get my head around. Here were all these people dressed in enough money to finance an African village for the rest of the century and beyond, yet they were picking their path around stacks of breeze blocks, bags of cement, prefabricated rafters and piles of sand and shingle. At home we would either have removed these and grassed the surrounds or, at least, covered them up with velvet cloths. Stavros had spent the money here but it didn't look as though he had; somewhere in all this there was a lack of what the Americans call "class".

Lorraine and I had dropped into the police station in the early afternoon to report the attempted mugging and it had been clear from the outset that the officer in charge did not believe a word of it. I saw him now in the crowd and he gave me a contemptuous look before averting his eyes altogether. He was sure that there were no guns on Cystos, such things would not be tolerated, but he made out a report and said it would be investigated. Whether it would or not was another matter. It's nice to read in the brochures that the crime rate on the island is zero. The tourists like to have confidence in the safety of their chosen resort. Lorraine waved and caught up with Caran and I, with Joyce in tow. The three of us made for the narrow gateway with its screen of running water spilling over the head of the mermaid on the rock. It was clear now that there was a pattern emerging; the crowds held the edges of the sandy pathway and would not budge to let us through. It was along here that the archbishop would pass and they wanted to be as near to him as possible.

"Come on, follow me and keep close. We'll find a spot."

I'm used to crowds and led the women to the slope which ran up to the raised bar-cum-restaurant. It was as far as you could get from the mermaid gate but gave us a good view over the heads of everyone. The theme park enclosure now filled rapidly and everything seemed chaotic: there were no barriers, no restrictions on movement, no direction. It was a free-for-all with pushing and shoving to get a good view, as the archbishop's black sedan drew up outside the Poseidon. Stavros made his way through the crowd which broke readily for him. Skeggy and the children were already on the footpath, the children lined up in height order, Skeggy behind the middle one with her arms resting lightly on the shoulders of the others. Several locals now joined us on the slope elbowing their way into the rail – it was all moustaches, cool sweat and gold accessories; one or two of the islanders smiled, but these were generally the younger ones. From the older people we received only blank stares or rather hostile glances; what were we doing here, taking up their space, watching their archbishop, drinking their drink, eating their food?

The archbishop, led by Stavros and followed by Skeggy and the children, now made his way through the crowd. He had already given his obligatory pat on the heads of the children and passed, almost oblivious to the noise and chaos of the movement around him, towards the restaurant on stilts. He had his crozier in his hand. Arms reached out to him and received a regal wave but no smile. He seemed almost solemn, a representative of another world. I could imagine him being glad to get back home and pour himself a sherry – or whatever Cystonian clergy drink.

Stavros and Skeggy were smiling now, the centre of attention, the epitome of achievement, graced by their children. As the archbishop approached the slope, I realised why most of the locals had avoided it; we were in the way and were about to be moved. Several men approached us – not the black-suited mafia types who still stood by the sedan but men who simply looked like business friends of Stavros. We were shifted without a 'by-your-leave' and gracelessly; there was no explanation, simply long gorilla arms which herded us down the slope and into the back of the crowd who gobbled us up. Lorraine laughed, Caran looked annoyed and Joyce offended as we turned to watch the archbishop tread his untroubled path up the slope. He paused at the top, turned and waved: a vial of holy water now appeared in his other hand and he began intoning a long adulation of the bar-cum-restaurant-and-children's-playground as he splashed this around the doorway.

I glanced at the locals who now blocked us from a clear view of the proceedings – you had to dip and dive to see properly – and on their faces was a look of utter respect, almost awe. I wanted to smile but didn't dare. I wanted to pass a comment to Caran, Lorraine or even Joyce but didn't dare; it just seemed to me, in that English way of mine, that there might be just be something more important that an archbishop should be doing. I could imagine this picture of the archbishop splashing his holy water around the door-jam popping up on *Have I Got News For You* and Paul Merton or Ian Hislop being asked to think of a caption.

Eventually I looked across at Lorraine and caught her eye; she wasn't thinking of Paul Merton or Ian Hislop. Somewhere in the crowd would be Dakos; what would be the expression on his face?

Day 10: Jeep Safari

Joyce:

I really wasn't looking forward to this but, when our rep had gone on about how wonderful it was, Lorraine and Caran were over the moon, as they say, and persuaded me to go; I noticed the rep was not with us, but I supposed she would get her cut! She had warned us "*not* to wear anything we intended to wear again!" in that hysterical way they speak when they are working up the crowd, and so we didn't really know what to expect.

Not that Caran would have "dressed down" for anyone, anyway; she was wearing something from Noa Noa – a white, singlet top over a pair of faded-blue, hipster jeans. The phrase "mutton dressed as lamb" came to mind but that wasn't really fair – she did look gorgeous. The accessories did, I have to admit, enhance the outfit – the white bucket bag slung from her shoulder and the hair band. The rest of them had their sunglasses pushed self-consciously up into their hair, but not Caran – hers rested casually on a white hair band, which matched the white belt in the jeans. "It's always nice to be able to see through your glasses when you wear them, isn't it?" she said, archly, as we waited for the jeep to turn up. I couldn't but agree with her. One of those French actresses – Brigitte Bardot or someone like that – started the "sunglasses in your hair" fashion way back in the fifties and, the thing is, you can never see through them when you put them on because they are always smeared with something from your hair. Looked good for the cameras, no doubt! Mind you, she slept with just about anybody, didn't she? That dirty devil, Vadim, was doing the rounds of the young actresses at the time. I've never seen the attraction myself.

Lorraine was her usual self; she had the inevitable low-cut top flopping carefully over a pair of straw-coloured three-quarter length trousers and a sleeveless safari jacket. I noticed all the men eyeing her as the jeeps pulled up. I was wearing a floral dress – I really dislike trousers – and a straw hat. There's something so English about a straw hat, isn't there?

I say "jeeps" pulled up because there were four of them. I don't know why, but we'd expected a single jeep with people from our hotel, and it was a little disconcerting to find hordes of strangers on the same safari. It was apparent from the start that that this excursion was going to cater for the vulgar. The lead driver was a short, stocky man who told us to call him 'Rambo'. Well, I ask you, we'd have been better off turning back there and then – never mind the money! Rambo was a typical swarthy foreigner – one of those men who assume that they are automatically attractive to women, especially foreign women, and that they have some preordained right to paw you. To be fair, he didn't actually paw us but the hands were all over the place. Call it courtesy, if you like, but an Englishman would have helped us into the jeep with a little more delicacy.

Robert and I had been part of a group of friends once and one of them – nice though he was – was one who couldn't keep his hands to himself. I'd never known quite how to deal with it and all Robert had said was "Go with it. He's harmless enough. It's the quiet ones you've got to watch." How true that turned out to be! Anyway, this Rambo helped us into his jeep – hosed down from the previous trip but not exactly clean. Caran annoyed those already seated by insisting on spreading her beach towel to sit on; Lorraine said she wasn't bothered, but I appreciated the gesture and sat next to Caran.

Rambo turned out to be more than just a "pawer": he was also one of those self-styled comedians. It was obviously going to be an exhausting day. I can't quite capture his style of speech but it went something like:

"I am Kypros Andreastophilus but you may call me Rambo. See – I have the muscles."

He pulled up his rolled sleeve further and exposed a bicep that looked and felt (Caran touched it, I didn't) like a rock.

"I am the safari leader! This is my jeep! You are in the best jeep on the safari, but we shall stay together."

He was dressed in African safari gear. He wore a khaki shirt with sleeves rolled to his biceps (I suppose they wouldn't go any further) and with the neck open to show his sweaty, hairy chest. He had a body warmer full of pockets and loops and things, and combat trousers – also full of pockets – tucked into leather boots and secured around the waist with a wide leather belt. Around his head was a red neckerchief – what Caran called a "bandana". Not exactly Stewart Grainger and I couldn't see Deborah Kerr falling for him, but everyone else seemed to love him. He made great play with Lorraine's safari jacket, touching her pockets and his, and – of course – with Caran's head band. Trust her to catch the right note before we'd even started! He looked like one of those American character actors who always turned up in those 1950s Westerns: smaller than Charles Bronson and uglier, but if you can imagine Bronson's face screwed up around the eyes and mouth even more than usual, you'll get the general idea of what this Rambo looked like.

"First we go for the petrol and the hoses!"

A great roar went up at this; we later discovered that some of these people came here every year and *always* went on this trip because Rambo was such fun. The jeeps careered through the streets of the resort, clearly expecting everyone to get out of the way, ending up in a back alley next to a line of dirty petrol pumps. You couldn't actually imagine the petrol from these working! A maze of hoses appeared as the drivers leaped from the jeeps; you could smell the petrol as the nozzles clanked into the tank. The other drivers were all much younger men than Rambo who must have been well into his forties, but looked fifty or more because of the time he had spent in the sun. After the tanks were full, they rushed about with large plastic containers – the kind you see people using on caravan holidays – filling those from other hoses. The people in the jeeps were obviously better informed than us because they too rushed out and filled empty Coke bottles and the like; there was an air of excitement I didn't understand at that moment. Rambo grinned and began handing round a collection of plastic bottles he kept under the seats.

"Fill, fill. We are the best jeep."

There was a moment's pause when all the bottles had been filled and I thought we were waiting for somebody to come for the petrol money but nobody did; then Rambo and the other drivers turned the hoses on the jeeps. It was pandemonium; there was yelling, screaming and laughter – all delivered at that hysterical holiday pitch – and we were sprayed from head to foot. So much for Caran's outfit! Mind you, she didn't seem to mind; I suppose she thought it would be a good idea to make the best of it! Rambo and the other drivers were creased up with laughter and then they turned the hoses on themselves. A few moments before we had been well-turned out holiday-makers – now we looked like drowned rats! It was right up Lorraine's street, of course; her big laugh filled the alley. Rambo appreciated this, gave her what he thought was a sexy look, jumped aboard and we were off!

The trip out of town was maniacal, with Rambo determined to keep his jeep in the lead and the younger men equally determined to overtake him; as the jeeps passed each other and criss-crossed through the other traffic the holiday-makers shook and squirted the water from their bottles over the other passengers until all of us were soaked to the skin yet again. Caran had obviously decided that there was everything to be gained and nothing to be lost by joining in, and she and Lorraine were standing, tumbling, gripping the cross-bars and shaking water from their Coke bottles with the best of them – as Robert would have said. I just held on to my hat and hoped the jeep wouldn't turn over in the road. The locals just jumped out of the way and cheered us on; even the odd policeman waved us past – glad to see the back of us, no doubt. We raced through villages, scattering market stalls; mothers grabbed their children's hands and ran for safety to the side of the road –

there were no footpaths. Traders held on to their produce and yelled with feigned anger.

"This is Rambo – eh? They love Rambo."

And they did: every now and then the jeeps screeched to a halt and he would stop and speak to someone or buy some fruit, and the villagers gathered round as though he was a favourite uncle. Once he bought four melons, sliced them up with what looked like a machete and handed them round the jeeps. We were now soaked with water, gritty with sand and sticky with melon juice; and then the jeeps were off on their mad race again.

"We are heading for the Koodos Hills. Soon we shall stop for coffee."

When we did, I must admit the place was lovely. It was all you would expect of a peasant village – white-washed walls, dusty courtyards, pergolas hung with grape vines, rustic tables and coffee hot from ceramic jugs. The women who served us, obviously the mother and daughters of this family taverna, wore headscarves and white aprons over the long skirts and billowing blouses; their forearms were still dusty with bread flour and they served the local equivalent of croissant with the coffee. There was no question as to whether we wanted this – it was simply served as though to welcome a stranger. For the children, there was a lot of fuss and jugs of homemade lemonade. Rambo was very attentive, making sure that everyone had what they wanted; he fussed around the tables, was quite taken with my straw hat and kept referring to me as "The Memsahib" which I rather liked although I wasn't sure whether he intended it as a compliment. He seemed very at home here and was welcomed with hugs and kisses. He also collected the payment; Lorraine smiled and said "I told you". There were the usual grumbles from the Brits used to all-inclusive prices but we stumped up and I, for one, was glad of the break and the coffee.

The jeeps sped on and we had almost the sense of an adventure; now that I was dirty, I'd given up caring. Here we were, out in the wilds of Cystos and in the hands of Rambo and his drivers. He stopped frequently as we raced through the foothills of Koodos:

"Here is the monastery for the saint who guided Paul and Barnabas through the Koodos Mountains. He lived in the cave – you see? He was a big man like Rambo. Each day the women brought him a sheep for his dinner – stewed in the juices of the vegetables, just like Rambo likes it! His skull is here, in the silver reliquary. Touch it and you will be healed. It has the powers of the miracles. The miracles are the miracles of Rambo's people. The nuns are meticulous. They tend the shrine. Here it is an oasis of greenery in the dry Koodos."

"What's a ... relick ... what was the word?" whispered Lorraine.

I must admit it wasn't a word I'd ever heard either, but didn't like to ask; it surprised me that someone like Rambo, who clearly wasn't educated, had even heard of it but he heard Lorraine's whisper.

"Reliquary?" he called, "Come I will show you. Rambo knows all the words!"

Arms around her shoulders, he escorted Lorraine through the immaculate gardens and into the little shrine; she grinned back at us as they entered. I saw Rambo cross himself when they passed under the arch. When they returned, two nuns came with them; Rambo showed great deference to these women, and Lorraine had her head covered. It's so strange in these places – the mixture of the religious and the carnal.

"It was lovely," said Lorraine. "A little silver casket set into a niche in the wall."

Most of us wanted to see it then, of course. Two by two, escorted by the nuns, we were guided into the shrine while Rambo stood at the door collecting the money. One or two of the youngsters couldn't be bothered to wait, of course, and hadn't the manners to feign an interest. They lolled about by the jeeps, flirting or chatting with the drivers. Sometimes, you're almost ashamed to be British.

Looking around as we waited I could well believe that half of us are overweight and one in five actually obese. There was one couple in particular who seemed to make a virtue of their grossness. She was a big woman with a slab face and rotten teeth – decayed from bad eating and yellow from smoking. She had what used to be called 'mutton chop arms' – great fleshy, muscular things. You could imagine her as a farmer's wife – carrying big buckets of slop for the pigs or lifting calves off the ground with one arm. Yet her husband doted on her: it was so obvious from his moony face and the way his arms were always around her shoulder as though protecting her from the world. He had the usual pot-belly, of course, and I noticed that when we were given that beautifully warm bread in the taverna, they asked for butter! Mind you, they didn't stand out from the general throng. As Caran said afterwards it was a bit like going on holiday with the Wobbly Men and Women: round shoulders, backs pulled forward by the weight of their stomachs, knees bent. Most of them simply slouched along looking like the letter S.

The jeeps sped on and I must admit, although I disapproved of the way they were driving, it was very exciting. As the road climbed, it twisted and turned on hairpin bends; usually we were "off road", as they say, and it was bumpy and dusty and always, it seemed to me, skirting along the edge of an abyss. There were cherry trees everywhere, and Rambo stopped and picked some, handing them round, opening his own mouth and stuffing huge bunches in; they were delicious, although I was careful to wipe them clean after they'd been in his hands.

"The village there is Medoulas. Maybe we shall come back this way in the afternoon when they are all asleep or having the siesta – yes? The memsahib will like that?"

He passed his toothy leer round the jeep with more cherries.

"Faith is alive and well in Cystos. You see – a new church to the Virgin. The church is built with money and muscle."

He pointed out a beautiful sand-coloured building as he yet again flexed his biceps. All turrets and domes, the church must have been three stories high. How could they afford to build such places here in this peasant country?

"We are to cross the bridges built by the Venetians five hundred years ago. The camels would carry the copper from the Koodos down to Craphos. Ah but there are no camels now. Then – thousands. Now – two, giving rides to the tourists. Hold tight."

I cannot describe the next part of our journey; I had my eyes closed most of the time, but caught glimpses of long, narrow bridges with short stone walls on either side as the jeeps careered across them. They were so narrow: fine, no doubt, for a camel, but not designed for jeeps racing each other – while the passengers squirted water – at sixty miles an hour. How many times we tottered on the edge I was too nervous to count, but I did catch occasional glimpses of the ravines which fell away from the road. Eventually, Rambo – whose jeep always regained the lead if ever he lost it – led the others to a clearing by the side of the road. Our off-side tyre was poised on a rock from which there was a drop of hundreds of feet.

"Careful as you get out, ladies, sweet ladies. Rambo will lend a hand. Come make way for the memsahib first."

Yet again, the helpful paw was proffered and we had no choice but to take it! The "clearing" was, in effect, a rough (and I mean 'rough') car park. No toilets or neatly arranged picnic benches here: find a rock or a bush if you couldn't wait until you got home! Behind this, through a small belt of trees, Rambo led us to yet another church or mosque or something. There was an air of expectation as Rambo opened a small, heavy wooden door and gestured us inside. The place looked more like a museum now but had once been the home of some religious sect.

There were lots of little rooms, not larger than cells and plainly furnished, around a central hall; this was complete with a splendid minstrel's gallery. From the roof hung a series of iron rings – candelabra, in fact – and these would have illuminated the central space of the hall. To one side, there was a collection of costumes, and to the other a collection of musical instruments. I didn't recognise any of them, but there were things that looked liked bassoons and balalaikas or lutes. Rambo's face was a picture of pride and expectation. He said nothing, and the other drivers followed his example as he gave us a tour of the building. As we left his eyes sparkled in the sunlight and then he spoke.

"This was the home of the Dervishes! The Whirling Dervishes! This was their home seven hundred years ago. In the big space you saw, under the candles, they would pray and dance."

I'd heard of them, of course; the old butcher in *Dad's Army* used to talk about them. What was his name – Corporal Jones? The nutty one played by Clive Dunn.

"The minstrels would play and the Dervishes would stretch out their arms as they prayed. They would lower their heads like a charging bull and spin. Watch. We will show you here. We are not allowed to perform in the museum."

What followed is barely describable. Rambo, followed by the other drivers, slowly removed his shirt and the body warmer with all the loops and pockets so that we gradually received the full benefit of his chest. It was a bit like one of those fifties movies when the hero – someone like Clark Gable – takes off his shirt and the heroine gasps as though she had never seen a chest before. One could scarcely believe that: from what David Niven had to say, on *Parkinson*, most of them were tarts. I thought for one horrible moment we were going to have to watch a complete striptease but they did stop at the waist. Rambo was obviously proud of his body – one of those physical men who like displaying themselves – and there wasn't an inch of spare flesh on him. I will say that. He was broad and extremely muscular; his torso from shoulders to waist formed a triangle of rippling muscle – not that I'm very impressed with that kind of thing myself but I could see that both Caran and Lorraine were enjoying the spectacle. Caran said afterwards – not to me but I overheard her whispering it to Lorraine – that she could imagine those arms around her waist and she wouldn't mind if he broke her back. It was comments like that which made me look forward to going home!

The dance started slowly enough as though they were meditating; they seemed to spin on one foot and push it round with the other. As they danced the four of them seemed to give out a humming noise and gradually the dance got faster and faster. It defied anything I'd ever been taught at the gym about turning constantly in one direction and they didn't just turn: they did spin, at everincreasing speeds. The midday sun beat down on their bodies until the brown muscles glistened with sweat. Occasionally, perhaps to break the intensity of the spin, they would leap into the air and lash out with their arms. It seemed to last forever and then, suddenly, was over; they knelt on the ground arms akimbo. We applauded, of course – what else could you do? Like it or not it was impressive.

You might guess what happened next: oh yes, we were invited to try it out! I ask you – the Wobblies among us looked as though they would have difficulty leaning on their trolley as they pushed it round the supermarket. You wouldn't expect them to walk anywhere, let alone dance, but they had a go! Caran and Lorraine, naturally, were easily persuaded; it was enough for them that Rambo had his arms around them with his hands running up and down their thighs as he "taught" them how to spin. At least they looked all right, but the

Wobblies were simply gross – flab flying everywhere; it was hard to see in which direction they were spinning. Lorraine said later that you had to admire the Brits – they'd have a go at anything. I'm not quite sure that admiration is the word I would have used as they flopped on to the ground, paunches and bellies everywhere! But they didn't seem to care: struggling to their feet they laughed and hugged each other, the sweat pouring off their white fat. Rambo gave me a grin and said something about "The Memsahib" enjoying herself!

The drivers' chests were now on full display as we drove on to where I hoped we might stop for lunch. Some of the young girls on the excursion were fascinated by this exhibition of naked muscle – well, they're brought up on it, aren't they – fascination with the flesh? I remember reading a story in one of those women's magazine, once; it was a magazine that used to be quite decent – *Woman's Weekly* or something. This young girl was off to get a job in a holiday resort and on the way she meets this young man who steps out of the sun – naked except for a pair of shorts and leather boots. Of course, he's all "rippling muscle" and "breathtakingly handsome". She shares her lunch with him, her skirt rides up, her bra is skimpy and before we know where we are, it's all "muscular thighs" and "groans". We hear a bit about his being "a red-blooded male with a red-blooded sex drive" and then a bit more about "muscular torsos" and before you know it she's handing him a … well it's not a word that was mentioned until recently in any nice paper – and it's her who's handing it to him!

I was right; we soon pulled up by the side of a river. Somehow, the jeeps must have driven down into the

valley and Rambo told us that this was our lunch stop –
our siesta time, he had to add!

"Swim. You will swim while Rambo makes the
lunch."

Across the river were countless numbers of – what
shall I call them, couches? They floated on the water and
families sprawled in them. It wasn't as it would have
been at home – clean plastic seats and tables to picnic on:
these were like little rooms complete with carpets, blan-
kets, cushions and a sun canopy. They were attractive
enough to look at, but you couldn't help wondering how
often, if ever, they were cleaned and how many families
had used them. The riverside clearing was packed not
only with tourists but with local people. Caran and
Lorraine wasted no time in finding a room to spread
ourselves out in, but I wandered up to what turned out
to be a restaurant. It's best not to describe the toilets, but
they were better than a bush – if one had had the fore-
sight to bring some paper. The restaurant menu was
filled with afelias, kleftikos, mezes, moussakas, souvlas,
stiffados ... and so on, but Rambo and the other drivers
were already lighting a fire.

"They're going to make a barbecue. Lunch is
provided as part of the trip," said Lorraine, "I've seen
this before, in Bulgaria – you watch."

They made the barbecue from wood they had
picked up on the way. I'd seen them foraging in the
woods for sticks and had wondered why – now I could
see. They burned the wood to make their own charcoal
and used this to cook kebabs on the shore in a circle of
stones. The kebabs were also wooden sticks they'd
picked up, with the meat and vegetables skewered on
them. I suppose the heat from the charcoal sterilised

them, but they didn't look as clean as the ones you get out of a packet at home, and I wondered why they didn't catch fire. Robert always used to soak his skewers in water for hours, and still they caught fire and the meat fell off into the barbecue.

The food they produced was very plain, simply some kind of meat on sticks interspersed with pieces of what looked like pork fat; with this we were offered salad and bread. The salad was – thank goodness – pre-packed; I was glad about that – I wouldn't want to think that they had washed it. It was all I ate; great chunks of meat have never really appealed to me and the lumps of fat were the deciding factor.

I was the first to eat because everyone else was in the river, splashing around; it was very rustic with ropes hanging from trees and rope bridges strung across from bank to bank. Rambo had brought me my lunch on a tray and handed it over with a little bow and his "memsahib" remark. While the younger drivers prepared the charcoal, Rambo had enticed everyone into the water by pretending to piggyback Caran across. Of course, she had been keen to volunteer – not that she had much choice, really, because Rambo just picked her up, but she climbed on to his back readily enough. When he got her out into midstream, pretending to take her to the opposite bank, he tipped her off; I don't think she was too pleased – her hair was soaked right through and hung in rat's tails. She rather looked her age at that moment. But it got everyone else into the water, including the Wobblies, and then Rambo left them to it while he supervised the cooking of the meat.

"Not exactly your 'Maple Chicken with Orange and Watercress', is it Joyce?" said Lorraine as she sat in our water-borne couch stuffing her face, meat juices running down her chin. She gave that big laugh of hers.

"Or 'Skewered Meatballs with Chilli, Olive and Nut Sauce'," laughed Caran.

"Is that what Simon cooks at home?"

"Yes. It impresses our friends, of course, but it all seems a little pretentious now."

"I'm sure he's only doing what he thinks you want," I said.

I felt sorry for Simon; I didn't socialise with them at home, but I did know him because I worked with Caran and he came to various "dos". He seemed a nice man.

"I know, but these are real men, aren't they? They don't spend hours discussing with their wives what they are going to cook. It's onto the skewer and into the fire."

I couldn't resist it: I didn't want an argument, but there was a point of principle at stake here.

"And that would be the kind of man you prefer – someone who just 'gets on with it' without a by your leave?"

"It looks good from where I'm sitting at the moment, Joyce."

I didn't reply. A lot of wine went with the meal and Caran and Lorraine were swigging it back. As we ate, the young drivers swam past and took a bite of the meat and fat Caran and Lorraine offered them; it was all getting a little carnal. I wasn't surprised at Caran's behaviour, but I was surprised that she tucked in so ravenously to the food. She was clearly someone who normally watched her figure. I wondered whether, if she ever actually lived out here, she would end up as one of those old Cystonian women – fat and slumped in a cane chair. There was no doubt in my mind that Lorraine would!

"You are enjoying the food?"

Rambo's head popped up from the water and he climbed aboard without being asked; he was virtually naked now and the legs on him matched his chest – huge calf muscles and heavy thighs. I could see Caran looking him over; there's nothing more embarrassing than naked lust in a woman.

"Come on Rambo's 'Ethnic Night' and his family will cook the special food for you."

"This is lovely, Rambo," said Lorraine.

"But the special food is better. We have the shish kebab where we make the onion puree ourselves and then, in a large bowl, mix it with the lemon and the oil and the cinnamon. And then we marinate the lamb in this for three to four hours or, better still, over the night."

"And do you cook this, Rambo?"

"No, no – the cooking at home is for the women. My wife would throw me out of the way," he laughed, "My wife and daughters cook for the guests."

"You have daughters?" asked Caran.

"Three. They are most beautiful. The eldest is Marjoria. She is a blonde Aphrodite. An unusual beauty. She moves with such grace, it is like sleepwalking. She is tall and long-haired and gentle. Her voice is low and slow – such a wonder in a woman. I never knew her to lose her temper. She will be a natural mother and skilled with her needle, making clothes for all her children and she will have many. Dorottea, the next one, is a devil. She is pretty and dangerous like a cat. She is a spark and the boys do well to know that. Dorottea is quick and noisy.

The boys like her. The youngest is quiet Phyllida. She is fragile and looks up to her sisters. She is the odd one and loves to help her mother and put her brothers to bed. She sings them to sleep with hymns."

"How old are they?"

"Marjoria is seventeen, Dorottea is sixteen and Phyllida is fourteen."

"And you have sons, as well?"

"Of course – three boys. They are like Rambo."

"And younger than the girls?"

"Oh yes, but full of spirit."

He then gave us a detailed description of each of his sons who were twelve, eleven and nine. I thought I had never heard a man speak so fully and so affectionately about his children. When the women at work speak of theirs it is always with an apology – especially if they are teenage girls. And how many of us are so certain how our children will be when they grow up?

"You have a big family, Rambo," I said, perhaps foolishly.

"Ah, Memsahib, I do, and one day, with all the grand-children, bigger!"

"You're sure you'll have grandchildren, then? These days children do not ..."

"All Cystonian girls marry young. The young men will come to me and say, 'Rambo! I love your daughter and I want to have her hand in marriage'. And I shall look him up and down to see if he is worthy of her, and then I shall speak to his family and all will be ....well!"

"And then she'll have lots of babies?"

"Many grandchildren, as beautiful as she is."

"What would happen if you didn't like him?" said Lorraine.

"It will not be like that. He will be a fine boy. My daughters have 'good taste'," he laughed.

"Do your girls sometimes marry … foreigners?"

"Like the English? Yes. Only last month my cousin's daughter Toula married an English boy from Grimsby."

"Grimsby?" queried Caran, as though she couldn't imagine anyone marrying someone from Grimsby.

"Grimsby – where the fish come from."

"And he will be a good husband – like the Cystonian boys?"

"Or he will find himself hanging by his heels from one of the Venetian bridges," laughed Rambo, and something told me that he meant it.

Once the Wobblies had eaten, the scene in the river became bedlam again; they say that fat people swim easily, and it was certainly true of those on the Jeep Safari. They flopped and splashed in the water like so many whales – rocking the couches and sending great waves across us. They all seemed so much in love with each other; they were forever groping and kissing in the water, and the slab-faced woman with the rotten teeth and her husband were never out of each other's arms. They staggered up to the rope bridge, stumbled across it and leaped into the river with their arms around each other and their mouths open, screaming into the air: that really started a trend!

All the youngsters copied them and soon we had dive-bombing non-stop. Lorraine and Caran joined in: as Lorraine put it - "The couch will soon be under water so we may as well be in the water!" I've never liked that kind of thing. I can't see the point of insisting that our swimming pools at home are of a certain hygiene standard and then wallowing in foreign rivers with a crowd of strangers with whose habits one is unfamiliar. Besides I didn't really want to be part of all that canoodling; thank goodness Robert wasn't like that.

It must have been mid-afternoon before the jeeps once again took to the mountain tracks. Rambo was ebullient although the rest of us were wilting in the heat. He certainly wasn't going for the fashionable "pale look" the tourist brochures talked so much about. Even the breeze, as we raced along the side of the abyss, was warm but at least we did have the scenery: everywhere out of the sun was green and in a very short while we arrived at the famous waterfall Rambo had promised us. This fell into a little grotto and would have been beautiful if the pool beneath it had been clear but, of course, the mud had been stirred up by jeep and bus loads before us. Rambo was quick to make a virtue of the mess – wouldn't he just!

"The Pool of Love, where the people of Cystos come to increase their fertility."

Where did he get words like that? It was like his knowing "reliquary" when none of us did.

"Here we make babies ...but first we prepare ourselves."

He had all of them lined up at the edge of the pool – except me, of course; I had no idea what was coming but it clearly wasn't going to be pleasant. When I declined, Rambo led me to a rock some way from the pool edge and with a courtly bow said:

"The memsahib will sit here?"

Once again, he had them all strip down as much as they dare. It was a disgusting site – all those pale, fat, almost naked bodies bleached even more by the sun. Only Lorraine, Caran and some of the young people looked reasonable and that didn't last long because Rambo and the other drivers began to daub them with mud. It was gross – how many others had been daubed by the same mud?

"The marks are the marks of Rambo. The marks ask the gods to bless the baby making."

The marks were his excuse for running his fingers over as many of the women as possible, and soon they were covered – faces, bosoms, arms, shoulders, stomachs, legs – with curves, swirls and stripes of green mud; all of this was accompanied by the usual hysterical laughter as though it wasn't possible to enjoy oneself without screaming.

"We have the wings of birds, the bodies of snakes, the heads of lions. Rambo makes all these for the making of the babies."

He had now tied a green handkerchief over his red bandana – I suppose because green is always associated with fertility – and proceeded to join the line along the edge of the pool. I thought, for a moment, that he was going to push backwards and take them all in with him, but no; nicely placed between Lorraine and Caran – by far, I must say, the most attractive women there (not that there was much competition) – he began to teach them a dance.

"Watch Rambo. The Cystonians know how to dance. We taught the Greeks and, before them, the gods. Rambo will show you. Legs apart and bring your right leg up to your left. Sway a little. Move your left leg away from your right. Bring it back. Sway a little. Move your right leg back then together with your left, but a little behind. Sway a little and move to the left."

This went on interminably with everyone falling over (more hysterical laughter) and stumbling against each other (more opportunity for wrapping your arms around your neighbour) until they were falling about in all directions.

"Now watch Rambo's arms."

These were then placed at shoulder height – he'd obviously been watching Anthony Quinn in *Zorba the Greek* – and round the shoulders of your neighbours: more groping, and from two people at once, but Lorraine and Caran loved it, and the whole lined swayed to and fro, and danced to the left and then back to the right. I must say it was impressive. None of our dance teachers at evening class ever taught Robert and I to dance as quickly as Rambo taught the Jeep Safari! By now the mud pictures were baked hard on everybody and Rambo said:

"And now – follow Rambo."

He went to the head of the line and led them a circuitous dance along the edge of the pool and then up a wet, muddy track through leaves and fronds to the top of the waterfall. As they approached it, the dancers all realised what was coming and the screams and laughter approached epidemic proportions. Rambo came out first at the head of the fall. I don't know how high it was – I've no idea – but it seemed very high to me and the water plunged noisily into the pool below.

"Watch Rambo."

He stood, with all his muscles flexing, and raised his arms like an Olympic diver about to do a plain header; a little bend of his knees and away he dived, arms coming together as he entered the water. There was a tremendous round of applause – in admiration, envy and fear, I suspect – as his head bobbed up from the pool.

"You see?"

He reached his chest up from the water with a little kick of his legs and then duck dived to show us his legs.

"All the paintings are washed away. The god of the waterfall has accepted Rambo's gift. Rambo now makes good babies. Come and make good babies with Rambo."

In the melee which followed, some dived, some jumped, some climbed down the rope ladder beside the fall and others turned and returned by the track, but all ended up in the pool. Caran won an enormous round of applause for her dive, and a heavy cuddle and kiss from Rambo when she rose from the water.

"The Goddess of Love," he kept shouting as he swam with her round the pool.

Lorraine took one look at the drop and returned along the track laughing all the way. She didn't seem bothered in the least that she hadn't attempted to jump or dive. I must say, I felt rather mean that I hadn't had a go.

By the time Rambo had had his way – so to speak – in the pool, it was late in the afternoon. Filthy with mud that didn't quite wash off, hair in lank strands and sticky with suntan lotion, everyone made their way to the cliff above the fall and climbed back into the jeeps. I suppose I was the only one who looked remotely respectable and Rambo ushered the others aside while he helped his "Memsahib" aboard.

"We go now to Medoulas, where they will all be asleep and having the siesta – yes? The memsahib will like that?"

The jeeps raced back to Medoulas – dust flying, brakes screeching – and roared to a halt in the village square. The silence then was absolute, and Rambo held his finger to his lips as he looked around and helped us from the jeep. You couldn't call it a smart place; many of the buildings were ramshackle or old or both, but it did have its own charm. Cherry trees were everywhere and the residents seemed to be dozing under them as the heat of the afternoon passed into the evening. There was no litter, I must say that – just dust. The people were well-dressed – not expensively but smartly – and the older men were handsome in that Mediterranean way: deeply tanned faces and silver hair.

"This is the favourite resort of my people. We come here to escape the heat of the coast."

The streets were narrow and the shops unchanged by time. There were no designer labels here – the goods seemed to fall back into the interior of the shops. Awnings stretched out over the streets, protecting fruit and vegetables from the heat of the sun. People were beginning to stir now, but slowly, with no bustle or sense of urgency, going about their business calmly. They were very courteous and helpful, emerging from the dark of their shops to interest us in their goods. Soon, of course, we were buying something from each shop we passed and Rambo greeted everyone with that toothy grin of his as he led us to another sunlit square and another café. This time it was tea – scented and fragrant. I'm not impressed by the current fashion for herbal teas – it's just a fad like any other – but this was very pleasant and, as we sat at the rough wooden tables drinking it, I really did feel like the Memsahib. Plates of biscuits accompanied the tea.

"Baklava," said Lorraine, "They are a speciality of the island."

"How do you know?" I asked.

"Dakos told me. We ate them at his cousin's restaurant in the hills."

"Dakos – you know Dakos?" said Rambo – missing nothing, as usual.

"He took me for a day out."

"Ah – you are the Lorren! He talks of no one else."

"You know Dakos?"

"We all know Dakos. Rambo knows all the big men in Craphos. Rambo is the entrepreneur!"

He then went on to gild the lily somewhat, saying that this Dakos talked of no one but "Lorren". We were led, yet again, through the usual spiel about "the island of love", lots of stuff about "philosophers and poets" and the inevitable trip down Mythology Lane to Aphrodite, "the goddess of love, beauty and sexual rapture". I must say, listening to him and thinking about the way he had talked of his children, I could see his charm. It was certainly more impressive than the kind of thing you got from Englishmen of any age, and I felt a certain admiration for the way in which he flattered and cajoled; it was better than the loutish approaches English males seem to make, and I could see how the locals might "poach" female holiday-makers.

Lorraine was subdued on the final race back and I could see Caran watching her with interest. I really couldn't believe that Rambo had renewed her interest in that Dakos. Why couldn't she just be satisfied with what she'd got?

Caran:

It had been a great day! I may have ended up looking like the bag lady and it isn't everyone who could cope with having their Noa Noa outfit washed in mud, bleached by the sun, covered in dust and drenched time and again in water, but it was nice to know that I could afford to – and that I was worth it! I'd really fancied Rambo; if you wanted a bit of rough in a foreign country, you couldn't go far wrong with him! These foreigners are so uncomplicated, aren't they? Simon never wasted too much time as far as that kind of thing was concerned, mind you!

Lorraine and I had enjoyed the day, and I think Joyce did too, in her own way; she hadn't taken much part in the festivities, but she was one who enjoyed watching others make a fool of themselves and her comments about the "Wobblies" when we arrived home had Lorraine and me in stitches – so, all in all, a good day out.

The return journey was just as mad as the rest of the day, with the jeeps racing each other to, and through, the town. I wondered how real the excitement of Rambo and his drivers was – I mean were they always like that or was it an act for the tourists? They'd flashed a mobile phone or two, but hadn't dropped everything to respond to its demands; they hadn't spent the whole day "checking their e-mails" in case there was something that "couldn't wait"; they hadn't had to "pop out" to get something; they hadn't had to turn round and drive into town to collect a daughter who couldn't be bothered to walk from the bus station; they hadn't dashed from one job to the next. Yet we had crammed so much into the day – and, when we did get back to Craphos, they'd sat around with us at a local bar. They'd been so relaxed, so totally absorbed in us, in what they were doing. They hadn't been on holiday, but they had made a holiday of what they were doing, and they'd been men – real men – in everything they did, not the half-men you get at home now who are virtually indistinguishable from the women in what they do.

Watching them, I'd thought of Simon. Around the house, he's no different to me: he does exactly the same jobs I do – cooking, cleaning, ironing, taxi-ing the girls, cutting the grass, loading the dishwasher. I just couldn't see Rambo or his young drivers doing any of that at all! "If you treat your man like a doormat, you can't expect a tiger in the bedroom." Who said that – some smart aleck who'd lost her tiger!

This was our tenth day. We were over halfway through our holiday now and had only four days left; soon we'd be back to the treadmill and the daily routine. The girls hadn't rung me – although I'd phoned home each evening – and neither had Simon. Lorraine said that she and Barry had agreed not to ring unless there was an emergency; otherwise, she said, you end up worrying about what's going on at home instead of enjoying your holiday. Mind you, I can't see Lorraine worrying about anything too much; she isn't the sort – there aren't many worry lines on her!

Now, following Rambo's remarks, she had the hots for Dakos again and planned to see him, if she could, that night. Good luck to her! It was going to leave me with just Joyce for another evening, but I thought that we might meet up with Frank or Noel and Tony – not that my memory of the night with Noel was something to dwell on; the least said the better – but we might have a laugh in company.

I'd taken a long time over my bath, partly to shorten the evening with Joyce but also because it's a pleasure you don't get at home; there's always a daughter knocking on the bathroom door – and no, she can't use the other toilet because she doesn't like it! So I relaxed in my Aromatherapy Dermo Gel Bath which contained eight anti-oxidants, both rapid and delayed-release which were dedicated exclusively to my skin, helping it look strong, instantly smoother and more radiant, reducing those visible signs of ageing – commonly referred to as lines and wrinkles. I must say, I felt better for it. I dressed in my creamy rayon top and slate-blue linen-mix shorts, and finished my appearance off with a chain-link necklace of Celtic silver which Simon had bought for me on one anniversary. I'd seen the look in one of those glossy mags on some celeb who was "flying the flag for normal women", in an outfit where the shorts alone cost her nearly three hundred pounds. Mine weren't exactly Stella McCartney; Joseph did the trick for me!

As it turned out, Joyce was OK company, if somewhat pensive. She wanted it both ways, really – wanted a man without the bother of having one! I suppose we're all like that sometimes, but she was no longer married and couldn't afford the luxury of switching off; when you're dating you have to keep turned on and that wasn't in Joyce's line. I found her Robert De Niro story strange. I just couldn't imagine her arranging to meet an unknown man like that; it shows what you'll do when you're desperate.

As we sat after dinner, Joyce with her "dry, white wine" and me with my "French Whore" (well, why not, it embarrassed the young waiter when I asked for it) she began telling me about a 'love letter' she had written after her divorce. It had taken her three days to write.

"I wanted to get it right. I didn't want to meet him under false pretences. I wanted him to know where he stood. It was someone I'd known years before. It wasn't a real love letter, of course – just a letter to say what had happened with Robert and how it would be nice to meet up again. Young people today are so 'laid back' about that kind of thing that they wouldn't have given it a second thought. I mean, women actually ask men out, don't they? – and buy the drinks and pay for the meal! But I wasn't used to that, not even when I was courting. You'd have had to be a bit of a slut to approach a man in that way, and he would have taken it the wrong way. It would have been a sure sign that you were after him. Not that any decent man would have accepted, anyway – he would have been ashamed to have a woman pay for him. I did trust Vic. I knew he wouldn't try anything on if we did meet. It just seemed such a nice idea and I was so lonely. It really is a couple's world, isn't it? You can't go far on your own without a man.

We'd worked together before Robert and I married. At one time, people thought we might make a go of it, but there was always Robert – in the background in those days, but always there. We'd got on very well then. We used to go to evening classes together. My Dad had gone mad because he thought that Robert and I were a certainty and that I had no right to be going out with another man, but Robert didn't mind. 'What's in an evening class?' he used to say and so Vic and I went to French Conversation together. Anyway, after the divorce, as I said, I wrote this letter to him. We had kept in touch over the years – Christmas cards, that sort of thing, so it wasn't too out of the way. I would sit at the bureau in our lounge and think about him. I knew he'd grown a bit fat but he'd always been on the plump side – an over-fed bachelor, I suppose – but he had a nice smile and was easy company, so I suggested, in the letter, that we might meet up for a meal or something.

I knew it wasn't going to be a meeting of "similar spirits" as it had been with Robert and me – just companionship. I wrote the letter and kept re-reading it, wondering whether it was too forward. I must have written it a dozen times. The waste basket was filling up with my screwed-up rejections! I kept wondering, too, what my friends would think if they knew I was writing it. I kept reminding myself to empty the waste paper basket when I had finished. I didn't want the cleaner to find what I'd written ...."

"Well what happened?" I said, impatiently, I suppose; her story was getting nowhere.

"I never posted it."

"Never posted it?"

"I couldn't. It would have been too embarrassing answering the phone if Vic had responded, and even worse if he hadn't."

Day 11: Evening Cruise

Lorraine:

I'd decided – well, almost decided – to leave the Dakos thing alone until Rambo's comments. It wasn't that I had changed my mind about him, but more that I could see no way forward; but it had played on my mind and so, when we got home from the Jeep Safari, I went looking for him. I can't say I was easy about this; our conversation on Saturday had been – well, fairly blunt. He had made it clear what he thought of Englishwomen on holiday, and me in particular, but what the hell? Nothing ventured, nothing gained – and I could give as good as I got in any argument with any man. More than that, I wanted him to understand a few things about me. I wasn't prepared to be dismissed, and if he was still interested in me – as Rambo had suggested – well, there might be a way forward.

I discovered that he would be at his family restaurant – the Ariadakos – and so I made my way there, leaving Joyce and Caran to have another quiet night in. I was in no hurry. If I was to have any conversation with him, it would be after the restaurant closed in the early hours. I didn't want to appear too eager, of course – that would have given exactly the wrong impression since he already needed "squaring up" as far as "Englishwomen" were concerned – so I had decided to take the line that I simply wanted to "clear the air" and see where it went from there.

The restaurant was as beautiful and peaceful as I remembered it, with the walled courtyards. It was more like an oasis than a restaurant. In the very centre, a grapevine climbed skywards and seemed to cling to a pergola which was supported by the surrounding walls. It was shady and I could see roses, clematis and what looked like honeysuckle. It was paved with old stone slabs, laid rather higgledy-piggledy. Shade was the key feature here, with strong masses of leaves, while some-one had cared enough to see that seasonal colour was achieved by the use of bright blossoms in tubs and pots. Dust is usually everywhere abroad, but it was clear that someone cared for these courtyards – the plants dripped water and the slabs were clearly hosed down each day. It was a nice place to eat – cool in the heat of the Cystos night. The waiters recognised me from my previous visit and fussed around. I guessed that Dakos would be cook-ing and so I ordered a kleftiko on which, I knew, he prided himself; besides, I enjoy eating and wanted a meal that would last.

"Would madam like a drink while she waits?"

"Yes please, I'll start with a jug of wine. There's no hurry. I have all night."

"Madam is expected?"

"Possibly."

He was a young man, probably one of Dakos' nephews, and he frowned as I spoke. The vagueness of "old people" is always puzzling to the young, which is nicely ironic, if you care to think about it. He assumed that Dakos had invited me and couldn't make out why I would be there if he hadn't; but then the young don't have our cheek, do they?

He poured the wine when it came and fussed around me with dainty slices of Cystos bread and olives. He was perplexed as to why a woman would be eating alone in a public place. Several men from the neighbouring tables were eyeing me up but they had their wives with them so I smiled back, freely. The young waiter just glared at them. He had assumed the role of my bodyguard for the evening. Young men are attracted to older women, aren't they? I remember Barry talking about it once. We were chatting in that way of ours, and he recalled an occasion when he had been about fifteen. His parents had taken him to visit a friend of theirs and they'd met a young married neighbour. He said he couldn't take his eyes off her; she would have been thirty-something, he said – quite old to a teenage boy – and all evening, she had been fiddling with the lacy cup of her bra. He hadn't realised it then, of course, but her movements had been quite deliberate; flattered by the attention of a young man, she had held him in her power all night with the flicker of a finger on lace.

"What's your name?"

"Stevos – I am Dakos' nephew."

He laughed; I laughed.

"You are learning the art of the family restaurant?"

"I only work here in the holidays. I am a student at the university ...."

"In Abydos?"

"Yes. You know the university?"

"No, no."

"Then you must go. We are very proud of it. The standards are very high and when I qualify, I shall go to England."

"What are you studying?"

"Chemistry. I am going to be a chemist."

"And work in England?"

"Yes. I need to get away from Cystos. All my life I have been here. I shall work in England and see Europe – France, Germany, Italy, Luxembourg ..."

"Everywhere?"

"Everywhere ....you must excuse me."

He dashed off to take another order. Isn't it wonderful to be young? Stevos had his whole life before him – but then, don't we all, all the time? 'Tomorrow is the first day of the rest of your life': someone once said.

The kleftiko arrived (after five hours on a bed of cinders in a sealed clay oven steaming in its own juices) and with it a brief appearance by Dakos, who arranged the dishes before me – the lamb, the potatoes, the broad beans in lemon, the vine-ripened tomatoes, the couscous salad – and left with a smile. Stevos continued to see that my glass was never less than half-full, and so I ate my way leisurely through into the small hours.

Other tourists drifted in and out during the night, in couples or groups, and the courtyard was ablaze with their bright holiday outfits, and a-bustle with the sober blacks and whites of Dakos' family as they served table. The joy of their service was so European; even in someone as young as Stevos, waiting was refined to an art form. They guided us all through the menu, swirled tables into new formations as different groups arrived, whipped off old cloths and replaced them with crisp new ones, dusted away crumbs between courses and provided water without being asked.

"The dessert, madam – let me recommend?"

"Go on."

"The roasted stuffed nectarines – or, if you prefer, peaches."

"No, no – the nectarines sound fine to me."

"We halve the nectarines and discard the stones. They are then placed, flesh-side up, in a shallow dish. The biscuits we crush in a plastic bag with a rolling pin. The butter is melted over a low heat and the crushed biscuits stirred in with the honey. A little of the mixture is spooned on top of each nectarine. The orange juice is poured over the fruit and they are baked for twenty minutes. While they are baking, we put the soft cheese in a bowl and beat in the sugar and orange zest. It is served to you straight from the oven."

And this was just the waiter talking! I use the word "just" with the greatest respect.

"Forget the chemistry, Stevos – you'd be wasted."

"Wasted?"

"You've never thought of being a chef?"

"Uncle Dakos is the master. I walk new ground for the family."

Later, as I sipped my brandy, an old man appeared from a side door that must have led from the kitchen; I knew at once that this was Dakos' father. He was one of those sexy old men, in the Omar Sharif mould: you know – even if he was eighty, you'd drop your knickers for him. It wasn't what he said or did or how he dressed; I'm not talking here about those old British men who dress like teenagers, drive round in open top cars, are forever making suggestive remarks, have their shirts open half-way down their chests and really fancy their chances. I'm talking about sex appeal – in the eyes, in the smile, in the manner, in the courtesy. At eighty he could still make your knees feel like jelly simply by handing you a glass of wine. He was in touch with something that we've lost.

He smiled and, when I returned it, he walked over to my table.

"I am pleased to meet you. I am ..."

"Dakos's father. I know. I can see it in your face."

"And you are Lorren?"

Oh God – to hear it said like that at eighty!

"Would you like to join me?"

"Please. My name is Georgios and I am a fisherman."

As soon as he sat down, the young waiter appeared and, after a brief exchange, two more digestives appeared.

"Metaxos. Please, you will try one with me. My son speaks so much of you and you are so lovely. He is right."

What can you say? I just smiled and looked at him. His hair was thick and nearly grey and his moustache was white; he wore a blue denim shirt that looked as though it had been made for him, it fitted so perfectly across the shoulders, and a pair of brown cord trousers. His face was tanned to the colour of Spanish leather and his hands – strong, gentle and marked with those little sunspots old people have – lay on the white table, hovering around his drink. On his wedding finger was a gold ring which was thinning now, and looked as though it had never been removed since the day he was married.

"I fish for the Ariadakos and for our other restaurant on the beach – the Karousos. There we serve only fish – fresh every day from the sea. Tonight we are taking the boat out. If you wish to join us it will be our pleasure."

The faint smile never left his eyes as he spoke and he looked directly at me.

"We?"

"No, no – not Dakos. He has done his work for today. We – the old men!"

He laughed as much to say – "You will not want to join the old men."

"I would love that – maybe another night?"

"You have only to say. You are enjoying your holiday?"

"Oh, yes, Cystos is a lovely island and for us – the Brits – it's so nice to be able to go out in summer clothes and feel the warmth all evening and through the night."

"I could not live without the warmth. During the war when we were on the mainland in the mountains it was cold. I hated the cold more than I hated the Germans. We would sit huddled together all night, the young men, for warmth."

He laughed.

"Can you imagine us – eh? – all huddled together like children to keep away the cold."

He laughed again and I laughed with him.

"But the world is a better place for it, a better place for us and for our children – all children – and our grandchildren."

Listening to him, watching him, I realised what he was "in touch" with: it was his past. His generation had fought for our freedom, as we "fought" for a comprehensive education; what would our children find that was worth the struggle?

"But you are coming nearly to the end of your holiday with us?"

"Yes, I'm afraid so – three, four more days....."

"My wife and I have lived happily together for all of our lives. For sixty years, we have loved each other and the love has grown and changed. It is the way it should be. Tonight, I shall kiss her when I leave for the sea and she will worry and scold me, but we will still love each other, even though she thinks I am a foolish old man. For your generation, it is different – things change not always for the better, but you must find your own way. My son is a stubborn man, but he is a good man. Do not let him "bamboozle" you."

He laughed; I laughed, but wasn't quite sure what to say.

"I thought you and your wife lived in the hills. You have the little shop?"

"We have a little room down by the harbour, at the Karousos. That way, she can watch the sea and the fishing boats bobbing up and down. She does not worry then – so much."

As we talked, the restaurant had cleared and begun to turn down its lamps; when I looked around, we were the only ones sitting in the courtyard. Georgios smiled.

"You must excuse me. It is later than I thought. Your company has been so enchanting. Thank you. It is not always that an old man has so much time with a beautiful young woman."

He called out to the young waiter and said something I did not understand, but Stevos hurried away to the kitchen; then he stood and kissed my hand as he left, and turned and waved when he passed out through the little arched doorway that led from the courtyard of the restaurant on to the street.

"My father has charmed you?"

Dakos stood in the doorway of the kitchen and walked over to me; I knew by his manner that his father had sent Stevos with a message to the effect that I was waiting.

"He is a very charming man."

"Yes. The old have a tolerance, born of time, which lends itself to charm."

"Charm is what you have, Dakos. It isn't only the province of the old."

My comment wasn't flattery and he knew it; it was said in defence of his father. It was also a comment on the nature of charm itself; that it oiled the works, maybe, but that there was more to life – and love – and that, perhaps, he had his father to thank for whatever charm he might have inherited?

We looked at each other for a while, neither of us quite sure how to take the evening forward; after all, he hadn't expected me and was probably unsure about why I was sitting in his courtyard with a stomach full of his kleftiko. I smile at him.

"We need to talk, Dakos. There are things between us that cannot be left unsaid."

My God, I sounded like one of those Regency novels – was it the Regency? – Georgette Heyer and that sort of thing.

"I do not feel that there is much point in pursuing such a conversation."

Had he read the novels too? "Pursuing" – where had he come across a phrase like that?

"Don't be such a prig. You fancied me enough to show me round the family estates and then you proposed to me. We have a lot to talk about and – even if you don't – I have a lot to say. I'm not prepared to be dismissed by you as yet another hot-arsed English-women who fancied a bit of Cystos."

His face was a picture. Whatever the outcome, it was going to be a formative night for Dakos. He could have walked away, of course, and simply left me to it, but I knew he wouldn't. His "charm" was a lot deeper than that; it was part of what he had inherited from his father – a natural courtesy and an inborn respect for women. I remember Steph going out with a boy once; they'd both got drunk and hired a taxi home. When he'd vomited in the taxi, the taxi driver had turned them out on the road-side. She'd been made to clear up the sick and left to pay the fare. When she turned round, her "friend" had disappeared; he'd staggered home, drunk, leaving her on the edge of a busy road to fend for herself. Dakos was not like that – could not be like that; he was, at least, a real man, and I knew he would behave like one.

"We cannot talk here, Lorren."

"Then shall we walk to your apartment?"

"My son is sleeping in the apartment. I would not wish to wake him."

"And Caran will be sleeping in our apartment and I wouldn't wish her to overhear what we will have to say. Maybe we can walk and talk?"

"Then we will walk to my apartment and talk quietly there. Michael is a sound sleeper."

Round One to me?

Craphos is beautiful at night. I'd walked it before –
once, when I'd left Dakos at the Andria on the beach and
met Frank, who'd listened and then taken me back to the
hotel. Tonight, I was with Dakos again with my whole
future strung out before me. The streets are never
deserted in Mediterranean resorts, but we walked the
back ways along by the harbour where it was going to be
as quiet "as it gets", as they say.

Dakos was ill at ease and I knew that the running, at
least at first, was going to be made by me. I didn't want
to beat the feminist drum – to sound like Germaine
Greer, but less intelligent – but I did want to fight my
corner. It wasn't just a matter of winning him over so
that he would propose again; I wanted him to see my
point of view.

The moon was out that night – although the air wasn't
filled with romance as we walked – and the houses of the
town were silhouetted against it. We walked in silence for
a while, talking about nothing – how his day had been
and what I had done and how happy his parents seemed:
you know the kind of thing. It wasn't until we were sitting
in his apartment with a cup of coffee each that we began
to really talk. I remembered the first, and only, time I had
been here. I remembered the neat little flat with one bathroom, two bedrooms and what we would call a lounge-
dining room which opened off the kitchen. I remembered
his son's bedroom, Dakos making his way around the
room tidying the books and toys, and all the while looking at his son with that expression of unremitting love.
I remembered Dakos moving around the apartment,
drawing curtains almost to close, putting on lights and

then sitting beside me on the couch, his hand brushing my hair aside, his caressing kiss, the open windows and the light breeze blowing through the lace curtains against us. The breeze still drifted from the harbour, but this time it didn't enhance our mood in quite the same way. Eventually it was Dakos who halted the flow of inanity and said, simply:

"Lorren, say what you have to say. Let us understand each other."

"I was wondering where to start."

"I fancied you enough to introduce you to my family, to take you for a trip round my island, and then to propose to you."

"Yes."

"You then told me that you already had what you call a 'partner' and could not accept my proposal. I understand that and I accept it."

"But there was more said than that. You did not approve of me."

"I was upset. I had not expected that you had a 'partner'."

"You then asked me if I would have slept with you."

"Yes – I had no right to ask that. I apologise."

"No, no, I didn't mind. It was your reaction to my answer that upset me."

"That you were prepared to be unfaithful to your 'partner'?"

"Yes. It was not a fair conclusion to draw."

"I do not want to argue with you, Lorren. I accept that your ways are different to mine. You must accept that mine are different to yours."

"But we need to understand that difference."

"Why?"

"Because you love me enough to propose to me and I feel the same about you."

"But you are not free to feel that."

It was the first time in at least thirty years that some-one had told me I was not free. I'd always been free, damn it; Barry never told me I wasn't free.

"But I am free – that is what you must understand."

"OK. I will listen."

"Barry and I never married – as I said, we wanted to remain free, to be able to 'do our own thing', as we put it in those days. The word 'partner' wasn't current coinage then. Barry and I simply 'lived together' because we wanted to – without making the commitment of marriage. We saw marriage as society's way of imposing its will on individuals, of controlling them, of making them conform to a set of rules laid down by someone else. Marriage, too, had all the trappings of turning the woman into a possession – something, like the old idea of the 'dowry', which belonged to the man."

"You are talking about 'feminism'."

"Yes – in a way, but it wasn't just women who felt like that. Men like Barry also felt that things needed to change – that women had become a 'chattel'.

"Chattel?"

"Someone else's property."

"Ah."

How much disagreement can you express in a single grunt? I was determined that he wasn't going to get away with it and pressed on:

"We also felt that women did not have the same rights within marriage, that it was an institution cre-ated mainly for the benefit of men."

"What rights were these?"

"Domestic rights ... sexual rights ... financial rights ... personal rights ... social rights ..."

"Tell me about them, Lorren. I do not understand."

I couldn't be sure that he wasn't 'drawing me on' – making me talk myself into realising that my beliefs were nonsense. I couldn't accept that he knew nothing of what I was talking about. As I hesitated, he said:

"What are these domestic rights you talk about?"

"Traditionally, women did everything around the house – cooking, cleaning, washing, looking after the children ..."

"While the men went out to work?"

"Yes – we felt that women had the right to go out to work, too."

"But your husbands were stopping you?"

"No, but women who did work also had the house to run. It wasn't fair."

"I can see that – and feminism stopped this? You now share the work and the housework?"

That wasn't quite how any of my friends saw it, I must say. Most of them reckoned they still carried the burden of the house, and the articles in women's magazines bore this out. Barry, I must say, had always done his bit, but then, that was Barry!

"Not always – though Barry does his share."

"So your feminism has achieved nothing for you?"

"Don't push me, Dakos – modern women in Britain feel better about themselves than our mothers' generation did."

"How do you know that?"

"Young women are more confident."

"How?"

"In their relationships, in the way they think about themselves."

"Their sexual rights?"

"Partly."

"What are these, Lorren? Tell me."

"A woman has the right to do what she wants with her body – to give it, to with-hold it if you like."

"And when you were younger this was not so? Your husbands or partners took you at will?"

"Once a woman was married, her husband had certain rights – conjugal rights."

"You mean Western men treated their wives like whores?"

"No – but they could."

"And this is why you and your partner did not marry – he would have treated you differently?"

His tone was still inquisitive – that of someone who was learning something new, something strange. There was no hint of condescension in his voice, and yet I couldn't help but think he was setting me up to shoot me down.

"No – Barry isn't like that. Barry would have behaved decently as husband or partner."

"Lorren – I still do not understand. Your partner treats you honourably; he shoulders his share of the domestic duties. He is a good man – a man who is out-side what this feminism of yours seeks to change."

"Yes."

"Then why did you not marry? What is this freedom you talk about? How were you more free as an unmar-ried woman?"

"It was the principle of the thing."

"Principle?"

"Yes – marriage represented the old ways. Men and women chained into relationships that imposed domestic, sexual, financial, personal and social constraints upon them. It was a chain we wanted to break."

"And your new ways do not impose these things? Today, the women of the West are domestically, sexually, financially, personally and socially free in a way that the women of your mother's generation were not?"

"Yes."

"Because of the stand your generation took?"

"Yes."

I nearly added "I suppose so", but thought it might weaken my argument and yet I couldn't quite believe it. Were Steph and her generation free-er than us? Well, she was at the moment: she was still young, had no responsibilities and could do as she pleased. Domestically she did nothing about the house at all whereas I'd been able to run a home before I lived with Barry. Sexually, she'd been bonking since she was sixteen although I don't think she was any the happier for it – she hadn't kept a boyfriend for more than a few months. Financially, she'd had her own bank account since she started the part-time job that she had to do because she needed the money to fund her social life, which was non-stop from Thursday night to Monday morning. Personally – did she feel any better about herself than I did at that age? I don't know – maybe. She certainly looked more confident but, like me then, could never find anything she looked good in and was forever changing her hair colour. Socially – yes, well, she could go where she liked and was free to ask a bloke out, buy him a drink and even pay for the meal.

Would I have been happier married to Barry, doing the things women traditionally did: spending time with my children when they were young (would I have had more than one?), cooking and baking for the family, keeping their rooms the way I like to see them and getting the beds made, arranging the family appointments with doctors and dentists, spending time in town when the children were at school, getting to know the local shopkeepers, being able to look after them when they were ill, actually getting the washing done and put away, sorting things out (the drawers, the holiday snaps – my mother kept a family album!), making sure the food cupboards were full (pickling, bottling, preserving), organising the house the way you wanted it to run and making sure everyone knew what was expected of them, remembering birthdays before they happened, preparing for Christmas before it arrived, planning family outings …?

I looked at Dakos. It wasn't easy, was it? Mine was the first generation of liberated women – the one that was to have a career and run the family, and there's no good bleating that it's expected of us. We did the expecting! I couldn't explain all this to Dakos: that this notion of freedom, of 'having it all', was somehow tied up together. The "sexual revolution", as they call it, wasn't just sexual; it wasn't simply that suddenly there was THE PILL and women could actually go and buy condoms. It was a whole new way of looking at women and their role – their rights, their responsibilities.

"Women are not men in my country, Lorren. They are respected as women. They are the centre of family life. There is no confusion. You and your partner both do two jobs – you both run the home and the work. Here we do one. I do not understand this sexual freedom of yours, but I understand it is to do with how you see yourself. What you say men have been able to do, now you are free to do – but it is not what you want to do?"

"No – and yes."

I wasn't going to let him get away with it – God, thirty years of fighting for the right to have your own pay packet, not to be solely responsible for bringing up the children, not to be tied to the home, to be as sexually active as we wished, to have a career, to gain the self-respect and self-esteem that came from being better than men at what we did ...

"But your women are not financially free, Dakos – therefore they are not personally free or socially free. They depend upon their husbands to bring home the money. Do you give them an allowance? I do not have to ask Barry for anything. We contribute to the home together and then my money is my own."

This wasn't quite true, of course: in fact it wasn't in any way true because once we started to earn a living prices went up, we all expected more and found ourselves committed to bigger mortgages, more holidays and additional clothes ....yeah, OK!

"Did you make your wife an allowance?"

Well, when you feel you're on the run, get in with the hatchet.

"We had an arrangement – yes."

"Which was?"

"My wife had so much for the house and so much for herself."

"And who decided that?"

"It was discussed between us. My wife is an educated woman."

Isn't it interesting? Suddenly, with the mention of his wife, the issues became personal; here was something real. I couldn't help going on:

"So what happened?"

"The divorce, you mean?"

"Yes, if you don't mind."

"No, no. My wife divorced me. Women do have that personal freedom on Cystos, you see."

"I'm sorry, Dakos. I didn't mean ..."

"No, no. I made comments about you and your man. It is right that you should ...be able to ask."

I waited – wouldn't you have done so? He looked uncomfortable but went on:

"My wife felt that I was neglecting her, spending too much time with my work. She was quite happy to spend the money, but felt I did not need to spend so much time earning it. It was true. Most of my waking day was spent in the restaurant. It was always the way of things on Cystos. I had expected more children, and that my wife would look after the family. I was happy to earn. I wanted to build up a successful business so that we could have a good life."

"Was your wife keen to earn her own living? Didn't you think you might run the restaurant together?"

"It was not my way. Look around you at the hotels run by the husband and wife. Where are the children?"

"But your son ..."

"I have no choice. I have to work and my wife has left me. I do the best I can."

"And your wife?"

He paused before he answered, as though he thought it was none of my business, but then said:

"She is very comfortable – thank you. She is free to work in the office in Porfos where she enjoys the social life."

"I see."

I also wondered: why had he asked me to marry him? He seemed to want a family, but I was past child-bearing age.

"Your wife is what we would call a liberated woman then, Dakos?"

"Liberated from what?"

But she was: I could just see her. She would be dressed in the latest fashions – dressed, in fact, to kill. She had a job, an additional income from her husband's restaurant and probably a share in the restaurant. She had a child, but no responsibility for her son because Dakos took that on; each night and most weekends, she was free to go where she wanted and with whom she wanted. Doubtless she had her own flat in Porfos and would need a car so that she could visit her son and – if she ran out of money – Dakos was always there to provide for her: after all she was the mother of his child. I said as much to Dakos – although not in quite those words – and he just smiled:

"She has no such rights under our law. She chose to leave her family, and must fend for herself. She has access to Michael, of course. The boy loves his mother. Your feminism would have given her all the rights you describe?"

"Yes – that's partly what feminism was about, Dakos."

"Giving a woman the right to lead her own life, but still be supported by her husband?"

"Feminism set out to establish rights for women under the law – among other things. It did not set out to exploit men."

"But that it what it does, if my wife's rights under English law would be as you describe them."

We seemed further apart than ever, so I decided to go back to the beginning and take one last tack down the river.

"You can see what I'm saying, can you – about Barry and me: that we took the decision not to marry together – freely? That I am not bound to him by the promises of marriage, that I am free to make choices about my own future, that divorce is not an issue for us as it was for you, that I am not betraying him, as you put it, because this was our agreement?"

"I think I can see that."

"If we were married, it would be different."

"But you must still have a loyalty to him?"

"Yes – but that's between Barry and me, and I know Barry, and how he will react. It may even be a relief to him."

"Relief?"

"It's not just that I've been with him thirty years – he's also been with me! He might welcome the break!"

"Do you believe that?"

"I don't know. What I do know is that he has always understood me."

"Then why do you consider leaving him?"

"We're going round in circles, Dakos. I've told you ....."

"Yes, yes – you have many more years ahead of you, and wish to make a new start."

"Which is why I accepted your proposal."

"You refused my proposal."

"At the time."

"You are changing your mind?"

"That is one reason I am here. I came to you to say 'yes' but I needed you to understand that I wasn't a tramp."

"I did not think that, Lorren. I simply could not understand how you would have agreed to sleep with me while you have a man at home."

"But you do now?"

"No. This feminism of yours is simply a way of having your cake and eating it. Your duty to your partner is no different from your duty to your husband."

"It is to me."

"Then we must agree to differ."

Are men exasperating, or are men exasperating?

"So you got nowhere?"

"I cleared the air. I made my case."

"You'd have been better off seducing him. Get him between the sheets, Lorraine. That'd change his mind. Have you arranged to meet him again?"

"Yes – before we leave. We're going out for a meal together. We can, at least, part friends."

"You can part more than that. Go for it."

Such was Caran's advice, when I returned, as we got ready for the evening cruise; but I remembered Frank's advice – that what was "normal" in our way of looking at things was so different from Dakos' world: "It's a long bridge you have to cross, Lorraine, to get back to that other world".

We'd decided that this was going to be a sophisticated evening and that we would dress accordingly. Caran's view was that "the roughs, the Wobblies and the beer-bellies" wouldn't be attracted by the idea of a Champagne supper cruising along the coast, and that we would find ourselves with a crowd of "civilised people".

Caran had chosen the black dress she'd worn on that first night, with the black silk panties and black bra, and it did look good against her naturally tanned skin and dark hair: all her clothes from Hobbs, of course! I decided on a little gold number which Barry had bought me from either Monsoon or Kookai; he had good taste in clothes, never asked me what I wanted, but just arrived with something so right and so special. This dress plunged at the neck (wouldn't it just?) and then dropped from the breasts, so that my belly was hidden, and yet clung to the back and hips. He'd been so excited when I tried it on that he'd promptly taken me from behind, which had set the evening back a while, but got us off to a nice start. Joyce was in one of her Laura Ashley dresses but very cool and summery. She did look lovely, like something from an Edwardian sketchbook.

Frank:

I'd been looking forward to meeting the three weird sisters again and I knew from my conversation with Joyce on that third day that they would be coming on this evening cruise. To be honest they were nice women – each in their own way, and I hadn't picked up anything since my night on the beach with Caran. Not that I'd tried: at my age you can usually take it or leave it, but it is nice when it comes your way and I wouldn't have said "no" to Caran. After all, we were nearly at the end of our holiday and it would be another nice little memory to take home with me.

The boat – the *Beachcomber* (will you comment or shall I?) – was more or less a floating restaurant with plenty of space both above and below decks. They do these things well, the Cystonians, and had just enough people aboard; any more and we'd have been vying for space and spilling our drinks over each other. That would have been a shame, because I was wearing my white jacket and feeling a bit like James Bond – Sean Connery's 'Bond', that is – not the other ponces that tried to follow him. I'd felt scruffy that night at Stavros' theme park opening, and had had this jacket made by a local tailor who'd measured me on Monday and delivered a perfectly fitted jacket this morning; it went well with my black trousers. I'd been tempted by the idea of a bow tie but was glad I'd stuck to the open neck when I arrived. There were few jackets around, but smart shirts (most blokes there wouldn't have got them for less than £35 a throw) open at the neck were the order of the day. The women – as always – were well dressed; my three ladies stood out, but more in the quality than the style since this had a certain uniformity.

I waved when I saw them, but they didn't notice me, and seemed to be making their way towards two other blokes. One of them was one of those 'life and soul of the party' types; as a young man he would have been considered handsome but now, at fifty-something, had allowed his paunch to sag. He reminded me of that French actor, Gerard Depardieu; he had the same kind of bulbous nose. His friend was lean to the point of being cadaverous and looked as though he had been hen-pecked over many years. I wouldn't have thought he'd held much appeal for women but you never know. He had thick wavy hair and you can never tell with women – they find

the strangest things attractive. I gave up trying to understand it – and therefore worrying about it – years ago.

The crew were obviously pleased that everyone had
taken the trouble to turn out smartly dressed; they, too,
were sharp as pins in dark blue trousers, white shirts,
and – yes – snappy bow ties.

The boat pulled away from the town and made its
way out to sea between the two arms of the harbour
mouth. This had once been a fishing village but was now
completely renovated as a marina. Each morning,
however, you could still sample the days catch on the
beach if you could be bothered to walk to the northern
end. I'd been there several times and was fed by the fisherman with barbecued sardines straight from the smoking wood. As we pulled away from the marina, the
tavernas were lit ready for their nightly trade and the
vibrant colours sparkled along the quayside. It was
another world away from Karavi Limani – the 'Clubbing
Capital of the World' – which was just a few miles along
the coast.

The *Beachcomber* was well lit, and you felt as though
you were adrift in your own little world as she pulled
away from the harbour and headed east along the coast.
The tables were all covered in blue gingham tablecloths
with matching condiment sets – no crappy sauce bottles
here! The crew drifted among us with trays of champagne and we were invited to toast Aphrodite who, it
seemed, was responsible for these vineyards having been
planted over seven hundred years ago. Having been on
Cystos for nearly two weeks I was beginning to swallow
the bullshit myself!

Our first view was to be that of the sea caves at Cap
Greco "where the rocky coastline has been sculptured

through time by wind and waves". The Cystonians had taken the trouble to illuminate the caves at night. It wasn't something I was used to here; most things seemed to have been done on the cheap – like the cafes, terraces and steps at Coral Beach. This was the most easterly point on the island and a popular diving spot. "The sunsets are spectacular, sir. Bring your woman for a walk along the coastal path and breathe in the panoramic views that reach over the sea to the mainland." The waiter said that, and I only wished that my Cystonian was as good as his English – or was I just being sucked in to the tone of the place? Whatever, I felt that "going native" that night would not be such a bad thing!

I was on my third glass of Aphrodite's Champagne when I heard Lorraine's voice hail me from across the deck – "Frank!" She had one of those voices that curled your toes and pulled in your pelvic floor – warm, lush, sexy: enough to make a man feel he could go on all night. I waved to her and threaded my way through the tables where guests were already beginning to seat themselves. "Come and make up a table with us!" I saw the two men look up and eye me; I thought I saw Caran's mouth twitch although I couldn't think why, and then I was standing with them. We went through the introductions interspersed with one-liners and self-put-downs which we Brits find necessary on such occasions and then settled to the cruise, the chat and the meal.

This was – you've got it! – a meze and we were promised thirty different dishes. In that rather tedious way of mine, I actually counted them through the evening and there were at least that; the fish dishes alone included swordfish, red mullet, whitebait, sea bass and the inevitable calamari, spelt with a 'k'. It's a shame we've become so blasé at home over food; we take it for granted, don't we, that these things appear on every pub menu? Spoilt, aren't we? This food, however, was fresh in a way it can never be at home: some of it was almost still cooking as it hit the table. Apart from Joyce and Tony, everyone really tucked in. I was glad of that because I can't bear people picking at their food; this was classic cuisine and deserved our respect. How many times at home have you seen fat Brits shoving their food to the edge of their plates?

The women had secured a table by the rail and so we had a good view of the coastline as we passed. Two pillars of rock stood out from the main cliffs, with a suggestion of caves behind them. "The Gateway to the Lost City of Atlantis," said our waiter. How many Mediterranean islands are the Gateway to the Lost City of Atlantis – the "prehistoric cultural source of civiliza-tion"? The waiter explained that a new expedition was being set up and that they already had "maps of the sea bed showing clearly a sunken landmass. Maps made possible only by modern technology." A Cystonian scientist was on the verge of proving that "Atlantis was a real place and not a myth. New maps show fifty features described in Plato's writings". The women took this all in while the men remained sceptical – as always. It's one of the wonderful things about women isn't it – their readiness to be taken it, their social gullibility?

The boat cruised on past Napia Beach, "home of bungee jumping", and the women regaled me with the story of Noel's heroic dive. I must say, I didn't envy him that – heights aren't something I have much toler-ance for and I could just see myself climbing back the way I'd come. "Nothing, dear boy, nothing; a mere thread in the tapestry of life," said Noel, and we all laughed.

Sitting there, and watching her, I wondered about Joyce. Throughout the evening, Caran had been elbowing her in the direction of Tony and I couldn't for the life of me think why. Here were two extremely tidy, house-proud people. They would be forever clearing up behind each other. Joyce didn't need that – she wanted someone she could look after; she and Tony would simply make each other redundant. His friend, Noel, seemed to think the same as Caran, however – that she might turn out to be Tony's cup of tea. You could see them crying on each other's shoulders, but how long can you go on crying? In Joyce's case would it be forever? To be honest, it was easy to see why her husband had left her: how long could you stand that nit-picking manner of hers?

Looking round the table, listening and picking up the threads of past conversations, I realised that we were a mixed bunch: Lorraine had never been married and was now tempted into it by a local she'd met on holiday. Joyce was resentfully divorced, hated the singles life, wanted to find someone but didn't like looking. Tony was widowed, loathed every moment of being alone and was still in love with his wife. Noel had been divorced for a while, was enjoying every minute of it and clearly had no intention of re-marrying. I was recently divorced and bemused: only Caran was still married. Was that typical of the state of modern, middle-aged Britain – one married but loose, one widower, three divorcees and one "living in sin" as they used to say? When my parents had been our age it would have been six married people sitting round the meze table cruising through the Mediterranean night.

Noel and I got on splendidly and sparked each other off for the benefit and amusement of the women. As we cruised past Mykronisis Beach with its "two miles of white sand reflecting the yellow face of the moon" (another nice one from the waiter who, by now, had us well and truly tipsy) the talk turned to feminism, something at which Lorraine, in particular, pricked up her ears. Noel, of course, took the natural chauvinistic line – that men and women are different, should be treated differently, that the world was a better place when we acknowledged this and that women should stop trying to "have their cake and eat it". He told the story of an American woman he'd "once had the misfortune to meet" who had said that she could think of nothing more wonderful than having your cake AND eating it; as he said, it never actually occurred to her that, since she'd already eaten her cake, it might be someone else's she was tucking into. "An example, you see, of the essentially selfish nature of feminism. It's all about what men can do for women; nothing about what we might get in return."

I disagreed with him; my view was that "feminism has been one of the most liberating influences in our society. It set up rights for women. It established rules for the way that women are treated not only in society but also in relationships. It made us think again about the way we behave towards each other. And what you need to remember, Noel, is that in establishing rights for women it also established the same rights for men. What was sauce for the goose was also sauce for the gander." The feminists never thought of that did they? It was always assumed that men had these rights and, of course, in the cut and thrust of marriage we didn't. How many men do you know who are verbally abused once and month, every month for most of their lives? No need to put up with that now; we all have the right not to be abused in any way, don't we? I've always been a staunch feminist; it was my road to freedom.

When we returned to Porfos the village was still in full swing, so we strolled through the shops and stalls along the harbour with the chance to buy anything from "designer clothes" to backgammon sets. We paused and chatted, warm and flowing with drink, by the sixteenth century monastery "built to mark the spot where an icon of the Virgin Mary, our Lady of the Forests, was found". The coaches picked us up, to return to Craphos, under the "six hundred year old sycamore tree". It had been a good night; no promises of sex but I was looking forward to tomorrow. It turned out that Noel and Tony were also coming on the Eco Day Out and I was eager to see our rep, Vera, again. I hadn't cast eyes on her since the 'Welcome Meeting' and it transpired that she was leading the trip.

Day 12: Eco Day Out

"This will really give us a chance to get to know each other," said Vera. "If, by the end of the day, we're not all on Christian name terms – or even nicknames – I shall want to know why!"

Vera's eagerness to get to know us, especially since our holiday was so close to its end, was no doubt commendable, and her schoolmarm manner promised an educational experience as we toured the villages of Cystos.

I remembered her sales pitch on that second day which now seemed like a hundred years ago. She'd come rapidly to what those 'welcome meetings' are really about – booking your excursions through the rep. There were plenty of places to go, she'd said, and she would take the hassle out of organising it by doing all the tedious stuff (like walking down to the tour operator on a sunny morning) for us. So what was on? Well, it was a democratic country so we could choose anything we wanted – which was nice. I'd given Karavi Limani – "the Club Capital of Europe" – a miss so far. I'd been tempted by the "whole-day two-centre visit to the dream-like beaches of Trootaras in the morning and inland to the mountains of Graphos, where I'd find the coolest shower on the island – the waterfall at Koodos, in the afternoon;

and which was an absolute must for fun-lovers and nature-lovers alike". I then realised it was going to cost me as much as the rest of the holiday put together. The sophistication of Abydos had bypassed me – not being enamoured of markets and souvenir stalls.

I remembered how Vera had wiggled her hips and moved her forearms backwards and forwards, rather like a child imitating the movement of a train but actually intended to give the impression that she was a party person and couldn't wait to boogie. She was doing it again now as we bordered the coach, pumping up her enthusiasm for the day. "This is a crazy island" – yes, she'd said that before and followed it up with reminders about slapping on the factor 20, chilling out to the max, putting on a few pounds, pumping some adrenalin and dropping all those inhibitions. So we were ready to go, doing the tour of the town first as we picked up fellow tourists from other hotels.

As I sank into the doze of the coach and watched for the others to board, my mind wandered to Vera and something I'd thought about her early on. Isn't it irritating when you can't remember little things like that? As I watched her, it came back to me – it was something about the hidden tension behind her eyes and the question, "Why is she doing this?" I'd known all my life why I'd done my job – apart from having to earn a living, it was a service to the community; but why was Vera herding tourists round the island? Vera (I remember thinking she was as English as steak and kidney pie and just about as stoutly built) had retired early to Cystos, and dropped immediately into this nice little earner, because British tour operators liked to employ home grown talent where they could. She had given us the usual warnings about avoiding the drinking water, watching the exchange rates, keeping out of the sun, adapting to Mediterranean time, going out late, eating late, not rushing, taking everything as it comes and so on. I remember thinking that it didn't sound terribly convincing because had she taken her own advice, Vera would now be relaxing in the shade of a convenient tree, sipping the local wine – so why wasn't she?

"This, my dears, will be 'village crawling' – pub crawling on a grand scale – but we shall take in the ecology of the island as we go. I've been fascinated by the natural balance here. My partner and I are heavily into ecology and we're responsible for several of the 'green projects' on the island. Ooh, yes, my partner is an islander. I met him when I came over here. I was fed up with England and the rain, and had just got divorced so I decided to make a fresh start. Came here with a girlfriend for a holiday, met Andreas and fell in love, so I stayed on."

So now we knew; so much for the reserve of the British! Were there any male islanders whose names didn't end in 'os' or 'as'?

"Our driver today is Miklos ..."

Well, that certainly fitted the pattern.

"... and he's going to be taking us round the island. Miklos is one of the best drivers we have ...."

Isn't it strange how your driver is always "one of the best"?

"...... so you're very lucky. He knows every inch of the roads round here and we shall be perfectly safe in his hands".

That was, of course, reassuring; for a moment there I'd had the impression that perhaps he didn't know where he was going, and was as safe as one of those boy-racers back home on a Thursday, Friday or Saturday night. Miklos smiled round the coach, ensuring himself a nice tip, which probably made up for the wages his company paid him.

By now, Lorraine, Caran and Joyce were aboard, and so were Noel and Tony; I was looking forward to the day immensely and once we were off – gliding gracefully along those Cystonian roads, "off the beaten track" as Vera put it with great excitement – I began to get that holiday glow. You know how it is on a holiday – great expectations largely unfulfilled. I had started off with a certain reserve. Coming here alone, I wasn't expecting much in the way of meaningful company – just the odd laugh with a drink or two – and then I'd had those two (how shall I put it?), 'encounters' with Caran, and had come to life. They'd been so unexpected I'd been in a daze ever since. I've never been one for casual sex and she had taken me by surprise on both occasions, but the last time was over a week ago and so I assumed that neither had done too much for her.

I've never been one for pestering women. In my experience they either feel inclined, or they don't. If they're going along with your advances without really wanting to, then the whole experience is like 'flogging a dead horse', as they used to say. It was a bit like that with my wife, really; when she wasn't easily persuadable, she was best left alone. You can't do it on your own, can you? All right, you can "get your end off" but what's the point? Lovemaking is either a shared delight or it's a waste of time. Worse than that, it's depressing afterwards when there's no feeling between you. I think the worst experience I ever had was when, after one abortive attempt to rouse her, my wife turned over and began talking about how we should think about redecorating the bathroom – meaning, of course, that *I* should think about re-deco-rating the bathroom. I was almost in tears. I waited until she'd gone to sleep and then went into the garden to be alone.

I remember, as a young man, I had expected sex to be a joyful experience and those first few years of marriage had been – at least, I think they had: I'm not so sure now. I had expected sex to be not only joyful, but liberating: you didn't even have to "come off together" to achieve that. When my wife had come to that point, I found I could hold it there and then take us back again and again until we'd both been satisfied: or so I thought at the time. It was that 'explosion' inside your head I used to love; everything drained away, and you and your lady were at one with each other. As Laurie Lee put it in that book of his – "I felt possessed by miracles ... fateful ... invulnerable ...." or something like that. I was now at the age when I had to acknowledge that it wasn't the same for women. I remember seeing that programme *Loose Women* once; the title implies both 'loose cannon' and 'loose sexually', so they cover themselves in terms of their feminist stance. During one cut and thrust exchange – they're usually like that with each other, but all smiles – one of the younger women had said some-thing like, "You just have to accept that men need sex in a way we don't, and give it to them if you want to keep them". There was a moment's stunned silence. You could feel the others bowled over by a level of honesty that none of them wanted to acknowledge. I knew, too, that – if challenged – the young woman would backtrack: to keep her credibility she would have had no choice. The moment passed – for her, for the others all bouncing their 'sexuality' around the studio and for the audience, but I never forgot it.

Anyway, my times with Caran had quite bucked me up, but I'd now reached that point when you're looking forward to going home. You've done as many excursions as you can afford, tried out the best looking restaurants (only to find that all of them are selling the same food presented in the same way as all the others), walked backwards and forwards to the beach umpteen times, slumped remorselessly by the pool time and again, read more books than the average person reads in a year, gone for that last nightcap up one side of the street and down the other, and so on. So it was quite a surprise to be looking forward, immensely, to the day – but I was: Lorraine had sat by me when they got aboard, and her chatter always enlivened me.

Our first stop was by a cactus at the roadside – not an orthodox stop, but an interesting one. Vera held our attention by asking:

"Has anyone got a sore place?"

Laughter – well, you're obliged to, aren't you?

"No come on – stop messing about ...."

More laughter: she did Kenneth Williams well.

"...has anyone got a sore spot? What's your name?" she said, looking at me.

"My ex-wife used to call me Hawkeye," I said.

On my reply, there was tremendous, almost uncontrollable, laughter as the coachload attempted to bond for the day. Vera had extracted her first nickname and was jubilant.

"Hawkeye? Why did she call you Hawkeye?"

"Because I never missed anything."

More laughter – hysteria increasing, with Vera reposting:

"We wouldn't want that, girls would we?"

Why wouldn't they? Were they all so busy with lovers on the side that they were worried about getting caught out? I don't think so, but it did for the moment, and Vera was grateful – the first stop and we were all laughing! She gave me a smile – a big, firm smile to match her steak and kidney looks – and proceeded to explain.

"This is your local chemist shop or – as the Americans would say – drug store."

Well, yes – and we're catching up with the Yanks aren't we. How long before our chemist shops are all called 'drugstores'? She got another laugh at that – why do people always laugh at the American way of life and of talking, when the whole world is busy copying it? Vera broke a piece off the cactus and squeezed the juice on to my sore spot.

"Tell everybody how that feels … Hawkeye."

More laughter; it was going to be Pavlov's dogs all day.

"Soothing, very soothing. It's taken the roughness of the mosquito bite away."

"Does anyone know what it is? You're all buying it, from your chemist shops. It comes in hair shampoo and creams …"

By now she was handing round the nodules from the cactus for everyone to try; the substance had a gentle, soothing smell.

"Aloe vera! That's right, go on, say it – Aloe vera!"

"Aloe vera," we all replied, and the coach exploded in further gales of laughter.

"It grows naturally here and is being farmed for the pharmaceutical industry – but please leave those that grow by the roadside alone. They are like wild flowers – don't pick them."

The coach pulled away and moved on to cries of "Aloe Vera".

"Did your wife – your ex-wife – really call you Hawk-eye, Frank?" said Lorraine.

"Yes, as a matter of fact she did."

"And were you?"

"Yes. It wasn't so much what Vera implied. It was just that I noticed changes. I could walk into a room and know that she had moved a vase or a book or a pen or whatever."

"But not a lover?"

"No."

"Did she ever have one?"

"No – I don't think so."

"But you're not sure?"

"Yes I am sure. I was just being fair on my wife."

"You didn't wish to imply she couldn't?"

"Yes. What is this, Lorraine? You should have joined the police force. I didn't expect ...."

" ...the Spanish Inquisition? No one expects the Spanish Inquisition!"

We both laughed, although we didn't have to; I knew she was curious, and that she would persist – we were coming to the end of our holiday now. The possibility of offending anybody didn't matter so much, and this could be the last chance to satisfy our curiosity: ask now or remain forever ignorant – and no women likes to be that when a question will settle the matter.

"How are you doing with Dakos?"

"Don't change the subject."

"I'd reached a point in my marriage when I didn't want to go on. That's all."

"Another woman?"

"No. Despite what you might think – after Caran – I've never been one for casual sex."

"Then why?"

I looked at Lorraine and wondered. I felt no need to tell her, and yet I didn't want to appear rude; also, I didn't really want to talk about things that concerned my ex-wife and me, intimately. The fact was that Stella had been a nagger and, after thirty odd years, I'd had enough of it. It began with the monthly period which spread over five days, once a month, every month, for a quarter of a century. She'd choose that moment to offload every grievance she had: nothing momentous – I'd never been unfaithful or anything like that – just complaints about what I hadn't done or said or, indeed, what I had done or said. Then, when she went through the change, and no longer suffered from periods, the nagging went on. It had become a habit, you see – an addiction – and I didn't like it. Verbal abuse had never appealed to me. I got enough of that in my job.

"It doesn't seem fair on my wife – ex-wife – to talk about it, Lorraine."

"OK. I understand that. Do you still love her, Frank?"

"Well, of course. You don't stop loving someone just because you don't like the way they behave."

She looked at me oddly when I said that, as if she found the remark strange, then we both laughed, as on the night she told me about Dakos; laughed as though we shared a mutual knowledge.

"But you still divorced her? So now you're both alone?"

"Yes."

"What precipitated it?"

It's always wonderful talking to an educated person, isn't it? How many people do you know who would have used the word "precipitated" in that way? I looked it up when I got back to the hotel (I always take a dictionary with me on holiday, because I read a lot and there's always some word that's new to me) and it said: "acting very suddenly or with undue haste: rash". Yes – well that wasn't far off. It probably had been, but we'd gone one row too far: who needs it? Counsellors always tell you to plan that kind of thing out of your life, and that's what I'd done; I said so to Lorraine.

"You're a very decisive chap, then, Frank?"

"I think I tend not to make those kinds of decisions. Like most men I go along with it and then …"

"Snap?"

"Yes."

"It can seem ruthless to a woman."

"Yes."

"We prefer to have it out."

"I know. It's a bugger, isn't it?"

The coach was now passing through a dusty village, and I watched the locals sitting in the kafenias, silent and tanned as the walls themselves. This was a wine-growing region of Cystos and the vines had lined the roads as we approached, stretching back as far as the eye could see.

"Pub crawling on a village scale, and this is our first stop-off!" cried Vera.

"Don't forget the cactus," called some wag from the back seat.

"Aloe Vera," chorused the coachload.

Tremendous laughter.

"This is Ayios Frenosios," said Vera, "the island's first ecological winery and it was built in 1987. It's a very young winery on a very old island. Can anyone tell me why it is ecological?"

Vera paused dramatically; previous coachloads had obviously been puzzled by the idea of an "ecological winery". In Britain the term "ecological" had been long since reduced to such concepts as reusing your shopping bags and not leaving your heated towel rail on; both vaguely linked in some way to the abstruse idea of global warning. No one answered so she said, very impressively:

"The grapes are grown organically!"

"My husband tried that on his allotment," called out a thin woman, in a red dress, from towards the back of the coach, "but all we got was a load of weeds."

Laughter – loud and tinged with irony; I don't want to sound xenophobic, but is it only the Brits who can manage ironic laughter?

"You have to keep hoeing," laughed Vera, "but your grapes are then free of pesticides – and so is your soil for generations to come."

"And you know what you're eating," cried out another woman, "My husband just couldn't be bothered to hoe. He said he'd better things to do with his weekends."

I've never been one hundred percent convinced by the organic argument. Fertilisers have increased crop yields beyond anything we could have expected, and the only reason we can get precious about organic food now is that we buy so much so cheaply from foreign growers – poor sods who are prepared to sweat under the sun for bugger all while we sit at home congratulating ourselves on our healthy eating habits. Kate Fox had something to say about 'food fads' in that book of hers, *Watching the English*; it went something like "middle-class busybodies getting the working classes to eat up their vegetables ... the interfering classes on a moral crusade ... amateur dieticians talking about food advertising corrupting the nation's youth ... no chattering class dinner party taking place without an advance survey of the guests latest fashionable food allergies ... food taboos becoming the main means of defining one's social identity".

In short, it's more about social fad than food, and I agree with her; not that I said so at the time, and we found ourselves sitting, congenially and in accord with each other, in one of the *kafenias* for our coffee break – drinking that wonderful thick rich coffee they serve abroad, with a creamy cake called *mahallebi*: very organic, very healthy!

The *kafenia* – I couldn't work out how it was different from a taverna, but it was the word Vera used and was, perhaps, more ecological – was situated in a new pedestrianised area in the centre of the village.

At the winery, Yiannis had explained to us his "genuine winemaking techniques", talked about "the birth of new wines", referred to his "father and grandfather's wishes to have their own vineyards" and advocated "tradition and new technology", which included his pneumatic press, stainless steel tanks and stabilization equipment. It all sounded fine and dandy and was, together with New World wines, giving the French a run for their money, so it couldn't be all bad. We sampled a glass of wine – "indigenous Mavro blended with the Grenache grape" – from his yearly output of fifty thousand bottles, and bought a bottle ourselves, of course. I did ask him whether it was "Soil Association Approved" and he laughed, but without understanding what I meant; I got the impression that they haven't reached Cystos yet. He told us that "expansion has been cautious, to maintain the high quality of our organic wines" – and he waved us off with a cry of:

"Drink responsibly during your village wine crawling!"

"People are strange, aren't they?" said Lorraine.

"Go on," I said, curious. I've always loved talking with women; they have such a strange take on things.

"Well, let's take Caran. What is she after? Does she really want an affair? Does she really want to wave goodbye to Simon and her daughters, the home they share and the affluence she clearly enjoys? No, decidedly no! So why the …fling … with you?"

"Simon and the girls? You mean she's married?"

"Didn't you know?"

"She wasn't wearing a ring. I assumed …"

"Oh! You mean you wouldn't have got mixed up with a married woman?

"No. I had no idea."

"Don't let it worry you. Her marriage is Caran's responsibility – not yours."

"I'm not sure I go along with that entirely."

"Caran is driven, Frank. She has to prove something to herself. I don't think even she knows what it is, but it strikes me that nothing has ever been quite good enough for Caran. She 'could' have married a doctor but 'ended up' with a nurse."

"Did she say that?"

"Not in so many words."

"Perhaps she fears what she sees as the 'inevitable slide into old age'."

"She certainly puts a lot of effort into looking after herself."

"I always think that there's a sexual drive to 'keeping in shape', don't you –body image and all that? What did you all come out here looking for?"

"Now who's being blunt?"

"You don't have to answer."

"We told ourselves that we were coming to 'pull'," she laughed.

"And were you?"

"Who knows? Joyce was certainly after someone – or something ...."

"But isn't the pulling kind."

"No. It was Caran's suggestion that we all came. She and I go to the same gym. She thought it would do Joyce good."

"And, of course, it's getting quite fashionable, isn't it – for husbands and wives to take separate holidays?"

"Barry and I often have – at least weekends and 'leisure breaks' as they are now called."

We were skirting the issues we were pretending to discuss. As far as I could see, here you had three women all discontented with their lot, nice though they were. Each of them was looking for greener grass on the other side of the hill. Joyce, because she wanted to be married, or at least re-establish some normality in her life – and, to her, that meant a home and a man.

Caran, because she had a sexual image of herself – she needed to be desirable and be desired and her husband had long since given up on that kind of thing; but she didn't, in her heart, want to be bothered with an affair or anything that was going to disrupt her social life. Lorraine, because she valued her freedom and "freedom" with Barry had become a rut, not a way of life. But what did I know – a mere man?

We "crawled" our way through several more wineries, all blending their local wines with Cabernet, Chardonnay and Grenache grapes and ageing them in French oak casks – so that heartland of great wine had contributed something after all – and then came to the highlight of our Eco Tour – the Caves of Graphos.

As a kid I lived in a two-up, two-down terraced house with a kitchen and scullery. The toilet was outside and there was no running hot water. On Fridays we all bathed from water heated in the "copper" in which our mother did the washing. The only heat in the house was a coal fire in the living room. In winter you could see your breath condense in the air of the bedroom as you breathed out. We did have electricity, although our country cousins did not. I'm talking here about the late forties and early fifties. If you can picture living like that, you'll have a good idea what these caves had to offer. They were the dwelling places of the indigenous islanders before "western civilization" overtook the island. We're not talking about cavemen; we're talking about how the islanders lived fifty or sixty years ago. They had been "faithfully restored" to show us how "a natural life in an organic community" was lived not long ago.

Vera was ecstatic about the lifestyle they offered:

"They grew all their own food and composted the remains – there was no waste here and no supermarket carrier bags to clutter up the landfill sites. Fresh food every day and no 'ready meals' past their sell buy date cluttering up the fridge because there wasn't a fridge – just a cold slab in the cave! There are butts to collect water. They washed in that as well as using it for the garden."

But they kept animals for food, didn't they? Was that eco-friendly? Didn't I read somewhere that animals are the biggest source of the greenhouse gas methane?

She led us down to the river at the bottom of the slope.

"And here they washed their clothes and dried them and aired them. No wasteful Pampers, but reusable nappies and no need for that big no-no – the tumble dryer. They dried on a line in the fresh air! And further up stream, they drank the fresh water!"

No bottled water, then – a major waste of plastic. But not much time for popping to the shops and looking at the racks of clothes, having a coffee with your girlfriends or going to the cinema. I remember my mother used to take a whole week to do her washing.

She took us into the caves themselves, which were, I have to admit, cosy; you could imagine the wood fire, the fumes from which seemed to escape through a hole in the wall, creating a pleasant winter's night in here, although my memory from childhood reminded me that, while your front was scorching, your back was like ice.

"No need for insulation – you have a mountain above you to keep in the heat – and one light illuminates the whole house. And do you see the children's toys in the corner – wooden! Plastic ones can take a thousand years to biodegrade."

Yes, well, I went with the wooden toys, but living in one large room didn't grab me as that exciting. On the other hand, you weren't going to lie awake all night worrying about energy-saving lightbulbs, dual flush toilets, radiators fitted against outside walls where they lost so much heat, the arguments about how long the central heating should be switched on for, whether you should really be using those plastic bottles of hand wash, or taking a bath after your teenage daughter to avoid wasting water.

"And we all know how they got about, don't we?" questioned Vera.

They certainly wouldn't be using a car, would they, or, indeed, any means of public transport, like buses, planes, boats and trains?

"Their impact on the environment was zero, then, Vera?"

"It certainly was, Hawkeye."

"And their carbon footprint?"

"Less than a tonne!!"

"Wow – how many tonnes would your average west-erner's be today?"

"Have an eco-audit and find out. One of our customers had a carbon footprint of over sixty tonnes."

"What on earth is a carbon footprint?" said Joyce, as we stood outside the cave.

Back on the coach, after an optional drink of ice-cold water from the mountain stream, having noted Vera's package holiday on which we could spend "a week or even two" in the restored cave dwellings, Lorraine and I turned to discussing Tony and Noel.

"Do you like them, Frank?"

"Yes, they're nice enough chaps."

"What do you make of them?"

"People are always more complicated than they look, aren't they? Noel comes across as the happy-go-lucky-don't-give-a-damn sort of bloke and yet he has artistic pretensions – listen to the "luvvie" way he talks – and he's clearly educated, like you. Do you remember him winding those kids up over the word 'wank'? He thinks, doesn't he? And if he thinks about one thing, he'll think about another. There's a lot going on in his head other than what happened on last night's soaps."

"Why do you think his wife divorced him?"

"You tell me, Lorraine."

"No, come on."

"Another woman?"

"Bingo!"

"How do you know?"

"We women have our ways! Anyway – I could have guessed as much without asking. He's here for what he can get, isn't he?"

"Or for what Tony can get. Maybe he thought he could take him out of himself. He's a kind man – as well as being a womaniser."

"And Tony?"

"You tell me ... no, come on. I gave you my view of Noel."

"He's still looking for his wife. He wants his Bev back, no one else will do."

"And the search will never end?"

"What woman could bear being compared to the incomparable?"

"You can see his life stretching out before him, can't you? From now to the grave …"

"Frank!"

"Well, can't you?"

"If he could just find the right woman …"

"You've just said …."

"I know – who wants to spend their life being compared to the incomparable? – but a woman, the right woman, if he could find one, would settle him down."

"You think that's essential, do you Lorraine – that we should all find someone, that we are happier that way than living alone?"

"Yes."

"But Noel is happy enough, isn't he?"

"On the surface – but someone will hook him, some-day."

"And what kind of woman does Tony want?"

"An untidy and disorganised cow – someone like me – whom he can look after."

"Would you boss him about?"

Lorraine looked at me when I said that, but I'd detected in her that streak of wanting to be in charge – under all the seventies creativity and artistic "living together" stuff, she liked control, and her Barry had gone along with it.

"You think he needs that?"

"I get the impression that his Bev had things organised the way she wanted them."

"What makes you say that?"

"Intuition – we men do have it, you know – and the way he likes to fuss around you women and please you … and his general eager-to-get-it-right manner."

"You don't miss much, do you Frank? What did you do for a living?"

"I was a police officer."

"A copper!!"

"Shhh! It puts people off. Mention it to no one – please, Lorraine. I don't know why I told you."

"Well, that explains a lot."

"What do you mean?"

"The way you are with people – you're so bloody curious aren't you," she laughed, with that Rubenesque laugh of hers, "I bet you were a good copper."

"Why?"

"Because you'd never do anything by the book – you'd use your discretion."

"Thanks, Lorraine – that's a really nice thing to have said, and it's true, I did ... Discretion's out of fashion now, of course, with the younger breed of police officer. They're so PC that they're scared of their own shadows. Anyway, we were talking about Tony and the single life. You think people are not meant to live alone?"

"It's a couple's world. It's easier to go somewhere with someone, than alone."

"You can go with a girlfriend."

"Unless she's going with her partner and then you're a gooseberry. No, no – it's handy to have a man around to take you places."

It was now quite late in the afternoon – at least by British standards; it was after one o'clock and we hadn't stopped for lunch. Vera assured us that "the wait will be worth it – where we are going for lunch is out of this world, sweethearts." She had progressed to the familiar "sweethearts" after coffee, over which she had winkled further nicknames from her coach party. Among others, we had aboard 'Scrumptious', because her husband would love to eat her, 'Punch', who had a large nose, 'Sugar Plum', because her husband thought she was sweet, 'Spike', for reasons his wife didn't acknowledge on the coach, 'Nobby', because his surname was 'Clarke' (but only to his mates and family – his wife never called him that in public) and the usual contractions of real names like 'Trace', 'Shel-w', 'Lil'w'. It struck me, at the time, how many of the men's nicknames referred to physical characteristics, while the women's related almost entirely to food. One woman, for example, was called 'Doughnut' by everyone who knew her. Vera lapped this up, and we were all soon using each others' nicknames – but only within our own group; the familiarity didn't extend to other people.

Lunch was at Kafenia Cystos. Have you ever been to the Rainforest Café? Well – this was like that, only real. Forget the electronic gorillas jerking around on cue, piles of plastic junk and cuddly toys from China, the artificial "forest" gathering dust on leaves that never photosynthesise, what amounts to a McDonalds menu dressed up with fancy names served in ridiculously small portions, and the girls inviting you to an "adventure", which simply means sitting down at a table and eating.

At Kafenia Cystos, you walked into a cedar forest four hundred metres above sea level, and sat down to eat at wooden tables under a canopy of trees, where the air was cool in the early afternoon heat. Real butterflies and other insects fluttered past on their way to the river. Occasionally, you heard the sound of a wild sheep crashing through the undergrowth. The children in our party were able to wander down to the river with their parents, cross the stone arched bridge and paddle among the boulders that lined the river bed. Grasses and reeds lined the banks and, now and then, a purple heron or other water bird could be spotted. Tracks led into the forest, vines hung from pergolas and real water dripped on to our table. Above the chatter, you could hear the trickle of water from a mountain spring. Under the tables, across the hot sand, lizards crawled and then pursued bugs up the dry, sun-bleached walls. Vera told us that, sometimes, on a really hot summer afternoon, lightning crackled in the nearby mountains and flash floods roared down the river-beds.

"And this is a café?"

"Oh yes, the area around the café is a protected eco-zone – fenced and secure. Here, we breed species that have become threatened by the spread of tourism and industry on the island."

"Are any of them on the menu?" said Noel.

"Noel!!"

"Oh yes – fresh from the land. Our kleftiko is made from mountain lamb and the taste is sweeter than anything you will find on the coast, our halloumi from the milk of the mountain goat is beautiful grilled; but, best of all, we have fresh trout straight from the mountain stream."

"I thought the mouflon was protected on the island," said Noel.

"It is! The Cystonians are like the French – they'll shoot anything that moves. The island was down to fifteen mouflon. We now have over twelve hundred but they still have to breed them on reserves. At Kafenia Cystos, our job is to show that they can be protected and eaten – if we get the balance right and *if* the hunters act responsibly!"

"Is there a vegetarian option?" asked Tony.

"Today, roast acorn squash with spinach and gorgonzola *or* roast peppers with halloumi and pine nuts."

"They sound wonderful," replied Tony, "When the halloumi is heated, the outside hardens and the inside softens, giving the texture of mozzarella, and its salty flavour will contrast well with the sweetness of the peppers."

I watched the women watching him; it was a delight to see their faces.

"Well, I'm for the trout, I think," said Joyce.

"Then you are in for a treat – trout with grilled ham straight from the barbecue, served piping hot."

"But first, a few appetizers – yogurt cheese in olive oil, walnut and goat's cheese bruschetta, marinated feta with lemon and oregano. Do I need to go on?"

"And what is there for the children?" called one woman who was surrounded by four of her own.

"We don't 'cook down' to children on Cystos," said Vera, "No turkey twizzlers or dinosaur nibbles here. On Cystos – like all the Mediterranean countries – children are treated with respect when they come to the table."

We ate like kings and queens. As we ate, I thought to myself how wonderful British cuisine was; there was nothing on this wonderful menu that I hadn't cooked, or eaten out, myself. The British, that mongrel race, now had a mongrel cuisine that was probably the best in the world.

Over lunch, Noel suggested that we all get together for the last night.

"It's Wednesday – do you realise that? We have just two more days, and then we'll all be packing our suitcases to go home."

"Shut up, Noel," said Caran.

"This isn't a rehearsal, sweetheart. Caran Shepherd – this is your life!"

He stood with a grand sweep of his arm and handed her the menu. Caran smiled suddenly, stood, and walked to the wooden bridge that led from the terrace down to the stream. I joined her, while we all laughed and Noel launched into one of his homilies, which began with, "The curfew tolls the knell of parting day". The British have a dark side to their humour; perhaps it's where we get our appreciation of irony. When I joined Caran, I noticed that she had tears in her eyes.

Lorraine:

I'd decided not to waste any more time with Dakos, but to go straight for the jugular – or, more appropriately, the crotch: nothing ventured, nothing gained. I remembered my conversation with Caran when I had returned that night – "So you got nowhere?" "I cleared the air. I made my case." "You'd have been better off seducing him. Get him between the sheets, Lorraine. That'd change his mind."

I'm not sure that I'd normally have followed Caran's advice – anyway, she was clearly thinking about herself that night – but there was a bit of truth in her remarks. An English actress (I forget who) had once said, when talking about the intellectual types she'd known in Cambridge, "Offer a man an intellectual conversation or a roll in the hay and he'll go for the roll in the hay every time".

After our last conversation, I felt that Dakos might be for turning. I wasn't sure, but if I was going to cross that "long bridge" Frank talked about, then I was going to have to make the next step.

We ate our meal, but I didn't try to hold him in conversation, nor he me. We both knew that something was in the air, and he didn't hesitate to drive me back to his apartment. After we got there, he explained, when I asked, that Michael was "sleeping over" with friends. He poured each of us a drink, but otherwise made no move towards me. On that first occasion, after our lovely day out, he had stroked and caressed me and kissed me lightly on the lips, but made no attempt to go any further. I remember this had surprised Caran, and rather pleased me – "Was he nice?" "Very nice. He's a lovely man." "And he treated you with respect?" "And he treated me with respect." "That's a shame." We'd both laughed – well, you do, don't you?

Dakos stood in the doorway of the balcony, his back just to me, looking out over the harbour. That light sea breeze blew the lace curtains against us again as it drifted from the bay. I felt tense, a sensation I'd never experienced with men, even before Barry. I began to talk – I forget about what, but Dakos responded in that quiet way of his and smiled.

"There's no bigger turn-on than a woman who's sexually confident." I'd read that somewhere, probably in one of Steph's glossy magazines giving advice to teenage girls. Somehow, however, I sensed that Dakos had to initiate this – or, at least, seem to – so I touched him on the shoulder and said:

"Dakos, a kiss would be nice."

He put his glass down on the balcony table, took mine and placed it beside his, then turned to me and ran his hands down the small of my back and over my buttocks, which he clenched not just firmly, but with force. I opened my mouth, so that it was soft and full – ripe, I think they like to say! His mouth closed over mine and took my lips; it was a full kiss, urgent, as though he were sucking the juice from a peach. I could feel from the pressure in his fingers and mouth that he wanted to unzip my dress and let it fall to the ground; I could play him now for all he was worth. I didn't doubt my "charm" once I'd got him to make the first move.

I took him by the hand and led him into the bedroom. He ran his hands all over me and began to kiss my body through the dress. I'd worn my midnight blue one, deliberately; it showed off my breasts and the cloth was thin. Underneath, I wore only a bra – with my breasts, I had no choice; they needed help now, standing up for themselves. He dropped to his knees and removed my shoes, running his hands up my calf muscles, lifting the dress and stopping just short of my buttocks. He kissed my feet and looked up at me. I smiled down at him and he stood, rising up along my body until he had his hands in that thick mane of red-blonde hair. He kissed me again on the lips and his hands dropped to my shoulders, ready to slip his fingers under the straps of my dress, so that he could slide it off and expose my breasts; but I delayed him then, reaching up around his neck so that the straps stayed where they were, and I kissed him on the lips and then on his cheeks and nose, under his chin, nuzzling the ticklish sensitivity of his neck. I wanted that unbearable tenderness again, that gentle delicacy he had shown only a week ago.

He continued his caresses, wanting to rouse me and gain his satisfaction, but this was an Englishwoman, not to be taken lightly – to be stirred not shaken. I could feel his urgency – a kiss always leads to this when you're both in the mood – but he could wait. He'd insulted me – although I'd forgive him that – and cast aspersions against my race; he needed to know that we were not an "easy" option, would not "sleep with anyone" and had at least as much "dignity" as the "women of the streets".

For a while longer, I would be all promise: sensitive skin, full mouth, tempting breasts, smooth legs, taut nipples, quivering thighs – you know the kind of thing. Then we could satisfy ourselves. I let him ease me down on to the bed and open my thighs – but only slightly. I let him linger around my shoulders, flicking his tongue along my collar bones; I let him slide his hands just between my legs through the dress, fondle me where he wished.

I'd been a dancer, so (though I was now, shall we say, bigger than I might be by NHS standards?) I was firm, and the curve of my back and even my waist to an extent, were still strong and well muscled. Men had always found that attractive and Dakos was no exception. I think it was the implied strength within me that they found a challenge. I sensed his excitement as he passed his hands over my body. I gave him every access and, of course, the more he had the more he wanted.

I knew his need to pull my dress off must become a torment to him, so eventually I wriggled further on to the bed, slipping out of it slightly and exposing my breasts; his mouth closed over my nipples, his tongue flicked around them, but Englishwomen are cool, aren't they? What's the expression the American film-makers use about us – 'cool as an English rose'? I thought I would provoke him just a little further, and said:

"Are you going to take your clothes off?"

I would have undressed him myself, but it gave me a feeling of power to lie there on the softness of his bed and watch him struggle out of his clothes. Don't get me wrong – I'm not a tease, nor do I enjoy being a bitch, but this Dakos had a lesson to learn. He had to acknowledge how much he wanted me – to himself, in front of me.

He looked puzzled for a moment and almost angry. Then he stripped quickly, throwing socks, jacket, shirt, trousers and pants across the room. I noticed he removed his socks first – realizing, I suppose, how funny a man looks standing in his socks. It was funny watching him undress himself. Naked, he was what I'd expected – muscled, broad, tanned and hairy. I wanted him now and opened my thighs under the dress. He lifted me from the bed just enough to get a grip on the dress, pulled down the zip and slung my midnight blue across the room.

The magazines tell us that men love it when you're selfish, so I was: I grabbed him by the hair and pulled him to me, snapped my fingers and began demanding! "Being at your sexual beck and call is a classic male fantasy", I'd read somewhere, so I egged him on – barking orders for him to "pleasure" me: nice phrase, isn't it? He did; his blood was up now, his eyes shone, his mouth never left my body.

"Take control", say the advice columns – so I did. I pushed him off me, turned him on to his back and rode him – girls on top stuff.

"Let yourself go": it was a hot summer night in the Med, and soon we were both bathed in sweat, crying out in excitement. "Men love the sight of their partner glistening with sweat" said the magazine: well, he got that, all right. It dripped from me like raindrops on to his cheeks, running into his mouth and my mass of hair – wringing wet – dangled over his chest.

"You can never be too loud in bed!" Really? Then Dakos had nothing to complain about; he got a "high-decibel orgasm". I let rip, and the louder I moaned, the more frenzied he became; finally he "took" me, as they say – meaning he felt free to satisfy himself.

He threw me from him, turned me on to my face, thrust two pillows under my belly to raise my buttocks at a good angle and came into me. Barry and I had never made love like that; he always said it was an insult, that a man should want to see his lover's face, not "take her like a dog", but I didn't mind. I felt his hands grip my shoulders and hold me in place and then he thrust hard and fast. I came again for Dakos, felt myself come, and then I had him and he collapsed on top of me.

Day 13: The Day after the Night Before

We made love again that night several times and each time he came, each time he satisfied himself, it was with the same forceful passion. Between times, we would lie together and talk, but he never took me gently as I'd expected; there seemed to be a silent anger in him as though, in some way, he bore resentment.

"So you took my advice?"

Caran had seen Dakos drop me off early that morning on his way to the market.

"What was that, Caran?"

"To get him between the sheets!"

"Yes."

My voice must have sounded slightly reluctant; I certainly felt that way – reluctant to think about it or, for the moment, talk about it. I wasn't sure that Dakos had seen it the way Caran was so sure he would. However, I could hardly play the 'innocent flower' – not at my age and not after the night I'd had – so I decided to go along with Caran's curiosity, but my voice must have betrayed my uncertainty.

"You don't sound very sure, Lorraine?"

"We didn't spend too much time lingering over the meal, Caran – if that's what you mean. Most of the night was spent "between the sheets", as you put it."

"And you're going to see him again?"

"Oh, yes."

I said it with an assurance I didn't feel, and Caran sensed this.

"What's the matter?"

"Nothing."

"Come on."

I didn't really feel that someone like Caran was in any position to say, "Come on." She, for all her verbal posturing on sexual matters, was hardly the essence of sophistication in that department, was she? Simon solo, for thirty years, and then two men she hardly knew on a holiday in the Mediterranean didn't really qualify you to give advice, did it? Still I didn't want to fall out with her so I murmured:

"I'm not one hundred percent sure that Dakos saw it the way I did."

"You mean he just took advantage of you?"

"No …."

Well, you wouldn't want to admit that would you?

" … Let's get ready for the trip to the market."

"The bastard!"

"You're jumping to conclusions, Caran. Dakos didn't take anything that wasn't on offer."

"Well, that's a funny way of putting it."

"I didn't force him into bed with me."

"No, but did he get there under false pretences?"

"I don't understand."

I did, of course: Caran's line was the traditional female bleat when a man 'lets you down'. It was the 'He had no business doing it unless he was serious about you' line of argument, but when you lead a man into the bedroom what's he supposed to do? I just wondered whether I'd made a bad judgement. I'd thought he loved me. He'd made no attempt on that first date to do anything out of line and he had proposed to me; the sex, last night, had been good as I knew it would be and I'd thought that would clinch it, but had it?

Tony:

"Come on, Tony, it's market day in Craphos. Some, it is said, go there and dally!"

Noel was in a high mood again. I don't know where he'd been the night before, but he'd come in late. I heard him stagger to his room in the small hours. I find it very difficult to sleep without Bev beside me. I keep the radio on most of the night and just lay there wide awake.

We'd been to a Lebanese restaurant – don't ask me why. Noel said it would "add the pure essence of the Middle East to our dining experience". In Cystos? I would have been quite happy with an English restaurant, or even a local one. As we ate, a belly dancer had "entertained" us: this meant that she twisted her way between the tables, expecting us to stuff money into her costume. She was a hard-faced woman, and when I'd ignored her, she'd bitten my nipples through my shirt. It was very painful. Noel, of course, was in his element. From the moment we arrived, led in by a young woman in a sequinned bra and panties, he had attracted attention with his loud comments. The waitress he had found "a little on the plump side but with a lovely movement". She'd arrived at our table with the menu and the, "Can

I get you any drinks?" question they always use, and when she'd arrived back with our order, it had been the wrong one! She'd had a big smile on her face but I'd complained – against Noel's advice. "Never complain about the food. You don't know what they'll do with it back in the kitchen."

This had attracted the attention of some woman at the next table, and her husband had launched into a long story about a friend of his who was a chef and who always wiped any steaks sent back around the toilet pan before returning them to the customer. Nevertheless, I did complain, and eventually the girl returned with what we'd ordered and, a little later, with that awful line they all use – "Is everything all right for you?" to which Noel had responded "No, darling, but with someone like you it could be."

He had ordered asparagus as a side vegetable because of what he called its "aphrodisiac qualities". "My ex-wife, whatever her faults, was a sexy cook," he'd said, "No one prepared, or ate, asparagus quite like her. I can see her now scraping the flesh from the tip between her teeth and lips. It's a pity her tongue was razor-sharp, too!" This got another laugh from a table next to us – this time a group of women who asked him what his favourite dish was; when he said "Toad-in-the-hole", the restaurant exploded. People were repeating it all night, including the waiters who couldn't ever have heard of the dish. I thought it rather vulgar, and when Noel had got himself caught up with one of the women, I took the chance to get away and back to the hotel. I made myself a cup of tea and went to bed.

I can't say I really understand Noel. We've been here almost two weeks and he has been in late nearly every night. He seems to pick up any stray woman who comes his way. He seems compelled to flatter them and lead them on. They're as different as chalk and cheese, too: you wouldn't get more of a contrast than Caran and Dot would you? Yet he seems to enjoy them all, and they swarm round him. Well, not that Caran: she seemed a bit prickly when we met her afterwards as though he'd taken advantage of her. I couldn't quite make her out. I don't think Noel could, either; not that he ever talks about them the next morning – he just sings as he showers.

To be honest, I was really looking forward to the end of the holiday now. I'd had enough, but this visit to the market might be all right. I cooked our breakfasts, trying to look forward to it.

Noel:

"Markets are the same the whole world over," said Joyce, when we bumped into her by the lace stall.

"Don't you believe it, Joyce," I said. "Is this your first visit to one on Cystos?"

"Yes, Noel, it is. Caran and Lorraine came before, but it was after a late night and I was tired."

"Come, gentle lady, let me lead you by the hand."

"Oh," said Joyce.

"The delights of a Cystonian market are not for the faint hearted or the uninitiated."

"I was just looking."

"A Cystonian market is a metaphor for life, dear lady. No one is ever – just looking!"

I took her by the hand and led her into the depths of the lace stall, rolling my eyes in that way I have at the stall holder who began, immediately, to close in.

My nickname at school was 'Popeye', because they do 'pop'. I think it's a thyroid condition but have never bothered to find out. Who needs to know? I was approached by the NHS once to take part in a bowel cancer survey. Being over sixty, it appeared that I fitted the criteria, but that was from their point of view, not mine. Whether those little drops of blood, which might or might not be in my stools, meant anything was something I'd rather not find out.

How these Mediterranean types fit so much into so small a space I've never worked out. The lace stall went back deep into the bowels of the earth. Row upon row of tables were stacked high with piles of lace and the stallholder, who did eventually close in, seemed to know exactly where everything was placed.

Joyce, who didn't know what she was looking for and probably wasn't looking for anything, kept glancing over her shoulder at the lace-man who followed us as we wended our way into the labyrinths of his trade.

"Fear not, I shall protect you, sweet lady."

"I wish he wouldn't keep following us. I feel under pressure to buy something."

"To traders out here, selling is an art form. If you leave with nothing, his manhood is on the line."

Joyce looked startled, but eventually found a lace blouse, high on the neck, long on the arms, frilled in all the right places.

"It'll keep the sun off," she said.

"You'll look like Lana Turner in *The Three Musketeers* in that. Try it on first."

"Where?"

"Madame, if you please?"

The stallholder closed in and, before Joyce knew what was happening, erected a make-shift changing room and called his wife, who fussed around Joyce muttering words, obsequiously. She did look lovely in the blouse and I told her so.

"It's nice to have someone take an interest. No one has, not since Robert."

The long negotiations began, with me keeping Joyce cool and calm until we had, in line with all the best advice, agreed a figure at around two-thirds of the asking price. The stallholder wrung his hands and his wife looked cheated, but they waved us off with beaming smiles.

I suppose a man could do worse than Joyce. Smiling and wearing, under protest, her new blouse, she looked a million miles away from the frumpy woman we'd met on the pirate ship. I remember thinking she might turn out to be Tony's cup of tea – him needing a shoulder to cry on and her looking the type – but I'd changed my mind about that; they'd organise each other out of existence. On the other hand, for a man who just wanted his washing done and his meals on time, she could be just the job. Mind you, she'd be a bit on the tidy side. You couldn't leave things lying around and might never find them again. I wasn't quite sure about how she'd be when you fancied a bit of 'how's-your-father', either; still, you can't have everything, can you?

Joyce:

It had really been nice of Noel to help me out in the lace stall. Without him that awful man and his wife would have cheated me left, right and centre. When we emerged into the sunlight Lorraine and Caran were waiting, talking with Tony.

"Come on, Joyce, what have you two been doing in there?" called Lorraine.

"Nothing, sweet lady, that one couldn't tell mother without a blush."

"Oh my word, Joyce, that is lovely," said Lorraine.

In two sentences, Lorraine had summed herself up; she had her vulgar side and was a bit of a tramp in some ways, but she was kind. It hadn't occurred to Caran to comment on my new blouse at all, but then Caran had eyes only for Caran. When we'd come on this holiday, there had been some talk about needing two apartments in case one of us "struck lucky", as Caran put it. What's so "lucky" about having a complete stranger pawing you all over, I can't imagine, but I think the idea had been that we'd have a spare bedroom if it happened.

Neither of them said much to me about that kind of thing, but I rather gathered that something had happened with Frank and Caran. I suppose it had been on that first night when Lorraine had been too drunk to notice what might be going on in the next room – I'm not really sure. I do know that Lorraine had met that Dakos several times, but at his flat. Anyway, neither of them had used the spare bedroom in my apartment.

I don't really understand what Lorraine is up to; by all accounts she has a nice home, a nice husband and daughter. What more can she want? It can't be the sex. After all, she's over fifty – she knows better than that by now. That's the trouble, isn't it? Women like her use sex to get what they want. Men are such weak creatures that you can "lead them around by the balls" as Robert once said in one of his vulgar moods. If she's tried to lead that Dakos on, then she has only herself to blame. I'm not racist but I wouldn't trust any of these foreigners an inch. They're out for what they can get – and can you blame them, the way Englishwomen behave when they're abroad? Still she is a kind person; I wouldn't want to see her hurt.

I can't imagine what her husband Barry would say if he found out but I get the impression that she'll probably tell him anyway. There's no accounting for how other people live!

"Joyce – we're moving on."

"Yes? You like the blouse, then?"

"You look lovely in it."

Noel and Tony had drifted away for a cup of coffee, but Caran wanted to look at one of the leather stalls and so we made our way down the avenues until we found one. The heat was indescribable by now, and I was glad of the shade the market offered. This was one of those permanent markets so every now and then a high, white wall cast cool shadows over us.

Haggling was going on everywhere. The locals seemed to thrive on it and some of the tourists used it as an excuse to be loud and show off. We passed one women who appeared to be buying a belly dancer's costume. The stall-holders were in fits as she tried on several styles and paraded up and down. There were cries of "Crazy women, crazy English women!!" and it drew a crowd who came to gawp. I felt sorry for her teenage daughter, who was cringing with embarrassment and pretending not to know her mother. The man with her, who wasn't her husband – neither of them wore rings – seemed to find it as funny as she did, but

I wondered what the stallholders and their wives really thought!

There were loads of leather stalls to choose from but Caran finally decided on one that looked "a little classier than the rest" although what she would know about "class", I didn't like to ask.

Caran:

The leather stall-holder was dishy, no doubt about that. He was tall and dark, with rock-hard muscles, hair cut close to his head and shoulders the width of a barn door. He was wearing a brown leather jacket himself, which gave him the appearance of an animal. He approached us the moment we paused and, before I knew what was happening, had me by the shoulders and was steering me into his shop. There was leather everywhere – coats, jackets, trousers, waistcoats, bags, belts and shoes were hung from across the whole ceiling, which seemed to be made of white cotton or canvas. It was like being inside a tent in the desert. I felt like a heroine in one of those forties or fifties films we used to watch on television when I was a girl – where they get whipped off by a sheik who ravishes them gently under the desert moon. The leather man didn't look particularly gentle but I would have minded him "taking me" on the leather; the smell was gorgeous. I'd only come to browse, really, but he began pulling out coats and jackets as though his life depended on selling me one. He was very determined, like one of those men in nightclubs who are desperate to "pull" and won't take no for an answer. Lauren, my hairdresser, was telling me about that type.

We'd got to the umpteenth jacket and I thought I'd learned all there was to know about Cystonian leather when I spotted Dot and Lorna – the ones Noel calls Siesta and Fiesta. They emerged from the back of the shop – one in a black leather jacket and the other in black leather trousers. It really put me off; I wanted to throw up. To think, I'd nearly bought a jacket (a leather jacket!) in a shop used by those two! I'd never have worn it – never in a million years!

God, how can I describe how awful they looked? The instructor at the gym (I have a personal trainer) once explained to me exactly what being a few pounds over-weight meant. He had a lump of artificial fat about a pound in weight – a bit like a tub of butter, or better still, lard – the white stuff our mothers used for cooking. "Imagine," he said, "seven of these hanging from your body – breasts, bottom or waist. That's you at half a stone, three kilograms, overweight. Imagine fourteen of these hanging from you everywhere – that's you at one stone, about six kilograms overweight! And it isn't just a matter of fat! We're talking here about slack muscle as well, untoned muscle ..." And so on. Well, that lump of fat, about forty times over and squeezed into a size twelve jacket and trousers, is what Siesta and Fiesta looked like – one in the jacket, the other in the trousers. They not only oozed over the trousers and out from under the jacket, they actually seemed to be seeping through the clothes as well; their fat rippled the leather as though it were part of a real, moving animal. Hills of flesh, tubs of lard – someone said that; I learned it at school.

The leather man saw me flinch and turn to the door. As I did, he stepped in front of me and blocked my way.

"Let me pass. I need to pass."

"One hundred and fifty English pounds I ask you for the jacket."

"I want to go."

"One hundred."

I dived under his arm – his muscles were hard and no mistake; I felt them as his arm came down to stop me – and dashed out into the sunlit street.

"Fifty pounds!"

His voice had risen to a scream now and Lorraine and Joyce looked up. We began running down the street. The leather man chased after us, calling:

"The jacket! I give you the jacket!"

We took no notice and didn't stop until we'd turned the corner.

"What on earth was he on about?" said Lorraine, "I'll give you the jacket?"

"They can't bear not to make a sale. It's an affront to their manhood," said Joyce.

"Who told you that?" I asked.

"Noel did, when we were looking for my blouse."

"Oh."

I couldn't think of anything else to say. I also couldn't imagine the leather man having his manhood 'affronted', as Joyce put it, by anyone. The men out here are so macho, I should think they simply 'take what they want when they want it' as they used to say in those fifties films we watched on television in the sixties. God – wasn't life simpler then, before feminism came along and messed about with all our roles? These modern 'I can take it or leave it' men aren't my cup of tea at all. The trouble is they could add, 'They'll be another one along shortly'. We don't seem to have the hold on them we once did, and whose fault is that?

I really thought that Lorraine had it made with Dakos. If she's as good in bed as she gives the impression of being, I don't see how she can fail. If he just took advantage of her last night, then – well, it's tantamount to rape, isn't it, a man taking advantage of a woman, leading her on to think he's really interested when he's only got one thing on his mind? My mother used to say that – "Men have only got one thing on their mind and when they've had that, they don't want to know. Don't lift up your skirt until you're married ..." and we never did, of course – not most of us, anyway. We were still hooked on *The Donna Read Show* and that kind of thing. Most of us were virgins when we got married, still mentally living in the fifties. It took a decade or more for the sixties free love to really catch on, but then, nothing's free is it? Sooner or later you have to pay.

Lorraine was ahead of her time, living with Barry as she did while they were still at university in the late sixties. My father would have gone nuts. But where's it got her? She's now hankering after starting her life all over again with a foreigner in a foreign land. She's lovely, I can see that, but even so, you can't be sure what Dakos was up to: he seemed to want to start a new life with her, he showed her his island, introduced her to his family. Why – if all he wanted was a bit of nookie?

Frank:

I was glad to meet the women again. They'd said they'd be at the market and I bumped into them when they joined Noel and Tony for coffee. We were all conscious, somehow, that this was nearly our last day – all out for those essential souvenirs without which you cannot return home. Joyce seemed pleased with her blouse, Caran seemed annoyed that she'd missed out on a leather coat and the rest of us were still looking.

Well, the women were: I'm not sure that men bother too much about that sort of thing. Noel obviously couldn't have cared less and I had always hated that last-minute dash to buy something for everyone in the whole family.

My wife drove me nuts with her insistence that we had to get something; the last two days of every holiday were always spoiled by that manic hunt for postcards and souvenirs. It didn't seem to matter what you bought – you could never find something suitable for everyone and simply ended up with a load of crap, which people ended up sticking in the loft or left languishing on the back of a shelf somewhere.

Take a look around your friends' houses the next time you get the chance; you'll recognise the holiday souvenirs – boxes of unopened Turkish Delight, windmills with sails that do not turn, fake glass paperweights, hookahs, soft toy animals, wall plaques with scenes from abroad, tea towels with sinew-stiffening slogans, 'local' craft items you later discover have been made in China or Taiwan, plastic bracelets no one would be seen dead wearing, sun-dials, … and all brightly and luridly coloured. Still, I shouldn't grumble. I was free of all that now – I'd decided to buy nothing at all unless something really genuine, which I thought one of the children or grandchildren might like, struck my eye – and I was actually enjoying sitting in this Cystonian market-place drinking coffee.

Tony was in a similar position, but not happy about it; he and Bev had always chosen a "holiday present" together – it had been the joy of their last day.

"We always left it to the last day. We really looked forward to it. We would go round the markets a lot – Bev loved markets – and then return to buy whatever had caught our eye on the last day. Bev could always remember exactly where to go. She never had any problem finding the stall again."

Noel fixed him with that quizzical look and smiled secretly at Caran, who smiled secretly back; Lorraine looked concerned but distant; Joyce was almost in tears. I could only admire the bloke. From what I'd picked up, his marriage had worked. He had worshipped his Bev, done everything for her and their kids while she seemed to spend a lot of time sitting on her backside. Noel had called him an idealist from the sixties who believed a man should do his share – change nappies, cook meals, clean houses, spend all Saturday afternoon shopping, Sunday in the garden, all week working and weekends and holidays decorating the house – while his wife busied herself worrying about when she was going to get everything done. Noel had a way of putting things! But it had worked: there'd been no arguments, no tensions about who did what. It had suited Tony and Bev. Now he had no one to choose his "holiday present" with, no one to share his excitement at returning home. You couldn't help feeling that it was always going to be like this for him now; no one was ever going to replace Bev, and if they did, Tony would drive them nuts.

"I've got my presents, Tony," said Joyce, "and I bought something for the children last week. I'd be happy to help you look for a present, if that's any use."

Glances passed rapidly round the table between Noel, Caran and Lorraine, but I put it down to plain and simple kindness. Joyce might be frumpy, sexless, houseproud, self-righteous, nit-picking and, in some respects, joyless, but she had a kind heart and knew misery when she saw it.

Dot:

When we saw the Tart run out of the leather shop, Lorna and I wondered what the hell was going on. We'd just pulled ourselves into this brilliant leather gear and were going to give it to macho-man straight in the face. If there's one thing these foreigners can't resist, it's an eyeful of Western tit and the black leather jacket I'd got on shoved mine up like a teenagers in a gel bra. There's nothing like leather, is there? It's erotic. You see it in all those porn movies. It brings out the animal in men – and women. Marianne Faithful had the right idea on that motorbike all them years back.

Well, macho-man didn't waste too much time chasing the Tart up the street. He was soon back to see to Lorna and me, and I wouldn't have minded him seeing to me, I can tell you! I watched his eyes bobbling. I feel sorry for these foreign blokes. Their women might seem all sexy – the thick hair, the all-over tans, the big dark eyes and so on – but you get the idea that they aren't up to much in bed, if you know what I mean. It's as though it's all on show but there's nothing much underneath, or why would their blokes be panting after us Western women? I always think they're a bit on the cold side: not so much frigid, as lying there thinking of England (or whatever their country is) instead of getting stuck in. I always put myself out to give a bloke a good time! They don't find me passive, I can tell you. I know where to put it and what to do with it when I'm on the job.

We did our little bit of business with leather man and then shoved and pushed our way round the rest of the market. Believe me, it was shove and push – like the bleeding January sales. Still, it's good fun; you never know who you'll get shoved up against. I reckon we could have a pulled a dozen times that morning.

We were taking a gander at some nuts – no, not that sort: these were ones you could chew on: well, you know what I mean, chew, like in eat – when we came across that Frank. We'd seen him once or twice with the Tart and her friends but never sort of spoken to him. I rather fancied him in a funny kind of way. When you're abroad, I think it's best to stick to foreign blokes because you're not going to get the chance at home, so you might as well try it out while you can; but this Frank looked a bit of all right, in a quiet kind of way.

I had the feeling you could get him going and, you never know, it might be handy to have a bit of steady on hand at home if he lived near. You know – someone you could ring up when you fancied a bit of the other. It's always nice to have a bloke you can rely on to hand, isn't it? A mate of mine at home has this bloke she can always ring up when she feels like that; he's a keen football fan, but he'll always fit her in at half-time and you don't always want to make a long night of it, do you? Sometimes a quick shag is all you're after.

Anyway, we hadn't got anything fixed up for the last night, so I chatted him up:

"All right, then? We've met before, haven't we?"

There's nothing like being direct: it takes most blokes' breath away. When I was younger, I noticed that they always ran their eyes over you – looking over your boobs, then your crotch, then leering in your face – so now I always do that and it really embarrasses them, just for a laugh, of course.

Don't get me wrong – I respect men. I'm not one of those women who get a kick out of making them feel small. I came across one the other day who kept a diary on the Internet – one of them blogs? Well, she called this diary 'Journal of the Twat' and the whole thing was taking the mickey out of her partner: he was the Twat. Fancy calling your bloke that, and writing down things about him to make him look stupid!

This Frank didn't seem embarrassed, though; he looked me straight in the face, deadpan like, and said:

"No, I haven't been that lucky. You must be mixing me up with George Clooney."

I didn't know what to say; it isn't often a bloke leaves me speechless, but he looked as though he might be good for a laugh, so I said:

"I've had ten fellers this holiday. Would you like to make it a football team?"

And he roared: it was corny, but I just knew it would work.

"Some of us are meeting up for the last night. Why not join us? Noel will tell you where. You know him and Tony don't you?" he said.

A night with the Tart didn't grab me, but you never know – it might turn out fun. Anyway, I said I'd see Noel. I couldn't make this Frank out. He seemed matey enough but I didn't get much out of him. He wasn't married so he must have been here on the pull but he didn't suggest that we met up that evening, so me and Lorna moved on. I thought for a while that he might fancy the Tart: there's no accounting for taste.

Frank:

Markets aren't my favourite thing, but it had turned out all right. We'd set up the last night, and I'd managed to get the couple Noel calls Siesta and Fiesta involved, so it might turn out to be fun, because I rather fancied that she and Caran wouldn't see eye to eye. That's one thing I miss about not being married, even after this short time – the wind-up: you can always get a laugh out of a group of women by winding one or all of them up. I don't get that anymore except at work.

I had lunch with Les Girls and Noel and Tony, so it was quite pleasant, and got back to the hotel in the early afternoon; siesta time but without Siesta, thank goodness. When she tried that daft line on me, I thought I'd been nabbed. You don't like to be rude, do you, but there is a limit. I imagine she's quite nice, really, but with a one-track mind, and I couldn't see myself in the sack with her. She'd shag the arse off you in no time.

Back at the Poseidon, I showered, changed, and sat by the pool reading a book. I wanted to bump into Vera, our rep; I knew that she was arranging a 'Booze Cruise Night' and would be about somewhere. People have always interested me and I thought Vera might have a tale to tell. I suppose being a copper makes you like that, and I've met a few novelties in my time.

Sure enough, Vera hoved into view when she thought the pool would be quiet and I hailed her:

"Fancy a drink? Rest your feet. Busy night ahead."

"Oh, hello Frank, don't mind if I do. I have a room here and was about to go for a lie down, but a drink would be nice."

"You have a room here?"

"It saves me driving back home. We live in the hills and there's no point when I'm 'night on'."

"I suppose not. Do you enjoy your 'night on'?"

She gave me a rueful smile and said:

"What do you think?"

"I love my job although I'm semi-retired now. There's nothing like the public to lighten your day."

"'Eco Day' – fine. 'Evening Cruise' – if the tour operator wants a rep – fine. 'Booze Cruise' – no thank you."

"Rough, hey?"

"Rough."

"Tell me about it."

The dark young man from Bangladesh studying Tourism and Systems Management at Abydos University, and who took my suitcase on that first day, served our pina coladas. Why does one drink this crap on holiday? I wouldn't touch it at home. I'd stuck to real drinks for the first few days, but had, somehow, 'gone native'. Not that the 'natives' touch this stuff. I'd kept on the right side of this lad – always left him a tip – and he'd looked after me: the drinks came more or less before they were ordered and Vera relaxed and began to talk. One thing about being a copper – the old-fashioned kind of copper, the ones people trusted because they used their discretion instead of the rule-book – is that you can get people talking. In fact, they want to talk to you. Talking is a pleasure for most people; my pleasure is in listening.

"Do you really want to know?"

"I really want to know."

"Well, these booze cruises aren't our idea. The local equivalent of the Chamber of Commerce wants them to encourage tourists to spend their money. They offer "incentives" like a cut-price 'booze cruise coupon' which entitles you to ten drinks. These kids don't need ten drinks! But, of course, they think they do when they get offered the coupon."

"It isn't just kids though, is it?"

"Oh no – men of your age are just as bad, Frank ...unless their wives are with them!! Some of these characters come here with the express purpose of getting drunk – it's their idea of a holiday! And, of course, the Brits don't get drunk quietly, do they? You can always tell them from other nationalities by their loudness. They even come out here for stag and hen dos now, you know – flights are so cheap. They're the worst. We once had a party of fifty-three women from Wales, all dressed as Tom Jones – that's right, blouses open to the waist, crucifix and all! It caused a riot, the locals were in uproar – even the archbishop got involved. Then you get calls to ban them, but commercial interests take over and everything dies down until the next time. A local saying goes 'The Americans are wild, the Germans are crazy, and the British are beasts.' I must say I agree, and tonight I have the job of getting them all back to their hotels in more or less one piece!"

"I'm surprised your company expects women to do that kind of thing. There must be male reps to handle drunks."

"Frank, your chauvinism is showing!"

"It's nothing to do with chauvinism – just plain courtesy and common sense. A woman shouldn't be asked to do that kind of thing."

"Thanks – but we are, and the younger male reps wouldn't take the same view as you do. They've been brought up in a different world."

"Maybe so. Have another drink. What's your worst experience?"

"A really bad one?"

"A really bad one."

"Drink or sex?"

"Either."

"I suppose it was that oral sex case on the beach. It got into the papers back in Britain, so a friend told me. Some young reps were in charge of a one of these 'booze cruises' and they'd been told that their job was "to ensure holiday makers have a good time – at any cost". They'd got this game going called 'Battle of the Sexes', where you split the boys and girls up, get them hammered and then put them back together and start chanting to gee them up. Well, you know how reluctant Brits can be until they actually do get going. This group was no exception, so the reps, who were as pissed as the punters, decided to show the way and began doing a blow job on the beach. The crowd were cheering them on and someone photographed it!

You can imagine the fallout when it hit the local press, who were "outraged", as the gutter press is everywhere in the world, but they printed the photos nonetheless. The tour operator was called to the mayor's office. Guess who represented the tour operator? Right – Vera! I apologised profusely, and then had to sack the reps concerned for their "unacceptable behaviour" while the board back home rubbed its hands in glee as bookings rocketed. Very unpleasant – I lost several local friends through that one – and we had an unforgettable summer as hordes of youngsters arrived on the promise of getting drunk and getting laid."

"Never a dull moment? But you survived it, and now you're the Eco Lady of Cystos."

She laughed and the Bangladeshi waiter-cum-university-student brought us our third pina colada.

"But you love the job, Vera – that's obvious – so it must have its fun side, too."

"Well, grossness and fun tend to mingle together in this job. You need to have a sense of humour to do it."

She laughed again; her mind was clearly running back over her time as a rep.

"There was an incident last year that cracked us up. We'd had a lot of bother from this particular group of youngsters. We're supposed to go easy on the sex – after all, that's why they come. But it can get out of hand – you know, doing it in the swimming pool upsets the hotel staff and it can be a problem when guests slip over on the condoms, so we try to encourage them to clear up after themselves. Anyway, one lad in this party was particularly foul – we'd caught him peeing up against the hotel wall a couple of times, for example, and he was on the verge of being thrown out when he decided to pull up this manhole cover. He's a bit upset that the bar is closing, I think, so he lifts the manhole cover over his head and throws it at the mirror behind the bar. Fortunately, the barman caught it. Unfortunately, the lad concerned steps backward with the force of the throw and falls down the manhole! Laugh – we never stopped! Multiple fractures in both legs and a broken wrist! He wasn't too frisky for the rest of his stay!"

"He was a Brit, I take it?"

"Ye-es."

"Is it only us, then? Do other nationalities misbehave in a similar way?"

"There was the classic German 'burping contest' a few years ago."

"Burping?"

"Yes. It's considered vulgar to call it a belch."

"What happened?"

"There'd been some racist trouble – well you know, what passes for racism these days. One of the reps had been indiscreet enough to suggest that *all* Germans – yes, all Germans! – were rowdy, arrogant, muscle-bound blondes who ate too many potatoes and burped in public. Can you imagine how a crowd of Brits would have responded to that?"

"Go on."

"We'd have said something like, 'You missed out the bit about farting', or something equally vulgar."

"But the Germans didn't?"

"Oh, no. They organised a protest of mega propor-tions! The whole party – and there were twenty or thirty of them – turned up at the hotel where this rep was staying – there was a restaurant there – and proceeded to eat as many potatoes as they could while drinking huge quantities of lager. In fact, the hotel began to run out of potatoes as the orders kept flooding in and had to send to their vegetable supplier for more. They ordered them in all styles – boiled with butter, mashed with onion gravy, chipped, wedged, sautéed, baked with various fillings including beans, creamed, sliced and fried, served as bubble-and-squeak, as dauphinesses, as potato salad with mayonnaise, pumped through an icing gun in whirls, toasted with cheese … and so on…"

"You're kidding?"

"No, no – and there's more. The women in the party, objecting to the "muscle-bound" stereotype, sunbathed topless on the lawn. And they were lovely looking women – not an ounce of shotputter's muscle on any of them!!"

"The rep was sacked?"

"Oh, yes, and the hotel and tour operator apologised in public. It made the papers, needless to say. Who said the Germans have no sense of humour?"

"And it doesn't qualify as misbehaviour – in the normal sense of the word."

"No."

"How did the locals respond?"

"They couldn't make it out. It was like something from *Monty Python* to them."

"They don't share the Nordic sense of the ridiculous?"

"No."

"How do you get on here? You're married to a local man, aren't you?"

"My partner's name is Andreas. He's an ecology warden. I was fed up with England, had just got divorced, came here with a girlfriend for a holiday, met Andreas and fell in love, so I decided to make a fresh start."

"And it's working out for you?"

"No complaints. It's just a completely different lifestyle."

"How do the locals view you – apart from Andreas, that is?"

"You're a nosey bugger aren't you Frank?"

"Sorry – I'm just curious."

"That's all right. I just thought I'd say so, that's all."

She paused only for a moment and then went on, quite rapidly:

"The locals are fine. It helps that I live with a local man *and* have a job here."

"Are *you* ever stereo-typed?"

"There's always that fight against it but, of course, I'm not your typical tourist Brit, am I?"

"No, obviously not – go on."

"Well you soon get over the 'loud and drunk' image because I'm clearly not either of those. I still get looks, as a foreigner, when I'm out with Andreas because associated with the drunkenness is the local view that English women are 'easy'. We'll never get over that while British holidaymakers continue to insist on taking up with anyone who chats them up and having sex in public, but Andreas treats me with respect and that rubs off on the locals we meet, so – yes – we're overcoming that one!

I don't sunbathe in public. I'd like to, but it simply isn't done out here – nothing would be more 'common'. Anyway, I'm in the sun most of the time, and I don't want to turn that horrible orange colour! I'm careful to dress like the locals, too. They do dress well. The Brits have that 'cropped top with breasts, thong showing, jeans-up-your-arse, belly-over-your-belt' image so I'm careful to avoid any style that would suggest that. And I eat local - none of your 'chips with everything, baked beans, HP sauce and PG Tips' image – but I love the local food anyway, and I can cook it!"

"And the language is no problem? I've noticed that however well they speak English for our benefit ..."

"And their benefit, Frank – they make money out of us!"

"But they speak their own language among themselves!"

"Oh yes, as you say, and they do appreciate your trying to learn it. There's a big expat colony out here – and the locals encourage it, there's a lot of money in selling property to the Brits – but they tend to stick together, taking over an area, and don't bother to learn the language. You know the attitude – "I've bought a house, haven't I? It's their hard luck if they can't speak my language".

"Yes."

"But that wasn't what I was about. I don't speak it well, but I try and that's enough. I'm careful, too, not to complain. Remember back home, whenever a foreigner mouthed off about Britain? What was your reaction?"

"Bugger off back where you came from then!"

"Exactly – so I'm careful. The Brits complain enough when they're abroad anyway – we've a reputation for it – so I'm careful not to, and you won't find me sitting on the patio at night swigging the local vino and singing the praises of home."

"Like the Irish anywhere out of Ireland – or the Scots out of Scotland?"

"Careful, Frank – your Union Jack underpants are showing!"

"It's true, though. What about Cystonian attitudes?"

"To what?"

"To animals, for example – the markets are rough, aren't they?"

"You mean all those chickens cooped up under the meat stalls?"

"Yes – that kind of thing."

"I didn't come here to change the world, Frank. We're used to seeing them as skinless breasts in plastic wrapping minus legs and everything else, but they weren't born like that, were they? The Cystonians prefer to buy them fresh and whole."

Vera suddenly laughed: obviously a thought had occurred to her unconnected with the plight of local meat in the market place.

"Hygiene," she said, "There is this belief that all Brits smell, that soap is something you won't find in their bathrooms and, if you did, they wouldn't use it too often, and that they've never heard of deodorants. Britishness and BO are inextricably linked in the minds of most Cystonians."

"Why? None of us smell."

"Don't we, Frank? How many of those kids roll out of bed in the morning, still wearing the pants they had on the previous day, and get straight into their trousers? They are our ambassadors and we have to live the image down. I always smell like a perfume boutique, myself – I make sure of it. You have to fight for your country when you live abroad!"

She laughed. It was a warm, comfortable sound.

"So you're settling in well?"

"Yes – I love it. Life is what you make it, isn't it? No one is put on this earth to make you happy; you're not born with your own court jester. You have to find happiness for yourself............. I must go now and get some shut-eye. As I said, I'm on the 'booze cruise' tonight. I've enjoyed our chat, though."

"Do you remember Lorraine?" I said.

"Yes. She's at the Captain Karas. Why?"

"She's got herself involved with a local man. Like you, she's thinking of making a life out of it. She might appreciate a chat with you."

"OK – I'll see if I can strike up a conversation. Who is he?"

"A man called Dakos. He seems to own a restaurant and work as a kind of maitre d' in others, as well."

"I know Dakos. He's well liked - a nice chap, hard worker. He thinks the world of his little boy. His wife treated him badly. Cleared off for the social whirl in Abydos and expects him to keep her – which he does! Your friend could do worse than Dakos."

"He took her round the island, she met his family but he seems to have this attitude that Western women are 'easy'."

"He wouldn't have asked her out if he thought that of her – and certainly she'd never have been introduced to his family."

"No, that's what she thought, but there's a problem there and you've crossed the bridge she has yet to step on to …"

"Well, I'm crossing it! Dakos is a nice man, Frank. He'll treat your Lorraine with respect. He's from an old Cystonian family. They have a code of honour."

"I'm sure. It's none of my business, of course. I simply feel that she needs to know what she's getting herself into, what the cultural differences are she's going to face."

"OK. I'll have a chat with her – if that's what she wants. You seem very concerned about someone you hardly know."

"Lorraine is a nice person. I wouldn't want to see her get hurt. There's a very fine line, sometimes, between your world staying intact and it falling apart – a very fine line. Just one little incident is enough."

"You speak from experience?"

"I'm divorced myself. It was my decision – wanted it – but if a conversation had gone the other way, it would never have happened. Lorraine could be on the verge of a new life or on the edge of a disaster."

"But you've no personal interest in the matter?"

"Hmm? No, certainly not."

"Then you're a nice man, too, Frank, for taking the trouble to help her."

After Vera had gone for her siesta, I though how funny it is – the way people see things: to Vera, at that moment, I was a "nice man", at another time, in another situation, I could be "the most ruthless man in the world" and yet, here I was – Frank – the same person in both places.

Day 14: Dionysus Night

Joyce:

I was sitting on my balcony enjoying my Robertson's Silver Shred on toast (not that the bread you get out here is a patch on ours at home) when I saw Lorraine walking back up the road with her morning paper, so I called down to her; she smiled, waved and joined me for breakfast. I made some fresh tea and she really tucked in! I was aware that this was the last full day of our holiday and I wanted to talk. I felt that I had achieved nothing, despite the good talking-to she'd given me at the beginning of it all. "You, Joyce," she said, "are on the lookout! You want a husband, someone to look after and nag at a little when you've had a bad day. You're not going to find one sitting at the poolside eating sundaes and going out for a quiet meal with Caran and me in the evenings." She was right, of course.

I really wanted to talk about myself, but thought it polite to ask about her first so I said:

"How are things with you and Dakos?"

"I don't know, Joyce, to be honest. How are things with you?"

I smiled; she'd guessed. I said:

"Well, I didn't really expect to meet anyone, and I haven't."

"And you don't really want to, do you? You just want Robert back."

"Yes."

"I don't know the details of your position, Joyce – I can only guess at things from what you've said – but it doesn't sound to me as though he's coming back. I expect you've been told that you need to move forward so I won't repeat the advice, but you can't keep living in the past."

"But I don't want anybody else – not in that way …."

"Then you'll end up living alone for the rest of your life. Is that what you want?"

"No."

"Then you have an unsolvable problem."

"Robert always said that."

"What?"

"That I created problems, asked him to solve them, and then didn't like the solution."

"You had rows over that kind of thing?"

"No more than most people. I blame her – the other woman. She latched on to him when he was vulnerable. We were going through a bad patch, but we'd have been all right if she hadn't been there!"

"Joyce, I hate to say this but – in my view – the 'other woman' is rarely to blame. The faults lie in our own marriages."

"You're not much comfort, Lorraine."

"I'm not trying to be. How often, once we get back home, are you and I going to sit down and talk about this? It's no help to you for me to fudge and mumble words of comfort now…"

"I don't see how you can say that she wasn't to blame."

"It's not the accepted wisdom is it, but given the number of 'decent men' – I use the term guardedly, because I don't actually know them all! – that seem to go for divorce these days, it does make you wonder, doesn't it?"

"You mean I'm to blame for him taking up with her?"

"Not just you – you and Robert. What was it in your marriage that he could no longer stand? I'm not saying that men aren't going to be attracted by 'Miss Hot Pants 2004' or whatever the latest bit of tit is! Of course they are, but they're not going to go off with it if they are happy in their marriage, are they? I don't know the answers, Joyce, so don't look to me for them. All I'm really saying is that I think the seeds of divorce are sown within our marriages and that the 'other woman' is not the main reason."

"She wasn't a young woman. She was about our age – a bit younger, but not much."

"I'm sorry. That must have been worse."

"She wasn't even that attractive ..."

"But she attracted Robert?"

"Yes."

"Was it an affair?"

"Yes."

"How long?"

"I'm not sure."

"Didn't you ask him?"

"I'm not sure he told me the truth. He said it had ended after a year, but friends said that they'd seen them together a lot longer than that."

"So he lied to you?"

"Robert wouldn't ..."

"But, unless your friends are lying, he did?"

"They worked together; they could have been seen together quite legitimately without it being an affair."

"But he left you for her?"

"Yes."

"And divorced you?"

"Yes."

"What grounds did he give?"

"It wasn't nice."

"What are you clinging on to, Joyce?"

"He was a good man, a kind man. I loved him. We had a lovely home – not materialistic, but homely. We'd brought our children up there. It's the only home they remember. We took such care with it, choosing everything together – curtains, furniture, carpets. Everything toned in, nothing jarred – it was a lovely, quiet, peaceful home, and I know Robert loved it. Some of the times we loved best were when company had gone and we were alone. We'd flop into a chair and just be with each other."

"How many times have you said this, Joyce – to friends, to family, to strangers, to yourself?"

I began to cry then, I hadn't done that for such a long time it was a relief. The tears rolled down my face. I choked and felt the sobs racking my chest and my heart. Lorraine came over to me, eased me from the chair and sat us both together on the settee. I put my head against her and just went on crying. I'd cried during the months of the divorce – to my daughter, who listened but was embarrassed: to my son, who sympathised but felt helpless: to some of my friends, who'd said things like, "He's a bastard" (which he wasn't) or "Forget him, move on" (which I couldn't). I'd always apologised to them, but

I didn't feel I needed to with Lorraine. She sat quietly, unhurried, and I sobbed it out of me – for the moment. At last, I said:

"It was love at first sight. Neither of us had had anyone else before we met each other."

"Things never work out as you expect, do they, Joyce?"

"I thought we'd spend our last years together – sail together into the sunset, so to speak. I don't want to be alone, Lorraine."

"Have you considered …just friendship?"

"What do you mean?"

"If you don't want a … full relationship why don't you find someone for friendship?"

"It isn't the same. Who else has the same interest in the children? Another man would just sit there with his eyes going blank. Robert used to fuss around me."

"Tea in bed, and that sort of thing?"

"Yes – although that stopped, suddenly, about five years after we were married."

"Why?"

"I don't know. I didn't like to ask."

I wondered about that, now; why hadn't I asked? Perhaps I had and Robert had given one of his evasive answers. I was still sobbing, still wanted to talk.

"I need someone who knows me, Lorraine, someone I can be comfortable with. When you love someone like that, you can talk, can't you? That's part of being in love – sharing your soul."

"You'd have him back, wouldn't you – even now?"

"I'd give anything to find him sitting in the chair when I arrive home tomorrow."

"And what would you do? What would you say?"

"I wouldn't have to say anything. We'd just be together."

"And the home would be there again – for the children?"

"Yes."

"Did you talk a lot?"

"We never stopped. There was always something to say."

"You say his affair with this woman ended?"

"Yes."

"But then it must have started up again if he left you for her?"

"Yes."

"Didn't you find reconciliation then?"

"No … yes! Yes we did, but it wouldn't go away. It was always there …between us."

"Did you talk about it?"

"Yes … but I couldn't understand it. We'd been so happy, such a close family. I never understood why he did it …I wouldn't let it go. I couldn't let it go! Every time there was something on television – you know, someone having sex, someone having an affair – it all came boiling up again. We couldn't watch anything like that without being embarrassed by it …"

"How were things between you?"

I looked at Lorraine. I couldn't think for a moment what she meant and then it dawned on me.

"They were alright. They'd always been alright."

"For you."

"And for Robert. Robert never complained."

"But he wouldn't, would he? He wasn't that kind of man …and, anyway, men never do, do they?"

"He said it wasn't sex that he did it for ..."

"I can believe that. He sounds a complex man and men like that don't just follow their dicks through life. So what was it? Did you ever get near to the answer?"

"As I said, I think things got on top of him. He just wanted ...."

"A respite?"

"Yes."

I didn't like that; I didn't like the idea that Lorraine thought Robert might want a "respite" from me – a rest from the family? But maybe he did, and when he came back, he didn't get it, did he? I wouldn't let it go. He'd felt guilty, I knew that; he'd found the whole adulterous business as difficult as I had. That's why I blamed her – if she hadn't been there it would never have happened.

The world's so full of it, isn't it – the sex thing! It's supposed to be the answer to all your problems: get a good sex life and the rest will sort itself out. 'Max your life in seconds!' They even have a website for it – 'spill your saucy secrets on the Confessions channel', as though the whole thing is a joke! 'Rate or slate your guy'. I didn't want to do either with Robert. I loved him; why would I want to 'rate or slate' him in a public place? Everything is trivialised. 'Feeling dodgy on the outside can make you feel dodgy on the inside, so treat yourself to a hot new outfit.' It's always 'hot' isn't it? They even refer to men as 'hotties' – 'choose your favourite hottie and download some seriously sexy eye candy.' It's all so flip and silly. People's real lives are caught up in all that nonsense.

"Did he want the respite?"

"Yes, perhaps he did. I do tend to go at things when I get my teeth into them. Robert used to say that I was like a terrier."

I laughed at the memory, and Lorraine laughed with me.

"You mustn't go on feeling bad about yourself, Joyce. You've lost your confidence."

"Robert gave me that."

"Yes – and divorce took it away. You feel less attractive than you ever did?"

"Yes – and the kindness of strangers doesn't help. I walked down here one morning and one of the shopkeepers gave me an orange. I know he meant well, but ..."

"It was also condescending?"

"An orange for the poor old lady."

"There's no chance of Robert coming back, is there?"

I looked at her; he and this other woman lived together ("partners" they call it, don't they?) but they'd never married. I always felt he'd kept the door open: that he could pack his suitcase and walk out any time he wanted to, and that one day he would.

"I just hope he will – one day."

Lorraine:

Poor old Joyce: I'd thought about her all day and when evening came and Caran and I were dolling ourselves up ready for the last night, I was still thinking about her. Her Robert seemed a nice enough chap, but he hadn't behaved very nicely had he – whatever the reason? If it wasn't sex that pulled him away, what was it – the lure of a new life? I couldn't help feeling that he hadn't been completely honest with her, and that a bit of bluntness on his part might have saved the day but "kind" men don't go for bluntness, do they? They store it up and then explode.

It was certainly the lure of a new life that was pulling me towards Dakos; I was well aware of that, and I was also sure that when the moment came, I would be more honest with Barry than Robert had been with Joyce. There's something in Shakespeare about "killing a woman with kindness". It's in *The Taming of the Shrew* and Shakespeare was right – kindness can be killing: far better to get things out in the open and give each of you the chance to see the other's point of view.

We'd all planned to meet up in The Square at – yes, the Square Pub. I don't quite know why, except that no one could make a decision and Frank had said that this was where we'd gone on that first night when I got plastered in Gasoline. The Square Pub was opposite the monastery, which gave it a sense of safety (false!) in Joyce's book. We were promised Demitri on guitar singing "classic pop", which sounded better than that "ear-shattering rubbish we normally have to listen to" as Joyce put it. Anyway, Frank seemed to think it might make "a good starting place". I could see that it was going to be difficult, keeping Joyce up beyond midnight – she'd packed already – so a good start was something! We were also promised "a party atmosphere", "many of our requests" and a "sing song", so Caran and I went dressed for a fun night tinged with nostalgia – she dressed by Kaliko and me by Next.

Frank:

I was looking forward to the evening, which is why I'd suggested returning to The Square, where it had all started fourteen days ago. Yes, I was hoping to end up with Caran when the night drew to a close, and thought that this might stir the right kind of memories. I'd enjoyed sex with her and was disappointed that we hadn't made more of a go of it during our stay on Cystos, but there you are – you can't have everything, but you can live in hope!

I was wearing my favourite holiday slacks and that white silk shirt which the hotel had washed and pressed freshly for me; the young man from Bangladesh had seen to that and tomorrow he would be tipped accordingly when I left. I decided to get to the pub-restaurant early – it always pays to be ahead of the game – and set off before eight o'clock, when all the locals and most of the Brits were still bathing or dressing. I hoped that Caran would be wearing that black Hobbs dress she'd had on the first night – the one with the low back – so that I could see the curve of the muscles of her spine as they flowed down to her hips.

I cut through the back streets, passing several families of locals hurrying home with shopping, and a few groups of tourists well tanked up; they'd probably arrived on an afternoon flight already half-cut from the booze served on board, checked into their hotels and had one of those 'Full English Breakfasts' which the bars serve all day. What makes me laugh is that it's unlikely that any of these kids actually have breakfast when they're at home – unless their mums cook it for them, of course.

Among the groups of tourists were two girls obviously "out on the piss", as they say, wandering around bra-less and "up for fun", hoping to pull later on in one of the clubs. They were reeling about across the street when they passed two local lads who seemed to be on their way home. The youths started calling out to them – more in hope than expectation, I thought – with phrases they had picked up from the Brits. One of these had the desired result – "Tits out for the lads" produced a huge pair of jugs as one of the girls pulled up her skimpy top. I hung back at this point, wondering what the hell was going to happen. Call it professional training – or voyeurism, if you like – but I had several worrying minutes as the boys (and they were little more than sixteen, if that) came urgently across and were all over the girls, who were both loving the attention. The next thing I knew, the girl who had lifted her top took both boys across to a stretch of wasteland. The other girl looked bored, but not unduly bothered, and began fiddling with her mobile phone. A few minutes later her friend came running back, grinning all over her face – "Two virgins in one day and it's not even nine o'clock!"

I slipped quietly away; obviously girls like that can take care of themselves – or can they? I felt uneasy about it but there didn't seem much I could do; they were clearly older than the boys – in their late teens or early twenties – and had probably lost their virginity years ago. I felt sorry for the boys; I don't think I'd have wanted my first sexual experience to have been on a piece of back-street wasteland with a drunken British girl while, presumably, my best mate looked on.

The Square was still relatively quiet, but it never got really busy until after eleven and I settled, somewhat thoughtfully, down to my first drink – a straight Scotch whisky: single malt and no nonsense. I watched as other tourists came in – people of my age, out for a last drink and meal, risking a final cocktail before the flight home. One man, bursting with flesh and sun, ordered a Blood and Sand while his wife protested – perhaps that was why he ordered it – and I watched the waiter pour the whisky, orange juice, cherry brandy and sweet vermouth into a mixing glass and stir them with ice before pouring the lot into a champagne saucer and garnishing it with a twist of orange. Joshing his wife and toasting his friend and his friend's wife, the 'Flesh and Sun Man' poured the drink down his throat. I was spared his next order by the arrival of Fiesta and Siesta.

Dot:

I was glad to see Frank sitting there when me and Lorna arrived. I always like to get stuck in early, but I had a particular reason for doing it that night. I fancied some last night nookie with someone – anyone, really – and thought I might get it off with Noel if I could get the Tart out of the way; and this Frank, from what I could make out, was just the bloke to do that. He was a real gentleman, I will say that. The minute me and Lorna walked in he stood up and asked what we wanted to drink. Never turn down an offer like that! Lorna went for a Cool Martini – she's always been a bit straight when it comes to drinks despite her being able to knock it back with the best of them – but I went for a Czarina. It sounded posh and vodka's in at the moment, right? A few of them and you're anybody's – provided you can get anybody.

I was glad to rest my backside, to be honest. It'd been a bit rough back at the hotel. Some newcomers had arrived and they were a right bunch, I can tell you. They'd come on one of those free drink deals. You know, everything paid for in the set price. Well, that's asking for trouble, if you ask me – especially when they're young Brits. Lorna and me were down at the pool when they arrived. They dumped their bags in reception and headed straight for the bar. They must have downed a dozen drinks in the first hour and then they were all over the place. Groups of the them running up to their rooms and taking showers with whoever they could grab, running along the landings – stark naked – between each other's rooms, vomiting over the balconies and screaming with laughter. They were soon singing – if you can call it that – at the tops of their voices, and ranting. Bloody hell it was only five o'clock in the afternoon, and they were shouting things like "slag" and "bitch" and calling out for sex! And that was only the women! It was embarrassing to be British, so Lorna and me went and got ourselves tarted up.

"You got anything planned for the end of the evening, Frank?"

"We'll have to see what happens."

"It's your last night. You might as well make the most of it."

"Right."

God, he was close. I wasn't getting much out of him, so I thought I might as well be blunt.

"You fancy that Caran, don't you?"

"What makes you think that?"

"Do you always answer questions with other questions?"

"You're the second person to ask me that this holiday."

"Well, do yer?"

"It's a habit."

"But you do fancy that Caran?"

"I like her, yes. Why?"

"Well, if you can get her out of my hair, I'd appreciate it, that's all."

Just as I said that she arrived, done up like a dog's dinner, with her two mates. It's funny how you take an instant dislike to some people, isn't it? If I could have poured some tomato ketchup down that dress of hers, nothing would have made me happier.

Caran:

Frank stood as we arrived and offered us a drink. I realised, when he did that, why I'd fancied him. The fact that he was sitting with the Roughs didn't take away from his quiet charm. He didn't, of course, look like George Clooney (I don't suppose even George Clooney does in the flesh) but he had the same kind of 'take-it-or-leave-it' charm; there's nothing more provocative to a woman than that, is there? You like to think they can't resist you, or that you can do something about it if they can.

I felt as randy as I had on that first night when we were all psyched up for it. It had been a funny holiday, but I had to admit, all in all, I'd enjoyed it. Coming away together had been a joke really, something Lorraine and I talked up after the gym. Simon hadn't minded. In fact, he looked rather pleased when I suggested it. Our own holidays had burned themselves out, really. For the past few years – once the children were off our hands as far as holidays were concerned – we'd been away with friends of our own age but the holidays never came up to expectations. I'd come to hate hotel rooms. You'd have a shower or whatever, and sit there thinking one of you should be making a move towards the bed and not really being that bothered. It was always a relief to get down for the pre-dinner drinks. Of course, when the other couple arrived you naturally thought they'd been "at it", which was why they were late.

Of course, this holiday hadn't lived up to expectations either; all that talk in the glossies about women of "a certain age" having at least three lovers in the two weeks, one in five having sex with a local, one in seven having sex with a club rep, two thirds of us cheating on our partners and the whole Mediterranean being one huge playground where Brits of our age "partied 'til dawn". But it would be nice to stay out until dawn once again in your life and walk home in an expensive dress, barefoot, with your shoes dangling from your hand, and I thought Frank might be up for that, if enticed. It wasn't the sex – it was the romance I wanted.

Noel:

We arrived late at The Square, because Tony insisted on packing before we left the hotel. "It will make it less of a rush in the morning," he'd said. "But we're rushing now!" When we did eventually leave, our suitcases stood in each of our rooms – "Flat, to reduce the chances of everything crumpling before we go." "What does it matter? The baggage handlers aren't going to carry them flat. We'll be lucky if they actually carry them at all. The normal technique is to throw!" But they were flat packed and our flight bags stood on the coffee table in the lounge, open in identical manners "so that we can just pop the last few things in." There was nothing to "pop in"! Everything we'd brought, bought or come-by had been packed or disposed off; every surface in the apartment had been damp-wiped and polished – the cleaners would be able to see their faces smiling back at them. Tony had even foil-wrapped the food we'd left – half a

jar of coffee, one portion of mini Shredded Wheat, a
quarter bag of sugar, four tea bags, a few scrapings of
Cystonian marmalade, three-quarters of a carton of
milk, several bottles of mineral water and two eggs – and
left a note on each wondering whether the staff would
like them. The fridge had been defrosted and opened, the
cleaning materials "wiped round" and left in the
cupboard under the sink. The only items that remained
unassailed were our tooth brushes, electric razors, two
bars of hotel soap and two shower towels, "which we
can hang on the balcony to dry out after we leave in the
morning" and our "leaving clothes" which were on
hangers *outside* the wardrobes.

When we left the hotel having tipped the concierge,
"in case we don't get time in the morning", I was
exhausted and insisted on sitting down in the English
Pub on the way to regain my composure. This proved to
be a mistake, but an interesting one. It was only just
touching nine o'clock, but already, those who had
arrived that day were on the streets overcome by a
mixture of tiredness, Full English Breakfasts and many
pints of lager. One group of lads was stopping at every
bar for one pint and by the time they got to us, they were
in boisterous mode. The locals were already watching
them closely so down went the trousers and out came the
pale English arses. Why are English arses always pale?
The inevitable digital cameras recorded each act of
obscenity from every angle, and the more sophisticated
types were also able to record the farts and belches.

Tony was for moving on rapidly, but I've always had
an interest in the wildlife of any region and watched,
fascinated, as a gang of five or six local lads arrived and
proceeded to strip the group of tourists "stark bollock

naked", as they would have said, if they could have talked at all. The crowd loved it. I suppose the attraction was more in the humiliation of the English than their backsides, but the youths were too far gone to care. The cheering crowd soon attracted a couple of policemen and before the lads knew what was happening, they were forced to the ground, handcuffed, covered up and frog-marched to the police van. They could hardly see at the time from the amount of drink they'd consumed, and the only words they could utter were "Fuck off!" which they did, many times with an exclamation mark, until the policemen thumped them in the mouths to shut them up. When we left the next day we heard that they'd made page four of the local paper, which must have pleased them enormously and provided an exciting souvenir for their mates back home.

Everybody else was there when we arrived. Frank brought us a drink, and we settled down – having moved the restaurant around a bit to make room for the eight of us at one table – while we regaled them with the story.

I was looking forward to the evening enormously and hoping for a bit of 'How's-your-father' at the end of it. I don't think Caran had been too impressed by my prowess as a lover – but then we'd both had a bit to drink that night – because she hadn't really spoken since, but there was always Dot. I'm not a fussy man. As long as the lady is enjoying herself, that's good enough for me. The dynamics of our little group hadn't gripped me too much, but I rather thought that Frank and Caran might have had something going, so if it could be manoeuvred that Tony walked the frumpy one home, it would just leave Lorraine and her breasts to worry about because I could see Dot and Lorna back.

Frank:

Why we couldn't eat at the Square Pub, I don't know; the conversation that moved us on was reminiscent of one of those you have when you're married. You know the kind of thing. You've discussed the evening, worked out the logistics, got yourself nicely seated with a comfortable drink and then the wife or one of the other women in the group (with whom your wife has to agree – despite all the discussions that went on in the bedroom, lounge and kitchen beforehand) decides that the restaurant down the road is better. She doesn't know that it's better because she has never been there but someone, whom she doesn't know, has told her by the poolside that it is, so we must try it. Listening to all this, I appreciated – not for the first time that holiday – the joys of not being married; on the other hand ...yes, it's something you get used to and rather miss.

So that's how we ended up at the Omar Khayyam. I know, don't ask! This not only had three outdoor bars, exclusive lounges, the Love Bites restaurant and hammocks in the garden but also *narghiles* which turned out to be a kind of hookah through which you smoked flavoured tobacco. None of us actually smoked, so why we'd ended up here remains a mystery; but it did have that air of decadence you need on the last night of your holiday. Caran smiled at me when we were found a seat and said, "Glad you came, Frank?" She must have been reading my mind.

The place was done out like a Hollywood version of the scenes you imagine from the Arabian Nights. I was reminded of the sensuality that oozes from those stories. As a kid – especially as a young teenager – I'd lapped up that kind of thing; it never occurred to me at the time that maybe the 'harem' hadn't been such a great thing for the women. They seemed happy enough in the movies in their sequinned bras and panties draped with fine lace: surrounded by hung curtains and tapestries of pure gold: lying on silken sheets, gazing at their faces in lily pools, seduced by oriental spices, attars of roses and damask clothes, dancing the night away in those lovely swaying movements while wazirs, sultans and other notables looked on, smitten and moony-eyed. They lived only to be loved by their men. Yeah, right.

I suppose there's a down-side to everything. I was also reminded of Fitzgerald's translation of the *Rubaiyat*: "The moving finger writes and having writ, moves on; Nor all thy piety nor wit shall lure it back to cancel half a line, Nor all thy tears wash out a word of it." Yes – well it does rather work out like that, doesn't it?

Not that the Omar Khayyam was exactly like that. The tapestries had faded somewhat and the chests of golden goblets, necklaces, bracelets and plate were plastic; the barrels of rubies no longer spilt like wine across the floor, nor were gold coins as plentiful as raindrops – and the Harem women had been surpassed by pole dancers. As we entered, a group of Brit girls were swaying – more drunkenly than provocatively – round the poles while the blokes stood around chanting and clapping; one of the girls had either removed her knickers or forgotten to put them on and this was attracting the usual plethora of digital cameras. It somehow lacked the magic of the Arabian Nights. Perhaps what you imagine is always better than what you get. We looked at each other and left.

As we did so, a young man was chatting up a girl in the doorway, trying to convince her that it would be a good idea to return to his "love tent down by the river". He had a can of lager in one hand, a cigarette lighter in the other, a cigarette in his mouth and looked as if he was about to puke over her shoes. The girl didn't appear terribly convinced, which was probably just as well since he seemed unlikely to be able to put one foot in front of the other let alone set his "love tent" aglow with the passions of the night.

"Why don't we just go to the Queen Vic and have a good blow-out?" said Lorna. "I'm buggered if I want to ponce around the town all night looking for somewhere posh."

This, of course, was aimed directly at Caran, who had suggested that we could do better than the Square Pub. She responded sharply:

"Some of us are just a bit fussy about where we eat and who we eat with, that's all."

"They serve everything there – all day. Breakfast, lunch and dinner, with yer plate piled high. And if you can still stand after a bellyful of their nosh, Costa and Markos will get you on the dance floor to round off the evening. It's fun!! Yer feel really at home and if you want to, you can catch up with *Eastenders* on Sunday with yer roast."

"Sounds delightful," said Caran.

"There is the Oracle", said Noel, "A truly stylish place. Tony and I had a great meal there, beautifully presented on the terrace by the award-winning chef. The whole ambience is set for the perfect night out. We could say a fond farewell to Kiri and Miklos who are both as sweet as chocolate."

I assumed that he was winding the two women up, but his smile carried all before him, won the day and we were soon walking along the main street – Noel between Dot and Lorna, Tony with Joyce and Caran, Lorraine and I bringing up the rear.

Joyce:

The street was as "lively" as ever when we – at long last – decided where we were going to eat. I really was quite tired by then of all the sparring between Caran and that other woman, and of the fact that it was after ten at night and we hadn't had anything to eat! I was glad to be walking quietly with Tony.

There was the inevitable loud music, the sounds of people yelling and shouting – why can't young people enjoy themselves without having to involve all of us in their noisiness? The bars that lined the street were full of them drinking and "having fun" – or, at least, their idea of fun. They were lining the bar with what they call "shots"; there were actually people of our age involved too, waving bottles of tequila round their heads and topping up the glasses. The nightclubs were beginning to tout for trade, enticing the young men in with half-naked girls thrusting their breasts at them. Another group of girls across the street were egging two men on to have a fight. They kept shouting "Waste him!" until the men started laying into each other and their friends just watched; it was like one of those fights that used to start up in the playground for no apparent reason. Then, just like a children's fight, one of them broke away and the others chased him; you can see how things get quickly out of hand. They were soon throwing stones and bottles, hitting passing cars and the swearing started – "F***ing this" and "F***ing that".

In one bar, a man was riding one of those mechanical bulls like at a rodeo. His friends stood round cheering him on and guzzling their beer. He only lasted seconds and was then thrown off on to the mat. He got up with a bloody nose and they all stumbled to the next bar, where young men and girls were dancing on the tables – the girls naked, or nearly so! I said to Tony:

"I've had enough of this. I shall be glad to go home tomorrow."

"I can't wait to put the key in my front door and walk inside."

I could see that Frank was keen to be with Caran – he hadn't left her side all night – and wondered if I might ask Tony to walk me home after the meal. I knew what it would be, otherwise – more drinking and silliness at some nightclub. Lorraine and Caran were obviously "up for that".

The police arrived as we passed the rowdies and they seemed very angry. One of the girls who had been doing the egging on began to cry – wanted her "Mummy", I suppose. One of the young men, more drunk than the rest, began to scream, "la Policia! la Policia!" Then another of the girls slapped one of the policemen round the face and ran off down the street. Whistles blew, there was a lot more yelling and some of the bouncers ran out of the clubs, and began to chase the girl and her friends, who had run off. Two of the youths jumped on to the police van and when one of the officers tried to intervene, they snatched his handcuffs and ran off with them – a fitting souvenir to show his friends at home, no doubt! It was too awful; the local shopkeepers came and stared from their doorways until the hullabaloo had died down. They say the police here are rough, but can you blame them? I just wanted to eat the meal and get back to the hotel, but looking at Caran I could see that she was quite excited by all the activity. I felt some sympathy for Lorraine – I don't know why, but I did; but I couldn't imagine ever looking Caran in the face again when we got home.

Noel:

Kiri and Miklos were indeed pleased to see us back, with our friends, and we settled ourselves on the terrace for a twenty-dish meze while the staff performed "Zorba the Greek". I felt settled in for the evening now; the dish was going to take us through until, probably, after midnight. I could see Tony was not going to enjoy the meal and would be keen to get back and I had the feeling that Joyce would go with him. So, if I made sure that Fiesta was knocked out with enough wine, the coast would be clear for Siesta and me to "party", provided I'd been right about Caran and Frank, and we could steer Lorraine in the right direction.

"This is lovely, Noel and Tony. So civilised," said Caran.

"Once you get through the peddlers," said Joyce.

"Joyce, Joyce, they are part of the ambience."

I tried my soothing voice; I've found with women that if you say their name twice it has that effect – but not, it would seem, with Joyce.

"Hmm, I don't really see why we should have to put up with them."

Along the street, we had negotiated our way through the usual hawkers selling designer watches, sweets, cheap cigarettes, anything in leather, designer jewellery,

designer perfume and so on, but when we arrived at the
Oracle a burly Cystonian made sure that only Western-
ers were allowed in. Frank had asked:

"Why?"

"For your protection, sir – you've come to enjoy your
meal, not to be pestered by these people."

"Better them than drunken Brits."

"We don't allow them either, sir."

Lorraine:

It was good to be sitting and eating at last and, as
the dishes arrived one by two by three, we all relaxed,
and I said:

"Let's share our holiday memories. Who's going to
start ....Dot?"

"All right, Lorraine – if you insist. The 'ethnic night'
Lorna and me went on was my favourite. It suited us
both – didn't it, Lorna? She got to eat and I got to pull.
It was great – eh, Lorna? You can't imagine the amount
of food they shovelled in front of us – it never stopped
coming. Lorna was so stuffed, she couldn't move from
her seat. Isn't that right, girl?"

"I should say. I don't know how I got it all down
me. By the end of the evening, I was fit to bust.
I should say I've gone up several dress sizes since I've
been here. Still you only live once, don't you?"

The expression on Caran's face was wonderful; it
wasn't so much the disapproval as the disbelief that
made me laugh. I know – they were vulgar and they
were coarse, but there was no pretence about Dot and
Lorna; what you saw – and heard – was what you got.

"And afterwards there was the dancing ..."

"Not that I could move from the chair – but Dot did."

"On the pull, Dot?" said Caran, apparently without spite.

"Too right. I landed myself a nice, muscley Greek that night. He'd come over to show the locals how to do Zorba's dance. He could do more than dance, let me tell you!"

There was uproar at the table; we all feel obliged to laugh at sexual jokes, bravado, innuendo, don't we? Why? Out of politeness? Even Noel, who I rather thought was hoping to follow where the Greek had been, joined in, but I felt just a little sorry for him and said:

"Lorna?"

"The same as Dot – I may have spent the next day creased up with the gut ache, but it was worth it."

"Tony?"

"I don't know that I had a favourite day, but the one I remember most vividly was the day Noel was obliged to dive from that cliff."

"Oooooooh!!!"

It was a collective "Oooooooh!!" All of us suddenly remembered Noel and the pirate ship.

"I jumped, Tony – that's all. Diving was beyond me at that moment. Indeed, I thought, while I was on that cliff face, that living was about to elude me forever."

"It took guts, nevertheless," said Frank.

"I had no choice. I was propelled. Destiny had me in the palm of her hand."

"Is destiny a woman, then, Noel," I said, with a laugh.

"For a man ...."

He paused, like an accomplished actor, for significant seconds and then said:

"... always."

"Frank?"

"I can't say – not in public. There was an evening – or two – that will live with me forever."

There was nothing sleazy about the way he said that; it was spoken softly and with feeling. Of course, he didn't have to say it – he could have simply made up a memory, but chose not to for whatever reason. Led by Dot, we all laughed. He knew we would – well you have to, don't you? I looked quietly at Caran; she was busy with a helping of halloumi.

"Got your act together, did you, Frank?" said Dot.

"Magic moments are seldom planned."

"How true," said Noel, quite taken aback by Frank's – how shall I say it – solemnity? 'You know how little while we have to stay; And, once departed, may return no more'."

Frank looked at him and said:

"Fitzgerald?"

"Fitzgerald."

"Who the F's Fitzgerald?" asked Lorna.

"A poet, dear lady, too decadent for this age."

"Thank God for that," said Dot.

"What about you, Joyce?" said Tony.

"The evening cruise'," said Joyce. "I loved the evening cruise'. I didn't think I would, but I did. It was so peaceful, I forgot where I was for a while. Oh yes, and when Frank was kind enough to take me back to our hotel on that first night. We walked along the harbour – do you remember, Frank?"

"Ooh yes," gushed Lorna.

"No, no," said Joyce, "We just walked and I talked, and Frank listened to me. It's nice to be listened to, sometimes."

"Thanks, Joyce – my pleasure," said Frank, "What about you, Lorraine – you're the one who asked us for our holiday memory?"

"My day out – I don't know what will come of it, maybe nothing, but I shall remember it."

Nobody laughed – the group, for a moment, seemed solemn, or was it just thoughtful; not, of course, that either Dot or Lorna knew what I was talking about. I said, to cover the moment:

"Noel – what about you?"

"Any moment that I spent with you ladies will always be precious to me."

"No, come on, Noel – one moment, don't cheat!"

"Then it must be Tony packing our suitcases."

We all laughed, whether we had to or not.

"Weren't you worried that they'd think you were queer?" said Dot, "I mean two blokes sharing a room?"

"No chance of that, Dot. Were you and Lorna mistaken for lesbians?"

"No chance of that either, sweetheart – I don't exactly look like a dyke, do I?"

"A what?" said Joyce.

"Never mind, Joyce; there are other worlds out there of which we need to know little – or nothing," said Noel.

"What about you, Caran?" I asked.

"I think my moment is yet to come, Lorraine."

Tony:

It was a nice evening. I was glad they all enjoyed themselves somewhere Noel and I suggested, but I didn't want to dance or go on to more drinking and neither did Joyce, so when the meal came to an end and the waiters began to pull people from their seats to join the bouzouki dancers, I decided it was time to go. We made our good-byes and left. I would never have dared to do that when I was younger; I would have sat there until everyone decided to go but, to be honest, when you get older, you don't care that much about what other people think.

"Thanks, Tony. I couldn't face another hysterical evening. None of them are going to be fit to fly to-morrow."

"I don't know. It's surprising how much alcohol they can get through."

"Will you be really glad to get home?"

"I can't wait. I've always been like it – even when Bev was alive, I enjoyed returning, rather than going. We always made an effort to leave the house clean and tidy so that it was nice when you came in. When we got into the house the children would always go to their bedrooms while I unpacked the suitcases, put any dirty washing in the machine and Bev put her feet up. Then I'd make her a cup of tea."

"What will you do tomorrow?"

"Unpack and put the washing in the machine ... I know, but it will still be nice to get home."

"You must find the house empty."

"I try not to think about it any more than I must."

"I can't sleep at night. I lie awake with the radio on to keep me company."

"I cried a lot at first. In fact, at first I cried all the time. Have you tried Valium?"

"The doctor did mention it, but I'm not one for drugs."

"It's prescribed. It gets you to sleep. My son recommended it to me. He used it as a student at university. He said it "eased the comedown after a hectic bout of studying". He used to get it from a pharmacist friend. In places like Thailand you can buy it over the counter – dozens of the little blue pills for a quid or so. He came back after his gap year with a stock of them. They do make you feel tranquil and then you fall asleep."

"Oh, I don't know."

"It's better than lying awake fretting, Joyce. Your doctor will make sure they don't become a habit. As my son used to say – "just neck a blue and then you're through"."

"Hey, fuck-face! It's him – Mr Cool from the pirate ship! Oi've bin waitin' to ketch up wiv you, mate!"

I did feel sorry for Joyce when I heard the voice; she so much wanted just a quiet walk home to her hotel. It was Neil, of course, or Keith or something like that – the ones who Noel had teased about "wankers", the ones with the size 14 girlfriends in the size 10 bikinis.

"Fucking get him, Neil, Give him fuckin' what for!!"

I noticed years ago, when I used to take my son to football matches – not that I ever enjoyed the game myself, but he was at that age – that it was often the girls who wound their boyfriends up to cause trouble, and here it was again. They were staggering from a bar; behind them a song was raging. "Keep St George in my heart, Keep me English, Keep St George in my hear I pray, Keep St George in my heart, Keep me English, Keep me English till my dying day ..." and so on. I couldn't help wondering why or what they thought was so English about them. They had bottles in their hands, and that worried me so I said:

"Cool it, or I'll have to call the police."

"Oh yeah, not so fucking cool now are we, wivout them sailors around?"

"Just enjoy your beer, son."

I knew he wouldn't let it go and I was right. With his girlfriend screaming, "Smash his face in, Neil. Glass him", he had no choice but to take a swing at me. It was a wild swing and had no chance of landing. I'm not particularly proud of what I did, but I had Joyce to think of and it was a tricky situation to defuse with all of them so drunk. I just took my hotel room keys from my pocket and with the metal fob curled round my fingers, I punched him on the nose. It's a delicate part of the body – the nose, and he bled profusely. Joyce looked shocked, the size 14 girl-friend looked shocked and then his mates closed round him and they left quickly.

We sat at a bar on the way home sharing a calming hot chocolate, and Joyce said:

"What kept you so calm – that Valium?"

"Oh no, I only take that at night to sleep. There was just no time to panic."

She laughed. It was a nice sound and I fancied that she hadn't laughed so naturally for a long time. We talked for a little while longer and then walked slowly back to our hotels.

Day 15: Homeward Bound

Lorraine:

I must say, it was a good finish to the holiday. Frank, who loved to dance, joined us on the floor and we showed those Cystonians a thing or two about dancing – even on their terms – and they loved it! I couldn't help but remember that night with Dakos at the end of that lovely day – the flirting that was the dancing, the intimacy of the whole day. I'd thought it was genuine: Dakos had been so sensitive, compliments had been paid: he had shown me off to family and friends. Everyone had seemed to love us – at the end of the dancing they all applauded. It had been wonderful. Dakos had smiled, and I knew he was happy; he had been so gallant all day. Foreigners take such pleasure in others admiring "their woman" and for that moment, I was his woman.

I'm not one to dwell on what has not happened – not one of those women who forever wonders about how it might have been, but I was disappointed. What had seemed a promise had come to nothing – or seemed to; something in me still said that we could not end it where we did. As we danced, I kept looking at the door, half-expecting him to appear: corny, I know, but time was running out for me.

We moved clumsily, compared with that night in the taverna where Dakos had taken me: not in pairs, but as part of a group, and we changed partners within the dance which was the general idea, of course. Dot, Lorna and Caran loved it; there was lots of hugging, arms across shoulders, knee bending, dips and rises and straight backs which thrust the women's breasts forward and we were enjoying the fact. The men couldn't keep their eyes off us. I don't mind being on display. In fact it was very nice.

I was also aware that Frank and Caran might have some goodbyes to say and didn't want to get in their way, so I chose my moment – between one set and the next – to disentangle myself and whisper to Caran.

"I'm getting a taxi back – don't make a fuss. I think you and Frank need to say goodbye. Anyway, I'm not sure where I'm going."

"Not sure?"

"No."

I kissed them all briefly – they thought it was the drink and the dancing – and then disappeared quietly.

Outside, the revels were still going on. A group of lads was stumbling along the middle of the road pushing a green wheelie bin. Someone was clearly in the bin because whoever it was banged repeatedly on the side of it. The youths were in stitches, holding their sides, aching with laughter, the tears rolling down their faces. I looked at the doorman who had ordered me the taxi, and he just shrugged his shoulders.

When the taxi arrived the driver leaped out and held the door open for me. You used to expect this, didn't you, but it doesn't happen at home anymore.

"Where would you like to go, lady?"

"I don't know."

He frowned and smiled at the same time; quite a feat on any face in any language but he managed it attractively.

"Do you know the Ariadakos Restaurant?"

"Oh yes, but they will not be serving meals at this hour."

"It's not a meal I'm after."

"There may be nobody there at all. They do not dance."

"Oh they do – they do; but you are right, there may be nobody there."

Even if there had been, I still wasn't sure – as the taxi pulled away – that the Ariadakos was where we were going.

Noel:

When Lorraine kissed us goodbye, I knew the evening was clinched for me. The dancing had pumped up my adrenalin with memories of Sharon and the rumbas we enjoyed on her sofa. Now – as long as Lorna didn't want three-in-a-bed, which at my age was not an attractive proposition – I felt sure that Siesta was going to bouzouki me through what remained of the night.

The dancing soon lost its interest after Lorraine left. Frank and Caran were clearly eager to be off and so were Dot and I – and Fiesta would now be quite happy tucked up in bed with a bottle of wine and something savoury. It was still warm when we left to walk back along the seafront. Frank and Caran had made the excuse of a final drink – which I noticed they didn't actually order – so that they could walk back alone, and

I set off with Siesta and Fiesta armed in arm, linked like life-long buddies.

It's amazing how much these old girls can put away; we'd been eating and drinking all night, yet they never showed any sign of it – perhaps the dancing had sweated it out of them. I could feel the heat of their bodies on either side of me. Not one of us was exactly lithe, of course. I had the usual paunch of any man over fifty – (well, any man over thirty, these days) and both Dot and Lorna were well timbered, so, with the humidity of the night and our eagerness to get started, we were soon sweating profusely. Dot and Lorna were both wearing tank-tops and their fat arms and chests glistened, while the sweat ran between us like water off a child's swimming ring. At that moment, I wouldn't have wanted to be in a lift with any of us.

As we reached our hotel, a taxi drew up and a young man fell out of it, completely out of breath, as if he had been running from some demon of the night. He ran round the back of the taxi, making for the hotel lobby as the taxi driver leapt out of his side of the cab and began to pursue him. The taxi driver was raging with anger and, although he undoubtedly spoke good English, his state of hysterics made him more fluent in his native tongue. Unfortunately, the youth didn't understand a word he was saying, and soon an argument broke out, each of them shouting in their own language. Before it could get far, however, two of the hotel staff emerged. They took both parties into the lobby, sat the taxi driver with a cup of coffee and proceeded to mop up the sick, which was the cause of the problem, in the back of the taxi. They then took the young man's wallet from his pocket, held it ostentatiously in the air for all of us to see and removed the fare and the fine; they then escorted the driver to his cab and the youth to his room, everyone smiling. It takes all sorts, I thought. We gave the two staff a big smile and tottered to our rooms; you have to admire these people – they cope with us brilliantly. Even I was slightly embarrassed, though; I just couldn't imagine a Cystonian behaving like that in Britain or our hotel staff coping with such aplomb.

Lorna had no sooner taken a bottle of wine from the fridge and (with a packet of Ritz biscuits and a lump of cheese from the cupboard) and disappeared into her bedroom, than Dot spun me round and pulled off my shirt.

"I hope you can get it up tonight, Noel. I'm as randy as hell."

"I'll do my best, dear lady, I'll do my best."

Dot was somewhat shorter than me, so that the kiss she demanded involved some stooping, which made my head swim; however, we managed and were soon involved in an all-in wrestling match with our mouths, while we proceeded to pull each other's clothes off. Dot and I had "enjoyed each other" (as the romantic novels are wont to say) before on the holiday, but then we'd been mildly plastered and relaxed: now were eager and a little desperate that things were coming to an end. I think it's a while since I've actually stood naked with a woman in the way I did that night. Usually you find one or the other of you in bed of you waiting, while the other gets undressed, hurriedly or chattily, on the side – if you'll excuse the expression.

"You're not half sweating, Noel. I like that in a man, but do you want me to take a shower first?"

"Why don't we both take a shower, dear lady?"

Had she needed any more stimuli, that comment would have been sufficient; we slithered and slid and soaped each other, laughing our way through the most interesting ablutions I've taken in years. If you can picture two fat people in a shower built scarcely for one, your imagination will do the rest.

By the time we reached Dot's bedroom, wet and exhausted, I was ready for some shut-eye or, at least, I was laid back and inclined to recline, but Dot wasn't. Once these old girls have worked up a head of steam, there is no stopping them; in my experience, which is considerable and spans many years and many countries, they are more of a "goer" than any young woman you'll find. They've lost all hang-ups and attitudes: sex, if they enjoy it at all at their age, is sheer, unadulterated fun – again, excuse the expression (not intended as a pun!).

She reached over and hauled me on top of her (they do tend to be a little on the traditional side, the experimental years have been left behind) and took my head between her hands, and kissed me. It was a lovely kiss, full of rough passion and a precursor to the main act; it lasted a long time and during that time, I felt myself rising, ready for action. She blasphemed once only and then her hands were everywhere. I think, perhaps, mine were a little tardy in getting going, because she took them and placed them where she felt the action was needed and then I was stroking – or perhaps, more accurately, massaging – her ample breasts, her solid thighs and her heaving rump. Our bodies came together in the orthodox manner (how could we feel through our joint fat?) and we climaxed together; DH Lawrence would have been proud of us, as far as I remember. I've always loved that moment – if you can pull it off together like that – and when it was over, I sank back and pulled her over on to my chest.

"Cor, that was fucking marvellous, Noel. I didn't know you had it in yer."

I felt satiated and could have slept, then, but I sensed the eagerness in her and felt her hands roaming over my chest and down to my thighs. She lifted my old chap into her hands and kissed it – a little chafed, of course (one might almost say chamfered) but Dot wasn't taking "No" for an answer. With the curiosity of a young woman, she began to kiss my body all over. I felt honoured, let me say; it doesn't happen often these days. I wondered what interest a fifty-something body could hold, but her lips must have found it somewhere, because they never stopped straying until she had covered all of me from head to each toe.

"Do you want a tablet, Noel?"

"Tablet?"

"One of the little blue rod rousers."

"Viagra?"

"Yes."

"You keep a supply, Dot?"

"At my age, I have to."

"No, no – no, indeed, your kisses are worth a thousand pills."

"Smooth talker!"

But they were: I've found, since I reached my fifties, that all you really need is a kindly lady and a helping hand – bugger the pills. By now it must have been four or five in the morning. We'd be lucky to get any sleep at all before we rushed out for the coach but "what the hell" – you only come this way once so let's come again!

"Would you like me on top? I can do the work then."

"Dear Dot, how thoughtful you are."

"Never mind the thoughtful. I want to get me end off."

And she did – time and again, with comments like "Bloody hell, I thought me top was going to blow off then!" or "Have I got steam coming out of me ears?" – until dawn's sweet glow appeared over the horizon. By then, we were two crumpled heaps of sweat and bedclothes, but it had been a great night; she might have been an "old boiler" but any young woman would have been proud of her head of steam that night.

"Thanks, Dot, you were wonderful."

"Don't mention it, you weren't bad yourself. Just leave me your home address before you go. You never know."

Caran:

We didn't have that last drink, that final digestif; it was just an excuse to give Noel and his ladies a chance to get away before Frank and I walked back to the Captain Karas Apartments. There's always a tension in me, I know that; maybe, it's even there when I'm relaxed during love-making, but tonight, that seemed to have gone. I was looking forward to the walk back; I wanted to walk barefoot and quietly, away from the noise of the street, so I suggested that we went by the beach.

I'd seen a film once – a French film – and this young couple had walked back, alone, late, through the streets of Paris; he was in a dinner jacket with his tie loosened and she was in a simple, expensive dress, carrying a pair of strappy shoes in her hand. I'd done it once – thirty years ago – after our 'graduation' ball (although we didn't call it that) through the streets of an English town. I'd never done it since, and wanted to: just once again, and it looked as if Frank was to be the man.

There's something, isn't there, about walking alone with somebody – just the two of you – while the noises of the city, muted by the night, go on around you unnoticed; not that Craphos was Paris, nor Frank the young man in the dinner jacket.

We walked along the shore together, our hands touching loosely, looking at each other occasionally, so that there was an intimacy between us. I could hear the swirl of the sea, its rhythmic pattern caressing the sand softly.

The shallow water lapped our feet without actually touching them. Frank kissed me once in a while but said nothing, respecting the silence. I felt the whole length of my lower left arm curled around his right, my fingers resting lightly in his; our bodies shared their warmth. His skin was rough against me and I could smell the faint traces of his deodorant in the warm, night air.

Neither of us seemed eager to break the silence of the occasion. I felt a quiet ache within me, almost as a distant thing, almost as though it were not part of this moment. We watched the sea – as the tide gradually brought the shore-lapping waves closer – and were part of its beauty. I felt small and vulnerable but it was a good feeling; at fifty-something, you need to feel like that again – recapturing what once was or you hoped would be. How many years had I left to know such a moment? Would there ever be another time like this?

"Thanks."

"Frank?"

"Thanks."

It didn't seem to need an answer. The quiet was enough, the quiet and the slight movement as we settled more firmly against each other. The moon had dipped by now, closer to the horizon, and the bars of Craphos were a far distant sound that seemed to blend in with the night; we were encircled, cut off from the world and the reality of our daily lives.

I felt my feet bare on the sand, and then on the pavements. I looked up at Frank; he put his arm round my shoulders and I leaned into him. We had only a few yards to go now and when we arrived at the reception door, he turned me to him and kissed me lightly on the mouth.

"Would you like to come in?"

"It would be very nice, but that isn't what you want, is it?"

"Is that selfish of me?"

"No."

He kissed me again, very, very lightly and I kissed him back. He hugged me with the same gentleness, held my hands and turned away. He waited until I'd gone into the hotel, and then I watched him walk off along the street.

Frank:

I decided not to try and sleep; it was four or five in the morning and I had an early coach to catch, so I took a cat nap. I've always been good at those – well, nearly always. I had a cool shower, put on a clean shirt and the new suit I'd had made in Craphos because I didn't want the baggage boys tossing it around in the case, zipped up my suitcase, took it down to the lobby and decided to get some breakfast. I tipped the Bangladeshi lad handsomely and could see the appreciation in his face; they are paid bugger-all here. Stavros and Skeggy were not around yet, so I left them a brief note of thanks, which I slid under the reception desk bell.

The breakfast was good – black coffee and warm croissant: for what more can a man ask? I thought about Caran – quietly, not eagerly, because I couldn't see, at that moment, that we were going to meet again – and was glad that I'd taken that last walk with her and read her mind at the hotel door. I avoided the English papers. I always do on holiday (after all, what can you do about it if the country is in chaos at home?) and strolled back to catch the six o'clock coach.

Stavros was there by now with his thick, curly hair and dark brooding eyes. He gave us that big, well-muscled smile, waved the coach goodbye and turned back into his hotel; today was another day and another coach-load of tourists would be arriving.

Vera was on the coach when it arrived and said in that steak-and-kidney way of hers:

"Well did you adapt to Mediterranean time, go out late, eat late, take everything as it came, enjoy your siestas, spin out your lunches, browse the bazaars, pick up on the local colour, stay sober in public and keep out of the sun?"

More or less. Anyway, we had or we hadn't – it was too late now. The coach twisted and turned its way through the endless side streets and half-finished hotels. It roared past the flashing signs of the burger joints; we caught glimpses of Chinese, Indian, and English restaurants, Irish bars and Scottish pubs. I was pleased to be on my way home – pleased, but mildly depressed at the same time: in touch, perhaps, with my feminine side?

At the Aphrodite, the blue floral trousers clambered aboard with her husband and three teenage children. A sense, a reassuring sense, of normality pervaded the coach. I recognised several other people, also. One was a short, blonde woman who seemed to have had her lips 'Botoxed' while she was in Cystos. Another was a father with a bossy wife and two bossy teenage daughters, all three of whom were angrily advising him on how to carry three suitcases without actually helping him to do so – the girls because they were concerned that it might not "look cool" to actually carry their own cases and the wife because she'd never had to do so.

At the airport we passed the black haired, dark-skinned, large-eyed, finely chiselled nose talent that comprised the local reps and airport staff, checked in our baggage, and then we were at passport control. Once again, the official looked me over several times before deciding that I was no real threat to security. But his scrutiny was probably diverted by a short, plump man who had joined the coach at the same stop as the pair of blue, floral trousers. This man had been sweating profusely throughout the coach journey and attempted to take a large, obviously heavy, bag through to the departure lounge. When questioned he explained that it was his television set, and the security man said:

"Why did you take your TV on holiday?"

"I wanted to listen to the football on the BBC with John Motson – not some foreign commentator."

The passport officer checked the bag, confiscated the set and waved us through. Not being in the mood for hassle at that moment I left the plump man arguing his case.

Once again, I was fortunate enough to follow that lovely backside in the blue floral trousers across the tarmac to the aircraft – some men get all the luck, don't they or is it just that some of us are more appreciative of what life, even in small ways, has to offer? I was over-come again by the gentle sway of her hips and how styl-ishly she was dressed: the snug-fitting, calf-length trousers, the flowing top with the slender shoulder straps.

The on-flight meal went into the gash-can, but this time the air-hostess didn't smile, seeming to take it as a personal affront to her dignity and professional status. Apart from that, and a little turbulence as we reached England, the flight was wonderfully uneventful.

It had been a good holiday; I couldn't have asked for more. Yes, I had been amoral and enjoyed it: to grumble would have been hypocritical. Good sex doesn't come your way that often and I had no regrets about what had happened between Caran and myself. I looked upon it as my *gap* fortnight – not much to ask after over thirty years as a father and holding down a demanding job, is it? I hadn't found promiscuity rife abroad. I hadn't had the three or four partners forecast – but a couple of weeks of sand, sea, sun and sex had livened me up no end. I was grateful.

Passport control and baggage collection went smoothly. I walked out of the airport towards my wait-ing car without any fuss or bother. I'd visited an open air theatre, found a quiet beach, had a drink in a village café and an alfresco meal off the tourist track, driven to a cliff-top for a view of the sunset, walked a forest trail and joined in a local dance – but not joined a plate breaking session, been invited to a wedding or water-skied: seven out of ten, then?

It was about lunchtime – the pubs would be open, wouldn't they? A good, Old English pub with a good Old English pub lunch un-rivalled anywhere in the world: what did I fancy – stew and dumplings, shep-herd's pie, sausage and mash, steak and kidney pudding, lamb cutlets, toad in the hole, macaroni cheese, fish pie, bruschetta with tomatoes, smoked salmon, beef Bour-guignon, chicken Kiev, spaghetti alla carbonara, moules a la mariniere, coq au vin ....and for pudding? Never mind, I'd wash whatever I had down with one pint of real English beer.

I drove slowly from the airport car park, still thinking of Caran, Lorraine, Joyce and the others. The holiday hadn't worked out as I planned, but then, I hadn't planned anything. It was a warm, gentle, English summer day, so I opened the sunroof. England: a little bit of sunshine and a little bit of rain, not a place of extremes. I didn't feel like going home – not yet, anyway, not on this lovely day; there was nothing waiting for me there, now. Men are foolish aren't they, in a way that women are not? We should keep our feet more firmly on the ground. As I drove along, looking for a nice pub, I kept wondering whether I should head north.

The Mediterranean	**2004**
Norfolk, England	**2006-2007**